WARTIME WITH THE CIDER GIRLS

MAY ELLIS

B

Boldwood

First published in Great Britain in 2025 by Boldwood Books Ltd.

Copyright © May Ellis, 2025

Cover Design by Colin Thomas

Cover Images: Colin Thomas, iStock and Andrew Palmer / Unsplash

A CIP catalogue record for this book is available from the British Library.

Paperback ISBN 978-1-83633-923-6

Large Print ISBN 978-1-83633-922-9

Hardback ISBN 978-1-83633-921-2

Trade Paperback ISBN 978-1-80656-051-6

Ebook ISBN 978-1-83633-924-3

Kindle ISBN 978-1-83633-925-0

Audio CD ISBN 978-1-83633-916-8

MP3 CD ISBN 978-1-83633-917-5

Digital audio download ISBN 978-1-83633-919-9

This book is printed on certified sustainable paper. Boldwood Books is dedicated to putting sustainability at the heart of our business. For more information please visit https://www.boldwoodbooks.com/about-us/sustainability/

Boldwood Books Ltd, 23 Bowerdean Street, London, SW6 3TN

www.boldwoodbooks.com

In times of war and trouble, many people of all walks of life discover that they are capable of far more than they ever imagined. This book is dedicated to unsung heroes – those who do their bit to protect and serve their community without fanfare, acknowledgement or reward.

PROLOGUE

3 SEPTEMBER 1939

'This morning the British ambassador in Berlin handed the German government a final note stating that, unless we heard from them by eleven o'clock that they were prepared at once to withdraw their troops from Poland, a state of war would exist between us. I have to tell you now that no such undertaking has been received, and that consequently this country is at war with Germany.'

Rose Flaherty's daddy turned off the radio. Her mammy burst into tears, sobbing loudly into her handkerchief. 'Oh my boys! What's to become of you? I can't bear it!'

Rose felt a pang that Mammy was weeping over her brothers, with not a thought for her only daughter. But she wasn't surprised. As they had listened to the news on the wireless in the past weeks, it was clear that war was coming and Mammy had been fretting something awful about the boys. All six of them were of an age that meant they'd be called up sooner rather than later. Only her oldest brother, Liam, who was married and a police constable, might avoid it for a little while. But the rest of them were already discussing what they would do. Declan wanted to join the air force. Sean and Patrick were set on the navy. Michael and Anthony were keen to join the army.

Truth be told, Rose was scared for them as well. She'd heard her parents' stories about the young men lost or maimed in the Great War. Daddy had lost three brothers in the trenches and another had come home so badly wounded he'd not survived long.

She glanced at him now as he tried to comfort Mammy. There were tears in his eyes. The shock of seeing him so distressed took her breath away and she felt her own tears well. Guilt over-whelmed her because she'd been selfishly looking forward to seeing her brothers off and spreading her own wings. She'd spent all her life in their shadows – the only girl and the youngest of the family. She knew that they expected they would all leave home and leave her behind, but she had other plans. She wanted a life where she wasn't watched over all the time by her family. It was all arranged and it made her feel giddy with the prospect of being free. Now, the reality of the situation hit her as she witnessed her parents' tears. What would they say when they knew what she'd done?

The boys might never come back, she realised. *How will I live with myself if they don't? I don't want them to be killed. I just want them to let me live my life.*

Mammy continued to weep as her sons gathered around, trying to console her.

'We'll be all right, Mammy,' said Michael. 'Don't fret.'

'Rose will look after you,' said Sean, glancing her way.

Rose glared back at him. Wasn't that just typical? She was always the one left behind, who had to help while her brothers sat on their backsides. Now they were rushing off to war, sure in the knowledge that their sister would stay home at Mammy and

Daddy's beck and call, when she wanted adventure just as much as her brothers did.

'Actually,' she said, her voice squeaking as her throat threatened to close up. 'I won't be here either.'

Daddy frowned. 'What are you talking about, girl?'

She took a deep breath. She knew they wouldn't be happy, but she had to get away before she ended up stuck, the spinster daughter left at home to care for her ageing parents. 'I saw the posters and I've signed up for the Land Army,' she announced, trying to inject some confidence into her voice. 'Just like Mammy did in the Great War. You said it was the making of you, didn't you, Mammy? Well, when they announced it was being re-formed back in June, I went along and had an interview and a medical with a couple of the girls from the button factory. I got my papers this week.' It had seemed so simple when she'd taken herself off to the recruiting office. 'I'm off in a couple of weeks for training, then I'll be working on a farm in the West Country.'

'But why didn't you say?' asked Mammy.

She shrugged, looking away from the hurt on Mammy's face. 'I didn't know if I'd be accepted, especially if Herr Hitler had changed his mind and we hadn't gone to war. There wasn't much point until I knew. But we're all going to have to do our bit, aren't we? I'd rather work on the land than in the factory.' She'd been working in a button factory in the Jewellery Quarter in Birmingham since she had left school. She hated it. She also hated the fact that her over-protective brothers chased off any lads who showed an interest in her. Maybe moving to the country would give her the chance to find a sweetheart without her family breathing down her neck. Lord knows, she'd had enough lads chased off by the Flaherty brothers that she felt sure no decent chap in the whole of Birmingham would take a chance on her.

Daddy frowned and shook his head. 'You can't go,' he said. 'You'll break your mother's heart.'

Rose blinked back tears, looking round the room at the angry gazes of her family. Only Declan seemed to understand. She sent him a pleading glance.

'I think it would be a fine thing for our Rose to do,' he said.

'She won't last five minutes,' scoffed Anthony. 'She'll get a whiff of cow muck and she'll come running back home to Mammy.'

'I will not!' she declared.

'That's as may be,' said Declan, as though she hadn't spoken. 'But we won't know until she tries.'

'I'm not happy with this,' said Daddy, comforting Mammy as her tears continued to flow.

'It's hard work, our Rosie,' cried Mammy. 'Out in all weathers. You don't need to do it. When will we see you?'

'But I've already signed up,' said Rose, her heart sinking. She loved them all, but she couldn't lose this chance to go out into the world on her own at long last. She wished they could understand how she felt. 'I have to go. They're sending me to Somerset. I hear it's really pretty down there. Please Daddy, let me try it. With everyone else going to do their bit, I really want to do something. I hate the button factory!'

'We all hate our jobs, my girl. But we need to work or we'll starve.'

'If I'm a land girl, I'll be helping to keep the whole country fed. That's got to be better than slaving away in the factory, hasn't it?'

'Do they even grow food down there?' asked Michael. 'I thought Somerset was all apple orchards. You really want to be a cider girl, our Rosie?'

She glared at him. It was typical of him to make a joke of

things she wanted to do. 'Don't be daft. It can't all be orchards, any more than Kent would be all hop fields to grow beer. No, I'm going to a proper farm. I've got to learn to milk cows and hoe crops, they said. I might even be taught how to drive a tractor.'

'God help us,' said Anthony, rolling his eyes. 'We'll be safer in the army if she's out on the roads on a tractor.'

'No drinking the local brew if you're driving, Cider Girl,' said Sean.

'Oh, hush you!' she scolded.

It took a good hour before Mammy calmed down and her parents finally agreed to let her go. Rose felt wrung out by it all. There'd been no such arguments about her brothers going off to fight, even though the prospect had reduced Mammy to tears. She didn't see what all the fuss was about – at least she'd be safe, working on a farm. It was hardly a battlefield, was it?

Once the fuss died down a bit, with her brothers talking excitedly about their plans, Rose escaped to her room. She had already secretly begun to pack what she needed to take with her in her duffle bag, so she was ready to go when the time arrived. She didn't need much – she would be issued with a uniform when she reported at the training centre. But she made sure to pack a couple of nice dresses in the hope that she could go dancing sometimes.

She could hardly believe it. She was going away; she would finally be free of her suffocating family. She loved them all dearly, and she knew she would miss them. But she couldn't help feeling that she needed to break free of them or she would never be able to live the life she wanted.

* * *

On her own in London, Elsie Bloomfield turned off the wireless, closed her suitcase and looked around the room. She'd stripped the bed and swept the floor. All her worldly goods were in the case or her large handbag. She'd left a few books and a pot plant on the chest of drawers. She couldn't take them with her, so she hoped the next tenant would want them. She'd also left a forwarding address in the hope that someone would send on any letters that arrived for her. Not that she expected any.

With a sigh she picked up her coat and gloves and put them on. She wasn't sad to be leaving this place. It was just the latest in countless moves over the years since her parents had died. Grasping her suitcase, gas mask box and handbag, she left the room. She wouldn't be back. There was nothing left for her here. Her sister Gertie had already left London – taking her baby out of the city with the first wave of evacuees who had left on trains just a few days ago, before war had even been declared. Her brother-in-law was already away in the Royal Navy. She wondered when she would see them again, if ever. They hadn't exactly parted on good terms.

Now she was completely alone. Her parents had gone years ago. Gertie had been her only family and chances were they'd never reconcile after the awful row they'd had before she'd left the city. Gertie certainly hadn't been willing to admit she'd done wrong and Elsie wasn't sure she could ever forgive her.

At least now, Elsie could put it all behind her and have a new start. Anticipating that war was coming, she had enlisted in the Auxiliary Territorial Service, glad of the chance to get out of London, away from her past and to do her bit now that war had been declared. It was funny, she hadn't truly believed that they would really go to war. Despite all the talk in recent months, she'd hoped that Mr Chamberlain's agreement with Herr Hitler would stand and the crisis would be avoided. But she'd enlisted anyway because it was her best chance of a new start. Now here they were, at war with Germany again.

I have to think positively, she thought as she made her way to the railway station. *It's a new start for me, and after the lies Gertie told, it's better that we part and I go on alone. Being in the ATS means I'll meet new people and have the chance of a better life without Gertie's lies hanging over my head. The army will be my new family.*

It was hard, though, especially as it meant she was unlikely to see the baby again. Even though the child was only a couple of months old, Elsie had grown to love her and it grieved her to know she was unlikely to see her again and the child would never know her. She just hoped that Gertie would do right by the little mite.

In the meantime, after her initial training, she'd been told that she was being posted to Somerset. She hoped she liked it. She'd never been out of London, apart from the odd day out to Southend-on-Sea when their parents had been alive. Somerset seemed like a different world. All she knew about the county was that it produced cider, Cheddar cheese and Clarks shoes. She wasn't sure what her duties would be when she got there, but she would do her best and hopefully this war would be over soon and then she'd be able to work out what she wanted to do with the rest of her life.

* * *

Daisy Selway let herself into her family farmhouse in the village of Walton in Somerset. 'Hello,' she called out. 'Anyone home?'

'There's my darling girl.' Her mother smiled as she came out of the kitchen, wiping her hands on a cloth. 'How was your journey?'

Daisy hugged her. 'I've only come from Bristol, Ma. You make it sound like I've been travelling the world.'

'Oh you, don't be daft. It's still a long way on the bus, isn't it? After you've been working so hard at the hospital as well. If it had been me, I'd have fallen asleep on the ride and ended up in Yeovil for my troubles.'

Daisy chuckled. 'You would not, and neither would I. I enjoyed the trip, although dragging my case from the bus stop has fair worn me out.'

'Well you're home now, thank goodness. I'm so proud of you, love. But most of all, I'm glad you're home. I've missed you.'

'Aw, Ma. I've missed you too. But I'm not going anywhere now.'

'It'll be so lovely to have another woman in the house again.'

Daisy smiled. 'I'll be glad of my own bedroom after sharing the nurses' hostel for all this time. I can't wait to start my new job tomorrow. I'll be glad to be off the wards, I can tell you! As you know, my last ward sister was a right tartar. None of us could please her, no matter how hard we worked.'

'Some people are never satisfied, are they, love? Let's hope the doctor you're going to work for will be better. Your brothers have sorted out your bicycle for you. It's all clean and the tyres are pumped up ready for when you start work. They even put a new basket on the front for your bag. Now, leave your case there, I'll get Pa or one of your brothers to take it upstairs when they get back. Him and Victor are round at the rectory, helping shift some furniture ready for the evacuees they've agreed to take. George is over at the farm cottage helping build some furniture. Did I tell you Tim got married and they're expecting?' She nodded. Tim had been working on the farm for a few years now, as had his father before him. He'd been sweet on Daisy for a while and she'd been glad to leave home to start her nursing training to get away from his shy glances as he really wasn't her type. She was relieved he'd found a girl better suited to him.

'Anyway, they'll all be back in a minute. Let's get the kettle on.'

She followed her mother into the farmhouse kitchen. She breathed in the familiar scents of Ma's cooking. With a sigh she sank onto the long wooden bench at the scrubbed table. 'How's Pa getting along?' she asked.

Ma shrugged. 'It's hard to tell. He swears there's nothing wrong with him, but he's lost weight and gets tired much quicker than he used to.'

'Hmm. It might just be his age,' she said. She knew that Ma was worried about him and had been trying to get him to see a doctor. She'd been sufficiently worried that she'd written to Daisy about it, which was part of the reason why she'd decided to take the district nurse's job in nearby Street. If Pa really was ill, she wanted to be on hand to help nurse him. She wouldn't know until she saw him.

'Talk of the devil,' said Ma as the front door opened. Daisy turned to see Pa and her brother Victor come in.

'There's my darling girl,' said Pa, grinning and opening his arms to engulf her in a hug.

'That's what Ma said,' she laughed. She hugged him back, noting that he had indeed lost some weight since she'd seen him a few months ago.

'Quite right too. It's good to have you home, lass.'

'Have you heard the news?' said her older brother George, rushing through the door after the others.

Daisy rolled her eyes. 'And hello to you, brother. I can see you've really missed me.'

'I missed you, Daisy,' said Victor, the baby of the family.

'Ah, thanks, Vic,' she said, kissing his cheek. She had to reach up on tiptoes as he'd grown so much since she was last home. It was a shock to her to realise that he was almost nineteen now. But he'd always be her baby brother. 'I missed you too.'

He pulled a face. 'There's no need to get soppy,' he said, scrubbing at the spot where she'd kissed him, making her laugh.

'Is no one listening to me?' asked George, frowning something fierce as he stood there, taller even than Pa and Vic now, with his hands on his hips. 'This is important!'

'What is it, lad?' asked Pa.

'It was on the radio just now. We're at war.'

The whole family paused. Daisy felt her heart stutter. Everyone had been talking about war for months now, but Mr Chamberlain had assured everyone that he had a paper signed by Herr Hitler and that their nations wouldn't be fighting. Daisy felt foolish, like she should have seen it coming. But she'd been so busy working in the hospital that she'd barely noticed the news lately.

'Oh no,' said Ma.

'Not again,' muttered Pa. 'Bloody hell!'

It was a measure of their feelings that Ma didn't scold Pa about his language.

'I know,' said George.

A shiver ran down Daisy's spine. Pa had fought in the Great War, even though as a farmer's son he could have claimed exemption. But he'd not been keen on farming as a lad and had gone to work at the Clarks shoe factory in Street when he left school instead, helping out on the farm in his spare time. His younger brother had stayed, happy to take it on instead. Pa had survived the trenches and had expected to go back to Clarks on his return, but his brother had been laid low with tuberculosis and was taken far too young, meaning that Pa had to return to farming. Eventually he'd inherited the land from his father and now Daisy's brothers were working it alongside him.

Pa didn't talk about the war – none of the men she knew did. But Ma had said he'd never been the same since.

'Oh, God,' said Ma, putting a hand over her mouth. 'I knew it was coming, but I kept praying Hitler would honour the paper he signed.'

Pa scowled. 'Can't trust the Hun,' he murmured before turning away.

Daisy shared a glance with Ma. They'd both noticed that he'd welled up.

'Will we be called up?' asked Vic. Neither brother looked thrilled at the prospect.

'No,' said Pa, shaking his head. 'You're both needed on the farm. You'll be given reserved occupation status. Don't either of you do anything foolish like enlisting. I made that mistake and believe me, I wish I hadn't. War is bloody hell.'

The lads nodded, sobered to see their usually mild Pa's fierce expression.

'But what about Mattie and Henry? They're Quakers. Will they be forced to go?'

Daisy felt her heart clench at the mention of Mattie. Him and his brother and their sister Ruby were the children of family friends, Lucas and Louisa Musgrove, who lived in Street. Pa had worked alongside Mattie's pa at the factory. She had been carrying a torch for Mattie for years – most of her life really. 'Of course not,' she snapped. 'Mattie's a doctor now.' That was part of the reason why she became a nurse. 'They won't expect him to fight.'

'And Henry's working full time for his Uncle Tom making prosthetics. They'll no doubt need more of those before this war's over,' said Pa.

They were all silent for a moment, thinking of Uncle Tom, as they also called him even though they had no blood tie, who had created a workshop to make false limbs and apparatus to help people with limited mobility after he had lost a foot and part of his leg in the trenches back in 1915. Unhappy with the false limb he had been issued with when he left hospital, he'd set about making a better version for himself. When people heard about it, he got a lot of requests for help. He'd done that work alongside his job as an engineer at the Clarks shoe factory in Street for a few years until it became clear that the demand for his projects was more than he and his friends could cope with as a part-time voluntary enterprise.

'Let's hope they get their exemption certificates,' said Ma. 'Lord knows it was hard enough for the Quakers who wouldn't fight in the Great War. I remember Quaker lads being sent to gaol for refusing to take up arms.'

Pa sighed and nodded. 'It's going to be rough. But I'll say it again as often as I need to – I don't want you boys rushing off to fight, you hear me? Don't be as daft as I was back then. War's no laughing matter.' He turned his attention to Daisy. 'And don't you go thinking you should sign up for anything, lass. We've only just got you home and your nursing skills are needed just as much here as anywhere else.'

'I know, Pa,' she said. 'Don't worry. I'm not going anywhere.'

But she couldn't help worrying about what would happen to her brothers and all the other lads she knew.

1

MARCH 1940

A thud against the wall next to her bed woke her. Rose sat up, instantly alert as she heard another thud and a woman's cry.

'Oh dear lord, not again,' Rose whispered. In the months she'd been working as a land girl at this farm on the edge of Exmoor she'd not had a decent night's sleep or a square meal. The farmer she worked for was a brute who seemed to delight in beating his poor wife.

Rose covered her ears as the thuds and cries went on, punctuated by the horrible man's snarling list of his victim's apparent sins. She didn't know how the poor woman survived it. Every day she had new cuts and bruises. But Rose had learned very quickly that she didn't care for the land girl trying to interfere. The first night she'd been woken by the sound of the beating, Rose had rushed into their room, sure that someone had invaded the farmhouse, only to find the enemy was living right there amongst them.

She'd been shocked to witness the farmer punch his wife so hard in the face that her head had snapped back and hit the wall. 'Now look what you've done, you stupid bitch!' he'd shouted at her, not caring that Rose was witnessing his cruelty. 'You woke her up. If she's too tired to work tomorrow, you'll be for it, d'you hear me?' The woman had barely whimpered while Rose had cried out.

He'd turned on her then, his face contorted with rage. 'Mind your business, lass, or you'll feel my belt across your back. Now get out!'

Rose shivered with fear and shame as she remembered how she had turned tail and fled the room, barricading the door to her own room from the inside by dragging a chest of drawers in front of it. She'd remained awake most of the night, still afraid that he would come for her, wishing she'd had the courage to stand up to him. She'd never experienced fear like it before, and she'd been hard put not to pack her belongings and rush home to Birmingham.

In the morning, Rose had wanted to talk to her, to offer support in whatever way she could. But the farmer had been waiting for her when she had left her room and he had ordered her to work without the chance to speak to his wife – or to have any breakfast for that matter. He was in a foul mood.

'Bloody stupid ministry, telling us to grow wheat,' he grumbled. 'Look at it. I could've told 'em it's no good trying to grow wheat round here. The peat's full of old seeds and as soon as we plough the top of it up, what happens? They germinate. That's what. Look at it!' he snarled again. 'Full of bloody weeds.' He gave her a sideways look. 'I'd have you pulling 'em out, but then you'd be behind with your other jobs. Ah sod it. This lot won't be any good for naught but birdseed. I'll not waste any more time on it. Get yourself over to the sheep pen and help the lad there with trimming their feet.'

She'd fled, glad to get away from him, even though the job of trimming the feet of a few dozen animals was a horrible but necessary job to make sure they didn't get foot rot. She fast came to the conclusion that she preferred the big, docile cows she had to milk to the recalcitrant sheep.

When she had finally managed a few minutes to have a quiet word with the farmer's wife, Rose had been firmly rebuffed.

'It's just his way, that's all. A man's entitled to run his home the way he wants to. If I've not done my duty by him, I should expect to be walloped, the same as the children do when they misbehave. So I'll thank you to mind your own business, young miss.'

'But he'll kill you one day,' Rose had pointed out as gently as she could. 'Then who'll care for your family?'

'He won't,' she'd said, not looking at Rose. 'Although he'll beat me again if he knew I'd let you talk to me like this.'

Rose had sighed. 'My brother is a police constable,' she began, but was quickly interrupted.

'He's not done anything wrong in the eyes of the law. I'm his wife. He's entitled to do what he likes with me.'

'Not to the point where you're covered in bruises,' said Rose, wishing she could get through to her that his treatment of her was so very wrong. No man should harm the woman he promised before God to love and protect.

'Even then,' she replied, her voice flat. 'And what would become of us if he was thrown in jail, eh? He puts food on the table and a roof over our heads and all that would be taken away if he wasn't here. So I'll thank you to mind your business and concentrate on doing your job. I don't need your kind of interference.'

Now, weeks later, it was still going on. The sound of the regular beatings, the sleepless nights. The brute ate the bulk of the food that was put on the table at mealtimes and Rose was reluctant to take more than the smallest of portions for fear that the children or their mother would have to go without if she took too much. The poor mites seemed so broken down that she couldn't bear to cause them any more suffering.

The combination of hunger, back-breaking work and lack of sleep was taking its toll on Rose. When she'd signed up for the Land Army, she'd expected to be put somewhere with lots of other jolly girls, working in the fields with plenty of sunshine and laughter. This bleak Exmoor farm where she was expected to work on her own or alongside a man who she feared and loathed was nothing like she'd imagined. The days had been rainy more often than they'd been dry, the cows were bigger than she'd expected yet never seemed to produce enough milk to satisfy the farmer so she'd been berated for her efforts, even as she'd been milking them out on the moor, soaked to the skin and shivering. The farmhouse was dark and draughty. Her mattress was made of straw and more than once she'd seen a mouse run from it when she'd approached her bed at night.

'I can't take this much longer,' she muttered to herself as in the adjacent room yet another blow was delivered. She'd thought to speak to her Land Army supervisor, but she hadn't seen the woman since the day she'd brought her here. It annoyed her because she was told that she would be checking on her regularly. There was no telephone at the farm, so she couldn't even call her to see why she hadn't been. Up until now she'd kept her letters home as cheerful and positive as she could manage. She didn't want Mammy and Daddy to worry about her, not when they were already fretting about all of her brothers. She'd done her best to fill her letters with silly stories of farming life, which was as far from her old life at the button factory as you could get. But now she was tired and felt as beaten down as the family in this house, even though the brute hadn't dared to lay a hand on her up till now.

Another thud. Another cry. Rose's nerves were frayed and she was close to screaming at the horrible man, telling him to stop it. For she truly believed that he would soon be the death of his poor wife and she felt so helpless in the face of the woman's refusal to stand against him.

Eventually the noises stopped. A few minutes later, Rose heard him snoring and breathed a sigh of relief that his wife could now rest while he slumbered. But it was hours before Rose was able to relax sufficiently to doze off again.

* * *

It was the farmer's dog that broke Rose in the end. She'd seen the animal being kicked more than once, so when she'd seen it whimpering in the shade of the barn when she had been sent there to return some tools after a back-breaking morning clearing a stream of weeds that threatened to block the channel and flood the fields, she immediately went over to see what she could do for the poor beast.

'Here, boy, what's the matter, eh? Did he kick you again?' She noticed there was blood oozing from a wound on the dog's flank. It was caked with mud, so Rose ran to the hand pump in the farmyard and filled an old can with water. 'Here now,' she said softly as she returned. 'Will you let me clean the muck off? You don't want to get infected now, do you?'

She carried on talking to the animal, trying to stay calm and gentle even though her voice and her hands trembled. The dog watched her, not moving. She supposed that he'd learned to remain still in the hope that the farmer wouldn't notice him. She quickly doused the wound, taking care not to hurt him and she was relieved to see that the dog seemed to relax as she tended to him.

'What the hell are you doing?'

The farmer came around the corner of the barn and bellowed at her. Rose dropped the can. As it clattered on the cobbles, the dog jumped up, snarling. Before she could react, the animal sank its teeth into her arm. Rose shrieked in shock and pain.

Moments later, the dog released its hold on her and ran off yelping as the farmer kicked at it. When the animal disappeared into the fields he turned to Rose. She was crouching on the ground, holding her arm. Her sleeve was ripped and she was bleeding, but he stood over her uncaring of her situation.

'Serves you bloody right,' he growled. 'Leave the dog alone. It's a working beast, not a damned useless lap dog. Oh, and that supervisor of yours has turned up. You're to go and see her at the farmhouse. But don't be hanging around yakking all day. Get rid of her quick. You've got work to do.'

'But I'm bleeding.'

'Your own fault, so stop whining. Now get yourself over to that woman and mind your tongue. I don't want her poking around my farm or into my business.'

By the time Rose got into the house, she was sobbing with pain and frustration. The supervisor, a no-nonsense matron with a brisk manner, took one look at her and marched her into the farmhouse kitchen and sat her down next to the range. The farmer's wife and children were nowhere to be seen. Rose supposed they were all out in the fields working. The last farm hand had left a week ago to enlist. He'd gone saying that he'd rather take his chances in battle than stay here. Rose didn't blame him.

'What happened to your arm, dear?' she asked.

Cradling it against her chest, Rose looked at the oozing puncture marks. 'His dog bit me. But it wasn't the dog's fault. He'd been kicked and I was trying to help it. That... that brute shouted at me for doing so and the noise frightened the dog.'

The woman studied her wound and her tearful face. 'But that doesn't account for the fact that you've lost a good amount of weight since I saw you last.' She glanced around the room. 'Or the absence of anyone else on the premises. This is the third time I've been here to see you only to be sent away or to find the place deserted. I had to go out into the fields to find the farmer this time to make sure I could speak to you today. Let's clean that wound now and perhaps you'll tell me everything that's going on?'

Rose looked at her in shock. 'You've been here before?'

'I have, as I said I would as there's no telephone here. The first time I came I was told that it was your day off and you'd gone into Minehead. But since then no one has ever answered the door, though I saw a child rushing away the last time I came. I think he must have thought I was from the education board, considering he should have been in school at the time.' She shook her head, frowning. 'It seems to me that this farm isn't being run as well as it should be.'

Rose let out a giggle. She tried to stem it, knowing that she was becoming hysterical. 'Sorry, ma'am,' she said as tears replaced her laughter. 'But it's certainly not what I expected.' She raised her arm. 'This is the least of it. I've not left the farm at all, not had a full day off in weeks. I've only been able to send my letters home when I see the postman and give them to him. I don't even know where Minehead is. Even if I wanted a day out, I can't because he hasn't paid me a penny yet. I've barely enough left of my own money to give to the postie to buy stamps for my letters home. I haven't slept more than an hour or so some nights because I lay awake listening to him beat his wife and children. He takes most of the food and there's never enough left over for the rest of us. Now the last farm hand has left and there's so much work to do...' Rose's breath caught on a sob, but she felt better for letting it all out. 'I want to do my bit, I really do. But if my daddy and mammy knew what it was like here, they'd order me home and never let me leave again. I haven't dared tell them how awful it is, I don't want them worrying. But I don't know how much more I can take.' She buried her face into her hands, sobbing in earnest now.

While Rose tried to stem her tears, the woman made her some sweet tea. She didn't speak until she handed Rose her drink.

'Here, lass. Drink this.'

'Thank you,' she said, taking the mug in trembling hands. She'd only been offered rough cider or water to drink since she'd been here. The cider had made her sick and the water had been brackish and unpleasant. In desperation, she'd taken to drinking some of the milk when she'd been out with the cows. She knew the farmer suspected, but she never had more than the equivalent of a cup or so, so it wasn't her fault that the milk yields were down. She wondered how the farmer would react if he came in and saw them drinking his precious tea, flavoured with the sugar that only he was allowed to have. In her current state, she decided that she simply didn't care any more.

While she sipped the hot tea, her supervisor took a clean handkerchief out of her handbag and soaked it with water. With brisk but gentle hands, she rolled Rose's sleeve up and began cleaning her wound. The girl took the woman's ministrations stoically, although she had to put her tea down because her hands were still shaking and she was afraid that she would spill it.

'That's the best I can do for now. At least the bleeding has stopped. I don't suppose they have any first aid supplies in here,' the supervisor told Rose. 'We'll pop into the doctor's on the way, just to check it over.'

'On the way where?' she asked, confused.

'Away from here,' came the firm reply. 'I'm more sorry than I can say that I didn't make sure I saw you before now, Rose. But now I've seen the true situation, I'll not be leaving you here. Nor will that man get another land girl. I'm disgusted by his treatment of you. I'll be reporting him to the appropriate authorities. He may well lose his government contracts.'

'But the country needs the food we produce.'

'Not at the expense of hard-working girls like you, my dear.'

'But what about his wife and children? They'll not be able to manage.'

The woman's stern expression softened. 'Don't fret yourself. I'll speak to some people. I'm sure there are folks around here who will help the family, even if the man himself has failed in his duty to care for them. A family thrives on love, not beatings.'

'I know,' she agreed miserably. 'But when I tried to talk to her, she told me to mind my own business and that it was how things were.'

She shook her head. 'Well, that's her choice of course. Now you mustn't worry. I'll make sure someone keeps an eye on things here.'

Rose felt a brief rush of hope for the family. Maybe someone could help them and be strong enough to stop the man from being so violent towards the people he was supposed to nurture and protect. But, whatever happened, Rose knew that she couldn't stay here any longer. It was so completely different from the warm, cheerful family home that she'd grown up in that the past months had almost broken her spirit.

She nodded, taking a deep, calming breath. 'Are you going to send me home?'

'Is that what you want, my dear?'

She shook her head. 'Much as I'd dearly love to see Mammy

and Daddy for a little break, I know that if I go home like this they'll know that I've been lying about what's been happening.' She grimaced and gave her a sheepish look. 'I don't want them to worry. It's hard enough for them with five of my brothers in the forces.'

'I understand. None of us want our families to worry, do we?' She smiled. 'So I propose that I take you away from here and we'll find you a better situation, where you'll be with decent folk who won't treat you poorly. How does that sound?'

Rose nodded, almost overwhelmed by the woman's kindness after weeks of brutality. 'That sounds lovely. Thank you.'

2

After spending the night at her supervisor's house in a warm, clean room, on a soft mattress with enough blankets to keep out the cold, Rose felt a little better. She'd been embarrassed by how weepy with relief she'd been when they'd arrived, especially when she'd joined the lady and her husband at their dinner table and been served with a generous portion of cottage pie. It was the best meal she'd had since she'd arrived in Somerset.

The next day Rose had been delivered to the Morgan family's farm in Catcott. She was nervous, hoping that this employer would be kinder.

'Oh my, you've been through it, haven't you, my love?' said Mrs Morgan after the supervisor had explained Rose's last situation. 'Well, don't you worry. There won't be no shenanigans like that on this farm, I can tell you. You'll be treated fair, paid a proper wage and have some time off like you're entitled to.'

Mr Morgan had nodded. He didn't say much, leaving his wife to do the talking. But he had kind eyes and when Rose saw him pet the farm dog as it lay on the flagstone floor in front of the kitchen range, she knew that he wasn't anything like her previous employer.

Their sons had come in from the fields after the supervisor had left, promising to see her in a few days to check that she was settling in.

'This is Ivor,' said Mrs Morgan, putting her hand on the shoulder of a tall lad of about twenty. 'And that's our Jimmy.' She nodded her head in the direction of her even taller son, who looked a few years older than his brother. Both had broad shoulders, fair hair and that tanned, healthy look of young men who spent most of their days out of doors. 'Lads, this is Rose, our new Land Army girl.'

Rose felt her spirits rise. They were nice looking. Maybe her dream of meeting a handsome young farmer away from the protective gaze of her brothers was coming true after all.

They both nodded at her, and muttered, 'Hello.' Ivor's gaze was curious. Jimmy was frowning. Her heart sank. After her experience of the past few weeks, his frown was making her nervous. Did he have a temper?

'Hello,' she said quietly, dropping her gaze, worried that he would see her fear.

He gave her a brief nod before he addressed his parents. 'I thought we weren't going to get another one unless one of the hands enlisted,' he said.

'I know son, but Rose needed a new situation. She's not been treated well and Pa and me agreed we'd give her a chance.' She turned to Rose. 'We've some other men and boys working for us. Some live in the village and the others are in cottages on the farm.'

She nodded. Hoping they were going to be all right with a girl working alongside them.

'You're not very big, are you?' Ivor said to Rose.

She glanced up at him, trying to gauge whether he was annoyed by that or not. She probably looked like a weakling after all the weight she'd lost. He didn't sound like he was criticising, but rather making an observation. 'I'm average height for a girl,' she said. 'And stronger than I look.'

'Where you from?' asked Jimmy. 'I ain't never heard an accent like that before.'

Rose hid a sigh. Until she'd left home, she hadn't realised she even had an accent. 'Birmingham,' she told him. 'It's a bit different from cider country.'

Jimmy didn't hide his own sigh. He ran a hand through his hair, making it look rather attractive, as though it had been blown by the wind. 'A city girl,' he said. 'Have you ever even seen a cow?'

Rose felt her spine straighten. Her fear faded as she caught his challenging gaze and held it. 'Yes, and I've been milking a dozen or so out on Exmoor, morning and evening for the past few months.'

He nodded. 'Fair enough. Just so long as you didn't change jobs to avoid milking, 'cause that's one of your jobs here. Me, Dad and Ivor have got enough to be getting on with.'

'I had no problem with the cows,' she said, her dander up now. Of course, she'd been scared witless of the beasts when she'd first encountered them – they'd seemed enormous! But the training she'd received before being posted to Exmoor had helped her overcome that and she'd soon learned that they were generally placid animals. She wanted to tell him it was the farmer who was the problem, not the animals. But she realised it wouldn't be a good idea to antagonise her new employers the moment she arrived. So she didn't mention that the horrible man at the last farm had tricked her into trying to milk the bull and laughed his head off as she'd screamed and run when the beast had taken against being handled in his privates. She'd learned her lesson and made sure she only approached cows with full udders showing after that.

She remained silent as they all sat at the kitchen table. Mrs Morgan served up bowls of a hearty vegetable soup and hunks of fresh bread.

'Have some butter on your bread, Rose,' she said. 'You'll be helping me to make the next batch.'

Rose smiled and thinly spread some, conscious of how precious the butter ration was. Mrs Morgan tutted. 'You can have more than that, lass. One of the perks of running a farm is that we don't need a butter ration. Same with bacon and ham. We have a licence to butcher a couple of our own pigs a year in return for giving up those rations.'

She nodded. She knew that. But at the last farm it hadn't mattered what rations she was supposed to have. The farmer had taken her coupons and barely given her any food in return and especially not his home-grown bacon. The supervisor had had to track him down on the farm while Rose was packing in order to get her ration book back from him. She'd even managed to prise a few shillings from him to cover some of her unpaid wages.

'Thank you,' she said. 'That's good to know. But I've got all I need at the moment.'

'Watching your figure, are you?' said Ivor with a grin, giving her body a thorough look. She felt her cheeks warm as Jimmy jabbed his brother in the ribs and told him to shut up. Their exchange reminded her of her brothers and she felt herself relax a little more.

'Not really,' she said. 'I just don't want to be greedy. No doubt once I start work I'll be happy to eat more if it's available.'

'Right,' said Mr Morgan, standing up when his bowl and plate were empty. 'We'd better get out in the fields, lads. We've a field of mangolds and one of willow withies to plant today and a couple of cows in the barn looked like they were ready to calve when I checked on them this morning.' The brothers finished their meals and got up as their father turned to his wife. 'I'll leave you to show Rose around, my love. When you've finished, any chance of some help with the willow? I've only got old Vic out there at the moment and all the bending and planting is rough on his arthritis.'

'Yes, my love. I'll pop over there as soon as I can.'

He smiled. Rose was glad to see this after the awful way her last employer had treated his poor wife. 'Do we still need to cover the milking later?' he asked.

'Oh, no, I'm ready to work,' said Rose, although in truth she still felt exhausted and out of sorts. 'If someone can show me where the cows are, I'll do the milking. And I'll come with Mrs Morgan to help with the willows if she can show me what to do.'

She'd heard that a lot of farms in Somerset grew willow as the low-level moors had the perfect growing conditions for it. Apparently, while the government had banned the production of willow baskets for domestic use for the duration of the war, the authorities were encouraging willow crops as they could be used to make woven pigeon carriers and hampers to contain supplies that would survive the impact of being dropped from planes by parachute.

He nodded. 'Good lass. The missus will show you what's what.'

'I will,' said his wife. 'We'll see you all at dinner time.'

'We won't be late in. We've got to be on parade at seven.'

'Parade?' Rose asked as the menfolk left the kitchen.

'The LDV – Local Defence Volunteers,' said Mrs Morgan as she collected the dirty dishes and took them to the sink. 'There's a unit in the village, mainly farming men and boys.' She sighed. 'I shouldn't complain. At least the farmers aren't expected to go away to fight. And the LDV are being trained to defend us if Hitler sends his stormtroopers over here. We'll be glad of that in an invasion, I'm sure. But I worry that they're burning the candle at both ends. Some nights they get sent to guard somewhere or to have practice exercises, which is all well and good, but when's a man to get a decent night's sleep after working and soldiering?'

* * *

As March gave way to April, Rose settled into the Morgans' farm and things were much more comfortable. The farm was much better run than the last one and the family treated her decently. She regained the weight she'd lost and had more energy.

She was still getting the measure of the sons. She didn't have much to do with Ivor. He was often out on the tractor in the fields or driving the farm truck to make deliveries of milk, eggs, butter and cheese around the area. Mrs Morgan mentioned that he also had a sweetheart in nearby Street.

Jimmy had been given the task of showing Rose the ropes after that first day although he'd made it clear that he would rather not have the job. It was a shame, because when she'd first arrived, she'd thought he was a fine-looking chap – tall and broad and with just the right amount of muscle, the result of his hard work on the farm. But although he'd been polite, he certainly hadn't made any effort to be particularly friendly.

'You don't smile much, do you?' she'd challenged him one day when she'd had to go with him across the moors to track down some of the farm's cows after they'd wandered too far. Like most local farmers, their small herds were grazed on the low-lying moorland and it was one of Rose's jobs to go out and find them morning and evening to milk them. She had to lug a heavy metal churn onto a wheelbarrow, along with a three-legged stool, a bucket and her gas mask and push it to wherever they were, fill it with their milk and trudge back to the farm with it. On this day she hadn't been able to find the cows and so Jimmy had been sent out with her to find them.

'I might be inclined to smile if you got on with your job and didn't create more work for me.'

'It's not my fault your cows have run off. Why don't you keep them in a proper field that they can't escape from?'

He rolled his eyes. 'All the decent fields are needed for food production,' he reminded her. 'Ministry of Agriculture said we had to plough up some of our grazing land for crops.'

Rose had heard about that. The government paid farmers two pounds for every field they ploughed. Wheat and potatoes were needed to keep the population fed without relying on imports. German blockades and attacks on merchant ships meant the country had to produce as much food as it could to make sure the population didn't starve.

'And anyway,' he went on. 'Why waste good land on grazing when we're surrounded by moors full of grass and wildflowers that the cows enjoy?'

'But they could be miles away,' she grumbled.

'Yeah, they could. But they usually go to the same places unless something's scared them off.' He glanced at her, not breaking his stride as they trudged across the land. 'You been frightening our livestock, have you?'

'No I have not,' she huffed, trying to keep up with him. She'd learned early on not to waste time trying to find a dry or cowpat-free path across the land, so her boots were clogged with mud and worse. She had to give them a good clean when her working day was finished. 'I even sing to them. They seem to like that.'

He laughed at that and Rose enjoyed the sight of this grumpy lad's face lighting up with amusement. 'Well, there you are, then.

You've frightened 'em off with your caterwauling. They won't be used to a city girl singing to them when the only singing they usually hear is when the farm workers have had too much cider.'

'My voice isn't that bad,' she giggled. Although she knew she wasn't the world's best singer, she was pretty sure that she was good enough to entertain a few cows while she was milking them.

He glanced sideways at her, grinning. 'Well, try not to frighten them off again, city girl, all right?'

Rose couldn't help but smile at his teasing. It reminded her of her brothers calling her cider girl now that she was working in Somerset. It was silly that they persisted in teasing her like that, because as far as she knew cider was made all over the West Country, not just in Somerset, and even nearer to Birmingham in Herefordshire. She hadn't met a girl yet who habitually drank the rough brew that all the local farms made for their workers, apart from the farmer's wife at her last place. She suspected it was that poor woman's way of coping with life with her horrible husband. But at least her brothers didn't make jokes about how much Cheddar cheese she was enjoying now that she lived in the county where the cheese was made. Why, she was even helping Mrs Morgan to make it as well as butter from the milk she collected. She supposed she should be grateful her brothers didn't give her a ridiculous nickname relating to the cheese-making or milking cows.

'There they are,' Jimmy said, pointing to a small herd of animals a few hundred yards away. 'Looks like the beggars are trying to get to the neighbours' hayrick. Lucky they don't like swimming, eh?'

The only thing keeping the cattle from the tempting hayrick was the long channel of deep water between that field and the edge of the moor. It reminded Rose of the canals that cut through Birmingham on which barges would travel, carrying raw materials into the factories and finished goods out of the city centre. These channels cut endless straight lines across the moors and fields, helping to drain the low-lying land, taking the water out to sea via the rivers that flowed into the Bristol Channel. She knew that the cows could swim if they had to, but preferred dry land to the cold, dark waters.

'I'll herd 'em back towards their usual grazing spot. You run back and get the churn. They look like they're all full of milk and they'll be glad to get rid of it, I reckon.'

Rose nodded. They'd brought the churn as far as the edge of the moor, but Jimmy hadn't seen the point of dragging it all over the place with them while they looked for the beasts and she'd agreed. She set off at a fast clip to retrieve it while Jimmy started rounding up the cows. She was puffing hard by the time she met up with them, but she didn't complain. No one appreciated someone whining all the time. Her first employer had been downright nasty if she showed any weakness, and Mr and Mrs Morgan were nice enough that she didn't want them to think she wasn't happy or pulling her weight.

She picked up her bucket and milking stool and approached the first cow. As she settled down to start milking she noticed Jimmy striding away back towards the farm.

'Typical,' she huffed. 'As soon as he finds them for me, he runs off and leaves me to it!' She supposed she should be grateful that he had helped her in the first place, but she had been hoping he'd hang around for a bit longer to help her get the churn back up the hill to the farmhouse dairy. It was bound to be heavier than usual now that the milking was a few hours late. But Jimmy was probably behind on his own chores now, so she shouldn't blame him. It was just that she had been enjoying spending time with him for a change. Once she'd been shown what she had to do, she'd tended to be left to work on her own, so any company was welcome. That was probably why she enjoyed spending time with Mrs Morgan in the dairy. She hadn't made any friends her own age yet and wasn't sure how she could get to meet anyone. She might pretend to be confident, but she couldn't imagine taking herself off to one of the local dances all on her own.

At home in Birmingham, she'd complained that she never had time to herself with so many brothers around to annoy her, but now she missed their chatter and teasing and would give anything to have them around her again. Of course, all but one of them was away in the forces now, so she didn't know when they might ever get together again as a family.

She was about halfway through the milking and the churn was almost full when Jimmy returned with another one.

She looked at him, surprised. 'I thought you'd gone off to do something else,' she said.

He shrugged. 'I could see these cows were full to brimming, so I reckoned you'd need another ten-gallon churn. I brought a bale of sweet hay as well. If we leave it here for them to snack on, they'll be less likely to wander all that way down to where they got to earlier and they'll be easier to find for the evening milking.'

'Thank you.' She smiled at him as he took her full pail of milk and poured it into the galvanised steel churn before handing the empty bucket back to her. 'That was kind of you.'

He frowned. 'Needed doing, that's all,' he said, as though he didn't like the idea of being thought of as kind. 'Now I've got plenty else to be getting on with. I'll take the full churn back and leave it in the dairy.'

She nodded, her smile fading. He was an odd one was Jimmy Morgan. She thought sometimes he didn't like her at all, but then he did something like this. He seemed to hate it when she smiled at him, as though he was suspicious of her motives. His mother had mentioned that they'd had a land girl before her who had set her cap at Jimmy and often followed him around the farm when she should've been getting on with her own work and not interfering with Jimmy's. Apparently, that had ended in tears, so Rose took care not to give Jimmy the wrong impression. Yes, he was quite handsome, and yes, he did kind things sometimes, but that didn't mean she was going to make a fool of herself over him if he wasn't interested. She knew enough from watching her brothers around girls to know when they were interested and when they were just being polite and Jimmy was definitely not interested in her.

She sighed as he walked away. It would have been nice if they could have been friends, though.

3

APRIL 1940

'Well that's that, Bloomfield. Driver training done, thank Christ. Are you coming out to celebrate tonight?'

Elsie smiled at her colleague, Maggie, a cheerful cockney girl who had occupied the bunk above her during their weeks of training. 'What did you have in mind? Only I've got an early train to catch in the morning.'

'Me n'all, love. But we've gotta mark our achievement, eh? Who'd've thought anyone would let me behind the wheel of anything with a motor?' She laughed, the sound raucous and joyful. 'I can't wait to see my old dad's face when I tell him I can drive a lorry. He'll be chuffed to bits.'

Elsie's smile became a little fixed. She had no one to share her achievements with. Her sister Gertie wouldn't care, even if Elsie knew where she was. Her natural shyness made it difficult for her to make friends, so she'd concentrated on her army career. Basic training, followed by clerical training and then learning to drive a variety of vehicles had kept her busy in recent months. While her fellow ATS trainee drivers were heading home to spend a few days with their families, Elsie had been ordered to head off to a place called Coleshill House. She'd been told not to tell anyone where she was going, so she'd let Maggie think that she was going to visit her sister.

'How about we nip to the local pub for a swift port and lemon?' asked Maggie, unaware of Elsie's thoughts. 'Them squaddies we met there last week might still be around.'

Elsie laughed. 'You weren't so impressed with them as I recall.'

Maggie shrugged. 'They're all right for an evening's entertainment. It ain't like we're looking for romance, is it? Just someone to share a drink and a laugh with before we move on again. I mean, who knows? We could end up posted in some dump in the middle of nowhere without a decent fellow in sight. My sister joined the Wrens and thought she'd be surrounded by sailors. But she's in an operations room with fifteen other girls and a couple of old, married officers.'

'I think I'd rather like that,' Elsie mused. 'Look, I don't mind having a drink this evening, but I'm really not looking for a man to keep me company. What's the point in meeting someone if we're leaving tomorrow?'

Maggie gave her an exasperated look. 'You know there's a war on, don'tcha? No one's expecting a fancy courtship or romance. We're leaving, they're leaving. So why not just have some fun?'

Elsie looked away, pretending to be engrossed in packing her case which lay open on her bunk bed. She supposed that Maggie was right. There was no harm in a little light flirtation. However, after seeing where that had got her sister, Elsie was far more cautious. But Maggie had been good company while they were on this course and she didn't want to let her down. 'All right,' she said, carefully folding a blouse. 'But I want to finish most of my packing before we go so that I don't end up trying to do it at midnight, squiffy after drinking.'

'Fair enough,' said Maggie cheerfully.

* * *

The next day the girls said their goodbyes and caught their respective trains. Elsie would miss the fun-loving Maggie and she wondered what the next posting would hold for her. She knew nothing about the place they were sending her to, and she'd been told not to ask – that she'd be properly briefed when she got there. It was all a bit strange. Her orders were to get to a place called Highworth in Wiltshire and to report to the postmistress, a lady called Mabel Stranks. Her instructions were quite clear. She was to arrive in mufti, so her uniform was carefully packed in her case, and introduce herself to Miss Stranks. She was to have her papers checked by the said lady, who would then make a telephone call and see that she was transported to her final destination, a place called Coleshill in neighbouring Oxfordshire.

The white-haired postmistress was nothing like Elsie had expected. But the elderly lady politely asked her to wait outside on the bench in front of the post office. 'Someone will be along to pick you up soon, my dear,' she said as she ushered her out of the door and greeted a new customer coming in at the same time.

Ten minutes later, a lorry pulled up and after checking her name, the driver told her to climb in the back with her luggage. Glad that she'd chosen a loose skirt to travel in rather than a fitted one, Elsie clambered onto the lorry hoping that no one had seen her ungainly entrance. As the vehicle pulled away, she found a space to sit on her suitcase against the wall of the lorry amongst various crates, hoping that they were well secured and wouldn't slip and squash her if the driver took a sharp corner.

When they finally stopped, Elsie was tired, stiff and completely lost. She'd understood that the house wasn't far from Highworth, but she suspected the driver had taken a longer, roundabout route to get to their destination – a fact cheerfully confirmed by the officer she was taken to meet once she'd been allocated a room and given the chance to change into uniform. The first order of the day was for her to be reminded that she had signed the Official Secrets Act and that divulging any information about this place would have dire consequences.

'Of course, sir,' she replied when he asked her if she understood this. She didn't add that she couldn't think of a single soul she could tell now that she'd said goodbye to Maggie and her other colleagues.

'We can't be too careful, Bloomfield. The work carried out here is top secret. The less people know about it the better.'

She felt a shiver of excitement run up her spine mixed with a little fear. When she didn't comment, he went on. 'You're aware of the speed of the German advance across Europe?'

She nodded. She read the newspapers, although she suspected that the press didn't know the half of it.

'To be frank, it's not going well for us, Bloomfield. Word is that we'll have to retreat over the Channel before long. If that happens, the enemy's next target will be Britain. We have to be prepared for the invasion.'

Elsie swallowed around a lump in her throat. The prospect of the enemy landing on British soil was terrifying.

'The purpose of this place is to help coordinate a special network of personnel who will stay behind if our forces are overcome in order to become an active resistance movement whose aim will be to stem the advance, make life as difficult as possible for the enemy.'

'I see. So, am I going to be your unit clerk, sir? I've also passed my driver's course.'

He shook his head. 'It's not your clerical or driving skills we need, Bloomfield although they'll no doubt come in handy. Now I understand that you used to be a telephonist. Is that right?'

'Yes, sir.'

'Then you'll be more use to us as a radio operator, although we'll utilise your other skills as a cover in the meantime.'

'Oh! I hadn't thought of that,' she said. She'd thought she'd left her old life as a telephonist behind, but it was good to know that her skills in that regard might be useful to the war effort. 'I'll be happy to do whatever's necessary, sir.'

'It will mean having to stay behind when the invasion comes, living either underground for weeks in a bunker, or more precariously amongst the civilian population with a portable radio. If the enemy takes control of our usual communications networks, rogue radio operators will be vital to keep the fight going. But be aware, Bloomfield, your life will be in danger. The Nazis will be seeking out our hideouts and eliminating anyone within them. Any man or woman found with a radio will be shot as a spy, probably after they've tortured them to extract information about who they're working with.'

That lump in her throat got bigger and she blinked hard as she tried to take a calming breath. She felt a kick of pride that she'd been selected for such an important role, even as her heart faltered at the thought that she might not – in fact, probably wouldn't – survive.

'It's up to you whether you accept this posting or not. No one will think harshly of you if you prefer to play it safe. We've plenty of clerical and driving jobs to fill as well. Take yourself off for a walk around the grounds before dinner to think about it. Just remember that anything you encounter in the grounds is top secret and never to be spoken about to anyone. We can talk further this evening.'

She stood and saluted before being dismissed. Elsie left the Clock House building where the offices were and skirted around the stable block where she had been billeted on the first floor in one of the smaller dormitories of just four beds. These buildings were a way from the main house, an imposing three-storey building with long, elegant windows and tall square chimneys. She stood in the shadow of the woods that covered much of the grounds, staring at the edifice. It glowed gold in the afternoon sunshine. She wondered about the people who had lived there before the war.

A movement caught her attention and she turned her head to see a small squadron of soldiers emerging silently from the woods. They seemed to be wearing LDV uniforms, but they marched as smartly as any regular army unit. Their faces were blackened and they wore knitted caps rather than uniform head-wear. Rubber boots instead of standard army issue meant their progress was silent. Elsie stood motionless, watching them, not wanting to draw attention to herself. It occurred to her that, one day, it might be German soldiers walking by rather than British and her life might depend upon them not seeing her. She fought the urge to shrink behind a tree, knowing that to move at all would make it more likely that she would be spotted. No, she was safer staying exactly where she was. Her khaki uniform helped her to blend into the browns and greens of the trees. She stayed there, frozen, until the last man disappeared around the corner of the big house, then she turned and walked swiftly back to the stable block and the sanctuary of her billet.

She would do as she'd been asked, she decided. It gave her a purpose, a reason to go forward in her life. Surely it was better for her to do this than someone with a family who would miss them? She would give it her all and maybe, one day, the world would be at peace and a better place for all those who survived this war. Her only remaining family would never know her part in the process, but at least Elsie would know that she had done her bit.

4

Daisy Selway finished changing the dressing on her patient's ulcerated leg. 'There you are, Mrs Lambert, all done.'

The old woman sighed. 'Ah, that feels better. Thank you so much for coming out to see me, Nurse. I don't think I'd have made it to the surgery, it's so painful to walk these days.'

Daisy packed away her medical bag and smiled. 'It's no trouble. You must keep it as clean and dry as you can, and I'll pop in again next week to see how it's coming along.'

'How much do I owe you?' she asked, reaching for her purse.

'The doctor will send an account. You don't need to pay anything today.' Daisy didn't get involved with payments for the work she did as a district nurse. Her job was to make house calls and provide whatever treatment the doctor told her was needed. It was up to him to issue accounts.

She took her leave, loading her bag into the basket on the front of her bicycle and checking her notebook for details of her next call. There was another elderly patient to check after a fall had left him with broken ribs. There was little that could be done for the old chap but to keep him comfortable while the bones healed themselves, but his family welcomed Daisy's support.

'Listen to the nurse, Pa,' his daughter told him when he grumbled about staying in bed. 'You'll get better quicker if you do as you're told.'

'You will indeed,' said Daisy with a professional smile. 'I know it's painful, but we can prop you up a bit better with more pillows to help take the pressure off. Then you can read your newspaper and try and rest. No pipe smoking in bed, though. You know the doctor has strictly forbidden it.'

The next call was to examine an evacuee child. 'It's definitely measles, I'm afraid,' she told the woman caring for him. 'So he'll need to be isolated from other children. I'm a bit concerned about those spots in his ears. Try and stop him from scratching them. If they get infected he could lose his hearing.'

'Ah, the poor mite. I'll do my best, Nurse Daisy. Thank you for taking the time to come and see us.'

'You're very welcome.' She smiled.

'I'll bet you miss working at that big hospital in Bristol, don't you?'

She shook her head. 'Not at all. I'm glad to be home.' And she wasn't lying. She'd enjoyed her training and work as a nurse in the city. But she'd missed her home, the family farm in Walton, just outside Street in Somerset. When her ma had confided that she was worried about Pa's health at about the same time when the threat of war was becoming a reality, Daisy had made the decision to come home. She'd had no trouble getting this job as a district nurse in Street and she had no regrets.

As she cycled home after her last appointment, she reflected that Ma had been right to be worried about Pa. He'd lost weight in recent months and some of his strength as well, even though he stubbornly refused to admit that anything was wrong. Daisy was thankful that her brothers were able to take up the slack on the farm, while she and Ma did their best to make sure Pa ate and rested and didn't overdo things. He needed to see a doctor soon, though.

She parked her bike in the shed and made her way into the farmhouse, taking a deep breath as she entered the kitchen. She found Pa asleep in his chair by the range. She didn't disturb him, but stood watching him for a few moments. He was ill, whether he admitted it or not. He was pale, his breathing was wheezy and he looked exhausted.

'Hello, love,' said Ma as she came in. 'Had a good day?'

She nodded and hugged Ma. 'How long has Pa been asleep?' she asked softly.

Ma sighed. 'About half an hour. He's not right, is he?'

Daisy shook her head. 'Try not to worry. I'll get a doctor to check him out if it's the last thing I do,' she whispered.

'I'm so glad you're home, lass.' She kissed her cheek. 'Now, let's get the kettle on, shall we?'

5

MAY 1940

Daisy pedalled her bicycle along the lane, enjoying the sunshine and the wind in her hair. It was her day off. She'd hoped that one of her old friends would be free to come out for a jolly trip on their bikes, but no one had been available. It seemed as though, since she'd gone away to train as a nurse, everyone had moved on with their lives and she no longer fitted in with them. The lads were either working or had already enlisted. Most of the lasses were now married, some had children already. She supposed that, at twenty-four, she should have thought about settling down by now. But her life-long adoration of Mattie Musgrove, the son of family friends, meant that no other lads had ever lived up to his image. And anyway, after working so hard to qualify as a nurse, she wasn't in any rush to give it up. So she'd set off early and come out for a ride on her own.

In her basket was a packed lunch, a bottle of elderflower cordial and a small picnic blanket, fitting snug over her gas mask box. She didn't know where she was going, but she wasn't bothered. She knew these lanes across the low-level moors well, so she wasn't likely to get lost, even though all the road signs had been removed. It was a precaution against an invasion by the Nazis. Without signage, it was hoped that they'd soon get lost in the lanes.

She barrelled along, reacquainting herself with the local area. She passed cider orchards, willow plantations, peat works and farms, waving to people in the fields. She had missed this when she'd been training and then working in Bristol after she'd qualified as a nurse. It had been a long time since she'd had a day out like this. Her studies and then her shifts at the hospital had made it difficult to get home very often. She was glad she was home for good now, because she really wanted to keep an eye on Pa. He was certainly slowing down, but still flatly refused to see the doctor. However, this week was one of his better ones, so she had decided to have a day out and enjoy the sunshine.

In an orchard alongside the lane in Catcott, a few cows were grazing. She noticed they were all huddled together and at the gate stood a milk churn. Daisy frowned. Most milk was collected early in the morning and then late afternoon. If someone had left a full churn there, the milk would be going off in the heat.

Daisy was almost past the gate when she heard a strange noise and slowed, frowning. She could have sworn she'd heard a whimper, not at all the sort of sound that usually came from cows.

She got off her bike and turned towards the gate again, propping the machine up against the gatepost. She peered into the orchard. With the blossom over and the fruit too small yet to identify, she didn't know whether the forty or so trees were tart cider apples or some of the sweet eating varieties. Some farmers had half and half, others had separate orchards for the two different kinds.

'Hello?' she called. 'Is anyone there?'

'Oh thank God,' a voice exclaimed. 'Over here. Please, help me!'

Daisy went through the gate, careful to avoid the cowpats as she approached the animals. 'Can you keep speaking to me so I can follow your voice? It sounds like you're in the middle of these beasts.'

'I am! The stupid cows knocked me off my milking stool, then one of them trod on me and I can't get up because they're all crowding round.'

She could tell that whoever it was surrounded by the herd wasn't a local. Her accent was strange, not at all like the soft Somerset lilt that most folk spoke in these parts.

Daisy held her arms out wide as she approached the animals. 'Go on, girls, move yourselves!' she cried out. 'Let me see the patient.' She only hoped they didn't tread on their victim again as they slowly lumbered away.

'At last!' A red-headed girl in a Land Army uniform of breeches and an aertex shirt sat up, reaching for her hat, which had come off worse than its owner. She scowled and punched it back into shape and plonked it on her head. 'Thank you so much. I thought one of the farm lads would have come to find me by now, but I shouted and shouted and no one came. I reckon they're already on the cider.'

Daisy hid a smile. She knew a lot of farming lads would play tricks on the land girls, or would conveniently forget they were supposed to be working alongside them. 'Are you injured? You said something about being trodden on.'

The girl sighed. 'I think it's more a case of injured pride,' she admitted. 'I've been coming out here to milk these cows twice a day for weeks now. I thought it would be easier when they were moved into the orchard to graze between the apple trees and I didn't have to search across the moor for them. But suddenly they decided to knock me about. One walked over my ankle. That hurt, I can tell you and it's still throbbing. Then they all crowded round me and it didn't matter what I tried, the damned beasts wouldn't move and let me up.' She held out a hand. 'Can you help me, please?'

Daisy took her hand and pulled her up. As the girl put her weight on one of her feet, she winced and staggered. 'Ow! Damn and blast it!' she cried as she clung to Daisy to stop from falling over again.

'Where does it hurt?'

'My ankle,' she said, tears springing up. 'What am I going to do now?'

'It'll be all right. I'm a nurse. Let's just try and get you to the gate in case the cows decide to come back. Lean on me and hop on your good leg – that's it.'

The two girls made slow progress across the uneven ground, the curious animals watching from a distance.

'I like your accent,' said the land girl. 'You sound like a proper cider girl. When my brothers found out I was coming to Somerset, they started calling me Cider Girl, the fools.' She gasped in pain as she jarred her injured foot.

'Steady now. That's it. I'm Somerset born and bred. We've got orchards on our family farm although I'm not a great cider drinker. The farm hands appreciate it, though.' Daisy smiled. 'But I don't recognise your accent,' she said, hoping to get the girl's mind off her injury. 'Where are you from?'

'Birmingham,' she said, breathless with the effort of getting over the rough ground. 'Never met a cow until I got here. They frightened the life out of me at first, especially at my last job on

Exmoor. Those cows were as mean as the farmer was. But once I moved here, I soon got used to 'em and thought I was going to be all right. Then this happens.' She huffed out a pained laugh. 'That'll teach me.'

Eventually they got through the gate and Daisy closed it behind them.

'Right, let's get you sat down so I can examine you,' she said. 'Just stand there a minute, holding onto the gate. I've got a blanket in my basket.'

The girl hung onto her arm. 'Oh no, please don't make me sit on it. I'm pretty sure I've been lying in a cowpat for the past hour or so. I'd be mortified if I got muck on your blanket.'

Daisy smiled. She'd suspected as much, but hadn't liked to tell a perfect stranger – one who was in pain at that – that she was smelling a little ripe. 'I'll lower you onto the grass verge then. Is that all right with you?'

She nodded, letting Daisy guide her until she was sitting on the side of the road.

'I'm Daisy Selway. I'm a district nurse in Street. What's your name?'

'Rose Flaherty.'

'Nice to meet you, Rose. Look, I need to get your gumboot off so I can examine you. It might hurt, but I'll try to be as gentle as possible. Are you ready?'

Rose took a deep breath and nodded. Daisy knelt before her and slowly pulled the boot off, aware that the girl was hissing in pain even though she didn't complain or tell her to stop. At last it was off and they could see that Rose's ankle was swollen. When Daisy gently peeled her sock off, there was extensive bruising starting to show around the ankle and foot and she knew it would only get worse in the coming days.

'Ouch,' said Daisy, giving Rose a sympathetic smile. 'I'm afraid

I'm going to have to touch it, to assess the extent of the injury. I'll try not to hurt you, but I might not be able to help it.'

She shrugged. 'It's got to be done.'

'That's the spirit. Ready?'

Rose nodded again and Daisy began to probe around the swollen area, watching her reactions as she did so.

'Can you wiggle your toes?'

Rose moved them, although it clearly hurt to do so.

'And move your ankle by flexing your foot?'

She had barely moved it before she yelped in pain. 'Ow! God, that hurts.' She lay back in the grass, covering her face with her hands.

'I'm sorry,' said Daisy.

'Not your fault. Is it broken?' she asked between her fingers.

'Probably, although it might be a bad sprain. But I think we need to get you to a hospital to have an X-ray to check it.' She frowned, trying to work out how on earth she was going to get the poor girl there.

'But the milk...' Rose pointed at the churn by the gate. Next to it was a wheelbarrow on which it would be conveyed. 'I lost a bucketful when the stupid beast knocked me over, but the rest is in there. My bucket and milking stool are somewhere around, I think they tried to play football with them.'

Daisy pulled a face. 'I doubt the milk is much good now it's been out in the sun for a while. Your stool and bucket won't have gone far. But at the moment, my priority is to get you some help. I think I'm going to have to use the wheelbarrow to get you back to the farmhouse. How far away are we?'

'About half a mile that way.' She pointed. 'I'm at the Morgan farm.'

Daisy nodded. 'I know it.' It was on a slight incline, above the low flat moors around them. Pushing an injured girl there in a wheelbarrow that looked like it had seen better days wasn't going to be easy, but it was either that or leave her here on the roadside while Daisy went to get help. Maybe it would be better if she cycled there quickly and got the farmer to come back on one of his vehicles to pick up Rose.

Before she could make up her mind, she heard a shout and looked up to see a lad running towards them. Rose struggled to sit up, wincing as the movement jarred her ankle. 'Jimmy,' she addressed the lad, muttering something under her breath that sounded to Daisy like, 'and about time too.'

'What's going on here? You should've got that milk back to the dairy an hour ago, and here you are gossiping and lazing about. If it's spoiled, it'll come out of your wages.' He scowled down at Rose who glared back at him.

Daisy stood up, pulling her best nurse-in-charge persona around her, despite her lack of uniform today. 'Excuse me, but we are not *gossiping* or *lazing,* young man. I'm a nurse and this poor girl has had an accident.' She pointed at Rose's still swelling and bruised ankle. 'I was just assessing her injuries after getting her out of the field where those cows trampled her. She needs urgent medical attention, so perhaps instead of standing there haranguing the poor girl, it would be more helpful if you could find a vehicle so we can move her.'

Jimmy seemed to notice Rose's injury for the first time, shock replacing his angry scowl. 'Damnation! That's all we need.'

'I'm sure Rose feels the same, but cursing about it isn't helping. Is there a telephone at the farm? I think she needs an X-ray. It might be broken.'

He stood there for a moment, scratching his head. 'Yeah, there is. Look, I'm sorry, but Ma sent me to get the churn. She needs it to make butter this morning.'

Daisy rolled her eyes. 'Well, I'm very sorry, but Rose is injured and in pain and she's my priority right now.'

'I can see that now,' he said. He squatted beside the injured girl. 'Are you all right, lass? What happened?'

Rose sighed. At least his tone was a bit gentler now. 'I'd milked all but Bluebell. She was a bit twitchy this morning so I left her 'til last. When I touched her udder, it felt hot and the milk that came out looked yellow. I think she's got an infection.' She winced. 'Anyway, I think I must have hurt her when I started to milk her and she kicked out and shoved me over. Then all the others gathered round so I couldn't get up and one of them trod on me.'

'Sounds like mastitis,' said Daisy. 'Our cows get it now and again.' When the lad looked confused, she explained, 'I'm a district nurse in Street, but my family farms over at Walton.'

Jimmy nodded. 'I'll check the beast once we've sorted Rose out.'

'Take the churn in the barrow,' Rose told him. 'We'll manage. If you can help me, Daisy, I should be able to hop, like we did across the orchard.'

He shook his head. 'Don't be daft. It'd take you hours. Look, let me get the milk to Ma then I'll come back with the horse and cart.' He held up a hand before Daisy could object. 'My pa's taken the truck to Glastonbury, so it's the cart or the tractor, and my brother Ivor's out with that on the other side of the farm.' He paused. 'Or... I don't know...' He turned to Daisy. 'What if I carry her and you follow with the churn in the barrow?'

'Oh God!' Rose lay down again and covered her face.

Daisy hid a smile at Rose's distress. As a farmer's daughter, she was no stranger to pushing a barrow, so she had no problem with that. She also had no doubt this tall, well-built lad could manage to carry Rose all the way back to the farmhouse without breaking a sweat. He would be used to hauling bales of hay and sacks of grain and milk churns, but carrying an injured woman who would be jolted with every step he took wasn't quite as simple. She was sure that Rose would not take kindly to being flung over his shoulder, or having to hang onto his broad back, which was no doubt his usual method of carrying heavy objects.

'Um...' she began, before a noise behind them stopped her. She turned to see a car coming round the corner towards them. She held up her arms and ran out into the road as she called out. 'Stop that car!'

There was a screech of brakes. Daisy had a glimpse of two startled faces through the windscreen before the vehicle stopped just inches from her. She let out a breath in relief, realising that rushing out in front of a moving car was not the most sensible thing to do.

'Bloody hell,' said the lad.

'Oh my, Daisy,' said Rose. 'Be careful.'

For a moment there was just the sound of the rumbling engine and the lowing cows, who had come to the gate to watch what was going on. Then the driver's door opened and a young woman in an ATS uniform got out.

'What on earth are you doing?' she asked, her accent clipped and posh, like the announcers on the radio. 'I could've run you over.'

'I know, I'm sorry. Thank you for stopping. I apologise if I startled you, but I'm a nurse and I have a casualty here.' She turned and pointed towards Rose, lying on the verge. 'She's been trampled, and her ankle might be broken. Can you give us a lift to the hospital?'

'Oh goodness! I'd like to help, but' – she glanced towards the car – 'I'm on official business.'

Daisy looked through the windscreen at the passenger who

remained in the car and frowned. When she recognised him her expression cleared. She put her hands on her hips. 'Uncle Ted, is that you?' she called out.

She saw him sigh before he opened the door and got out. 'Morning, Daisy,' he said with a nod. 'What have you been up to, lass?'

'It's my day off, so I was out on my bike. Poor Rose here was milking in the orchard and got trampled. I couldn't leave her here, she's been stuck for hours already.' She directed a disapproving glance at the farmer's son. Why he hadn't come to find her earlier, she would never know. She turned back to her godfather and his companion. 'She needs to get to hospital in case she's broken something. Can you help?'

'Captain Jackson, sir,' the ATS girl said, looking at her watch. 'We have to get to Bridgewater.'

'I'm aware of that,' he said. 'But Daisy here really is a nurse, so if she says a casualty needs to get to hospital, we must take it seriously. It won't take us far out of our way to drop them at the infirmary.'

'Hang on,' said Jimmy. 'Who's paying for this?'

Daisy rounded on him. 'She's your farm's employee, and she was injured while working with your animals, so who do you think should pay?'

'Actually,' said Uncle Ted in his usual calm manner, 'as she's a Land Army girl, I'm sure the authorities will cover her medical costs. Right now the important thing is to get the poor lass some help, isn't it?'

'Sorry, sir,' said the lad, looking shamefaced. 'But it's the first thing my pa will ask, so I had to put the question.'

Ted nodded. 'I understand. You're the Morgan lad, aren't you? I recognise you from the LDV parade last week. I know your pa.

I'll speak to him. Now, help me get the patient into the back seat, lad, then you can get on with your work.'

It took just a few minutes to get Rose settled on top of Daisy's picnic blanket – she had worried about getting muck on the leather seats and so had reluctantly agreed that it could be used. 'I'll wash it for you,' she promised.

'No need,' said Daisy with a smile. She handed Rose her gas mask, having retrieved it from the wheelbarrow. 'Here, you'll need this at the hospital.' It was compulsory for everyone to carry a gas mask with them at all times. 'Remind me to get mine out of my bike basket before we go in or someone will be sure to tell me off.'

She climbed in beside her with a smile after Ted had put her bike in the boot, and they were off, leaving Jimmy to lug the churn back to the dairy and explain to his ma what had happened.

Uncle Ted turned around in the front passenger seat to smile at the two girls.

'So, Daisy, even on your day off you're treating patients, eh?'

She chuckled. 'I had a nice bike ride this far before duty called. This is Rose, by the way. You already know she's a Land Army girl at the Morgans' farm.'

'Hello, sir,' said Rose with a shy smile. 'Thank you both so much for stopping. I'm sorry to be a nuisance. But if it wasn't for Daisy, I don't know what I'd have done.' She sighed, her skin pale. She was clearly in a lot of pain after all the jostling about.

He gave her a reassuring smile. 'I'm sure young Jimmy would have found you eventually. But you're certainly in good hands with our Daisy.' He looked over at their driver. 'And we have young Elsie here to thank for her quick reactions on the brakes. I'd have hated to have to explain to Daisy's pa that we'd run his daughter down. Elsie Bloomfield, meet my goddaughter, Daisy

Selway. Her ma and I are cousins on my ma's side. And her patient is Rose...?' He raised his eyebrows in question.

'Flaherty, sir,' said Rose, her voice laced with pain.

'Nice to meet you both,' said Elsie, keeping her eyes firmly on the road ahead. 'I'm very glad I stopped in time.'

'I thought you were going to knock her down for sure,' said Rose. 'I nearly screamed.'

'So did I,' laughed Daisy. 'Thank you, Elsie, for not hitting me and for the lift. I'm so glad you had Uncle Ted with you and not some other officer, otherwise I might have been in real trouble, seeing as how you're on official business.' She paused. 'And speaking of trouble, Uncle, I've been meaning to ask you for a while – how much of it are you in for getting back into uniform? I don't suppose Auntie Kate is happy about it.'

He chuckled. 'Don't worry, I'm just a Local Defence Volunteer like your pa and most able-bodied men who aren't enlisted. I'll be staying at home this time. I'm still teaching, and in my spare time I'm working with the LDV to defend family and friends from invaders. I promised Kate I wouldn't rush off to fight like I did in the last conflict.'

Despite his smile, Daisy noticed the bleak look in his eyes as he said that, and she wondered what he'd really done in the Great War. Her ma and pa had hinted that he'd been more than a regular soldier and he'd come home an officer – a captain no less. But like Pa and all the other men who'd fought in the Great War, he never spoke about it.

'But anyway, it's the Whitsun half term and I've been invited to a meeting with a chap in Bridgewater who kindly sent Elsie to fetch me, which is lucky for you lasses, because otherwise I'd have been tempted to make the journey on my motorbike to save my petrol ration. It's a fine day to be on two wheels, eh, Daisy? Not so good for transporting casualties to hospital though.'

Rose groaned, shifting her foot. 'I hope it isn't broken.' She explained how the cows had caught her off guard that morning. 'I hope they don't send me home.'

'Would it be so bad?' asked Ted, his tone curious.

She shook her head. 'Not really. I love my family and I miss them a lot more than I expected to. But all my brothers have left the nest now, so if I went home, my mammy and daddy would smother me with love and I'd never be able to leave again. This is my first time away and, despite missing everyone, I'm rather enjoying the freedom.'

'How many brothers have you got?' asked Daisy.

'Six.'

'Good grief!' said Elsie as though she couldn't help herself. 'That's a lot.'

'I know,' sighed Rose. 'And I'm the youngest. They drive me mad.'

Daisy laughed. 'I can imagine. I've got two brothers and they're enough for anyone to deal with. How about you, Elsie? Do have any siblings?'

Elsie cast a quick glance at Ted, her cheeks going pink. 'Don't worry, lass,' he said. 'I don't stand on ceremony. You have a good natter with the girls.'

Daisy grinned at him. She'd always liked Uncle Ted. He hadn't been her original godfather – that had been one of Ma's other cousins, but that poor man had been killed in the last war and Daisy had no memory of him. When Ted had come home after the Armistice, her ma and pa had asked him to step into the role and he'd agreed. He was good fun and a brilliant teacher. Even though languages were his speciality, he always took time with the youngsters of his acquaintance to help them with their lessons if they struggled, whatever the subject. That was probably why he was deputy headteacher at his school in Wells now.

'I've just one sister, that's all,' said Elsie. 'I can't imagine having lots of brothers. It must be nice,' she concluded a little wistfully.

Both of the other girls made identical scoffing noises at the same time, then giggled as they realised what they'd done. Uncle Ted laughed out loud.

'I had brothers, but no sisters,' he said. 'Every family is different, isn't it? You know Tom has five older sisters, don't you, Daisy?'

Tom was the husband of his wife Kate's good friend Jeannie. 'I know.' She grinned. 'Didn't he move to Somerset from Northampton to get away from them all?'

Rose sighed. 'I know how he feels,' she said, making them all laugh.

'Well, the joke's on him,' said Ted, 'because he's got four daughters now.'

'Goodness, more cider girls,' said Rose, her voice a little woozy.

Daisy chuckled, even as her keen eyes checked her patient to make sure she wasn't about to pass out from the pain. 'Rose told me her brothers are calling her a cider girl now she's living in Somerset.'

'You don't sound like a cider girl, Elsie,' said Rose.

'No, I'm not. I'm from London. They're more partial to beer there. But I'm not much of a drinker. I've never even tried cider.'

Uncle Ted laughed. 'Well you're all Somerset cider girls now, ladies. At least for the time being.'

'My lot drink Guinness, on account of Daddy being Irish,' said Rose, grimacing as her ankle was jolted. 'I don't much like that, either. Give me a nice cup of tea any day. It's a shame it's being rationed now, isn't it?'

They reached the outskirts of Bridgewater and Ted directed

Elsie to the infirmary, where he went in and emerged with a porter and a wheelchair for the casualty.

'Elsie will see me home after my meeting, so we'll hang onto your bike, Daisy, love, and come by here and get you when we're done.'

Daisy nodded and thanked them, relieved that she wouldn't have to find her own way home, then followed the porter as he pushed Rose into the building.

6

Rose's ankle was indeed broken and had to be painfully reset. She spent a couple of days waiting for the swelling to go down before she was put in a plaster cast that would have to stay on for a few weeks. Despite telling her employers she had done so, she didn't write to her parents to tell them, knowing they'd immediately demand that she return to Birmingham to convalesce. She knew that if that happened, it would be even harder to leave again when she was healed. As it was, she was kept in hospital for a week before she persuaded them to discharge her back to the farm.

She'd been scared that the Morgans would say she had to leave, because she wanted to stay. They were nice people and even though the work was hard she was much more comfortable at their farm than she'd been at the last place. To her relief, they had agreed that she could stay.

'You've been working hard, lass,' said Mrs Morgan. 'So I'm not inclined to lose you. We'll need you to help as best you can while you're laid up though. I know you're not supposed to do domestic work, but would you mind doing a bit of darning and mending, and maybe peeling veg and the like while I go out in the fields in your place for the time being?'

'Of course I don't mind,' she'd said. 'I'm happy to do anything that keeps me busy while I'm stuck with this.' She scowled at her plaster cast. 'I'm so sorry to be such a nuisance.'

Mrs Morgan had laughed. 'Don't you fret, lass. I swear the great-great grandmother of that cow what got you did the exact same thing to me when I was a young bride on the farm.'

So, three weeks on, Rose was caught up with all the Morgan family's sewing jobs and she was sitting sideways on at the kitchen table in the farmhouse, her injured foot elevated on the chair next to her while she peeled and chopped vegetables.

She heard the outer door open and the thud on the stone floor as someone shucked off their muddy boots before Jimmy came into the kitchen. He barely glanced at her as he went over to the range and checked the kettle warming there.

'Good morning to you, too,' she said.

He turned towards her. 'It's nearly afternoon, and anyway, I said morning to you when I came in for breakfast.'

Rose raised her eyebrows and stared at him. She'd thought he was softening a bit that day he'd helped her find the missing cows, but she hadn't seen much of his nicer side since she'd broken her ankle and everyone had had to take on her chores while she healed.

He reminded her of her older brother, Liam, who had been a miserable beggar until he'd met the girl who was now his wife. She hadn't put up with his grumpiness, teasing smiles from him until he was full of the joys of love and spring. Rose had been astonished that anyone, especially someone as sunny and nice as Sheila, would put up with him and even more surprised at the transformation in her brother. As she looked at Jimmy, she couldn't imagine having the patience to bring about such a change in him. Although she was tempted sometimes.

She gave herself a little shake. No, Jimmy Morgan was her employers' son, so it would be foolish to set her cap at him.

'A simple hello would've been nice,' she said, her tone dry. 'I'm sitting right here. Didn't your mammy ever teach you it was rude to ignore people?'

He sighed and rolled his eyes. 'Hello, Rose. Do you want a cuppa?'

She beamed at him. 'There, that wasn't so hard, was it? And yes, please, a cuppa will be lovely.' She checked the clock. 'Your ma should be back soon. I expect she'll be ready for a cup as well.'

He nodded as he spooned tea leaves into the pot and then poured hot water in. 'Pa and the others are staying out. We could've done with your help hoeing. This good weather's brought on a damned great crop of weeds in the mangold fields.' He pointed to her plaster cast. 'When is that coming off?'

She grimaced. 'Another week before I go to have it checked. If it hasn't healed enough by then, they'll put another cast on.'

'We need you back in the fields soon,' he said. 'You're no good to us peeling spuds.'

'I didn't want to break my ankle,' she said, stung by his words. 'And I've been doing more than peeling, in case you hadn't noticed. I've never known anyone like you for losing buttons off their shirts or splitting seams.'

'I can't help if I'm doing physical work and things get ripped.'

'Your brother and pa don't have the same problem.'

'Yeah, well Ivor's always driving the tractor or the delivery van, so he ain't likely to be busting any seams, and Pa don't want you sewing up his britches, so he's being a bit more careful when he bends over until Ma gets back to her normal jobs.'

She chuckled. 'So you're the only one working hard enough to ruin your clothes, is that it?'

'If you like.' He grinned, his gaze challenging her. 'I can't help it if a cotton shirt can't handle the strain of my manly muscles.' He raised his arms out to the side and flexed. Rose could see the strain it put on the seams of his shirt, and – truth be told – she did feel a little bit of a thrill at the sight, but she kept her expression neutral.

'How about you concentrate all that *manly muscle* power on pouring me that cuppa you threatened me with?' she said, her tone dry.

He narrowed his eyes. 'Not impressed by a real man, eh? I suppose you prefer them skinny, pale city boys.'

She laughed out loud at the idea, the joyful sound echoing around the large kitchen and making him blink. 'I'm not impressed by any male – man nor boy. I've spent all my life with six big brothers. Peacocks and show-offs, the lot of them.' She looked him up and down. 'And it seems you're no better. Why, you can't even make a girl a cuppa when she's dying of thirst. If I could get up, I'd make it myself.'

He laughed and turned away to grab the strainer and pour the tea. He placed a large mug in front of her and pulled out a chair opposite her to sit down and drink his own.

'You could get up, I reckon. You've managed to get yourself down here from your room every day, haven't you?'

Mr Morgan had carried her downstairs and back up again the first couple of days she'd been allowed out of bed. But Rose hadn't felt comfortable being manhandled by her boss, even though Mr Morgan was a nice man who was nothing like her previous employer, so she'd learned how to help herself.

'Crutches,' she explained. 'I've been using them to get to the stairs. Then I sit on my bottom and slide down.'

'And how do you get back up?'

'Slowly. That's not so easy, but I can still manage. I sit on the stairs and use my good foot and the crutches to push myself up, one step at a time.' She didn't mention how ungainly she felt, especially trying to stand upright once she reached the landing all hot and breathless. Thankfully no one had seen her struggles yet, and that was how she wanted to keep it.

'Well, if you can do that, you can make your own tea next time, can't you?' he said, his eyes sparkling with mischief. 'I haven't got time to be running round after you.'

She gasped at his cheek. He'd offered to make her a drink, after all. But before she could respond, the back door went again and Mrs Morgan came into the kitchen carrying a basket of fresh eggs.

'Ah, there you are, Jimmy lad. Is there any more tea in that pot? I'm gasping.'

Jimmy nodded. 'It's still fresh. I'd better be off. Pa needs me to take another keg of cider down to the mangold field. It's hot work, all that hoeing and the men are complaining they've run out of anything to drink.'

He tipped his mug and finished his tea before he got up and left the room without another word, completely ignoring Rose. She ought to have called him out again for being so rude – her brothers wouldn't dare walk away from their mammy without at least giving her a peck on her cheek or acknowledging a guest in the room. She supposed he didn't think of her as a guest, but rather another employee – one below him in status and not worth the bother. The thought riled Rose even more. He was an arrogant toad!

But as Mrs Morgan didn't seem to mind her son's surly manners, she kept silent. She was starting to realise that, as much as they infuriated her, her family were uncommonly loving towards each other and sociable towards anyone visiting the family home, so long as they weren't there to court their sister. She stifled a sigh. She missed the affection Mammy and Daddy doled out on a daily basis.

'D'you want a top-up, lass?' Mrs Morgan asked as she poured her own drink.

I'd rather have a hug, she thought as she shook her head. 'No thanks, Mrs M.' Drinking too much meant she'd need to use the lavatory, and negotiating the path from the kitchen to the outhouse across the cobbled farmyard was not easy on crutches. 'I've nearly finished the veg. What do you want me to do after this?'

'Well now, let's have a think. There's a leg of lamb ready to go in the oven, and I've an apple pie and some cream in the pantry for pudding.'

One thing Rose couldn't complain about was the food. Despite rationing, the Morgans made sure she was well fed, which wasn't the case on all farms, as she'd found to her cost at the last place. She'd heard that other girls had been half starved by their employers as well, so she knew how lucky she was with the Morgans. If she hadn't been working so hard in the fields, she'd have been bursting some seams of her own by now. She'd been careful not to eat so much since she'd broken her ankle for fear that she wouldn't be able to get back into her overalls when the plaster cast came off.

'Unless our Jimmy splits another seam showing off, all the mending is done for now,' Mrs Morgan went on, winking at Rose.

Rose grinned, although she felt a little pang in her heart that it was clear that Jimmy liked to show off to everyone, not just a silly land girl who had more time on her hands at the moment than was good for her.

'He certainly seems to enjoy it,' she said. 'But as we're done with mending for now, is there anything else I can do?'

Mrs Morgan sat in the chair that Jimmy had vacated and took a sip of her tea as she thought about it. 'To be honest, lass, I've been too distracted to think about it beyond getting meals on the table. The young woman who does the farm books every quarter has got herself a job in Bath and moved away, so she's up and left us in the lurch.'

Rose studied her hands, trying to hide her excitement. 'I might be able to help,' she said, hesitantly. 'You'd have to show me the ropes, of course. But my best subject at school was arithmetic, and I used to help my auntie with the books at my uncle's shop on Saturday afternoons after I finished work at the button factory. I really enjoyed it. I was even hoping they might take me on and I could leave the factory, but they never had the money to pay me for it full time.'

Mrs Morgan put down her cup with a thud. 'Well, I'll be! Who'd've thought it? When they said we was getting a girl from the big city who used to work in a factory, I'll be honest, lass, we thought you'd be as useless as the last one. But you've got on with it and not complained, even when our beasts did you an injury. And now you're offering help with a job that none of us wants to do. I swear, you're an angel in disguise, young Rose. If you really mean it, I'd be delighted if you took the paperwork off my hands, and I've no doubt my James will gladly swap some of your hours round so you can do the office work. Since the war started, we've been getting a mountain of extra forms that need filling in, and the new rules coming from the Ministry of Agriculture week after week have been driving us round the bend.'

Rose smiled, her excitement growing. But then she remembered what she was here for and her spirits fell. 'Do you think my Land Army supervisor will let me do it? I mean, I'm supposed to be here to help grow more food for the nation, not hide away in an office. You know how funny they get about us girls even being asked to do domestic work.' They'd had to pretend to her supervisor that she wasn't doing any work when she arrived for her inspection last week. Rose had assured her she was convalescing at the farm and doing nothing more taxing than reading magazines until her plaster cast came off. She felt bad about lying, but she'd have been bored out of her skull if she hadn't been able to do *something*.

'We'll worry about that when she shows up for her visits, lass,' said Mrs Morgan. 'If you want to do the paper and number work for us, you'll be freeing up the rest of us to take up the slack in the fields.'

Rose frowned. 'Actually, I like doing the field work as well. Most of it anyway. I'm mighty glad to be missing the hoeing in the mangold fields this week – that's back-breaking work. How about I have a look at the office while I'm laid up and see what I can do to get it in order? I'm sure I'll be able to get on top of it fairly soon. Then, when I'm fit for farm work, I can go back to my duties and do an hour or two in the office in the evenings, or on my time off, so that everything stays in order.'

Mrs Morgan nodded. 'If you're sure. But you mustn't let us take up all your spare time. You still need some time off or you'll wear yourself out.' She gasped and put a hand to her head. 'Oh my lord, I completely forgot to tell you! Talking about your time off just reminded me. That nurse who found you in the field – Daisy Selway, isn't it? I met her when I was in Walton yesterday while I was delivering eggs. She asked how you were and said she'd like to come and see you on her afternoon off on Thursday. I told her she'd be welcome. I hope that's all right? From what you said, it seemed like you girls got along, so I thought you'd be glad of the company.'

'Oh, that will be lovely.' She smiled. 'I'll look forward to seeing her.' Rose had indeed hit it off with Daisy, and Elsie had seemed nice too, though she was clearly nervous about being too friendly while she was on duty and in the presence of a captain, even if he was only an LDV officer and not a regular soldier. Rose had sent them all thank you letters, care of Daisy at the surgery as she didn't know their addresses. It would be nice to be able to thank Daisy in person now that she wasn't feeling woozy with the pain. She had been so kind, staying with Rose while she was examined in hospital and making sure she was settled into the ward before she finally took her leave.

'Lovely,' said Mrs Morgan. 'Right, how about I get your crutches and help you into the office along the hallway there? You can have a look and see if it's something you really want to do. Now if it's too much chaos and you don't want to take it on, you must say, my dear. We'll manage somehow, although it might make my James a bit grumpier while he tackles it.'

Rose took her crutches from her. 'Don't you worry, Mrs M. I'm sure I can sort it out. Let's go and have a look.'

It wasn't until she saw the piles of unopened official letters, seed catalogues, and invoices that she realised that this wasn't going to be as simple as her aunt and uncle's tidy bookkeeping.

Oh well, Rose, she told herself silently while Mrs Morgan lit the paraffin heater so that she wouldn't get cold in there. *You wanted something to beat the boredom of darning and peeling spuds, so you can't complain.* She just hoped that Jimmy didn't start accusing her of skiving if this took up more time than she spent in the fields.

7

JUNE 1940

Elsie was busy typing up reports when her new boss Captain Crick entered the office. She immediately stood and saluted.

'At ease, Bloomfield. No need to leap to your feet every time I walk in the room. We'll never get anything done if you do that.'

'Yes, sir,' she said, sinking back into her chair. 'I've almost finished the last of the reports and your post is on your desk. Would you like me to get you a cup of tea when I've done this?'

'Splendid idea.' He nodded and walked through her office into his own one.

Elsie turned back to her work, relieved. This CO was a different kettle of fish to her last boss, who had been transferred a week ago. She had got used to his taciturn manner and strict adherence to military procedure – especially saluting whenever he entered the room. But as the captain had just said, having to jump up and down all the time didn't help her concentrate on the work she had to do.

She allowed herself a small smile. She much preferred this chap. He wasn't very chatty, but not many officers were. But at least he was polite and didn't treat her as though she shouldn't be in uniform simply because she was a woman, like one or two of the others she'd encountered. *Didn't they know that it was all hands on deck with the war on?* By doing this clerical work and driving, she was freeing up men for combat, so those old stuffed shirts should be grateful she was here. But they seemed to think that the Auxiliary Territorial Services wasn't as good as the men's army.

She huffed at the thought, banishing it. She was in the army and that was that. She was doing her bit, although she'd be happier if there were more ATS girls around. She'd done her basic training with lots of really nice girls and she'd hoped to end up working with some of them. But first she'd had to do a clerical course, then a driving course and by the time she'd done those most of the girls she'd started basic training with were scattered far and wide and she didn't see any of them. Then she'd been sent to Coleshill and she knew she wasn't likely to be working with any other ATS girls for the foreseeable future. However, nothing seemed to have come of it since she'd arrived in Somerset. She wanted to ask someone about it but, as she'd signed the Act, she didn't think she could talk to just anyone about it and had no idea who might be privy to what she'd been told.

She'd ended up at this office in Bridgewater where she only saw a few soldiers and Local Defence Volunteers and no other women and no mention was made of her trip to Coleshill. Her billet in the town was with an elderly widow who resented her presence and was fully prepared to bolt the door at eight every evening, whether Elsie was home or not, so she daren't take herself off to the cinema or a dance. Between her duties and her strict landlady, Elsie had no chance of meeting new friends, so she was feeling rather lonely.

She finished the report and pulled it out of the typewriter. After a quick scan for errors, she was satisfied it was up to standard and put it in the file on her desk. Ten minutes later, she tucked the file under her arm and picked up the tea tray and took them through to Captain Crick.

He was on the telephone, so she went to put them on the desk and leave. But he held a hand over the receiver and told her to wait. He scanned the tray. 'Bring your cup in,' he said. 'I need to talk to you.'

She nodded, but he had already turned back to his call. By the time he finished, she had brought in her own cup of tea and a pencil and notepad so that she could take notes. She sat in the chair opposite him and waited as he scribbled some notes on his own pad before reaching for his cup.

'Ah, that's better,' he said after his first sip. 'I was ready for that. My last clerk was a chap who'd never learned how to boil water, let alone make a decent cuppa.'

She smiled but didn't say anything. She was still not sure how easy-going he really was, so she wasn't about to push her luck by getting too friendly with him. He could well be testing her. They'd been warned in basic training not to get too chummy with soldiers, especially officers, because some would take that as permission to take liberties with them, while others would see it as proof that women shouldn't be in the forces. It wouldn't only make life difficult at work, but could ruin a girl's reputation. As Elsie had no home to return to and no family she could rely upon, she couldn't afford to blot her copybook. The army was her home and family now, and she wanted to keep it that way.

She took a sip of her own tea, enjoying the brief respite after hours hunched over the typewriter. 'You said you needed to talk to me, sir,' she reminded him.

'Ah, yes. It seems that our plans are about to come to fruition and it's been decided that we need to move these offices out of town. You're going to have to pack up everything over the next two days. Oh, and you'll have to change billet I'm afraid.'

She couldn't hide her smile. 'That's all right, sir. It's not the most comfortable place, so I'll be glad of a change of scene.'

He regarded her thoughtfully. 'Good. Hopefully your new billet will be a bit more to your taste, although I can't promise anything.' He glanced at his watch. 'Now, it's 1600 hours. An LDV Captain Jackson is due here, but I understand he's a schoolmaster, so he'll probably arrive late and in mufti.'

'I know him, sir. He came here before. Should I go and collect him?'

He shook his head. 'He tells me he's got his own transport. Just show him in when he arrives. In the meantime, see if you can source some tea chests and start packing. All classified documents are to be kept separate and all boxes must be clearly marked. Keep an inventory of what you pack so that we can make sure it all gets to the other end. You wouldn't believe the stories I've heard about office supplies going missing. Everyone's an opportunist these days.' He chuckled. 'But they're not going to get their sticky hands on our supplies, Bloomfield. D'you hear?'

'Yes, sir,' she replied. She hesitated. 'Er... permission to ask a question, sir.'

'What is it?'

'Can you tell me where we're going, sir? Not that it matters. I'll just be glad to get out of my current billet. My landlady...' She realised she was rambling as he stared at her, so she shut up.

When she subsided, he spoke. 'We're going to an estate on the outskirts of Glastonbury. I think the enlisted men will be billeted in a dormitory. Officers in the main house. Not sure where we're going to put you, but we'll find somewhere.'

She nodded. 'Sorry, sir.'

He shook his head. 'That's not the first time you've apologised, Bloomfield. What was that for?'

'Um, well... I realise that having a female clerk causes problems in terms of accommodation.'

'So what? You're a valuable member of the team, so we'll find a way to make it work.' He narrowed his eyes. 'Did they tell you why you were attached to this unit?'

She shrugged. She wasn't sure how much she could say about her time at Coleshill. 'Not really, sir. I had understood that my previous experience as a telephonist would be utilised, but that hasn't been mentioned since I got here. I believe the previous CO thought I was useful because I can type as well as drive. Is that it?'

'Mmm. Not exactly, although your office skills and driving ability are jolly useful. No, I understand that your experience as a telephonist did have rather a lot to do with it. You signed the Official Secrets Act, didn't you?'

She nodded. 'Yes.' She paused for a moment then made the decision to speak out. If she got into trouble, so be it. 'I had to go to a place called Coleshill a while ago and they got me to read some things out loud. But none of it made sense and I haven't heard anything else about it. They said I might be selected for special duties, but I've heard nothing since, so I assume I failed the test.'

He made an impatient huff. 'Of course you didn't. What the hell was your last CO playing at? It's quite clear from the orders I received that you're to be the unit's communications officer. I did wonder why he hadn't sent you on the course yet. Damn! Make a note to get yourself on the next radio operator's course at Coleshill. You should've done it by now, and with the news of our forces retreating back to the Channel in France, it's even more urgent.'

She felt a shiver of excitement. 'Does that mean I'll be one of the Stay Behinds after all, sir?'

'Of course. I thought it had been made clear to you.'

'No, sir. Your predecessor said my role was to keep the office running smoothly, drive the staff car, and to leave the rest to the men.'

The captain swore. 'Damned incompetent fool,' he muttered. He sighed. 'Well, I'm your CO now and I expect you to be a full member of the team.' He caught her surprised glance with his own cool gaze. 'You realise what that means, Bloomfield?'

She gulped. 'I think so, sir. They said at Coleshill that, in the event of an invasion, I'm to go underground and do my best to keep communications open while auxiliary units do their damndest to halt the German advance.'

'That's right. Are you going to be able to do that?'

She paused, knowing that the Stay Behinds, as they were referred to, weren't expected to survive for more than a few weeks, but that their work sabotaging supply lines and key routes across the country would give the Allies vital assistance and maybe help defeat the enemy before they had a chance to establish themselves in Britain. As the communications officer she would be the key link in communications between the secret underground units in the area and whatever allied authorities that remained. Without adequate communications, the unit would be isolated without orders and unaware of what was going on elsewhere. It would make their position far more dangerous.

She took a deep breath, holding his gaze. 'Yes, sir. Once I've had the radio operator's training, I'll be ready and willing to do my part.'

He didn't smile, but she could see approval in his regard. 'That's the spirit,' he said. 'I'll make sure you get priority for the next course. You should've done it weeks ago. We've got a lot to do. Now, I understand that Jackson has a contact who will be able to organise our move to save us waiting on official channels. I'll ask him about that. The quicker we can get organised, the better.'

Elsie rose to take the tea tray away. She would make a start on finding some tea chests before she left the office for the day so that she could begin packing everything up tomorrow. Her typewriter would be the last thing to pack so that she could type all the inventory lists as she went along.

There was a knock on the outer door and Captain Jackson came into her room as she left the CO's office. As expected, he was in mufti. He looked every inch a mild-mannered teacher now, nothing at all like an officer.

'Hello, Elsie, lass. How are you? Are you used to being a cider girl yet?'

'Good afternoon, Captain Jackson.' She smiled. 'I'm fine thank you. I'm not sure I qualify as a cider girl, but I'm getting used to living here in Somerset. Anyway, you're to go straight in, sir.' She nodded towards the CO's office.

'Right. Better not keep him waiting. I hear you're on the move.' He winked at her, rapped on the CO's door and entered when told to do so.

She smiled, thinking about her last encounter with him, when his goddaughter, Nurse Daisy Selway, had flagged down the staff car. She'd been quite fierce. Elsie had admired her and her easy chatter with her godfather.

Elsie was thoughtful as she sat at her desk and picked up the local directory to start her search for tea chests. So Captain Jackson already knew about the move, even though he was a volunteer rather than a regular soldier. He was clearly in a position of trust and she wondered again what his role in the unit might be.

She was still feeling a little light-headed after the CO's confirmation that she would be one of the Stay Behinds. If the Germans did invade, which everyone expected they would, it would be highly dangerous and she knew she might not survive. Part of her was scared witless at the idea. But... it wasn't as though she had anyone who cared much about what happened to her.

She'd had a curt note from her sister, informing her that she'd gone back to London from the village in Mid Wales where she'd been evacuated with her baby, because she hated the country and the papers were saying that all the fuss about possible bombing raids on the city were just hot air. 'The Phoney War,' they'd called it. But Elsie wasn't so sure. There had been some terrific battles at sea and enemy planes were constantly testing the British defences. They'd even been spotted over Somerset. The Germans were advancing on all fronts and, since the recent chaotic withdrawal of British forces towards the French coast, it was only a matter of time before they had this island in their sights. She had asked her sister to reconsider, if only for her baby's sake. Any invasion force would be heading to London to take over the government of the country. But she hadn't heard anything else from her, so she had no idea whether she had stayed in London or not. That had been months ago. So now Elsie really did feel alone, and it hurt.

It's better this way, she decided. *This way, I can do my bit for king and country without leaving behind anyone who might grieve my passing.*

8

Rose was trying to add up a line of figures when there was a knock at the front door of the farmhouse. It was unusual in itself because most people used the back door into the mudroom that led into the kitchen.

Knowing that she was alone in the house, Rose sighed and grabbed her crutches. As she made her way from the office to the front hallway, whoever was waiting knocked again.

'I'm coming!' she called as she hobbled towards the door. 'Hold your horses.'

It occurred to her as she reached it that it might be her Land Army supervisor, who wouldn't be happy to see her up and about when she was supposed to be on bed rest, but now that she'd called out she knew she had to let her in and face the consequences. She just hoped she didn't get the Morgans into trouble.

Bracing herself against the wall, she opened the door and breathed a sigh of relief to see Daisy Selway standing there.

'Oh, thank goodness it's you,' she said, opening the door wider so that Daisy could come in. 'Sorry I took so long to answer.' She inclined her head towards her plastered foot. 'I'm still getting the hang of all this.'

Daisy laughed. 'Don't worry about it. You'll just get used to it and as soon as you do, the cast will be off.'

'The sooner the better as far as I'm concerned,' said Rose. 'It's getting mighty tedious, I can tell you, and it's so itchy under the cast it's driving me mad.'

She led the way slowly down the hallway and into the kitchen. 'Would you like a hot drink?'

'Ooh, yes please. I brought some bread pudding. You're all right, my ma made it. You wouldn't want to eat anything I cook.' She got it out of her basket, wrapped in waxed paper, and put it on the table.

'Thank you. I love bread pudding.' Rose filled the kettle from the water pump and put it on the hotplate on the range. 'I'm sorry, I lost track of time, otherwise I'd have had this ready for when you arrived. Is camp coffee all right? We're all trying to eke out our tea rations.' She was actually getting a taste for the chicory coffee substitute, although she still preferred a good cup of tea.

'That's fine. Don't worry, I'm in no rush. It's nice to be out without having to call on a patient – although, I suppose you're unofficially a patient of mine, aren't you? How's your ankle feeling?'

She shrugged. 'It's not bad. It aches something terrible sometimes, but I'm getting used to it and it definitely feels better than it did just after it happened.'

'Well, that's good. It will take time, so don't try to overdo it.'

'I won't, although I couldn't stay in bed all this time. It would've driven me mad. That's why I didn't want to go home to convalesce. Mammy would have fussed so, I couldn't bear it.'

Daisy chuckled. 'Aren't all mothers like that? It's what they do.'

'I know,' Rose agreed. 'But I was just getting used to my freedom, so I wasn't about to go back to all that coddling.'

The kettle boiled. Daisy helped Rose to get cups and saucers and plates out of the dresser and then nipped into the pantry to get the milk jug.

'Sorry I can't offer you any sugar,' said Rose.

Daisy waved away her apology. 'Don't fret on it. We've never had sugar in our drinks at home. Ma and Pa got out of the habit when it was in short supply in the Great War and never went back to it. Our sugar rations go into baking.'

'Mine were the opposite – they always say we should enjoy it because life was far too miserable without sugar. Of course, that means now it's rationed they're missing it all over again.' She sighed. 'And it doesn't look like it's going to get any easier for anyone any time soon, does it? Have you heard the news about the retreat at Dunkirk? I heard it on the radio this morning. I hope they manage to get our boys home safe.' She thought about her brothers Michael and Anthony who were both in the army. She didn't know whether they were in Europe or not. But wherever they were, she prayed they were safe.

Daisy nodded, looking grim. 'It doesn't sound good does it? All those men having to be rescued from the beaches. Thank God for all those brave sailors who took the small boats over to pick them up. I can't bear to think about the casualty rates.'

'And if Hitler's troops have chased our lads all the way to the English Channel, what's to stop them from following them over here?' She shivered. 'It's so frightening. We could wake up one morning to Nazis running the place. What will we do then?'

'My godfather says we shouldn't worry about what *might* happen but concentrate on what's actually happening now. He said the Channel is like a huge moat around a castle, giving us a better chance of keeping them out.'

'Your godfather? Isn't that the chap who was in the car who got us to the hospital?'

'That's the one. Uncle Ted. And let me tell you, Rose, he might act all jovial and mild-mannered, but he's a dark horse that one. Ma told me he was incommunicado during the Great War – he just disappeared and no one knew where he was. Came back a captain with a chest full of medals. Pa reckons he was a spy, but you'll never get Uncle Ted to admit to anything. Anyway, if Uncle Ted says something, I'm inclined to listen to him.'

Rose nodded. He'd seemed a nice man, she remembered, not making her feel like a nuisance to be taking him out of his way. In fact, his intervention had made the trip to hospital a lot easier than it might have been if he hadn't come along.

'Mind you,' Daisy went on with a smile. 'Uncle Ted's taught all of the lasses he knows to defend themselves and cause a bit of damage if we need to.'

Rose laughed, delighted. 'My brother Liam did the same for me. That's how I can best my big brothers if I need to.'

The back door slammed, followed by the familiar thud of boots on the stone flags. Both girls looked towards the sound. A moment later, Jimmy came in, carrying a brace of rabbits, their pale fur dripping blood. He grinned and held them up. 'Got the beggars. They'll make a good pie.' He stilled and frowned when he realised that Rose wasn't alone. 'Oh, sorry. Didn't know we had company. You're that nurse, aren't you?'

'That's right,' said Daisy. 'And you're Jimmy Morgan.' She inclined her head towards the carcasses. 'Those look like fine rabbits, but I don't suppose your ma will appreciate you dripping their blood all over her kitchen floor.'

'Damn!' He winced as he looked down and saw the mess. He

threw the rabbits into the sink and pumped some water from the hand crank over them, rinsing off the worst of it.

'There's a mop and bucket in the boot room,' said Rose, levering herself up from the table and fitting her crutches under her arms. 'I'll get it.'

'No,' said Jimmy. 'Sit yourself down and see to your guest. I'll do it.'

She raised her eyebrows at that. 'Really?'

He rolled his eyes at her as he laid the now dripping wet carcasses on the draining board. 'I'm not completely useless, you know.'

The girls looked at each other, both trying to hide their amusement as Jimmy got the mop, sloshed some water in the bucket and began cleaning up the bloody mess. Rose didn't like to tell him that he needed to wring the mop to leave less water on the stone flagstone floor. He was creating a worse mess than when he'd started.

'Oh for goodness' sake,' said Daisy as she stood up and held out her hand. 'Give it here before you flood the place. Take your rabbits and do what you need to do with them while I sort this out.'

Jimmy looked nonplussed by her brisk tone. Rose could imagine her speaking to her patients like that, taking no nonsense. She kept her expression serious as he meekly handed over the mop, but he must have seen how much she was enjoying his discomfort when he caught her eye because he turned away, his cheeks going red.

Daisy made quick work of the mopping up while Jimmy showed surprising skill in gutting and skinning the rabbits with a sharp knife. Within minutes, he'd hung the meat on hooks in the meat locker and carried the fur and giblets out. She knew he'd feed some of the innards to the farm dogs and the fur would go into the barn, where Mrs Morgan would clean and dry it and save it to sell along with other rabbit, fox and mole skins.

When he'd gone and Daisy was sitting back down again, Rose began to apologise.

'I'm so sorry. He shouldn't have let you do the mopping. Like he said, you're a guest.' She glared down at her injured foot. 'I feel so blinking useless.'

'Don't worry about it,' said Daisy. 'If you were fit for work, you would've been out toiling in the fields so I wouldn't even have been able to visit today. And the mopping didn't take but a minute. Men can be so daft sometimes. He was so pleased with his catch he completely forgot it was dripping blood.' She paused, studying Rose's face. 'He's quite handsome though, so maybe that makes up for his shortcomings.'

Rose felt her cheeks warm. 'Handsome is as handsome does. The grumpier he gets, the uglier he seems to me, thank you very much. He reminds me of my oldest brother. I've no idea how Liam managed to persuade his girl to marry him. I'd not put up with him.'

Daisy laughed. 'I reckon it just takes the right woman, although no sister can see the attraction of her brothers, can she?'

'I know,' she agreed. 'And as for Jimmy, it won't be me. I want a man who warms my blood with a smile, not rage. Every time Jimmy talks to me, he gets my back up. So if you want to get to know him, be my guest.'

She shook her head. 'Not my type. I think he fancies you, though. He looked like he was trying to impress you with his hunter-gatherer skills.'

Rose shook her head and laughed. 'More likely he expected me to have a funny turn at the sight of a dead animal. He's always making comments about me being a useless city girl.'

'For God's sake,' said Daisy. 'If you were so useless, you'd have used the excuse of your accident to run home to your ma and pa and leave them in the lurch.'

'Exactly,' agreed Rose. 'I might be a city girl, born and bred, but I'm not afraid of hard work and the sight of some blood isn't going to make me faint. I've seen more blood on my brothers after they've had an argument.' She was getting a head of steam up now. 'And I'm hardly useless, even when I'm stuck indoors. I've been helping to sort out the farm office because clever-clogs Jimmy and his brother never set foot in there. If it wasn't for me filling in all the forms the ministry wants these days, they'd be in trouble.'

'Good for you. I knew you had a backbone after seeing how you kept your head when you were stuck in that orchard with a broken ankle.' She grinned at her. 'I think you and I are going to be great friends, Rose.'

Rose felt her heart swell. 'I'd like that,' she said, suddenly shy. 'I've kept in touch with my girlfriends back in Birmingham by letter, but none of them want to hear about me working on a farm. I made some new friends when I started my Land Army training, but we all got posted miles away from each other so we don't get to meet any more. I could do with some new friends around these parts.'

'I'm surprised the Morgans didn't get more than one land girl,' said Daisy. 'We haven't got any at our farm as my brothers are still home and our workers are older or have been granted their exemption certificates so we don't need extra help. But some other farms have lost their younger workers to the forces and need to have a few Land Army girls working for them.'

Rose shrugged. 'I think the Morgans would take more girls, but they don't have enough lodgings for anyone else.'

'Nevertheless, you must be lonely.'

'I am,' she confessed. 'Although don't get me wrong, Mr and

Mrs Morgan are lovely and have done their best to make me feel welcome. Not like my last job on Exmoor. That was awful. It's just... I don't know. After living with all my brothers all these years, I was hoping that I'd be sharing with other girls for a change.'

'When all you've done is swap them for grumpy Jimmy,' Daisy teased.

Rose laughed, even though she was welling up. 'Exactly, and right now I can't even escape him because of these stupid crutches. There's him calling me a useless city girl and my brothers calling me a cider girl. What's wrong with calling a girl by her own name?'

'Aw, bless your heart,' said Daisy, squeezing her shoulder. 'As for the name-calling, just ignore it. I find it annoys them if you don't react. You'll soon get the cast off, then you can run away as fast as you like every time you spot him.'

'Either that, or I'll be chasing after him to box his ears, like I do with my brothers when they vex me.' She grinned at Daisy, even though she was still blinking away her tears. 'There's a lot to be said for catching them by surprise when you're as little as I am. But I've brought all of them down one time or another, so they don't underestimate me these days.'

'Well then, that's your plan – first chance you get, bring Jimmy down. That'll sort him out.'

Rose closed her eyes, imagining herself shoving him face first into a cowpat and then standing on his back, her fist raised high in triumph. She smiled as she opened them again. 'Yeah,' she said. 'He'd better watch out. It don't matter if I'm a city lass or a cider girl, I'll take him down.'

'Cheers to us cider girls,' said Daisy, lifting her cup of camp coffee in a toast.

The girls were still laughing about it when Mrs Morgan bustled in.

'Hello, lass. You found us all right then?'

'Yes, thank you, Mrs Morgan,' said Daisy.

'She brought some of her ma's bread pudding,' said Rose, indicating the plate piled high on the table.

'Ooh, lovely. I'll have a piece of that with me cuppa. D'you want another, girls?'

'We're having camp coffee, Mrs M,' said Rose.

'Oh, right. I'm getting used to it slowly, but I still need a good cup of tea now and again.'

A few minutes later, they were all enjoying a piece of bread pudding with their drinks.

'Oh, my, this is hitting the spot,' said Mrs Morgan. 'You're from the farming Selways over at Walton, aren't you, lass?' she asked Daisy.

'That's right,' she said. 'My pa runs it, although he didn't really want to go into farming. He started working at Clarks when he left school, thinking his brother would take over the land. He and Ma married in Street and I was born there just as he went off to fight in the trenches in the last war. But then his brother died from tuberculosis after the war, and Pa had to take over the farm. We've lived there ever since.'

'Aye, that's right. I heard about that. Must have been hard.'

Daisy sighed. 'It was, but he's used to it now and both of my brothers enjoy working the land, so it's easier with them doing their bit as well. I think both Ma and Pa are relieved they've got their exemption certificates and won't be going off to fight like Pa did.'

'Amen to that,' said Mrs Morgan. 'I feel for all those mothers and wives seeing their menfolk off to war. I don't think I could bear it. It's bad enough that they rush off for LDV duties most evenings.'

She glanced at Rose. 'I know there's more land girls ready and willing to come, and if they were all like young Rose here, we'd be glad to have 'em if only we had the room for 'em. But I want to keep my boys close as well. No offence, Rose, love. They've spent all their life on this land and work hard. I don't know how we'd manage without 'em.'

Rose shook her head. 'None taken, Mrs M. I'm glad they'll be able to stay home. My mammy is beside herself with five of my brothers away. Only the eldest is still in Birmingham as he's a policeman as well as in the LDV. I think Mammy's driving him and his missus mad by popping over to see them all the time. She says she needs to see at least one of her children on a regular basis. Chances are, Liam will take himself off to the recruitment office to get away from her fussing!' She winked at Daisy.

'Oh, surely not!' exclaimed Mrs Morgan as Rose and Daisy laughed. 'Oh, you lasses are teasing me, aren't you?' she chuckled.

'Sorry,' said Rose. 'I couldn't resist.'

She smiled at Daisy, feeling hopeful that at last she'd found a friend who she could have a laugh with and maybe, once her broken ankle was healed, someone she could go out dancing with and let off some steam. Maybe then she wouldn't get quite so riled up about Jimmy.

9

The war finally came to Somerset in the coming weeks as the enemy attacked from the air, their aim to wear down the British people. In July, the Luftwaffe raided the Westland factory at Yeovil. In another raid, two civilians were killed and seventy houses destroyed by bombs dropped on Weston-super-Mare. British forces fought back, with support from the anti-aircraft batteries stationed across the county. In Upottery, over the county border in Devon, a German pilot was captured after he bailed out of his stricken plane. All LDV units were on high alert, guarding the coastline, factories and utilities. The whole population was holding its breath, praying that the enemy wouldn't be able to breach Britain's defences.

On a cloudless sunny day at the end of July, Elsie sat in the staff car outside a house in Street. She'd been here before, to collect Captain Jackson to take him to see her last CO in Bridge-water. That was when she'd nearly run over the captain's goddaughter. She wondered how she and the land girl were getting on. It had been a few months since then.

She'd hoped to be able to see the captain and ask after the

girls. She hadn't had a chance when he'd come into the office before their move. Then she'd been busy with packing up the office and her own meagre possessions. A letter had arrived from the land girl, Rose, thanking her for her part in her rescue, and she'd sent a note back. But she'd barely been able to settle into her new billet just outside Glastonbury before she'd been sent off on the radio operator's course.

Glastonbury was a strange little town with the ruins of a once-rich abbey at its heart and dominated from above by the famous Glastonbury Tor – a huge conical hill topped by an ancient tower. The Tor loomed over the area and could be seen for miles across the low-level moors. The countryside around was beautiful, although when the wind was in the wrong direction they could smell the urine and chemicals used to treat hides at the Morland sheepskin factory on the other side of town. She wasn't sure if this was as bad as the smells she'd had to put up with in Bridge-water, where there were numerous brick kilns which left an unpleasant stench of damp river clay hanging over the town. All the odours seemed equally unpalatable.

She was billeted at Edgely Hall, a small manor house and farm on the outskirts of the town. The hall had been requisitioned by the army. She lived and worked there alongside regular army and LDV personnel. She was the only woman, apart from the cook and housekeeper who came with the house.

This was her first week back and she'd been surprised that Captain Crick had chosen to be driven to Street for this meeting with Captain Jackson. It seemed strange, because the Local Defence Volunteers were usually expected to come to the unit office. Maybe it was because he was a captain? She didn't know. All she did know was that she had to sit here in a hot car in the midday sun and wait for them to conclude their meeting.

She hoped he wouldn't be much longer. She could feel the

sweat running down her spine and she was desperate to take off her jacket, but she knew she had to remain in uniform while on duty at all times in public. She had already taken off her hat and put it on the seat beside her on top of her gas mask box. She would have to remember to put it back on when the CO came out.

She wound the driver's side window down a few inches, hoping to get some air flowing into the car, but she was reluctant to do any more with so many people around. It was late July and the village of Street was in the middle of what was known as Factory Fortnight around these parts, when all the Clarks shoe factories closed for a summer holiday. The road was full of young lads and lasses who would normally be working hard in one of the numerous factory buildings around Street, as well as their little brothers and sisters, enjoying their freedom during the school holidays. Their fascination with an army vehicle outside one of their neighbour's houses meant that Elsie was being openly stared at. She squirmed in her seat, hating the attention. But she managed to keep calm and act as though she wasn't bothered by all those eyes on her.

While keeping her gaze steady out of the front windscreen, albeit with half an eye on the front door of the house in case the CO came out, she didn't notice someone approaching the car from the other side until they knocked on the driver's window.

Elsie jumped, whipping her head around to confront whoever had dared to touch the vehicle. She was startled to see Daisy Selway's smiling face peering at her.

Breathing a sigh of relief, she wound the window all the way down.

'Hello, I thought it was you,' said Daisy. 'It's Elsie, isn't it?'

'Yes, that's right. Hello. It's nice to see you again.'

'I'm glad I saw you. I've been visiting with Rose and we've been wondering how you were getting on.'

'Oh, how is she? I was just thinking about her.'

Daisy nodded. 'She's grand. The plaster cast is off at last and she's back out milking the cows again. But this time, they're making sure someone works nearby to keep an eye on her while she's out with the beasts so she doesn't get left lying there for hours again if one of the herd decides to play up.'

'That must've been quite frightening for the poor girl. I'd have been terrified, but maybe that's because I'm from London and have never been close to a cow,' she said with a smile. 'Anyway, I'm so glad we were able to help her.'

'You and me both. Mind you, I reckon if your passenger hadn't been my Uncle Ted, you might have been ordered to keep driving.'

She smiled. 'Probably. My CO at the time wasn't the easiest of men.'

'Oh, do you have a different one now, then?'

Elsie frowned, wondering whether she shouldn't have said anything. The government were issuing all sorts of notices about not talking about anything that could help the enemy. Did saying her old CO was difficult count as loose talk? She blinked, realising it was too late to worry about it now. 'Yes,' she said, not elaborating.

Daisy looked up at the house. 'And is that who's visiting Uncle Ted?'

'Er... I really shouldn't say.' She took out her handkerchief and wiped her forehead. It seemed to be getting even hotter, the longer she sat there. She was starting to feel quite light-headed and had the beginnings of a headache behind her eyes.

'Fair enough. It's pretty obvious anyway. I wonder how Auntie Kate is reacting to all this. She's likely to be interrogating your boss, I'd say. She's something fierce when she gets riled and she's not best pleased that Uncle Ted's back in a uniform, even if it is for local defence.'

Elsie nodded, taking a deep breath. She'd have thought that having the window open would have brought some cooler air into the vehicle, but if anything she felt hotter.

Daisy glanced at her and frowned. 'Are you all right?'

'Of course. Why?'

'Because you've gone very pasty-looking and you're sweating. How long have you been sitting in there?'

Elsie glanced at her wristwatch, but the numbers and hands blurred and she couldn't work out what the time was. 'I... I don't know. We got here at about 11.30.'

Daisy exclaimed and pulled open the door. 'For God's sake. You've been sitting in there for over an hour. You shouldn't be stuck inside that metal box in this heat. Come on, out you get before you're roasted alive.'

Without waiting for Elsie to respond, Daisy grasped her arm firmly and helped her out, holding her upright when dizziness overcame her. 'Whoa, there. Take a deep breath now, that's it. And another. Feel the cooler air on your skin, that's the spirit.'

Elsie stood there, doing as Daisy bid. The dizziness receded and she began to feel calmer. 'I'm all right now, thank you.'

'No, you're not. You're overheated and possibly dehydrated. Come on, let's get you in the house.'

'Oh no, I can't! I've got to stay here and guard the vehicle.'

'Stuff and nonsense. No one's going to steal it.'

'Nevertheless...'

Daisy huffed and looked around at the group of youngsters watching them with interest and pointed at the tallest one. 'You lad – you're Mrs Vowles' boy, aren't you?' The lad nodded and approached when she beckoned him. 'I'm putting you in charge of this car. It's an official vehicle, so no one is to touch it, you hear? Not a single person is to go near it, or there'll be trouble and I'll hold you responsible. Have I made myself clear?'

He nodded and stood to attention as Daisy closed the driver's door and led Elsie through the gate and up the path to her godfather's front door. Elsie looked back, torn between her duty and the nurse's brisk orders. But she felt light-headed and a little nauseous, so she was hardly in a position to countermand her.

The door was opened in response to Daisy's knock by an older woman with brown hair. 'Hello Auntie Kate,' said Daisy. 'This is Elsie. I found her just about overcome with heat stroke out in that car, so I insisted she come in and cool down. Her boss is in with Uncle Ted.'

Kate Jackson frowned. 'Good lord, did they leave you out there all this time? I'm so sorry, lass, I had no idea you were there. Come in, come in. Let's get you a cold drink and a sit down.' She drew Elsie inside. 'Thank goodness Daisy came along. You wait 'til them men come out of their meeting. I'll have some choice words to say to 'em, I can tell you.'

'Oh no, Mrs Jackson, please don't,' said Elsie. 'It's my own fault. I should have opened all the windows. I didn't realise I was getting so hot.'

'That's as may be, lass, but that husband of mine and your boss are sitting comfortably in my parlour having shed their jackets and enjoyed some elderflower cordial, and I'm cross with both of them for leaving you out in that heat. The cheek of 'em!'

Elsie cringed at the thought of her CO getting a dressing down from this woman. He'd been a decent chap thus far, but he could take against her if he was humiliated on her account.

'Auntie Kate, you're upsetting the poor girl,' Daisy chided softly. 'Let's get her comfortable and worry about telling them off later, eh?'

Mrs Jackson immediately softened as she took in Elsie's distress. 'Sorry, lass. I shouldn't go on so when you're not feeling right. Take your jacket off now. Daisy, give her a hand, love. Hang it up on the hook and come into the kitchen. I'll get a damp cloth to cool your skin.' She bustled off, leaving Daisy to help Elsie out of her jacket.

'How are you feeling, Elsie?' Daisy asked as she hung it up.

'A bit shaky,' she confessed. 'I'm sorry to cause so much trouble,' she said as they arrived in the kitchen and Daisy guided her into a chair at the table.

'Nonsense,' said both women at once, causing her to smile as they both laughed. 'Daisy's right,' said Mrs Jackson. 'It's no trouble at all. If I'd known you were out there, I'd have invited you in earlier.' She patted Elsie's hand and gave her the cloth she'd dampened under the cold tap. 'Hold that against your neck, lass. It'll help cool you down. Truth be told, I'm afraid I couldn't bear to look out the window and see that car. In the last war, I was but a lass and Ted was my sweetheart. I went round to visit him one day and there was an army car outside his parents' house. An officer had come to recruit him for a secret mission, but he didn't tell me that at the time.' She shook her head, looking sad. 'That day was the last I saw or heard of him for years. Most of the time I didn't know if he was dead or alive. I still can't bear to see one of those vehicles outside the house without remembering how my heart was broken.'

Elsie didn't know what to say to that. She knew nothing about Captain Jackson's war experience, but she did know that her CO held him in high regard and that they were having discussions that she wasn't privy to.

Perhaps sensing her discomfort, Daisy changed the subject. 'How's Peggy getting along, Auntie?'

Mrs Jackson beamed at her. 'Ah, she's grand, lass. Enjoying

every minute of her training.' She turned to Elsie. 'My daughter Peggy started her nurse's training just as the war started. She's always admired Daisy and wanted to follow in her footsteps.'

Elsie smiled. 'How nice.' She was beginning to feel more like herself now that the cool cloth was doing its job.

'And the boys?' asked Daisy. 'I haven't seen them around this week.'

'No, they're off camping with the Scouts until tomorrow. No doubt they'll come back with a knapsack full of grubby clothes and a clean flannel. I might have to hose them down in the yard before I let them in the house.'

The girls laughed at the image and Mrs Jackson smiled as she poured some cordial into glasses and gave them to her visitors.

'Now,' she said as Elsie drank, grateful for the cool liquid. She hadn't realised how thirsty she was. 'I was just about to make some sandwiches for dinner. It's nothing fancy, just meat paste, but you're both welcome to join us.'

'Oh, that reminds me, Auntie,' said Daisy, reaching for her basket. 'Ma sent some fresh tomatoes and some green beans. We've had so many in our kitchen garden, she doesn't know what to do with them all. We've enough chutney and other produce that she's run out of jars and bottles to preserve them, so these would only go to waste if you didn't take them.'

'Ah, lovely. Thank you. We can slice some of these tomatoes for the sandwiches. My beans aren't so good this year, so we'll enjoy these. But I've a good crop of peas, so you must take some with you when you go.'

'Perfect.' Daisy smiled. 'I love peas. Now, I'll put these in your pantry and we can help you make the sandwiches.' She glanced at Elsie. 'That's if you're up to it? Your colour is a bit better, but you mustn't overdo it.'

Elsie shook her head. 'No, I'm fine, really. I'd like to help. But I don't know if I should go back out...' She looked towards the door.

Mrs Jackson shook her head. 'Knowing my Ted and his love for the sound of his own voice, I doubt those men will be done for a while yet. I'll be taking some food in for them, and I won't let you miss your dinner on account of those gasbags.'

'Yeah,' said Daisy. 'They only need my pa in there with 'em and we wouldn't see 'em until Christmas. They're worse than any lasses for having a natter.'

Elsie couldn't help but laugh at that along with the others, although she would never dare call her CO or any officer a gasbag to their faces. She was enjoying the insight into these people. They seemed so kind in a no-nonsense sort of way. She liked it.

Between the three of them they soon had a pile of sandwiches ready. Mrs Jackson divided them between some plates, putting two on a tray with a couple of apples. 'You girls get started, while I take this into the parlour. If you hear raised voices, just cover your ears.' She winked at Elsie as she left the room.

'Oh lord, I hope I'm not going to cause a row,' Elsie groaned.

'You won't. Auntie Kate's going to give them a hard time anyway, don't worry. You heard what she said about army cars rolling up to visit Uncle Ted. But he won't mind, he's used to her. Calls her his fierce warrior maiden.' She took a bite of her sandwich. 'Ooh, that hits the spot. Eat up now. You were nearly fainting out there, you need to eat.'

Elsie did as she was told, wondering what it would be like to be married to a man like Captain Jackson, who apparently loved his wife's fierce nature.

She chewed slowly, remembering again that she didn't like the new 'national loaf', which had replaced the nice crusty white loaves she was used to. This government-approved wholemeal bread with added vitamins was grey, mushy and unappetising, even though it was supposed to be healthier. But the meat paste filling with fresh sliced tomatoes was tasty and she ate it gratefully.

She could hear Mrs Jackson speaking in the parlour, although she couldn't hear what she was saying through the closed door. She hoped she wouldn't get into trouble for leaving her post. 'Do you think that lad can be trusted with the car?' she said. 'Maybe I should check.'

Daisy shook her head. 'No, you stay where you are. The Vowles lad will make sure no one touches it and I'll give him a couple of coppers for his troubles.'

'You don't need to do that. I can pay him.'

Daisy shrugged. 'Either way, we'll see him right. But I'm not happy with you going back out in that heat yet. No, you must wait until your boss is done yakking with Uncle Ted, then when you drive off, keep the window open to get some breeze blowing through. How long will it take you to get back to Bridgewater?'

She shook her head. 'The office has been moved to a place near Glastonbury and I'm billeted there. So it's not far, thank goodness.' She yawned, covering her mouth with her hand. 'Oh, dear, excuse me, please. I've been away on a course for a while and only got back yesterday. It was an intensive couple of weeks. I think it's catching up with me.'

Elsie conceded defeat and stayed where she was. She still wasn't feeling brilliant, although she didn't feel sick now and the dizziness had gone. 'I'll definitely keep the window open while I drive back today.'

Daisy leaned on her elbows. 'See that you do. Anyway. I'm glad I saw you. In fact, it's perfect timing. Rose is getting a lift in to meet me on Saturday night and we're going to go to a dance at the Crispin Hall. They're raising money for the war effort. We'd love you to come with us, we've already talked about trying to get in touch so we could invite you. I was going to ask Uncle Ted while I was here how to go about it.'

Elsie flushed with pleasure. 'Really? I can't remember the last time I went dancing.'

Daisy smiled. 'Well then, you'll come? Do you have to get a pass from your CO?'

She shook her head. 'No, my shifts are office hours, with the occasional late shift or weekend working, but I usually get plenty of notice of those. I'm free this weekend, so I'd love to,' she agreed. 'Thank you so much for thinking of me.'

'That's agreed then. We'll meet you outside the Crispin Hall just before seven. If you're coming in on the bus from Glaston-bury, it stops right outside.'

10

Jimmy trudged back to the farmhouse, bone weary after a long day of working with his pa, brother and the other farm hands clearing weeds from the rhynes. These water channels across the low moors and fields had been man-made centuries ago and served to help drain the land to make it easier to farm. If they didn't clear them regularly, the slightest rain shower could flood the area, ruining crops and cutting people and animals off. It was a big job, but it needed doing.

His fatigue wasn't helped by the conversation amongst the farm hands about the latest news.

'It said in the *Western Gazette* that they had a practice in Yeovil, preparing for air raids,' said one of the older hands. 'You know, dealing with casualties and the like. Don't know why they bother. If a bomb lands on you, you're dead, ain't you?'

'Lots of folks are surviving raids,' Pa pointed out. 'Better that some folk know what to do than we all run around like headless chickens.'

'Maybe,' said the old fellow. 'But it said in the paper that one chap who was supposed to act as a casualty got fed up waiting for someone to find him, so he left a note. It said: "*Bled to death. Gone home.*'" He'd cackled at that, but it left Jimmy feeling as though no one seemed to be taking this war seriously enough.

'There's a letter for you, Jimmy,' said Ma when he came in from the fields on Saturday afternoon.

He frowned. He rarely got letters. 'Is it my call up?'

'Of course not, lad. You're already registered as working in a reserved occupation. The country's still got to be fed,' she said. 'Anyway, look, it's handwritten, so it can't be official.'

He shrugged and took it from her. Aware that she was watching, he opened it, hoping it wasn't a note from some lass. How embarrassing would that be?

He scanned the neatly written letter, getting even more confused. 'It's from the area LDV leader. He wants me to report for a meeting at five o'clock today.' He glanced at the kitchen clock and frowned. 'Strange time for a meeting, and on a Saturday as well.'

'Not really,' said Ma. 'There's a war on, isn't there? Hitler don't follow office hours.'

He glanced round. 'Speaking of office hours, is Rose in there?'

His ma gave him one of her looks. 'Yes, she is, and don't you go upsetting her. She's been a godsend, sorting out all that mess, the place has never been so organised. You could learn a thing or two from her if you're going to take over the farm one day.'

He scowled. 'Are you checking what she's doing? How d'you know she's not going to cost us all of our money? I mean, what does a city girl know about running a farm?'

Ma shook her head. 'You do talk a lot of nonsense, lad. Just leave her alone. I've been working with her and she's got a good head on her shoulders, that one. She'd make a fine wife for a farmer, not like that daft lass our Ivor is courting.'

He laughed. His brother was walking out with a lass from

Street. He was well smitten with her but she wasn't keen on farm life. She'd only been out to the farm once and had complained about the smells and the mud. Ivor went to see her in Street these days. 'Well, don't look at me. She's not my type.' He raised the letter in his hand, hoping that his ma wouldn't call him on his lie. 'Anyway, I've got better things to think about while this war is on. I'd best be off for this meeting. I'll probably go on to that dance in Street after, no point in coming all the way back here first.'

'Right you are, son. Ivor and some of the farm lads are going. Rose will be there with her new friends.'

He didn't bother commenting as he left the room. It was no skin off his nose what she did.

* * *

Edgely Hall was the other side of Glastonbury on the road to Shepton Mallet, so after changing into his uniform Jimmy got his motorcycle out of the barn. He'd bought it a couple of months back for a few pounds and spent all of his spare time on it. It had been old but the mechanics were all good and with some new tyres, clean spark plugs and an oil change, it was running well. It had taken him a few tries to get the hang of riding it. The first couple of times he'd driven it round the lanes, he'd dropped the damned thing every time he'd gone round a corner. But he'd soon learned how to control it and to enjoy the freedom of rushing along on two wheels. It beat the heck out of crawling along at a snail's pace on a tractor or in the old farm delivery van. It didn't use much fuel either.

On arrival, he was shown into a book-lined room where he was greeted by an officer he'd never met before, and a man who looked familiar.

'Good to see you again, lad,' he said, shaking his hand. 'I hear your land girl did a good job of breaking her ankle, eh?'

Jimmy realised who he was. 'You were in the car,' he said. 'I've seen you at the LDV parade as well. Captain Jackson, isn't it?'

'That's right. Well remembered.'

His colleague cleared his throat. 'No need to bother yourself with names. When addressing us face to face, simply call us sir or captain.'

Captain Jackson gave the other man a wry smile. 'Sorry. I never got used to military etiquette.' He turned to Jimmy again. 'But by some strange quirk of fate, I ended the last war with the rank of captain and now they want me to take on that mantle again. Come and sit down, lad, and we'll explain why we've called you here.'

When they were all seated, with Jimmy on one side of a large oak desk and the two men on the other, the one who hadn't introduced himself opened a file and took out a paper. He was clearly also a captain as he had the same pips on his epaulettes as Jackson, but judging by his stiff manner and superior air, he was clearly a regular officer rather than an LDV.

He looked up from the paper in his hand and Jimmy sat up a little straighter. He might only be an LDV private, but he knew authority when he saw it.

'Before we discuss with you the reason for calling you here, Morgan, I must ask you to sign this document.'

'What is it... sir?' He remembered his manners just in time.

'Official Secrets Act. Anything we discuss in this room today, and whatever results from it, whether you decide to proceed or walk away, must never be discussed with anyone. Not with your comrades on parade, nor your family, friends or sweetheart. This is top secret and the consequences of loose tongues could have catastrophic results. Do I make myself clear?'

It took him by surprise that the first image that came into his mind when the man said 'sweetheart' was of Rose, glaring at him with a fierce expression. He frowned, banishing the picture from his head. He looked at Jackson and saw his solemn expression matched that of his colleague. They were serious about this. He frowned. 'Have you got the right James Morgan, sir? Were you expecting my pa? I mean, I'm just a farm hand. I can't imagine anything to do with me would be that important.'

'Good lad,' said Jackson. 'That's the attitude.' That confused him even more. 'Now, sign the paper, Jimmy, then we can tell you what we have in mind.'

The other officer held out a fountain pen. It was clear they wouldn't say anything else until he signed it. With a shrug he took it and wrote his signature where he was told.

The officer blotted the paper and put it back in the file. He sat back and regarded Jimmy again. 'I am Captain Crick. My unit's official purpose is to support local LDV groups, supply them with training and equipment and so on. However, I am also an intelligence officer for certain auxiliary units in the area. But that part of my job is strictly classified and you are not to discuss it with anyone. You know who Captain Jackson is?'

'Yes, sir. I've seen him a couple of times lately. He's LDV but I don't know which unit he belongs to. He's helped with some of our training.' He glanced at him. 'And I hear he's the deputy headmaster at the grammar school in Wells.'

Jackson inclined his head in acknowledgement. 'I am,' he said. 'Not bad for a lad who left school at fourteen and worked as a clicker at the shoe factory before the Great War, eh?'

He blinked. 'Did I hear you right?' asked Jimmy. 'You left school at fourteen and worked at Clarks?'

He nodded. Jimmy was impressed. Clickers – the men who cut the leather hides into pieces that would be sewn together to make shoes – were highly skilled but hardly the same calibre as a teacher. He wondered how he'd managed to get from that to his current position.

'So how did you end up a schoolmaster?' he asked.

The other officer cleared his throat and Jimmy turned his attention back to him, realising he was speaking out of turn. 'Sorry, sir. I was just surprised.'

'Understood. However, the captain's rise to the heights is a subject for discussion another time when we're not on official business. That said, if you come across him in public, you are not under any circumstances to indicate that you know him any better than you did before you came here today. Is that clear?' Jimmy nodded. 'Good. Now, I understand you're an LDV, along with your father and brother?'

'Yes, sir. I wanted to enlist, but they said I was reserved on account of being in a farming family.'

'Noted.'

Jackson sat forward. 'But we're told you're a good shot and a useful mechanic when the need arises.'

He nodded. 'I shoot to keep the vermin down and fresh meat on the table. And I help maintain the farm machines, sir.'

'And I'm betting you did some work on that beautiful old Triumph you rode up on?'

'I did,' he confirmed, pleased that he'd been impressed by it.

'Good man. I've got a similar machine, only I've had to fit a sidecar to mine now. Makes it easier to haul school books back and forth and saves my petrol rations while I can still take the missus out for a trip now and again.'

Again, Crick cleared his throat. 'Yes, well, back to business. We've heard good things about you, Morgan. As well as your mechanical aptitude, you've a good reputation as a hard worker and your willingness to enlist has been noted.'

'So, you're going to let me go and fight?' he asked. The thought excited him, even while he knew his ma and pa would be dead against it.

'Not as such,' said Jackson. 'At least, not yet, and not in the usual way.' He leaned forward. 'No, we're looking for capable men like you to help us defend the home front in the event of an invasion, which after Dunkirk is looking more likely.'

He frowned, disappointed and a little confused. For a moment, he'd thought he might be able to go and fight like other lads his age. He felt bad that he was excused the call up when others had no choice. He'd heard stories from his pa about people giving him white feathers in the last war, when he was needed at home to keep those same people fed. No doubt someone would hand him one someday soon. 'But isn't that what I'm already doing with the LDVs?'

'That's the public face of our home defences,' said Crick. 'Their job will be to hold the enemy at bay long enough to allow the regular army to arrive and engage.'

'And while we know they'll fight to the best of their ability,' Jackson went on, 'the chances are they'll be overwhelmed by the superior numbers of an invading army.'

Jimmy felt sick. 'It sounds like you don't think much of our chances.'

Jackson shook his head. 'You misunderstand. I have every confidence in our chances, but I'm also a realist. I was in France and Belgium in the last war, working alongside local resistance. I know what I'm talking about when I say that the Nazis will be ruthless and we need to be prepared to take them by surprise. They're expecting the LDVs to fight back. But the auxiliary force we're putting together to work in addition to those brave men will be something they won't expect, because we're operating under the strictest secrecy. Not even our nearest and dearest must know about our operations. God willing, the enemy won't know we exist, which will give us the best chance to stop them in their tracks.' Jackson paused, watching him.

Jimmy was struck by how this man, who came across as cheerful and mild-mannered each time he'd encountered him, was transformed as he spoke. Jimmy could see the fervent belief behind his words, and the passion and desire to win in his eyes.

'The unit we're putting together here will be replicated across the country. But each one will work alone on the whole. It's better that way so that if captured no one will be able to reveal the true extent of the network.'

'But why here, sir? I mean, there ain't much of anything round these parts. Surely Jerry will head for Kent and London.'

'They probably would, considering it's the shortest route from mainland Europe. That's why the south and east coasts are so well fortified while Somerset has a coastline of fifty or more miles, much of it difficult to guard effectively. So, if Hitler has any sense, he'd send his troops around the defences along the other coasts and up the Severn Estuary to land right here. It would then be an easy matter of pushing North to Bristol and East to London if we let them. That's why it's important for us to build a well-prepared network of auxiliary units in Somerset ready to stop them.'

'Makes sense,' said Jimmy. It really did. It made him feel ill, thinking about his family being in the path of the might of the German army. His pa said he didn't think they would invade, but Jimmy thought that was just to reassure Ma. The Nazis had taken over the Channel Islands in June, so the next obvious step would be mainland Britain. 'So what can I do to help, sir?'

Jackson looked at his colleague, who indicated that he should carry on. 'We would like to transfer you from your local LDV platoon to a special auxiliary unit. You'll still be LDV officially, but you'll work separately and be taught the skills you'll need to offer an effective resistance against enemy occupation.'

Crick nodded. 'Officially the LDVs are going to be designated Home Guards soon and Auxiliers like yourself will be listed as Home Guard – Special Duties. But no one outside of your own unit will be told anything about your specific missions and tasks, not even your local Home Guard or regular military personnel other than those attached to your unit. It's vital that secrecy is maintained, otherwise, if an invasion does occur, local people could inadvertently betray the Auxiliers and that would prove fatal.'

Jimmy could imagine how disastrous that would be. What would be the point in training to fight if your neighbours gave you away the minute the Nazis started asking questions? No, he wouldn't be telling anyone about this. Better they remained in ignorance.

He nodded. 'All right. When do I start?'

Crick held up a hand. 'Before you agree, Morgan, you need to be quite clear about this. Should the invasion take place, you will be required to go underground – to cut all ties with your family and friends and disappear. You will be armed and have provisions for approximately one month. Your mission will be to disrupt enemy supply routes, destroy enemy arsenals and fuel depots, in short to do everything in your power to hold them up. You'll be trained to work with explosives, in armed and unarmed combat. If you're as good a shot as we've been told, you might be selected for sniper training.'

'Which all sounds very exciting and adventurous,' said Jackson. 'But let me tell you, lad, you need to be able to reconcile yourself to the fact that you could be called upon to kill or be killed. You'll be living on your wits, hiding out during the day and creeping around in the dark of night, with no one to rely on but your small unit. If you're captured, the enemy will be merciless. There's a good chance you won't survive. Do you understand?'

He felt a little sick at the man's blunt assessment. But if the enemy found its way to Somerset, he wanted to be trained and ready to fight back and protect his family and his neighbours. 'There's no guarantee for anyone, is there, sir?' he said. 'Look at how many of our lads have already copped it. Lads I went to school with fell at Dunkirk. I know that Jerry is just across the Channel. We're already being attacked by their planes. I want to do my bit to make sure they don't just march into Somerset and turn us all into his slaves like I hear they're doing on Jersey.'

Both officers nodded. No doubt they knew men who'd been caught up in the shambles at Dunkirk as well. Thousands of allied soldiers had been pushed back to the coast. Many lost their lives, most lost their weapons and equipment in the confusion. While many were rescued and repatriated, the British Army was now vulnerable and the possibility of an invasion even more likely. In fact, he was surprised it hadn't already begun.

'Right,' said Crick. 'Think about what we've discussed. If you decide it's not for you, we'll accept that. You can walk away now and stay with your LDV platoon, there's no dishonour in that. You'll still be doing your bit.'

'Agreed. There's no shame in refusing this mission, lad. But we need a special breed of men,' said Jackson, 'who are prepared to put their lives on the line in such a way that we can do maximum damage to any invading force. Don't imagine it will be easy, because I can tell you with certainty that it will be hell. But we'll do our best in the time we have to prepare you and equip you with the skills and tools you need so that, God willing, you'll still be in one piece at the end of it all.'

There was a bleakness in the man's eyes that chilled Jimmy's heart. Jackson nodded slightly, as though confirming that he knew what he was talking about – that he'd killed men, that he'd seen and done all these things they now wanted Jimmy to be prepared to do. Yet he was still here. He'd survived. If he could, then maybe Jimmy could – if he did as he was told and learned what they could teach him.

'I'll do it,' he said, raising his chin. Better to do this than sit by and do nothing but play at being soldiers in the LDV.

Jackson didn't react. He seemed to have gone somewhere deep within himself. It was Crick who spoke.

'You're sure? Or do you want to take some time to think it through?'

Jimmy shook his head. 'I'm sure, sir. I'm in. I'll do whatever's necessary to stop Jerry from taking over this country. I don't want them getting anywhere near my ma.'

Jackson blinked and nodded, back in the room with them. Jimmy wondered whether he'd ever find out the true story about the steely core behind this man's mild exterior.

'Thank you, Jimmy,' he said. 'With your help, we'll do our best to keep your ma safe.'

11

Rose and Daisy were waiting at the stop when Elsie got off the bus outside the Crispin Hall in Street. There was already a queue to get into the dance. It was the first time Elsie had seen the red-headed Rose since her accident, when she'd been pale and wracked with pain, and it struck her that the girl was very pretty now that she was rosy-cheeked and smiling. She couldn't help smiling in response to her cheerful greeting.

'Thank you so much for inviting me, and for your lovely note. I can see you're fully recovered from your accident.'

'I am,' she said. 'It healed well. I was so relieved when I went back to the hospital last week and they finally took the cast off. That's thanks to you two. If I'd had to rely on the Morgan brothers or any of the other farm hands, I'd probably still be there.' She rolled her eyes. 'Useless, the lot of 'em. Just like my brothers.'

'Oh yes, I remember you said you had a lot of brothers.'

'Too many.' She groaned. 'I'm only glad I managed to keep it from them that I'd broken my ankle, or I'd have been ordered home without a by-your-leave.'

Elsie thought it sounded quite nice, to have a large family

who all cared about you. She felt so alone these days that it was hard to imagine ever being cross about someone caring too much. But as no one had ever fussed over her before, maybe she'd grow tired of it like Rose after a while.

'Are they still calling you the cider girl?' she asked.

Rose rolled her eyes. 'They are. Every letter I get from them mentions it. It's really annoying.'

They joined the queue. Daisy greeted several people around them, introducing Elsie and Rose.

'Goodness,' said Elsie quietly to Rose. 'I don't think I'm going to be able to remember everyone's names.' She would definitely remember Peggy, who was Captain Jackson's daughter and looked just like her mother. There was a girl with her called Ruby; she was very pretty, with blonde curls and a friendly smile, but the rest were a blur. Daisy seemed to know just about everyone in the area. She supposed it was to do with her job as a district nurse.

'I know, it's hard to keep track of everyone if they're all introduced at once like this,' said Rose, 'but don't worry. They all seem nice enough. I find if you tell them you recognise their face but don't remember their name, most folk are happy enough to remind you.'

'I'm always worrying that people will be offended that I forgot who they were.'

'Don't fret,' said Daisy. 'Some of this lot will soon forget their own name once they've had a cider or two. The others will remind you, like Rose says.'

Elsie frowned. 'I didn't think they served alcohol here.'

Daisy smirked. 'They don't. But it doesn't stop a few of these reprobates sneaking in their own drinks.' She tilted her head, indicating the lads behind them who were already taking turns to drink from flagons of cider that they had secreted in their gas mask boxes. Elsie wondered what would happen if there was a gas attack and these lads were caught without their masks. She shivered, not wanting to contemplate the consequences for them.

'If they're caught drinking cider they'll be thrown out, but it doesn't stop them trying. Knowing that pair, they'll have finished the jug before they get through the door. Look out for 'em,' Daisy said quietly. 'They're inclined to get handsy when they're in their cups.'

One of the lads caught Elsie watching and lifted his flagon. 'Want some, darlin'?' he asked. 'I'll let you have a drink if you let me have a dance.'

Elsie raised her chin. 'No thank you,' she said, trying to keep her expression neutral rather than show her distaste at the way he leered at her.

The lad's friend nudged him as she turned away. 'Hark at her – *no thank you*,' he mimicked, making Elsie's cheeks warm. 'Where you from? I ain't ever heard no one round here talk as posh as that.'

'Oh, hush now,' said Daisy, her tone brisk. 'If you ever paid attention, you'd come across plenty of people who talk nicely round these parts. But you won't find any of them at the bottom of your cider jug.'

The crowd moved forward towards the entrance of the dance hall. Daisy linked arms with both Elsie and Rose. 'Come on, girls, let's leave them to drink themselves even dafter than they already are.'

Elsie was glad to follow her lead, putting some distance between them and the half-drunken lads. Rose caught her gaze and rolled her eyes. 'Take no mind of them, Elsie,' she said. 'I've yet to meet a lad who can hold as much drink as they think they can. The only difference here is that it's cider they're drinking. My brothers take after our Irish daddy and drink nothing but Guinness. If cider makes these lads as daft as the black stuff makes my brothers, I'll steer clear, thank you very much.'

'Don't they give you cider to drink at the farm?' asked Daisy. 'Most farmers I know drink more of it than water while they're working in the fields.'

Rose wrinkled her nose. 'I did the first time I was offered it at my last job, thinking it was harmless like apple juice. I mean, everyone else was knocking it back, even the farmer's wife, so I didn't think there'd be any strength in it. But I was as sick as a dog.' She leaned close, lowering her voice. 'And I threw my guts up again when I was sent to fill the jugs from the cider barrels in the brewing house. I saw a dead rat in one, it was just floating there. One of the lads laughed at me and said it was all right as it wasn't drinking any. Then he just hooked it out and threw it to the farm cats and filled the jugs from the same barrel.' She shuddered. 'I don't care what anyone says, I'll not touch the stuff now.'

Daisy laughed as Elsie gasped in horror. 'I've heard of worse things than dead rats ending up in the cider barrels,' she said. 'Some of our neighbours make mutton-fed cider.'

'What on earth is that?' asked Rose.

'They add a joint of mutton to the barrel,' she explained. 'The alcohol eats away at the flesh until only clean bones are left. Some say it adds to the flavour. But, like you, I'm not inclined to believe them. Yet plenty of folks are partial to it.'

Elsie was aghast. 'I don't think I'd like that.'

'Me neither,' said Rose. 'In this hot weather we've been having, the hands have been drinking gallons of cider.' She shook her head. 'At least Guinness is dark enough that you can't see anything nasty that might be floating in it. But I'm not fond of that either.'

'My brother-in-law is in the navy,' said Elsie. 'He's rather keen on his rum ration. It does nothing to enhance his demeanour.'

She knew that because he drank a lot of it when he was on shore leave. Maybe that's why her sister's marriage was in such a precarious state.

'One of my grandpas drank himself to death on cider,' said Daisy. 'By all accounts, he was a horrible man, especially when he was in his cups. No one misses him. I've never seen my parents touch a drop of alcohol, even though they make cider for the farm workers. We've always got plain apple juice for the temperance folk, and as there's a lot of teetotal Quakers round here, it's much appreciated.'

'The Morgans aren't Quakers,' said Rose. 'But like your family, they have apple juice for anyone who doesn't want to drink cider.'

'I wonder, why are there so many Quakers in these parts?' said Elsie.

'That'll be on account of the Clark family, who own the shoe company and built this hall and most of the village. They're Quakers. Mind you, there's Anglicans, Methodists and Baptists, as well as Salvation Army here in Street, and the temperance movement is strong in all denominations.'

At last they got to the head of the queue and paid for their tickets. Daisy led them inside, managing to find them a table. They piled their gas mask boxes onto it to mark that it was taken. 'Stay there a minute while I get us some civilised drinks. D'you want lemonade, blackcurrant squash or dandelion and burdock?'

The hall was filling up fast. An eight-piece band was playing on the stage and a few lasses were already dancing in front of it. Some lads were in uniform and were attracting a lot of attention, especially as there were far more young women than men in attendance.

'I don't know why they're not in mufti,' said Elsie. 'I was glad to wear something other than khaki for a change.' She smoothed down her pretty cotton wraparound dress. Its blue colour set off her blonde hair and blue eyes.

Rose eyed them with suspicion. 'They're just show-offs,' she said. 'Probably thinking they'll get lucky with some girl.'

'Either that, or they haven't got any decent clothes to wear to a dance,' said Elsie, her expression thoughtful. She'd overheard one young soldier say as much at her last posting. He'd previously been working in a factory and most of his clothes were hand-me-downs. He didn't want to wear his Sunday clothes because even those were quite shabby as well, so he'd been glad to have a smart new uniform to strut around in. When she told her new friend this, Rose sighed.

'Ah, bless him. I didn't think. I suppose there's some like that, whose uniform is the first thing they've had new,' she said. 'But I'll bet they still want to impress the girls.'

Daisy came back with a tray of drinks and sat down with them. 'Who wants to impress the girls?' she asked.

'Them fellas over there in their uniforms,' said Rose.

Daisy laughed. 'Oh, yeah. That lot are all Flash Harrys. Be careful around them. I was stupid enough to dance with one of them a few weeks back. He told me I should let him have his way with me because he was going off to fight for king and country and I'd have it on my conscience that he could die without knowing the love of a good woman. But he's still hanging around, and from the look of it he's still trying it on.' She nodded her head towards a lad on the edge of the small group who was trying to nuzzle a girl's neck. Before his lips could make contact with her skin, she stepped smartly away and slapped his face before walking away.

'Good for her,' said Rose as the lad's friends laughed and jeered at him.

'It seems to be a problem for all of us,' said Elsie, shaking her head. 'I've lost count of the soldiers who've propositioned me since I joined up. They can't accept that I'm there to work and support the war effort rather than to provide personal services to any idiot in a uniform. It was such a relief to be posted here with a smaller unit, where most of them are older married men who don't bother with that kind of nonsense.'

Rose leaned forward. 'So what does your unit do that doesn't involve young single soldiers?'

'Erm... I can't really say. I mean, it's nothing exciting...'

The others stared at her, not asking but clearly waiting for more. Elsie blew out a breath, wanting to share something with her new friends, but aware that she could be in serious trouble if she told them everything she knew. 'It's just a supply unit, really, working alongside the Local Defence Volunteers.' It was true, but not nearly all that her unit's work involved.

Daisy nodded. 'And the LDVs are all full of men like Uncle Ted who's too old, or lads too young to enlist.'

'Surely it's not all old fellas and boys. What about the men in reserved occupations?' said Rose. 'My brother Liam's a copper. He's just shy of thirty and he's an LDV in his spare time. So are most of the farm hands on the farms around Catcott who are in their twenties and thirties. Even they scrub up nice in a uniform.' She grinned at the other girls' expressions. 'Hey, don't get me wrong. I'm not likely to fall for a daft line from any of them. But it doesn't mean I can't appreciate a handsome lad in a smart uniform. I mean, after being guarded by my brothers all my life, it's nice to be able to appreciate the view when I see someone nice looking.' She looked around to make sure they weren't being overheard before leaning in again. 'I was surprised at how even some of the farm hands are well worth a second look. It must be all that fresh air and hard work, because they're all in fine shape, I can tell you.' She paused for a moment, as though thinking about what she'd said. 'It's just a shame that they spoil it all by opening their mouths and saying something daft like that lad outside.'

Daisy laughed. 'How old are you to be so cynical about lads?'

'I turned twenty-one last March. How about you two?'

Elsie sighed. 'I'm twenty-two, but sometimes I feel like I'm in my dotage.'

'At twenty-two?' said Daisy, raising her eyebrows. 'Well that would make me positively ancient at the grand old age of twenty-four.'

Rose shook her head. 'Well neither of you look old. I'm just wondering why you're both still single. I mean, you're both so pretty. I didn't stand a chance with my rotten brothers keeping guard against any lads who fancied me, not that there were many who were keen on a carrot-top like me. But you two have had the freedom to go out courting if you wanted to. Why hasn't some handsome chap snapped you up?'

'That's a story for another time,' said Daisy, standing up. 'Come on, let's dance.'

Elsie shook her head. 'You go ahead. I need to powder my nose.'

Daisy pointed her in the direction of the ladies and she left them to it. Rose got up and followed Daisy onto the dance floor.

'I think Elsie's a bit shy,' she said. 'We'll have to bring her out of her shell.'

'I know,' said Daisy as they began to swing around the hall. 'But I like her. Don't you?'

'Yes, she's lovely. A bit posh, but she doesn't have any airs and graces, does she?'

There were lots of girls dancing with other girls, given the reluctance of most lads to shake a leg until they'd built up some Dutch courage with illicit cider. Instead, they stood around the edges of the hall, watching the lasses and no doubt talking about them with their pals.

The music changed. 'Ooh, I love this song!' said Daisy. 'D'you know it? Come on, I'll show you the dance me and my friends at the hospital do to it.'

Rose was quick to pick up the moves and by the time the song ended, she was laughing, even as she put her foot down on the floor and winced. 'Ow! I think I'd better sit down for a bit. I keep forgetting I've not long broken my ankle.'

'Oh no, I'm so sorry,' said Daisy, offering an arm for Rose to lean on. 'I should've known better to have let you get that energetic.'

Rose limped back to their table and was greeted by a round of applause from Elsie.

'That was amazing. You two are really good. That looked like fun.'

'It was,' said Rose. 'I've never been so grateful for all the dance classes Mammy sent me to.' She grinned. 'I think she wanted me to dance so I wouldn't turn into a tomboy. It didn't stop me being the best tree-climber in the family though.'

'I love dancing,' said Daisy. 'Ma and Aunt Kate told me about the dances they had here in the last war and taught me some of their moves. I must tell them about tonight. They'll love it.'

'She worked at the Clarks shoe factory here in the village during the last war. She was even younger than us then.'

'Hang on,' said Rose. 'Jackson. Isn't that the name of the officer you were driving for on the day I had my accident, Elsie?'

'Yes. I saw him again when I drove my CO over to his house for a meeting not long ago. I met Mrs Jackson then.'

Daisy filled Rose in on how she'd found Elsie about to expire in the hot car and dragged her indoors to meet her aunt.

'Oh my,' said Rose. 'Men are so useless. They never realise, do they? Fancy leaving you out there like that. It's like the farm hands thinking I was just skiving when I was lying injured in the orchard the day we met. Well, thank God for you, Daisy, or I'd still be there. And now it looks like you're the guardian angel for both of us, doesn't it?'

Daisy laughed and shook her head. 'I'm no angel,' she said.

'You are,' said Elsie. 'I agree with Rose. You saved us both. I hadn't realised how dangerously hot I was getting. Thank you. I don't know how to repay you.'

'I do,' said Daisy with a grin. 'Come and dance with me while Rose rests up.'

Elsie hesitated. But Daisy wasn't having any of it. She took her hand and pulled her onto the dance floor. Rose watched them as she sipped her drink. She could see that once they started moving, Elsie began to relax and by halfway through the song she was laughing and throwing herself into it. Rose was smiling at their antics when someone sat down next to her. She turned her head, ready to tell whoever it was that the seats were taken, to find Jimmy Morgan sitting next to her.

'Oh, it's you.' His brother Ivor had driven her to Street with another couple of lads from Catcott village. They all had dates waiting for them. She could see them on the other side of the hall with their girls. 'I didn't think you were coming tonight. Been on parade, have you?' She nodded towards his LDV uniform. It surprised her that he'd wear it to the dance. He might be cocky, but she didn't think he'd be so vain as to think girls would fancy him better in uniform.

He took a drink from the glass in his hand. He looked grim. She wondered why he bothered if he was going to sit there with such a sour look on his face.

'I didn't say I wasn't coming,' he said. 'I had things to do first.'

'Like what?' she asked.

'None of your business,' he said, tapping the side of his nose. 'Had to report in.'

She laughed. 'Is that your excuse for wearing your uniform? 'Cause I've got to tell you, Jimmy, the girls here are more impressed by Air Force blue, not Local Defence khaki.'

'I'm not interested in impressing girls. It was just easier to come straight here than go home and change. But what about you? Got your sights on a pilot, have you?' He smirked. 'Think again, ginger. Most of the lads here are ground crew. The flyboys go to posher places than this. If they were here, they'd go for the top lasses like that blonde over there.' He pointed at Elsie, who was looking radiant as she finally let go and was enjoying herself. Sure enough, Rose could see a couple of young men in RAF uniforms eyeing her with interest.

She bristled at his rudeness. He didn't have to be so insulting about her hair colour. So what if she was a redhead? Plenty of people thought it was attractive, even if some boys had insulted her like Jimmy just because of the colour of her hair. Lots of girls were dying theirs to look like hers these days. Anyway, he was hardly a catch. Then she smirked as she had a thought. 'What happened? Did your girl stand you up?'

'No,' he said. 'I've more important things to do than fuss around a lass. There's a bloody war on, y'know.'

'As if we could forget,' she chided. 'Yet I can't see what that's got to do with you being late for the dance and turning up in uniform. What *important* business have you got on a Saturday night?'

'Nothing I'm going to tell you about.'

She shrugged, tired of his grumpy attitude. 'Suit yourself. But it better not be black market nonsense. My brother's a copper and he said I'm to report anyone I find is playing around with things they shouldn't.'

'Damned cheek,' he growled. 'I'm no spiv and you'd better not be telling anyone otherwise.'

She turned back to watch her friends, determined to ignore him. She believed him, but she wasn't about to give him the satisfaction of telling him.

'Are they the lasses who took you to the hospital?' he asked, pointing to Daisy and Elsie as the girls waved at her from the dance floor.

'Yes. They're my friends now. Daisy's a district nurse and Elsie's with the ATS.'

'She's a driver, isn't she?'

'More than that. She's a unit clerk and she's been on some sort of training course lately, but I don't know what that was for. She won't talk about her *important* business either.' But she was more inclined to believe that Elsie's work really was vital to the war effort, not like Jimmy and his grand ideas.

'I should hope not,' he said, still watching the two of them. 'So why aren't you out there dancing as well?'

'I was. If you'd arrived ten minutes ago, you'd have seen me and Daisy cutting a rug.'

He turned his head to look at her, his usual smirk on his face. 'Fall on your backside, did you?'

'No I didn't,' she said. 'If I say so myself, I was pretty good at it. Better than you'd be, no doubt.' She matched his smirk with one of her own.

'If that's your clumsy way of getting me to ask you to dance...'

She sat back, horrified that she'd leaned towards him without realising it during their exchange. She must have done it to hear him better over the music and chatter. Well, that was what she told herself. 'No, it isn't. Not at all. I don't want to dance with you. Why would I? You don't even like me.'

He shrugged, not denying it. 'I wasn't going to ask you

anyway,' he said, looking around the dance floor. 'Like I said, I've no time for flighty lasses.'

She rolled her eyes. 'Good. Because the feeling's mutual. You've been a miserable so-and-so ever since I arrived at the farm. Your ma says it's because the last land girl wouldn't leave you alone. Well, don't worry, I've no time for daft lads, thank you very much. I left enough of them back at home, so you're safe from me.'

He grinned, making her want to slap it off his face. 'Feel better now you've got that off your chest?'

'I'd feel better if you'd get lost,' she snapped.

He barked out a laugh before he scraped back his chair and stood up. 'Well, you might not have time for me now, but you'll be looking for a lift home when Ivor disappears with that lass of his at the end of the dance. I'll be outside. Don't keep me waiting.'

He turned and left her gaping after him.

'Was that the lad from your farm?' asked Elsie as the girls returned to the table, breathless and laughing.

She nodded, frowning.

'What did he say?' asked Daisy. 'Was he trying it on?'

She shook her head, her frown deepening. 'No. I don't know what he was playing at.' She stood up. 'I need to find Ivor.'

'Who's Ivor?'

'His brother. He brought me in his pa's car with a couple of the lads. They all went off to meet their sweethearts.' She glanced around the crowded hall, finally spotting him off to one side, his arm around a pretty girl who was making puppy-dog eyes at him. 'I won't be long. I've just got to check something.'

She limped over to Ivor, regretting her enthusiastic jitterbugging. She felt awkward, interrupting what looked like a special moment between the couple, but Jimmy's words had worried her.

'Um, Ivor, can I have a quick word?'

The couple looked at her, the lass glaring at her. 'Who's this?' she asked.

'Just our land girl, sweetheart. I told you, I had to give her a lift in.' He glanced at Rose. 'If you've had enough already, you'd better start walking,' he said, making his girl giggle.

'No, it's all right. I just wanted to check that you *are* taking me back to the farm when the dance finishes.'

'No, he's not,' said the girl. 'He'll be seeing me to my door and we might just take our time about it. So maybe walking's your best bet, eh? It's only, what? Six, maybe seven miles back to Catcott from here.'

Ivor looked uncomfortable. 'It's all right. Jimmy said he'd see you back. You don't need to wait for me.'

'What about the other lads?'

He smirked. 'They'll be seeing their lasses home n'all. There ain't no one but you in a rush to get back.'

She wanted to point out that no one but her was having to get up to go out on the moors to find and milk the cows at the crack of dawn. But she held her tongue.

'Fine,' she said, bristling as the girl giggled and wiggled her fingers at her before turning and pulling Ivor's head down for a frankly indecent kiss. She turned away, her cheeks burning as she made her way back to Elsie and Daisy. Behind them, leaning against the wall watching her was Jimmy, the familiar smirk marring his handsome face.

12

After a while, the heat and noise in the dance hall began to get on the girls' nerves. They'd danced their fill – well, Daisy and Elsie had while Rose had sat and rested her throbbing ankle on another chair. She was quite cross with herself for being so careless, but she wasn't going to let it spoil her evening out with her new friends. Every time they came back to the table for a break, she greeted them with smiles and compliments on their dancing skills and they all had a good natter.

Elsie even had a dance with an airman. He escorted her back to her seat when the song was over and stopped to chat with them all for a little while before his pals beckoned him over. Rose could see that they were asking him about their chances with her and Daisy, but he shook his head and directed them to the refreshments instead. She smiled, because when he'd suggested introducing his comrades to them, Daisy had thanked him politely but firmly told him she wasn't interested. Rose had agreed with her friend and he'd shrugged, smiled at Elsie and thanked her for the dance and left them to it.

'Phew, that's a relief,' she said. 'He seemed nice enough, but his friends look at bit too cocky for my liking.'

'Airmen,' said Daisy, shaking her head, making Rose think about Jimmy's disdain for them. 'There's plenty of them based around here, all thinking they're God's gift.'

'The one I danced with was quite nice,' said Elsie. 'I enjoyed dancing with him. But I'm not looking for a relationship.'

'Why not?' asked Daisy. But before Elsie could answer, she put up a hand to stop her. 'Hang on, it's really noisy in here. Shall we go outside for some peace and quiet?'

They all agreed and within a few minutes they were outside, sitting on the wall of the library just across the road, their gas mask boxes at their feet. In the dwindling light, Rose admired the garden in front of the library and noted that the date carved in stone above the window was 1924, so the building was only sixteen years old.

'I miss my local library,' she sighed. 'If I could get into Street more often, I'd be glad to join this one. I'll have to check the bus timetable and maybe come in on my half day.'

'We're lucky round here,' said Daisy. 'The Clark family have been running their shoe business in Street for over a century now and they give a lot back to the community.' She pointed at the Crispin Hall building. 'They built that back in the 1880s and there was a smaller library in there that the Clarks stocked. Then Miss Alice Clark decided we needed a bigger library and she was the driving force behind getting this one open.'

'Who is she?' asked Elsie.

'She's dead now, God rest her soul. She was the first woman to be a director at the shoe factory, and she was in charge of the day continuation school at the factory.' When the others looked confused, she explained, 'Any lads and lasses who left school at fourteen to work at the factory would have time set aside in their working week to carry on with their education. My friend Ruby's Uncle Peter had extra lessons through that scheme and got accepted onto an engineering apprenticeship. He's one of the best-paid workers at Clarks now outside of management. Not bad for a lad from one of the poorest families in the village.'

'That's impressive,' said Rose. 'And all thanks to this Miss Clark?'

Daisy nodded. 'They say she was right fierce.' She grinned. 'And you know we have a swimming pool just around the corner from here at Greenbank?'

Rose nodded. 'Mrs Morgan told me. I'm saving up for a bathing costume. I'd love to go there on my day off. The farm hands just swim in the river or the ditches.'

'D'you mean the rhynes?' she asked.

'The what?' said Elsie. 'Did you say *reens*?'

Daisy laughed. 'Yea, we say it like that but it's spelt r-h-y-n-e-s. They're the channels on the moors that have been dug out to stop them all flooding. Being on a lower level than the sea, all the rain ends up down there, so the rhynes are kept dredged and maintained so that the water can flow down them to the rivers and out to the coast. Otherwise we'd be overrun with water like it was in ancient times. You know Glastonbury Tor was an island in the middle of a shallow sea back in prehistoric times, don't you?'

Both girls shook their heads. 'I had no idea,' said Elsie.

'Anyway,' said Daisy, 'I got off track for a bit. Sorry about the history lecture. What I meant to tell you about was Miss Alice Clark and those lads swimming in the rhynes and rivers. It turns out she didn't like the idea of women and girls joining the lads there because they usually swam naked. So when she died a few years back, she left money in her will to pay for the new swimming pool so that lasses didn't have to put up with lads with no skivvies on whenever they wanted a refreshing swim.'

Rose shrieked with laughter. 'Oh my, that's precious! So is the pool only for females?'

Daisy shook her head. 'Sadly not,' she said. 'But at least the lads have to be decently covered in there.'

'Well, that's a relief,' she giggled. 'I haven't joined the farm hands swimming for that very reason. I've spotted a few bare backsides in this hot weather, and I've no desire to get any closer than a field's length from them, thank you very much.'

'Miss Clark sounds like quite a woman,' said Elsie.

'That she was. Lots of local lasses were inspired by her. Aunt Kate especially. Miss Alice was the director in charge of the Machine Room when she and her friends started working there at fourteen. Aunt Kate wanted to be an independent woman like her, so she took evening classes in typing and bookkeeping and ended up being promoted to an office job at Clarks. Now she's a secretary at the school where Uncle Ted teaches.'

'Impressive,' said Elsie, looking thoughtful.

'Gosh, your aunt must be ever so clever,' said Rose. 'Maybe I should meet her and get some tips, else I'll end up having to go back to work in the button factory where I've been since I left school. I always hated it, but there wasn't much else to do but work in a different factory. That's why I joined the Land Army.'

Daisy looked at Elsie. 'What did you do before the war? Did you work in an office?'

Elsie shook her head. 'Not exactly. I was a telephonist.'

'Ah, that accounts for your posh voice.'

She laughed. 'I'm really not posh,' she said. 'It was just me and my sister for years after our parents died within months of each other. We were barely scraping by, but my sister was working as a Nippy – you know, a waitress at the Lyons Corner Tea Shop?'

'Ooh, yes, even I've heard of them,' said Rose.

'Well, a lady who came in regularly befriended her and commented on her nice speaking voice. Our mother was a stickler for proper diction. We didn't dare drop our aitches, and after we lost her we didn't want to.' She smiled sadly. 'Anyway, the lady introduced her to a gentleman who was recruiting telephonists and he offered her a job. It paid better than working as a Nippy, and Gertie was glad to be able to sit down to work instead of being run off her feet all day. So when I left school, she got me a job as a telephonist as well.'

'That sounds nice,' said Rose. 'But I don't suppose they'll want a lass like me with a Brummie accent.'

'Any more than they'd want someone with my accent,' said Daisy. 'It's the King's English all the way in modern communications, isn't it?'

'I rather like your accents,' said Elsie. 'They're so much friendlier. I think my accent makes people think I'm a bit cold and formal.'

'You're not like that at all,' said Rose. 'A bit shy, maybe. But you're sweet.'

Elsie blushed. 'Thank you. I think you two are sweet as well. I'm so glad we've become friends.'

'Me too,' said Daisy. 'I might know a lot of folk round here, but all my old schoolfriends are married now and quite a few have started families. I don't have much in common with them these days. I only tend to see them when I'm called upon to treat them or their relatives. So I was glad to meet both of you.' She beamed at them. 'If you stay round here long enough, you'll pick up the Somerset accent and sound like proper cider girls.'

Rose laughed. 'I'd love that. I didn't realise how strange my Brummie accent would sound away from home. It seems a bit rough and flat here next to your soft lilt. Maybe we should call ourselves the cider girls? Even without the right accent, my brothers are convinced I'm a cider girl now.'

The others giggled. 'Why not?' said Daisy. 'I'll have to work on teaching you to sound like proper cider girls. It would be fun.'

Elsie nodded, laughing with the rest of them. There were more people outside the hall now, coming out for some fresh air after the heat and cigarette smoke inside. Some came over to say hello or to ask if the girls wanted to go back in for another dance. But the cider girls were content to stay where they were on the library garden wall, getting to know each other better.

'So, why did you join the ATS, Elsie?' asked Daisy after she'd turned down yet another offer of a dance.

Elsie looked down at her hands. 'My sister got married, so she gave up work. Then she had a baby while her husband was away in the navy and she joined the first evacuation last September. I didn't want to stay in London on my own. There's nothing there for me now.'

Rose put a hand on her shoulder. 'Aw, you must miss her and the baby. I'd love to be an auntie. Trouble is, I don't think any sensible lass will put up with my brothers. Liam's just married, but it's early days yet.'

Elsie sighed. 'Actually, we weren't getting on very well by the time she left. I've written to her, but I only heard back once or twice and nothing since. I'm not even sure where they are now.'

Rose felt her heart ache for her new friend. She couldn't imagine what it would be like to have no contact with her family. She might get a bit overwhelmed by the sheer number of letters Mammy and her brothers were sending, but she'd miss them if they didn't arrive.

They were silent for a moment as others came and went from the Crispin Hall, calling to each other to close the door behind them to stop the light getting out. Rose realised that it was fully dark now, with only moonlight to see by. Since the outbreak of war, the total blackout every evening had been strictly followed. No one wanted a stray light to attract the attention of enemy aircraft as they patrolled the skies above.

As if conjured by her thoughts, they all looked up at the sound of engines overhead. It happened regularly, day and night, although the planes flying during the day were often their own as more pilots were trained to fight off the Luftwaffe.

'It's all right,' called a man's voice in the darkness. 'Those are hurricane engines. Probably our lads on a night-flying exercise.'

'I hope so,' muttered Rose. She hated the sound of planes whatever the time of day or night. She couldn't help but worry that one day they would be enemy planes and they would attack Birmingham where Mammy and Daddy remained. It was a major industrial centre, so a likely target.

Her thoughts were interrupted by the sound of another engine, this one on the road. A motorcycle turned the corner, it's engine rumbling as the rider slowed, looking around at the people coming out of the dance.

He spotted the three girls on the wall and stopped in front of them and turned off his engine. He put a foot down to hold the machine steady. Rose's heart sank as she realised it was Jimmy.

'There you are,' he said. 'I'm off home now, so if you don't want to walk, you'd better get on.' He nodded his head at the seat behind him.

She swallowed against a lump in her throat. She'd never been on a motorcycle before and it scared her a bit.

When she didn't move, he shrugged. 'If you'd rather walk, just make sure you get back in time for milking,' he said as he kicked the machine back into life.

'Wait!' She jumped off the wall, rushing towards him as fast as she could with a sore ankle, suddenly more afraid of being left behind. She'd never find her way back to the farm in the dark.

He grinned as he waited. As usual, she felt the urge to slap it off his face.

'What do I do?' she asked.

'Climb on and hold onto me.'

She nearly told him to forget it, but then she felt a twinge in her weak ankle and knew she couldn't manage the walk, even if she knew where she was going. There might be a bus going that way, but she didn't know when. She had probably already missed the last one. It was Jimmy's way or nothing. Taking a deep breath, she wished her friends a swift goodbye, gathered her skirt and quickly got on behind him. She was still trying to smooth down her clothes so that her legs weren't on show to all and sundry when he revved the engine and moved off.

With a shriek, she forgot her exposed thighs and grabbed him around his waist. He laughed as the machine picked up speed and she held on tighter, until she was plastered against his back, her cheek against his jacket and her hands clinging to his taut belly.

She didn't open her eyes until he stopped and turned the engine off. They'd reached the farmhouse much quicker than the drive to Street in the car. But as she got off, she vowed to either make sure she could get a lift in a four-wheeled vehicle in future, or she would jolly well walk, no matter how far it was. Having to hold onto him for dear life like that had made her feel quite strange.

She muttered an insincere thanks as she left him to put the machine away as she made her way into the farmhouse, glad to have made it in one piece.

Jimmy's laughter echoed across the yard as she closed the door behind her.

13

The summer continued with all hands, including Rose and various neighbours, helping with the willow harvest, haymaking, then mangold harvesting – which was the hardest of all. The mangold beets had to be pulled by hand and lifted, wiped clean of mud and then carried in heavy sacks to a trailer at the edge of the field. They would be used for animal feed. Picking them left Rose with an aching back by the end of each day. She went to bed smelling of pungent wintergreen liniment which she applied to her aching muscles to ensure she could move the next day.

As August progressed, the war got closer and closer to the farm. German bombers dropped high explosives on West Huntspill and Pill. A good number of them failed to detonate and so the authorities sent in bomb disposal teams to make them safe and remove them. A Heinkel plane was shot down over Charterhouse. The crew survived and the local Home Guard unit captured them, preventing them from setting fire to their plane. Everyone was more alert to the threat after that and strangers were observed and reported to the authorities.

Then as autumn approached it was time to harvest the cider apples in the orchard and turn the fruit into the raw cider so beloved by the farm hands. Rose was given the task of picking up the fruit as it fell from the trees. After being bombarded with hard fruit from above a couple of times, she soon learned not to wander under a branch when the lads were shaking it with their hooks. It might amuse them, but it left Rose with bruises on her back and arms and a short temper.

Rose continued to milk the cows wherever they were on the moors or in the orchards morning and evening, as well as helping with the harvests. It was a good thing that she had managed to organise all the paperwork in the farm office, because with so much going on in the fields it would have been difficult for her to maintain everything in order. As it was, she simply spent half an hour or so keeping the office work straight after supper most evenings.

'Any excuse to get out of the washing up, eh?' Jimmy teased her.

Rose tried to ignore him. Land girls weren't supposed to do domestic work – or the office chores for that matter – so she wouldn't have been expected to help out in the kitchen anyway. That said, she did help Mrs Morgan whenever she had a chance because that's how she'd been brought up, so Jimmy's scorn was unwarranted.

'It's as good an excuse as yours,' she retorted. 'Off playing soldiers again tonight, are you?'

He seemed to go out most nights these days, while his dad and brother only seemed to be on duty two or three times a week. But she noticed that Jimmy didn't go with them any more. They walked along the lane to the church hall where the local Home Guard, as the LDVs were now called, met for parade. On nights like tonight, when they could hear German planes flying overhead and searchlights lit up the sky in the distance, she knew that Mr Morgan and Ivor would be put on watch duties, keeping an eye out for any signs that enemy planes or parachutists had landed. But Jimmy didn't go with them. Some nights he took off on his motorbike, other times she saw him head off across the moor towards the elm woods on the higher ground that surrounded Catcott. He'd been away for a whole weekend last week, and she'd heard him tell his ma he would be gone for an entire week as soon as the apple harvest was completed. No one questioned this and she didn't feel it was her place to comment on it. But it bothered her. What was he up to?

Despite her dig at him, he didn't respond. Moments later he left the farmhouse and yet again stalked off towards the woods. Mr Morgan had warned her from going there. 'We've had trouble with poachers,' he said. 'The woods are full of traps, so don't go in there, lass, it's too dangerous.'

So she did the farm paperwork then fell into bed, exhausted, every night. She slept deeply until a knock on her bedroom door from Mrs Morgan roused her the next morning.

Daisy had shown her how to bind up her weak ankle to give it a bit of support, which made it more comfortable to walk and stand on for any length of time, but it still ached at times and added to her fatigue. It didn't stop her from making sure she got a bus or a lift into Street on Saturday afternoons, though, so that she could meet up with Daisy or Elsie, with whom she was becoming fast friends. They would catch up on their news and later go to the dance, or watch the latest release at the picture house on Leigh Road. The Pathé news reels before the main feature were always depressing, as was the information filtering through the population about the increasing air attacks and downed planes all across the country, including London and Birmingham – which worried Rose – and, even closer, in Bristol and towns like Yeovil, which was only a few miles away.

'Did you hear the news from Filton?' asked Daisy one afternoon when she and Rose were waiting in the queue for the tea shop.

'What's Filton?' she asked.

'It's a place just outside Bristol. There's a factory making planes there, and a small airfield. It got attacked yesterday and the blighters hit the shelters where the workers were. Killed dozens, I heard. A friend of mine at the hospital in Bristol was called on to help with casualties, not that there were many left alive, the poor souls. She said only a young lad survived in one shelter. He reckoned it was because he wanted to read his book, so had sat right by the entrance. The blast threw him clear.'

Rose grimaced, her heart sinking. 'That's horrible,' she sighed. 'They're relentless, these attacks, aren't they? It terrifies me that my mammy and daddy could get killed by the bombings in Birmingham. They write and tell me not to worry, that they spend every night in the shelter on their street. But if the bombs can kill people in the shelters, how can I not worry about them? What are folks supposed to do to protect themselves?'

'I don't know,' said Daisy. 'I did wonder whether I should go back to work in the hospital because they're getting so many casualties from these bombings. But Bristol is a target, with the docks and such, so my ma and pa wouldn't be happy about it, and there's still patients here that need me. I'd rather be at home with my parents so they don't have to fret about me so much. Ma's worried enough about Pa overdoing it without me adding to their concerns.' She sighed. 'He won't admit it, but he's not well these days. He's lost weight and gets tired more easily than he used to.

He says it's just old age creeping up, but I'd be happier if he would speak to a doctor. But until he agrees, I'm not going anywhere.'

'I hope you manage to persuade him to get help, Daisy. At least it's safer here,' said Rose. 'Since the bombings started in Birmingham, my family are finally coming round to the idea that I'm better off here than in the city.'

'So long as you don't get trampled by cows again,' Daisy said, grinning.

Rose laughed. 'I'm wise to them now,' she said. 'And Mammy and Daddy don't know about that. I didn't dare tell them. Oh, look, there's Elsie.' She waved.

'Sorry I'm late,' said Elsie, joining them just as they were allocated a table. 'I wasn't sure I'd get back in time.'

They settled in and ordered tea and buns.

'Where've you been this week?'

'On another course,' she said.

The girls had got used to the vague responses the ATS girl gave to their questions and didn't ask for more details.

'Meet any interesting chaps?' asked Rosie with a smile.

Elsie shrugged. 'Not really.' She wrinkled her nose. 'Not that I'm looking.'

'Whyever not?' asked Daisy. 'Wouldn't you like a sweetheart?'

'Doesn't seem worth it, with so many men being shipped overseas, does it? I think I'd rather stay unattached while this war continues. There was a weeping woman on the train today. I heard her tell another passenger that she'd lost one sweetheart in France last year, then she'd met a sailor and she'd just heard this week that his ship was torpedoed and lost with all hands.'

'Oh my lord,' said Rose. 'How awful. I can't imagine losing one, let alone two sweethearts in a matter of months.'

'Exactly,' said Elsie. 'It doesn't make me inclined to give my heart away when there's no guarantee of anything right now.'

Their order was delivered and they enjoyed their fruit buns while the tea brewed in the pot.

'I see what you're saying,' said Rose. 'But that shouldn't stop us having a bit of fun with a lad if he asks, should it?'

Daisy grinned. 'Why, have you got your eye on someone?'

Rose laughed. 'Not really. Truth be told, I'm so tired most of the time, I've gone right off the idea of courting. I'd rather have an early night than have to get dressed up to impress a chap. I only came out this afternoon so the three of us could have a good natter. I just noticed there's a lot of extra airmen around here, that's all.'

Daisy nodded. 'They expanded the airfield at Weston Zoyland. The lads stationed there either come here, or into Bridgewater for their entertainment.'

'They look quite smart, don't they?' said Elsie.

'Yeah,' said Rose. 'Air Force blue is much nicer than khaki. No offence Elsie, love.'

She laughed. 'None taken. Khaki's not really my colour anyway. But look, I'm quite tired after my week away, so I don't think I'll stay long.'

Daisy nodded. 'I'm not feeling much like it either. I spent most of last night with a dying patient.'

'Aw, you poor thing. That must be difficult,' said Rose. 'I don't know if I could do your job. I'd hate it if people died on me.'

She shrugged. 'I don't think I'll ever get used to it, but I try to keep my emotions in check and stay professional. It's just that I knew this old chap. In fact, I've known a lot of the patients I deal with in this job all my life. It can be difficult to remain detached when it's a relative of an old school friend, like this chap was.'

'But I'll bet they appreciate having a familiar face around

when they're so ill,' said Elsie. She looked thoughtful. 'I know I was glad to have you there. You were so kind and capable when I was suffering in that hot car.'

'And I've never been so pleased to see someone as when you found me in the orchard and chased the cows away,' said Rose. 'But I know it must be hard on you, Daisy.' She yawned. 'It sounds like all three of us would rather be home in our beds than waiting around for the dance. Shall we have our tea and call it a day?'

Daisy poured their drinks. The tea was weak, on account of the shortages, but with just a small splash of milk it was palatable.

'How will you get back to Catcott?' she asked Rose. 'Is Jimmy going to ride up and carry you off on his motorbike again?'

'No he isn't,' she said, trying not to scowl at the thought of him. 'He's doing something with the Home Guard this weekend.' She checked the time. 'There's a bus in about half an hour, I think. I looked at the timetable before I came out, thinking I might not last till the evening. I'll catch that one.'

'My bus to Glastonbury should be around the same time,' said Elsie, yawning as she checked her wristwatch. 'I'm so sorry. Let's hope we'll be more in the mood for dancing next time.'

'Come on, then,' said Daisy, standing up. 'I'll wait at the bus stop with both of you. I'll go and see if Ruby's home and have a chat. It's not too far to walk home from there.'

A few jolly lads tried to persuade them to stay and go to the dance, but the girls wouldn't be persuaded.

'I suppose I should feel a bit bad, turning them down,' said Rose. 'But right now sleep is more appealing to me than anything else.'

'Mmm,' said Daisy. 'I agree.'

Elsie laughed. 'Listen to us. All worn out and no fun at all. Maybe we should have gone to the picture house matinee and fallen asleep in comfy seats. We're no good to anyone for dancing tonight.'

Daisy sighed. 'I'm all for fun, but not tonight.'

Rose nudged her. 'So who would you want to have fun with, eh? You never seem to have any inclination towards any of the lads we come across.'

Daisy rolled her eyes and put a hand over her heart. 'That's because I've been ruined by unrequited love,' she said dramatically.

'Ooh, do tell. Who's the man who's so daft as not to notice what a catch you are?'

Daisy sobered. 'He's not daft. That's the problem. He's clever and doesn't have time for anything but his work. I've known him all my life and no matter what I do, he just doesn't see me like that. He thinks of me as family, even though we've no blood connection.'

'Tell us about him,' said Elsie, her tone gentle as they crossed over the road.

With another sigh, Daisy sat on the wall of the library garden. 'His name's Mattie. He's Ruby's big brother.' The others nodded, encouraging her to go on. 'Well, he looks just like her, only taller and broader, of course, and he's dark-haired while Ruby's a blonde. They've got a little brother, Henry, as well. Their ma, Louisa, and Aunt Kate have been friends for ever and our pas worked together at Clarks when they were lads. Mattie's the reason I became a nurse. He's a doctor now, not long qualified.'

'Will he join the medical corps?' asked Elsie.

Daisy shook her head. 'No. He won't enlist, even in the medical corps. He's a Quaker.'

'Ah,' said Elsie. 'So he's a pacifist?'

'That's right. But thankfully, his job as a doctor exempts him from call up, so he doesn't have to fight his case with a tribunal like some conscientious objectors, thank goodness. I don't know what I'd've done if he'd signed up for the medical corps. Joined up myself, probably, in some ridiculous hope that we'd end up somewhere together.'

'Does he know how you feel about him?' asked Elsie.

She shook her head. 'No. I've never said anything.'

'Whyever not?' asked Rose.

'Because... I don't know. A lot of the time when I see him it's with other folk around – his family or mine or both. The few times we've seen each other alone in recent years, he just talks about work. I could hardly blurt out that I fancy him when he's talking about the latest treatment for tuberculosis or some other ailment, could I?'

'I expect he's glad to talk to someone who understands medicine,' said Elsie. 'It's a connection between the two of you.'

Daisy sighed. 'I know. But I'm beginning to think that I'm wasting my time pining for him when he doesn't see me as anything other than a nurse.'

'But don't most doctors look down on nurses?' asked Rose. 'You were saying that the ones in the hospitals were really patronising. Surely if this Mattie is discussing things with you, he must respect you. That's a good sign, isn't it?'

'I suppose so. But it's probably because we've known each other all our lives. I want more than that from him.' She crossed her arms. 'I want him to see me as a woman.'

'Then you must make him do that,' said Rose. 'Knock his socks off with your beauty as well as your stellar nursing skills, make him see what he's missing.'

Daisy laughed. 'Believe me, I've tried, but it's hard when we're surrounded by our families. Short of grabbing him and kissing the life out of him the next time I see him alone, I don't know what else to do.'

'That sounds like an excellent plan.' Rose smiled. 'I know that's what my sister-in-law did to attract my eldest brother's attention. She said she did it to win a bet, but I think she just got fed up of waiting for him to notice her.'

'Goodness, that was brave,' said Elsie, her cheeks warming. 'I wouldn't dare do anything like that.'

'Me neither, I'm afraid,' said Daisy. 'Because if he rejected me I'd be mortified. Can you imagine having to face him every time our families got together?' She shook her head. 'No, I'm going to have to think about finding someone else who doesn't make me compare him with Mattie all the time, or I'll be a spinster for the rest of my life.'

'Oh, don't say that,' said Rose. 'You're too young to be considering spinsterhood. If this Mattie is too daft to see what a treasure you are, then we'll help you find someone else, won't we, Elsie?'

Daisy smiled, glad that Rose's bus pulled round the corner at that moment. She really shouldn't have said anything. There wasn't much point, with Mattie being so clueless. But the last thing she wanted was for her friends to play cupid and parade a selection of lads for her.

'We'll talk about it next time, all right?' Rose called as she waved goodbye and hopped onto the bus. 'See you soon!'

'It must be hard,' said Elsie when they were left alone. 'I've never been in love.' She sounded wistful. 'But I know my sister has suffered for loving the wrong man.'

Daisy wasn't sure, but she thought she heard Elsie mutter, 'More than once,' under her breath. Before she could ask her about it, the bus going in the other direction arrived and they said their goodbyes. Once the sound of the engine receded into the distance, she stayed on the wall, thinking. The village was busy and folks who knew her called out greetings. Someone asked if she was going to the dance, but Daisy shook her head. Like her friends, she had had enough for one day.

She stood up and headed round the corner into the high street. She would stop off and say hello to Ruby at her home in West End, then walk the rest of the way home to Walton. It wasn't far. Maybe at the Musgrove house she would get some news of Mattie.

14

She ended up spending longer than she intended at Ruby's as her friend wanted some help with a dress she was making. There was no news of Mattie. He was still working at the big hospital in Exeter and was so busy the family rarely saw him.

It was dark as Daisy headed home. As she walked with only the moon to guide her, she wondered whether she ought not to have said anything about Mattie to her friends. She felt a little guilty that she might have made them think that he was unfeeling or standoffish, because he really wasn't like that. He had been her best friend for as long as she could remember. It was just that her feelings had changed over the years until he was the only one she could ever imagine being with, while Mattie hadn't changed in his attitude towards her. All right, so he liked to talk about work with her, but that was only because they'd joined the St John's Ambulance Brigade as children and had both been obsessed with all things medical ever since, practising bandaging and splints on each other. It was a special bond they had. But that wasn't the bond she wanted with him going into the future.

She was still pondering this as she reached the edge of the village. Despite the darkness, she walked confidently, knowing the route from years of walking to and fro to the high school in Street. There was no one else around and so when a shape moved swiftly into her path, it made her shriek in surprise.

'Halt! Who goes there?' A torch was shone in her face, making her flinch.

'Put that light down,' she snapped, stepping back.

A hand grabbed her arm, pulling her towards the light. 'Can't do that. We've had reports of an enemy pilot on the loose. Got to check everyone out and about.'

She shrugged off the hand. 'Well get on and find him before we're murdered in our beds.' She tried to peer around the bright light. 'Who are you? How do I know you're not this missing pilot?'

Whoever it was gave a dark chuckle as he grabbed her arm again. She realised he was in Home Guard uniform. He had a rifle slung over his shoulder. 'You don't, do you? But I'm the one with the gun, so you'd better do as you're told, missy.'

She frowned, not even sure if the Home Guard had enough bullets to shoot an innocent woman for sport. She doubted this idiot would be trusted with ammunition. Drawing her professional persona around her like a cloak, she said, 'I'm on my way home to the Selway farm. I'm the district nurse and I'm on duty early tomorrow, so I'll thank you to let me pass.'

'Not yet. I need to check you're not this pilot, dressed up in that nice dress of yours. He could've overwhelmed a pretty lass out for a walk and stolen her clothes. I hear they like those kind of disguises, does Jerry. They caught one in a nun's habit a while back. Left the poor sister tied up in her skivvies, he did.'

'What a load of nonsense,' she said. There were always fantastic stories like this doing the rounds. 'You can see I'm no German pilot.'

'It's not nonsense at all. You're fierce enough to be a man.'

She pointed at her long dark curls. 'And German men have long hair do they?'

He let go of her arm and grabbed at her tresses, pulling her head back as she yelped. 'Just checking it's not a wig. Can't trust 'em, you know. We've got to protect the population. Mr Churchill said so.'

She struggled against his painful hold, her fear feeding her growing anger and frustration. 'Let me go!'

'When I'm ready,' he growled, keeping hold of her hair, his warm breath close to her ear, making her shudder. 'Got one more check to make,' he said as he stuffed the torch into his pocket and slipped his rifle higher onto his shoulder by its leather strap and used his now free hand to latch onto her bosom and squeeze hard.

Suddenly, all the training she'd had with Uncle Ted came back to her and her anger turned ice cold.

With a furious cry, Daisy swung her fist towards his face, too angry now to feel anything but sheer rage as she felt his nose break under her knuckles. His grip on her hair and her bosom fell away as he staggered back, dropping his weapon as he went.

'Bloody hell! You bitch! I'll get you for that.' He scrabbled round for his rifle as blood poured from his nose.

Daisy was too enraged to be scared. Instead, she swiftly dodged around him, grabbed the rifle off the ground and used it to smack him across the back of his legs so that he collapsed onto his knees. Another blow knocked him flat onto the ground. 'Don't you dare move,' she ordered, sticking the barrel of the rifle into the middle of his back. 'I'm not an enemy pilot, as you well know, you filthy beast. But I am capable of pulling this trigger and ending you, so stay still.' She was shouting by the end of her speech. She took a calming breath and lowered her voice. 'Now give me the damned torch and don't do anything daft because I'm just itching for you to give me the excuse to shoot you.'

With a whimper, he carefully took the torch out of his pocket and held it up. She snatched it, keeping the gun firm against his back, and switched it on.

'Turn your head, slowly now, and look at me,' she said. 'I want to know who you are.'

He did as she said, revealing his bloody face to her. She recognised him as a lad whose older brother she had been at school with. She had no idea why he hadn't been called up yet, he was probably too young even though he was full-grown, but that was beside the point.

'Do you have a whistle, Ronnie?' she asked. He nodded, more blood dripping. 'Blow it. Call your comrades.'

He swore, but did as she said when she poked him again with the gun. A few minutes later boots clattered along the road.

'What the hell?' the first man to reach them exclaimed. 'Is that you, Nurse Daisy? Did he have an accident? Is it serious?'

'It is serious, but no, he didn't have an accident,' she said, her voice loud and clear as a couple more Home Guards arrived. 'This man assaulted me and I've requisitioned his gun after he threatened me. Now, I want this reported and I expect you to restrain him and take him to your superior officer.'

One of the men laughed. 'Come on, lass, I expect he was just fooling with you. He's only young. No need to involve officers, is there?'

She turned the torch towards the voice, recognising this man as well. 'On the contrary, Mr Underwood. He pulled my hair and I've bruises on my arm and chest. I think you'll agree that the fact that I had to break his nose in order to get his hands off me means that a young lad *just fooling around* is not an accurate description of this incident. However, if you won't report it, I'll go and see your commanding officer myself. I don't think he'll find it any funnier than I do. And my pa will have a thing or two to say about it as well.'

'The bitch punched me,' Ronnie snarled.

'And I'd do it again,' she snapped, ignoring the ache in her hand as she held tight onto the rifle. 'So be quiet.'

The other men stood there, apparently unsure what to do. Daisy sighed.

'Do I have to ask again?' she said using the torch to check the identity of all of them. 'Because I'll make sure you all end up on a charge if you don't shift yourselves.'

They all began to move, just as a car came along the road. The men were helping Ronnie to his feet when the vehicle stopped and a door opened.

'What's going on here, then?' asked a voice in the dark.

Daisy blew out a breath in relief. 'Is that you, Uncle Ted?'

'Daisy, lass? Are your nursing skills needed?'

'I'll not be laying another finger on him,' she declared. 'He's got a bloody nose because he assaulted me and I walloped him one.'

Ted Jackson walked into the dim light of the torch. He was in uniform, his expression hard and cold. The men who had been reluctant to take orders from Daisy all jumped to attention. 'Is that right?' he asked. 'This soldier laid hands on my goddaughter?'

'I was just joking, sir,' said Ronnie. He shrank back when he saw the captain's expression. 'I didn't mean anything by it. She just can't take a joke.'

'A joke?' said Daisy, her voice high with indignation. 'You accused me of being an enemy pilot in disguise.'

'That's what we was told,' he said, his eyes not leaving her uncle's. 'We had to look out for him.'

She scoffed. 'You shone your torch in my face and knew jolly well who I was. Then you grabbed me and pulled my hair,' she went on.

'Well, I had to check it wasn't a wig, didn't I?'

One of the men sniggered but quickly stifled it under the furious gazes of Daisy and the captain.

'And you grabbed my bosom!' she shouted.

Uncle Ted stepped forward holding out his hand. 'Daisy, lass, let me have the gun before you do someone another injury.'

She realised with a shock that she'd been brandishing the rifle in Ronnie's face. It pleased her no end to see how pale and frightened he looked. With a huff she handed it to her uncle. Ronnie sagged with relief as Ted checked the weapon, removing a bullet and slipping it into his pocket. His relief was short-lived though when the captain turned towards him.

'You, lad, are in a mess of trouble. Taking advantage of a young woman under the pretence of carrying out your duty is an act of cowardice and depravation that will not be tolerated. The fact that it was my own goddaughter – a well-respected nurse in this community – makes it something I take personally. Very personally indeed.'

'But, sir, it was a joke, I swear. I didn't mean anything by it.'

'You say that now, you toad,' said Daisy, 'but with that gun in your hand you thought you could get away with murder.'

Captain Jackson touched her arm. 'It's just as well you knew what to do, wasn't it? If he'd tried it on with some other unsuspecting lass, he might have gotten away with it.' He glanced around the men who were still standing to attention, eyes wide as they witnessed the scene. 'You should all know that I make it a point to teach all the lasses in my family – my wife, my daughter, my sisters-in-law and all my nieces as well as Daisy here – to defend themselves from attacks like this. No man has a right to take advantage of a woman, so anyone messing with my family will soon learn that being bigger and stronger than a woman will not give them the advantage – as you can see from this lad's injuries tonight. Spread the word. We might expect this from the enemy, but it had better not happen again with a local man. Touch my kinswomen or any women in this community and the consequences will be harsh, both at the time and with what follows. Am I clear?'

'Yes, sir!' the men declared in unison.

Ted nodded. 'Good. Now, take this man to your headquarters and report the incident to your commanding officer. I will be along to speak with him after I've delivered Nurse Daisy safely home. Then we'll decide whether this should be passed to the civil or military police.'

Daisy watched with a mix of frustration and satisfaction that they jumped to obey Uncle Ted when they had been reluctant to follow her orders. If they'd done as she'd said they might have gotten away without all of them getting into trouble, but now that Ted was involved, they'd all be facing the consequences she was sure.

'All right, Daisy love?' he asked, his voice far more gentle now that the men had disappeared in the direction of the Home Guard HQ in Street. 'Let's get you home, shall we?'

He gently guided her into the car and turned it around to take her home. As she sat beside him, she realised she was shaking. She clasped her hands together and took deep breaths, trying to calm down.

Ted glanced at her. 'It'll be the come-down after a stressful situation that's giving you the shakes,' he said, his tone reassuring.

'I know,' she said. 'Adrenaline in my system. Fight or flight response.'

He smiled. 'Exactly. Nothing to worry about.' He brought the car to a halt outside the farmhouse. 'I'd better come in and talk to your ma and pa,' he said, holding up a hand when she would have protested. 'They'll have to be told because you can guarantee it will be all round the villages by tomorrow. If I'm with you, we can reassure your pa that Ronnie will be dealt with. Otherwise, knowing your pa, he'll be rushing after the lad and giving him a good hiding, won't he?'

She sighed. 'He will. Which won't help matters.' She paused. 'You know he's not well? I've been trying to get him to see a doctor, but he won't.'

He nodded. 'I thought so. I heard they took him off the rota for Home Guard duties. Keep on at him, lass. He'll see sense eventually. In the meantime, I'll persuade him to let me deal with tonight's incident officially, so he doesn't end up in a police cell.'

'Thanks, Uncle Ted. You arrived just in time.'

He chuckled. 'I didn't do anything, lass. You sorted him out good and proper. I'm proud of you.'

She smiled, glowing in his approval. 'You taught us well. I didn't even think, I just reacted. Got him square on the nose.'

'Good. You know, Ronnie had an uncle, a lad called Stan. He tried it on with Jeannie Musgrove outside the Street Inn one night. She kneed him in the privates, left him screaming on the ground.'

Daisy's jaw dropped. 'Do you mean Auntie Jeannie who lives in Cranfield Road?'

'That's her. It was that night that she met her husband, Tom. He came by and found her standing over a whimpering Stan. Said he'd never seen anything more magnificent.'

'Oh my,' she exclaimed. 'That's unbelievable. She's such a gentle soul.'

'That she is, but she's not a woman any man should underestimate. A bit like you, our Daisy.' He grinned. 'You can guarantee no lad around here is going to mess with you from now on. Now, let's go and talk to your ma and pa before I go and deal with young Ronnie.'

15

In early September, almost a year to the day since war had been declared, hundreds of German planes bombed London. They came first with incendiary bombs, using the River Thames to guide them to the heart of the city where docks and factories and warehouses worked tirelessly for the war effort. The fires they set guided the next wave of planes, who dropped tonnes of high explosive bombs, destroying whole streets of houses. Hundreds were killed. The so-called phoney war was over. The real conflict and the fight for Britain had begun.

By mid-October of 1940, after weeks of air raids over London and across the country, with widespread civilian and military casualties, the Battle of Britain in the air didn't seem to be easing off, even as the RAF proved its strength against the Luftwaffe. The incident that upset Elsie the most was the killing of three young children in Bridgewater. It seemed that an enemy bomber had dropped the rest of its load over the town on its way back from a raid on Cardiff docks, across the Severn Estuary. The high explosives had landed on a street, damaging seventy homes and depriving a family of its children.

At about the same time, she finally heard from her sister Gertie for the first time in months. After Gertie had returned to the city, declaring that life in the country was too tiresome and that she'd rather die in an air raid than from boredom, Elsie had written to her, begging her to reconsider, and she'd heard nothing for ages. Finally, Gertie had replied, but still refused to listen to Elsie's pleas to take herself and her baby to a safer place.

'There's no safer place than London,' she'd replied. 'I go into the underground when the air raid siren goes. They stopped us going down there at first, but now they let us. Stop fussing. What I do with my life is none of your business!'

But that was three weeks ago, and Elsie hadn't heard from her since. She hadn't even received a birthday card. Elsie had turned twenty-three this week with no fanfare, no celebration. She had never felt so lonely in her life. She could have told her new friends, Rose and Daisy, but she hadn't wanted them to feel obliged to give her a present or a card.

The CO came into her office. 'Ah, Bloomfield. Are you busy?'

She smiled. She was always busy, but that was how she liked it. 'I've just finished the latest situation report, sir. Is there something you want me to prioritise?'

He shook his head. 'Leave the paperwork. You do a grand job of it, but I think it's time for you to join me on a field trip. I have some equipment to deliver to an auxiliary unit, including their radio set. You can instruct them on its use.'

'Yes, sir,' she replied, standing up, eager to get out and about. 'Shall I bring the car round?'

'Not this time. There's a lorry outside. We'll be going in that. You can drive it, can't you?'

A few minutes later, Elsie sat beside her CO, her concentration on the road as she drove the lorry south.

'This AU has just finished their new OB,' said Captain

Crick. She knew that an OB was an operational base from which the auxiliary units would carry out their missions in the event of an invasion. Auxiliary units, or AUs as they were referred to in the office, were officially designated Home Guard – Special Duties to the wider world. No one outside of the AUs and the army personnel who worked directly with them knew the true purpose of these men. Her own role, as a communications officer, would be rather different – she would be right in the centre of the civilian community, a 'Stay Behind' with a hidden radio set in order to keep in touch with other radio operators and to pass information and orders to and fro between them and whatever British authorities might remain after an invasion.

'Their arms store is also in the vicinity, but not so close as to create a risk to the OB,' he went on. He studied the map in his hand before addressing her. 'There should be a drove lane across the moor up here on the right. Follow this for a mile or so. It should then climb into an elm wood.'

Elsie looked around with interest. They had passed through Glastonbury and Street before turning and going down onto the moors. To their left the land rose to the ridge of the Polden Hills, to their right, across the low, flat moor, she could see Glastonbury Tor rising above the landscape like an island. She remembered what Daisy had said about it having indeed been an island in prehistoric times.

They were soon across the moor and climbing towards the woods. The CO checked his watch. She wasn't sure where they were, but she thought it was quite close to where Rose was living on the Morgan farm.

'Right on time,' he said. 'There should be someone looking out for us, so keep your eyes open.'

A moment later, Elsie saw a man step out from the trees and

wave in their direction. 'There, sir,' she said. It wasn't until they got closer that she recognised him. It was Jimmy Morgan.

He frowned as she got down from the lorry's cab with the CO. 'What's she doing here? This ain't no place for a lass,' he said.

Elsie kept her expression neutral as the CO turned on him. 'You will address a fellow combatant with respect, soldier,' he snapped. 'This young woman is a valued member of my team and has skills and expertise that are vital to your survival in the event of an invasion, so I suggest you wind your neck in and listen to her.'

Jimmy had the decency to look embarrassed. Elsie stifled a smile, understanding why Rose found him so objectionable sometimes. She only hoped he'd heed the CO's words. He could make life very difficult for her if they were forced to work together during an invasion.

'Sorry, sir,' he muttered, not looking at Elsie. 'But she's pals with our land girl. She could give the whole game away.'

Elsie glared at him. 'I would never put my comrades or my friends at risk with loose talk,' she said sharply. 'I'm aware of the importance of secrecy. Can you say the same when you've had a belly full of cider?'

'I don't gossip,' he snarled.

The CO stepped in. 'I'm glad to hear it,' he said. 'Now, let's get this equipment off the truck. Are the rest of your unit around to help?'

Jimmy turned towards the woods and whistled. Five other men appeared as if by magic. The CO nodded as they approached and directed them to unload.

'How far is it to the OB?' he asked.

'About ten minutes.' He glanced at the crates piling up on the ground. 'Three of us can get the supplies installed there. The others can take the rest to the arms store.'

While they were getting organised, Elsie spotted the leather suitcase that contained the radio set. It was the twin of the one she had stashed in the bottom of her wardrobe, ready to take with her when the time came. She picked it up. It was compact but heavy. It was her responsibility to see it installed and to instruct them how to use it, so she was prepared to lug it as far as was needed.

Under orders, some collected crates and started the trek into the woods with the CO, while the others went to the arms store. They would then go back to guard the truck until they were ready to return to base. Elsie followed behind the ones heading for the OB, trying her best not to get left behind as they all strode ahead on their longer legs. It didn't help that she couldn't stride out like they did because her straight uniform skirt wasn't suited to marching through the woods. She didn't dare complain. It was hard enough being the only woman in a group like this, so she had to keep up. The team needed her, she had to remember that, even when they patronised her. And if, God forbid, one day they were occupied, she was determined not to be the one to let her side down.

Despite her efforts, she fell a little behind and would have missed the entrance to the OB altogether if she hadn't seen the last man disappear into it before the trapdoor into the underground bunker closed silently.

With a sigh, she put down the suitcase and stood there, hands on hips, trying to work out how to open it again. She wouldn't put it past them to forget about her and leave her outside. A chill wind blew through the trees, making her shiver. She was about to give up and shout when she noticed a piece of old, weathered rope lying on the ground in the middle of the undergrowth. It looked as though it was just something that had been discarded and left to rot, but maybe it wasn't as old and useless as it appeared. She bent and grasped it and sure enough it was thick and strong, despite its rough appearance. Hoping it wasn't some kind of booby-trap, she pulled. To her relief, it moved a section of camouflaged netting to reveal the entrance. A swift tug on the lever that had been exposed and the trapdoor swung upwards silently. She marvelled at the ingenuity of it. What had appeared to be part of the woodland floor was in fact a box, planted with ground-hugging plants that fitted perfectly with their surroundings.

Below was a shaft with an iron ladder going down. With a self-satisfied smile, she turned and started climbing down, pulling the suitcase with her, remembering to pull the lever at the bottom of the shaft so that the trapdoor closed silently above her, leaving her in darkness.

She could hear the low murmur of voices, so she took a deep breath and followed the sound. Still in the dark, she moved carefully, one hand out in front of her, wishing she had brought a torch with her. Her fingers had just encountered a smooth metal surface when it swung open to reveal a room lit by oil lamps. Jimmy stood in the doorway.

'There you are, Bloomfield,' said the CO from further into the room. There wasn't much space with four full-grown men and a pile of crates. 'I was about to send someone to look for you. Just put that down for a minute and help us stow this lot.'

She looked around, surprised by the quality of this underground chamber. The thick metal door behind her was sturdy – no doubt to withstand explosions and to help suppress noise when the OB was occupied. There was an arched roof of corrugated iron, high enough for all the men to stand up straight. These metal structures were known as elephant shelters. They were larger than the compact Anderson shelters that so many people had half-submerged into their gardens, and she knew that the AU and some sappers would have had to have dug out a chamber big enough to hold such a beast before the shelter was lowered over it. They'd then have had to backfill the earth around it. How they'd managed to restore the surface above them to its natural appearance, she had no idea, but she was impressed. It fitted so perfectly into the landscape.

They all worked around each other, finding places for the crates under bunks and in plank-lined niches. When everything was cleared away, she could see that the OB was really rather spacious. There were three pairs of bunks against the walls, a table with a camping stove, kettle, pans, some metal cups and plates, and the oil lamp. A couple of folding chairs were propped up against the table. In a corner, she noticed a small barrel, marked Navy Rum. Apparently, the government felt that men risking their lives in this way needed a ration of hard liquor on hand as well as field rations to help them survive. Next to it was another barrel. She hoped that contained water rather than the cider favoured by locals. At the other end of the room was another metal door set in a brick wall.

'We keep flammables, fuses and other supplies in a chamber out there,' said Jimmy quietly when he saw her looking. 'And our escape chute. It leads straight into a stream, so we can throw dogs off our scent.'

She nodded. Although this was her first visit into an underground OB, she'd seen plans for them and knew the basic design. There would be a basic privy out there as well, and ventilation shafts. 'But not your arms store,' she said. If they were discovered inside the OB, they would only have hand guns and a few grenades with which to defend themselves. In their arms store would be a cache of ammunition, machine guns, sniper rifles, more grenades and bomb-making equipment. Keeping it away from the OB was a matter of common sense. Provided they could escape the bunker if it was discovered, they could re-arm and fight on.

He shook his head. 'No, that's safely away from here, but you don't need to know where that is.'

'Of course not. The less I know, the better. Don't worry, I doubt I'd be able to find this place again. I won't betray you.'

He studied her, still looking suspicious, but she held his gaze steadily until he nodded.

'Now, let's set up the radio,' she said.

'Over here,' said the CO, pointing to a niche above the table.

She opened the suitcase and began pulling out the components, fitting them together with quick efficiency, aware of the men watching her. She talked them through everything she was doing, pointing out that, should they need to abandon this OB, they would need to pack the radio away and take it with them if at all possible.

'Bear in mind, though,' she told them. 'If it seems likely that it will fall into enemy hands, you must make sure to destroy it.' She explained how to do that, as well as how to fashion new spare parts should they need to. When she'd done, she made each of them take it apart and stow it back in the suitcase before following her instructions to set it up again.

She wasn't surprised that the men picked it up quickly, although she had been surprised by Jimmy's astute questions. From what Rose had said, he was a surly beggar who could barely hold a civil conversation. Yet he must have something about him that got him noticed. The Auxiliers were all hand-picked men with certain characteristics. They had to have a thorough knowledge of the local landscape, the ability to move around it in the day or night without being detected, and a sharp mind that would help keep them alive. Some were farmers like Jimmy, and others were quarrymen, miners, or teachers who were exempt from fighting because they worked in reserved occupations. And then there were the older men, veterans of the Great War like Captain Jackson, who had experience of combat. Like the old soldiers, the farmers were decent marksmen and also had a good level of competence when it came to maintaining machinery; the quarrymen in particular knew their way around explosives. She knew that some units had even recruited local poachers for their nefarious skills.

'They might be tricky devils,' the CO had commented when she'd asked why they would consider known law-breakers as Auxiliers. 'But they know how to move around silently in the dark, to evade capture. They're also handy if rations run out and the men need some fresh meat to sustain them.' Captain Jackson had muttered something about poachers becoming game-keepers, and Elsie had accepted that even tricky devils had a part to play to keep the country safe.

After each man had mastered the art of building the radio and dismantling it so that it fit into the suitcase again, Elsie put it together once more and began instructing them on how to use it. An aerial had already been incorporated into the construction of the OB, running from the bunker up into the high branches of a nearby tree, hidden by ivy and moss. She showed them how to connect and disconnect it.

'You have the manual here, which must be kept secure and destroyed if there's any danger of it falling into enemy hands. Study it well, but then it's better if you can build your confidence in using the equipment without having to look everything up so that you're used to operating it. You won't be able to afford to waste time.' The men nodded, no longer looking at her with contempt. 'We'll set up some times to test the system and relay messages with my unit.'

Jimmy frowned. 'But when the invasion comes, you'll be rounded up with the rest of the uniforms, won't you?'

She didn't say anything. The CO spoke instead. 'Not necessarily. While she may not be embarking on the missions you'll be undertaking, she will be a vital support to the whole resistance operation.'

'I can shoot, though,' she said. 'And am prepared to fight if I'm needed. I have also been trained in unarmed combat.'

'Blimey,' said one of the men. 'What is it with women these days? I heard the district nurse took down one of the Home Guards in Street a while back.'

She laughed. Daisy had told her and Rose about the attack the last time they'd met. They had been full of admiration for her courage.

'Well, that might be because she's related to Bulldog,' said the CO. When the Auxiliers worked together, the officers were referred to by their code names. Captain Crick was Apollo, Captain Jackson was Bulldog.

The CO chuckled. 'The man's got a bee in his bonnet about women being able to protect themselves. Having said that' – his expression became stern – 'it seems that that particular incident involved a man who thought his Home Guard uniform gave him the right to take liberties with civilian women. He has been severely dealt with as will any man who dishonours his uniform and the fairer sex in such a way.'

'Quite right n'all, sir,' said the man. 'It's bad enough thinking about Jerry coming over here and interfering with our wives and daughters, without having to worry about our lads doing the same. I wasn't criticising the nurse, sir. I think she's a real little pistol. Good on her. And good on the young lady here, for learning to protect herself.'

'But our job is to make sure they don't have to,' said Jimmy.

'Quite right. Now, I think we've done all we can today. Well done, men. You've done a sterling job on this place. One of you can show us the way back, after which we'll both forget the location of this OB.'

16

Most of the conditions that Daisy's patients suffered from were treatable in the doctor's surgery in Street, or even their own homes. But occasionally it was necessary to transfer them to specialist hospitals. In early November, she volunteered to escort a lady with tuberculosis who was being transferred to the isolation hospital in Taunton.

'Thank you so much for coming with me, Nurse Daisy,' she said as they settled into the back of the ambulance. 'I was so scared of going on my own.'

'It's no trouble.' She smiled. 'I wanted to see you all settled there. Now, didn't you say your daughter is in Taunton?'

She nodded, her breathing laboured. 'That's why I asked to go there, so she can visit me when they allow it. If I'd gone to Wells or Yeovil or one of the other sanitoriums, I'd never have seen anyone from one week to the next.'

Daisy patted her hand. 'It'll do you good to see her, won't it? And the hospital is very good there. Now you must do as they tell you, rest and take your medicines and you'll be feeling better before you know it.'

The woman's eyes filled with tears. 'D'you think so, lass? Only my dear old pa got took with the consumption when I was but a girl. There was no hope for him.'

Many of the older folk still called tuberculosis that. Daisy had always thought it was a grim name, implying that the disease would consume them.

'I'm sorry to hear that,' she said gently. 'But treatment is better today. With total rest, plenty of fresh air and the expertise of the doctors, you've every chance.' It might take up to a year, but she knew of many cases of folk going into remission from the disease. Of course, there wasn't yet a complete cure and many were still dying from it, so she understood the woman's fear. 'Now, you must try to be positive. Think about how much easier it will be for your daughter to visit you there, and someone else will be doing all the cooking and cleaning for you, so it will be like being on holiday.' She grinned. 'Now have you got some books to read?'

'I have, lass, thank you. Everyone has been so kind, not least the folk at Clarks. Do you know, they said on account of my late husband having worked there all his life, that they would pay a grant to cover my medical bills?'

She nodded. Not only did Clarks look after their workers, but they also did what they could for their retired workers and their families when they were in need. Although the factory management oversaw the grants, she suspected it was often the Clark family members themselves who provided the funds for such support. It was one of many ways that the family cared for the community and lived out their faith.

She wondered if it was his Quaker faith, like that of the Clark family, that had led Mattie to become a doctor. Thinking of him distracted her, producing a hollow ache in her chest. She hadn't seen him for a while because he'd been working at the general hospital in Exeter.

Her patient began to cough. Daisy quickly passed her a handkerchief to cover her mouth. She supposed she should be concerned, sitting with a tuberculosis sufferer in close quarters, but if she let herself consider the risks of infection every time she dealt with someone – whether it be this or scarlet fever or measles or chickenpox or diphtheria or any number of other diseases that folk were prone to – then she'd never be able to do her job. She decided that she simply had to maintain strict hygiene, keep healthy habits and have faith that the good lord would make better use of her ministering to the sick than being one of them. There was no point in worrying.

They arrived at the isolation hospital and Daisy delivered her patient into the cheerful and capable hands of the nurses there. The driver and his attendant had disinfected the back of the ambulance by the time she came out.

'Are you ready to get back, nurse?'

'I am. I've got the afternoon off, so the quicker you can get me home, the better,' she said with a smile.

But as she was about to climb into the ambulance, someone called out, 'Daisy Selway, as I live and breathe!'

She spun round, astonished to see a grinning Mattie strolling towards her. 'Good grief!' she exclaimed. 'What on earth are you doing here?'

He reached her, took her hands and kissed her cheek. She felt his warmth flow from her fingers through her entire body and hoped that she wasn't blushing as he surveyed her. 'I'm visiting a pal who works here. I'm going to have tea with him and his wife in Taunton. What about you?'

'Delivering a patient. We're heading back now. It's my afternoon off,' she said, wondering what on earth she was doing, blurting that out.

'So you don't have to go back to work?' he asked. 'Then you

must come and have tea with us. I'll see you back to Walton. I've a few days off and I'm going to visit Ma and Pa anyway.'

She hesitated, looking at the ambulance. The driver leaned out of the window. 'We need to get going, nurse. Are you coming or not?'

'Say you'll stay,' said Mattie, squeezing her hands. 'It's been ages since we saw each other. I want to know everything you've been up to.'

'I'm not exactly dressed for going out to tea,' she said, feeling uncommonly flustered.

'Nonsense,' he said, his tone firm. 'Just take your apron and cap off and you'll be grand. My pal's a doctor and his wife used to be a nurse, so they'll understand.' Without waiting for her response, he turned to the driver. 'I'll see her home. No need to wait.'

'Hang on!' She held up a hand to stop them driving away. 'You've got my handbag and cloak.' She'd stowed them in the cab as she'd been planning on getting them to drop her off at home rather than have to go back to the surgery.

'Oh, right you are, nurse,' he said, reaching for them and passing them through the window to her. 'You sure you'll be all right with this one?' He looked askance at Mattie.

She smiled at Mattie's mock outraged expression as she pulled her cloak around her. 'Yes. He's an old family friend. A doctor. I'll be fine, thank you.'

Mattie chuckled as the ambulance drove away. 'Good to know people are looking out for you, Daisy. Although I hear you're quite capable of taking care of yourself.'

She looked at him, frowning, not sure what he was getting at.

'Didn't you disarm a handsy Home Guard and give him a bloody nose?' he asked, his eyes full of humour. 'I could have warned him he was asking for trouble.' Daisy rolled her eyes but couldn't help but laugh. 'News travels fast. I thought it was only going to be difficult to live that down in Walton, but clearly my fame is spreading.'

They stood there, smiling at each other. 'It's good to see you, Daisy,' he said.

She nodded, unable to put into words how happy it made her to see him. She could have stayed there, standing in the cold outside the hospital looking at him for ever. He was as handsome as he always was – tall, broad-shouldered, his dark hair in need of a haircut to stop his natural curls from exploding, his intense brown gaze holding hers. A gust of autumn wind swirled around her legs, making her shiver and blink. It seemed to bring Mattie out of his own trance and he moved forward, enveloping her in a warm hug. With her hands caught inside her nurse's cloak, she couldn't return the embrace. Instead she closed her eyes and relaxed into his hold.

'It's been too long,' she murmured softly, not intending him to hear.

Before he could say anything, they heard footsteps and looked up to see a bearded man in a tweed suit approach them.

'I can't leave you alone for a minute,' he said, his voice deep and hearty. 'Put that nurse down!'

Mattie laughed, stepping back to shake the man's outstretched hand. 'Don't worry. This isn't just any nurse, my friend. This is my favourite nurse in the whole world.' He turned and winked at Daisy. 'Dr Robert MacKay, meet Nurse Daisy Selway. She's an old friend. We've known each other our whole lives. I've just persuaded her to come to tea with us.'

Daisy suddenly had doubts. 'I don't have to, though,' she said. 'He shouldn't have invited me without checking it was all right first.' In these days of rationing and shortages, it was the height of rudeness to bring an uninvited guest to a meal.

Robert laughed. 'Nonsense. You must come. It'll only be fish-paste sandwiches and some tinned pears with condensed milk. If you've known this reprobate all his life, you're bound to have all sorts of embarrassing gossip about him. I know my wife will welcome you with open arms in return for a few snippets.'

Mattie groaned and covered his face with his hands. 'What have I done?'

Daisy laughed at Mattie's discomfort. 'Well, I don't know what he's been up to since he went to university, but I can tell you about all sorts of things he got up to before that.'

'That's the spirit,' said Robert, offering her his arm. 'Come and meet Shirley. She's going to love you.'

* * *

Mrs MacKay did indeed welcome her with open arms and they had a delightful tea punctuated by lots of teasing and laughter. Daisy glowed under Mattie's smiles and his friends swapped her stories of their childhood for their own anecdotes about his university and medical training days. He took it all in good form, giving as good as he got and reducing Daisy to a giggling mass of hysteria at times over remembered mischief.

Their visit flew by and before she knew it, Robert and Mattie were rushing out to buy supper for them all from the local fish and chip shop. It was one of the few meals that wasn't affected by rationing these days, so it was always popular.

When Daisy mentioned that her parents would be wondering where she was, Shirley showed her into Robert's study and let her use their telephone. She was glad that her pa had had a telephone installed at the farm, so she could call them direct.

'Where are you, lass? Ma says you missed your dinner. Are you going to be back in time for supper?'

'Sorry, Pa, no,' she said. 'I met Mattie at the hospital and he invited me to tea with some friends here in Taunton, and now we're going to have a fish supper, so don't wait for me.'

'How is he?' he asked. 'We haven't seen the lad in ages.'

'He's grand. It's been lovely,' she said, hoping her voice wasn't sounding as wistful as she felt.

'Good. Now, how are you getting home, lass?'

'Mattie's bringing me. He's got a motorcar and he was planning on visiting Auntie Louisa and Uncle Lucas anyway, so it won't be out of his way.'

'Mmm. He's doing well for himself is young master Matthew,' said Pa.

'He's Doctor Matthew now, Pa,' she reminded him.

'Right, so he is. Tell him to drive careful. He's got a precious cargo to deliver.'

She felt the familiar glow of love as she ended the call. She loved that her pa was never shy about letting his wife and children know how much he cared about them. Back in the Great War they hadn't seen him for years until the conflict finally ended and he was repatriated from his prisoner of war camp. She was too young to remember the emaciated stranger who came home, but Ma had told her that she had refused to believe that he was the same uniformed man whose photograph had pride of place on their mantle. Apparently it had taken a few weeks before Daisy would call him Pa and let him cuddle her. It made her feel guilty, thinking that she must have hurt him, not accepting he was her long-lost pa come home from the war. She had been a newborn babe when he had been conscripted, only knowing her pa through his photograph. But he had been patient and loved her all the same and she loved him with all her heart.

The familiar anxiety over her pa's health grew within her. She didn't want to lose him and his continuing refusal to see a doctor or to slow down made her afraid for him. She resolved to see if Mattie could talk to him while he was home with his family.

'All set?' asked Shirley when she returned to the parlour.

'Yes. I'm to tell Mattie to drive safe because I'm a precious cargo.' She smiled.

'Quite right too.' Shirley regarded her curiously. 'It sounds strange, you calling him Mattie. He's always been Matthew to us.'

Daisy shrugged. 'It probably suits him now he's a professional man. But we've always called him Mattie. In fact, for years he was "Little Mattie" on account of him being named after his...' She hesitated. She didn't know how much of his history Mattie had revealed to his friends.

'Ah, a relative who was no doubt referred to as Big Mattie?' Shirley smiled.

She sighed, wishing she hadn't said anything. 'Sort of,' she said. 'But the first Mattie died before our Mattie was born.'

The slamming of the front door heralded the return of the men. The pleasing aroma of fried fish and chips wafted in with them.

'Sorry we took so long,' said Mattie. 'Someone was telling us about a chap with a lit torch, walking the carnival route round Bridgewater. The Air Raid Precautions wardens were yelling at him to put the light out, while other folks were cheering him on. Nearly caused a riot, apparently.'

'Whatever for?' asked Shirley, looking confused.

'The Guy Fawkes Carnival,' said Daisy, realising the date. 'There's been a torch-lit procession in November through Bridgewater every year since the gunpowder plot was foiled and Guy Fawkes was executed.'

'Local groups create some splendid illuminated floats and the parade goes through the town to celebrate,' said Mattie. 'Then the carnival comes to a few other towns in Somerset through

November – Glastonbury is the nearest one to us in Street. It sounds like this chap in Bridgewater was insisting that, even though the full torch-lit carnival has been banned on account of the blackout, it's still important for someone to carry a torch around the original route to keep the tradition going. You can't let hundreds of years of history disappear just because there's a war on, can you?'

Shirley frowned. 'It sounds a bit reckless for the sake of a tradition. What if a German plane had seen it and attacked?'

'That was the ARP's argument, but apparently the man wouldn't be dissuaded. But he got round without attracting Jerry, so all's well that ends well.'

'And the carnival lives to run another day.' Daisy smiled, remembering how much fun it was in the dark days of Novembers gone by. 'Maybe if the war's over next year you can come and see it for yourselves. Then you'll understand what a spectacle it is and how much work folk put into their floats every year.'

'God willing,' agreed Shirley. 'I want to see what all the fuss is now you've told us about it. But in the meantime, let's eat.'

'Don't bother with plates, darling,' said Robert, unwrapping the packages. 'It always tastes better straight out of the newspaper.'

* * *

It was well past midnight when they finally took their leave of the MacKays, who invited Daisy to come back any time she was in the area.

'All set?' said Mattie as he put the car into gear and drove away. 'Sorry it's so late. I should've warned you it might have ended up like that. Hope you weren't too bored.'

'What nonsense are you talking?' she asked. 'I wasn't bored at all. They're lovely.'

He chuckled. 'Well, Shirley is. Robert's all right, I suppose. Will your parents be waiting up for you?'

She shook her head. 'No. They've grown used to me having to come and go at all hours with work. What about your folks? Were they expecting you hours ago?'

'No. I told them not to wait up as I wasn't sure if I'd be persuaded to stay in Robert and Shirley's spare room and drive over in the morning. They won't fret. I've got a key.' They never used to lock the house, but in these days, when everyone was being warned to be vigilant of strangers who could be German spies or parachutists, homes were locked up tight at night.

He drove on in silence, concentrating on the road. Driving at night was always difficult in the blackout, although in town the kerbstones had been painted white so that they could pick them out with the faint light that came from the hooded headlights. The country lanes would be harder to navigate, so Daisy could understand why he might have been tempted to wait until daylight. But she had to work in the morning, so she needed to get home tonight.

They hadn't reached the edge of Taunton before they were flagged down by an ARP warden, flashing his torch to stop them at a junction.

Mattie wound down his window and they showed their identity cards when asked. 'Everything all right?' he asked. 'We're heading to Street.'

'That road should be clear, but we need you to wait for a bit, sir. There's a fleet of ambulances coming through. Nasty derailment at Norton Fitzwarren.'

He frowned. 'A whole fleet?' he asked as several vehicles rushed by. 'There must be a lot of casualties.'

The warden nodded, his expression grim. 'It was the Paddington express. They say six of the thirteen carriages have left the track. It's bloody carnage over there.'

Mattie looked at Daisy. 'What do you think?'

'I think they need all the help they can get,' she said, feeling sick at the thought of the sort of injuries that could be sustained in a train wreck. 'Have you got your bag in the car?'

'Always,' he said. 'Just as well you're in uniform, isn't it?'

'You can move along now,' said the ARP warden as the last of the vehicles, which Daisy noticed also included a couple of fire engines, passed by.

'Change of plan,' said Mattie. 'I'm a doctor and my companion is a nurse. We'll follow the convoy to see what we can do to help.'

The ARP looked unsure. 'I don't know...'

'No time for uncertainty, man,' said Mattie briskly. 'Lives are at stake.' He didn't even bother winding up the window as he turned the car in the direction of the others and left the man standing in the middle of the road.

17

The warden had been right. It was bloody carnage. Mattie parked the car out of the way of the ambulances and got his bag from the boot. Daisy put on her apron and cap and pulled her cloak around her so that she was recognisable as a nurse. In the distance, they could hear the hiss of the derailed steam engine and the cries of the wounded as men called out for stretchers and dressings.

'Look,' he said. 'You don't have to do this. You could wait in the car. Try and get some sleep.'

In the moonlight, he saw her roll her eyes and place her hands on her hips. 'Don't be ridiculous,' she said. 'There are people who need urgent help. I'm not going to ignore them and have a nap. What kind of a nurse would I be if I did that? Now, come on, let's see what needs doing.'

He nodded and handed her a torch. 'You'll need this. Stay close to me, all right?'

They made their way along the embankment past dazed passengers who had emerged from the rear carriages. Near the derailed portion of the train, men were giving first aid to the walking wounded while others were attending to the more seriously injured on the ground. Some souls were beyond help and their corpses were covered with coats and blankets.

Mattie spotted a man with a clipboard and pointed in his direction. 'He looks like he's in charge. Let's see where we can be most useful.' He took her hand, pulling her along with him.

'Excuse me, can we help? We were passing and saw the ambulances. I'm Dr Matthew Musgrove from Exeter Hospital and my companion is Nurse Daisy Selway.'

'I worked in the casualty department at Bristol Royal Infirmary,' she said. 'And now I'm a district nurse in Street.'

The man nodded. 'We need all the help we can get. There are some people trapped in the first couple of carriages. They just telescoped into each other.' He eyed Mattie, who was tall and lean, and petite Daisy. 'Do you think you two would be able to squeeze in? Most of my men are too big but we know there are folks alive in there. We need someone to assess the situation and let us know what needs to be done.'

'We can do that, can't we doctor?' she said, slipping off her cloak and cap and giving them to the man for safekeeping. She looked at Matthew. 'I'll go first. I might be able to squeeze into the smaller spaces. Can you try and get in behind me so that you can pass me any dressings or pain killers I need to administer? I'll probably need your medical opinion as well.'

Mattie nodded, not happy at the prospect of Daisy crawling into the wrecked carriages which lay in a mangled heap. It didn't look safe. Yet he knew he was willing to go in there if he could get his shoulders through the gaps, so he could hardly object to her doing the same thing. He turned to the official. 'Can you get someone to crowbar a wider opening so that I can go in with her?'

Within minutes someone had handed her a first aid pack, which she slipped over her shoulder. She was helped up a ladder set against the roof of the train, now on its side. A couple of men were already at work with crowbars, trying to create more space within the crumbled wreckage so that she could lower herself in through a broken window. Mattie went after her, unwilling to let her out of his sight.

'If it gets too much, you must say and I'll pull you out,' he told her, his voice low. They could see limbs and body parts crushed between metal and glass. It was clear that many souls in these carriages were beyond help. But they could also hear signs of life – a woman weeping, a man groaning.

'We've got to help them,' she said. 'I can't crawl and use my torch at the same time. Can you shine yours ahead of me?'

She stopped at each exposed body part, checking for a pulse. With a shake of her head, she would move on, taking no notice of the blood and bodily fluids that she had to crawl through to reach the next casualty. Eventually, she looked back at him. 'I can see someone moving,' she said, crawling quickly towards them.

Mattie shone the torch over her head and saw a woman flinch against the light. He lowered the torch a little as Daisy crawled towards her.

'Stop!' the woman screamed. 'My baby! Don't hurt him! I can't reach him.'

They both froze and Daisy gasped as she spotted the child, swathed in blue, lying in her path. The poor little mite must have been flung from his mother's arms on impact. 'It's all right,' she said. 'I see him. I'm Daisy. I'm a nurse and my friend is a doctor. I'm going to check the baby and pass him to the doctor so that he can look after him while I look after you. Help is coming, I promise. We'll get you out of here, all right?'

She carried on speaking gently to the woman, soothing and encouraging her, promising some pain relief as soon as she could reach her.

'Take care of him, please,' the woman sobbed. 'Is he alive?'

Daisy quickly checked and nodded. 'He is. I'm going to pass him back now.' She carefully picked up the child who was limp and silent. He was breathing, but she wasn't hopeful that he was unscathed. With a bit of wriggling in the small space, she managed to roll onto her back and pass the baby over to Mattie. She silently begged him to do what he could. He nodded and took the child and Daisy immediately turned and moved towards the mother.

Mattie loosened the baby's clothes and began examining him. He was well swaddled and as the cold air touched the child's skin he opened his eyes and whimpered. Mattie breathed a sigh of relief as he continued to check him over. There was no blood on him and he seemed by some miracle to be unharmed apart from a few bruises and scratches. This was confirmed when the child began to wail.

'There, you see?' he heard Daisy say to her patient. 'He's got a good pair of lungs on him, hasn't he?' He could hear the smile in her voice and he smiled down at the little lad, glad of the noise he was making.

Above them, a face appeared in the broken window. 'Here, doc, let me take him.' Hands reached down and the child was lifted out, still bellowing his outrage. Mattie heard a cheer go up outside.

Taking a deep breath, Mattie crawled towards Daisy. 'All right?' he asked.

Daisy nodded. 'This is Muriel, and her baby is Albie. Muriel's leg is trapped.' She shone the torch to show him that the woman was caught between the metal struts of the seats that had been squashed together by the impact.

He reached for his bag. He found a phial of morphine and

quickly prepared an injection. 'Here.' He handed the syringe to Daisy.

'I'm going to give you some pain relief now, Muriel. Then we'll get someone to come and help us get you out, all right? Don't you worry now. We'll soon have you back with little Albie.'

The patient was soon woozy but thankfully pain-free and Mattie moved out of the way so that a man could squeeze into the space with a crowbar to try and pry the metal apart. Before they pulled her out, Daisy quickly fitted a tourniquet to Muriel's thigh above where she could clearly see the bone was broken. She was satisfied when the blood oozed from the wound rather than gushed. There was always a danger when a casualty was released from a crush situation that they could bleed out very quickly from damaged blood vessels. The compression would help prevent that. Within minutes, she was free of the wreckage and handed over to an ambulance crew.

'I hope she makes it,' said Daisy quietly as she watched her being carefully lifted out of the train. 'Right.' She took a deep breath, trying to steady her racing heart. 'What's next?'

'We keep looking for survivors,' he said. 'Want me to go first?'

She shook her head. 'No, it's all right,' and she began crawling forward again.

They found an unconscious man, blood pouring from a head wound. Daisy cleaned and dressed it while Mattie continued his examination. His arm was also broken. Mattie did his best to reset the bone and splint it in the cramped space before the patient was moved, thankful that the man was not awake as he treated him. It would have hurt like hell.

Further along the carriage, Daisy found an elderly man, bleeding and beyond hope, and sat quietly holding his hand and talking to him as he breathed his last. Beside him, his wife was already gone. Daisy closed the man's eyes with shaking fingers and said a quiet prayer over the couple's bodies. She wiped away her tears before she turned back to Mattie, but he could see her distress. His warm hand on her cheek calmed her a little.

'You can stop any time,' he said softly.

She shook her head. 'No. There are people needing our help. Come on.'

They searched every inch they could access before accepting that there were no more survivors in this carriage. Strong arms pulled them out and they started again on the next carriage. When they'd been through all of the fallen wreckage, they went to help the walking wounded who were still waiting for assistance. There was no time to think. Everything was taking longer than usual because they were working in the dark, unable to set up flood lights to guide them because of the danger of being spotted by enemy aircraft. Above them in the night sky there was the almost constant drone of enemy planes passing over, no doubt on their way to bomb the cities and ports. If they spotted lights around the crash, there was a serious danger that they would drop their explosives right onto the crash site.

Eventually, someone directed them towards a Women's Royal Voluntary Service mobile canteen van that had been set up on the lane. Daisy sank onto the damp grass verge, exhausted. She wanted to weep, but was too exhausted to do so. Mattie, who had managed to stay by her side all night, joined her a moment later, handing her an enamel mug of tea and a fruit bun.

'Ah, you're an angel,' she said, accepting them gratefully.

He smiled through his weariness. 'That fish and chip supper seems a long time ago, doesn't it?'

She nodded, sipping the hot, sweet tea. 'Do you think we've done enough?' she asked. 'I feel like there should be something else we can do.'

He looked around. Ambulances that had rushed off time and

again with casualties had returned and were now collecting the dead. 'We've done all we can,' he said. 'There's nothing more we can do. You've been a real trooper tonight, Daisy, gone above and beyond.'

'I did no more than you did,' she said, giving him a weak smile. 'I'm glad you were here.'

'I'm glad you were here, too,' he said, kissing her cheek. 'We made a good team, didn't we?'

* * *

The sun was rising over the moors, filling the levels with mist, as Mattie drove her back to Walton. When they pulled up outside the Selway family home, her father stood in the open doorway.

'Good God,' he said, coming towards her. 'What's happened? Are you hurt?'

Daisy shook her head but didn't protest when he enveloped her in his arms. 'I'm all right, Pa. There was a train wreck outside Taunton. Me and Mattie helped.'

Her pa looked at Mattie as he came around the car to meet them on the path. Mattie knew he looked as bloody and dishevelled as Daisy did. 'I'm sorry if you were worried, Uncle,' he said. 'But they had so many casualties, we simply had to muck in and do what we could. Daisy was a heroine.'

She scoffed but didn't say anything, taking comfort from her pa's embrace.

Her pa looked down at her, stroking her hair. 'You look all done in, lass,' he said gently.

She nodded. 'There were six carriages wrecked in the derailment, Pa. The whole train was full of people. Nearly thirty killed. Twice as many injured.'

'It didn't help that we had to observe the blackout, so we had to do everything in the dark while Jerry flew overhead,' said Mattie, running a weary hand through his hair.

'Was it an attack?'

'No, thank God, or we might have been dealing with unexploded bombs as well,' said Mattie. 'It was a derailment. Someone said the train was on the wrong line. They were lucky they didn't crash into a heavy goods train. Just missed it, I heard.'

'I hope we didn't miss anyone,' said Daisy, her voice thick with tears. 'There was so much carnage.'

Her pa kissed her hair. 'Hush now, lass. You did what you could, I'll warrant.' He glanced at Mattie. 'You both did.'

Mattie felt a lump in his throat at Daisy's distress. Maybe he should've taken her home before going back to help. But then again, she'd worked as hard as every man there and her gentle voice and calm manner had soothed many a man, woman and child caught up in the disaster.

Mrs Selway appeared in the doorway. 'What's going on? Oh my lord, Mattie, are you hurt? Where's my Daisy?'

Daisy lifted her head to look over her pa's shoulder. 'I'm here, Ma.'

Quick explanations were given as she fussed over her daughter. 'Come on in, both of you. George, we must get the bath filled so they can clean up.'

Daisy shook her head. 'There's no time, Ma. I'll just have a wash and change my uniform. I'm due at the surgery in half an hour.'

Mrs Selway looked at her askance. 'If you think you're going to work after being up all night doing rescue work, then you've got another think coming. You'll have a bath, get some sweet tea and some food in you, then you'll be spending the day in bed, young lady.'

'And you're not to worry about work, lass. I'll ring the surgery and tell them what's gone on,' said her pa. 'You can't be expected to work today.'

'I agree,' said Mattie. 'They're right, Daisy. You need to rest. Let your ma and pa look after you. You haven't let up for hours. I'll be doing the same, but I'll have to decline your kind offer of a bath, Auntie. I need to get home to Ma and Pa or they'll be worrying. I'll clean up there.'

'If you're sure, Mattie, lad. Give them my love.' She kissed his cheek. He hoped he'd manage to wipe off the blood and sweat that had caked his skin most of the night.

Mr Selway shook his hand. 'Thanks for looking after her and bringing her home safe.'

Mattie laughed as Daisy stiffened in outrage. 'Actually, Uncle, she was looking after me just as much. She's a fine nurse.'

'That she is.' He smiled. 'And it looks like you're shaping up to be a fine doctor. We're proud of you both.'

Mattie smiled, touched. He leaned forward and placed a soft kiss on Daisy's cheek. 'Do as your ma says,' he murmured. 'I'll see you soon.' He said his goodbyes to her parents and climbed into the car.

As he drove away, he saw her ma usher Daisy into the farmhouse and her pa watched him until he drove out of the farmyard.

18

As the chill winds of November swept across Somerset over the next couple of weeks, the Luftwaffe continued to wreak havoc from the skies. Their targets were mainly industrial centres, ports and military installations, but that didn't stop them dropping their excess payloads over the countryside as they made their way back to their bases in mainland Europe.

Just a day after the terrible train crash, an enemy plane fired shots over Taunton, hitting someone's bedroom window and shattering ornaments inside before becoming embedded in the mattress. Thankfully no one was in the room at the time, although the householder got a terrible shock when they went to retire that night and discovered the state of their bed. The next day, planes targeting the airfield and factories at Yeovilton also dropped bombs on nearby Yeovil. An officer and two men working on defusing an unexploded bomb down the twenty-foot-deep shaft it had created were killed when it detonated.

Rose read the news and listened to the wireless whenever she got the chance. Birmingham was taking a battering night after night, as was Bristol and London. On 15 November, Coventry was all but laid waste by a terrible attack. The pictures in the newspapers of the cathedral burning broke Rose's heart, especially when her mammy wrote to say that an old school friend of Rose's had been caught up in the attack.

'I can't believe she's gone,' she told Daisy and Elsie. It had been a few weeks since the cider girls had seen each other, but they all had a day off together at last and decided to make the most of it. They'd met in Street and got the bus into Wells. Neither Rose nor Elsie had had the chance to explore the tiny city and its beautiful cathedral, so Daisy offered to be their guide. 'She was newly married,' Rose explained, 'with a baby on the way. She'd been living with her in-laws in central Coventry while her husband was away fighting. They all died.'

'Her poor husband. Fancy being so far from home and finding out your whole family has been wiped out,' said Elsie, shivering.

'I know,' said Rose. 'I've been so afraid of hearing my mammy and daddy had been hurt in the bombings that it never occurred to me that girls my age were in as much danger.'

'My ma says we think we're immortal. That's why so many lads rush off to war, never thinking they'll be hurt or worse.' She turned to Elsie. 'Have you heard from your sister?' she asked. 'London's taking a terrible battering as well, isn't it? Surely she'll see sense and take her baby out of there, won't she?'

Elsie shook her head. 'She's a law unto herself, is Gertie. I've begged her. I'm sure her husband has as well. But he's aboard ship, we don't know where. So he can hardly make her, can he?'

They arrived in Wells and their talk changed to the charm of the historic buildings. 'I still don't understand why a small place like this has such a huge cathedral and can call itself a city,' said Rose, looking around at the quaint shops in the market square.

'It's to do with Glastonbury Abbey, I think,' said Daisy. 'It was one of the richest in the country before the Reformation and had a lot of power. Henry the Eighth had the abbey reduced to ruins, but let the cathedral stand so long as it changed allegiance to the Church of England.'

'Do you think that's why there's so many road blocks and defences around the town?' asked Rose. 'You can see they're determined to keep the enemy out, aren't they?'

Elsie remained silent. She knew that there were indeed detailed plans in place to defend Wells. But she couldn't say as much. In addition to the barriers that they could see, she knew that there were sniper stations on rooftops around road junctions. Homes at pinch-points, where disabling an enemy tank could hold up their advance, were requisitioned and machine-gun and mortar launchers were installed inside them, out of sight. Holes had been created between the party walls of terraced houses to enable men to escape a counter-attack and rear gardens were booby-trapped so that the enemy couldn't attack them from behind. If the Germans did arrive in Wells, they would find their path strewn with deadly obstacles. It was all part of what the military were calling 'The Stop Line' that ran across the county, aimed at slowing down the enemy's advance towards Bristol or London. And these plans were to be executed by the regular Home Guard, who were tasked with holding off the enemy for long enough for the regular army to arrive with reinforcements. The Auxiliers would be even more deadly as they sabotaged and harassed the German invaders from all directions, blowing up bridges, roads and railway lines as well as enemy vehicles, planes and arms stores, cutting off their supply lines and their onward routes.

She shivered again, a frisson of fear running down her spine as she thought about the role she was being prepared to play.

'They're determined to keep the cathedral safe as well,' said Daisy, unaware of Elsie's dark thoughts. 'They've installed a huge great water tank on Cathedral Green, ready filled so that they have enough water to put out any fires caused by incendiary bombs. I hear there's a whole team of volunteers who spend their nights on the cathedral roof, watching for fires.'

'It must be freezing up there,' said Rose, pulling her coat around her more snugly. 'Fancy being stuck up there night after night, in the cold and dark.' She shook her head. 'It didn't do them much good in Coventry, did it? I saw another picture of the cathedral ruins in the paper. Someone had painted a sign and put it next to the burnt altar. "*Father, forgive them,*" it said.' Her eyes filled with tears. 'If they take any of my family, I'm not sure I'll ever be able to.' She shivered. 'I feel sorry for them fire watchers. It must be miserable for the poor beggars. I could do with some heat right now,' said Rose. 'Doing the milking out on the moor at this time of year leaves me cold to my bones.' She wrinkled her nose.

Daisy laughed and held out her free arm for Elsie to take. 'All right, I can take a hint. Let's find a tea shop and warm up with a cuppa, shall we?'

They were soon ensconced in the warmth of a café just off the market square sharing a pot of tea and enjoying a fruit bun each.

'So, Elsie,' said Daisy. 'Are you seeing much of my Uncle Ted these days?'

She frowned. 'Not really,' she said cautiously. She did in fact see quite a lot of Captain Jackson. He was in and out of the offices at Edgely Hall a lot, having meetings with her CO that she wasn't privy to. He had also insisted she join some of the Auxiliers on his unarmed combat course. She'd been really nervous, especially when she realised she was the only woman there. But at least Jimmy Morgan hadn't been there. The captain had pointed out that she needed to be able to defend herself and talked her through techniques that allowed her to best a man twice her size if she had to. After she'd managed to overcome the men using the moves he'd taught her, her confidence had grown. But she couldn't say any of this to her friends, even though she wanted to. She'd love to talk to Daisy about it, especially since she knew that she'd benefitted from similar training from her uncle. That thought gave her an excuse to change the subject.

'By the way, what happened to that Home Guard who attacked you?'

Daisy grimaced. 'He's learned to regret it,' she said. 'He got a severe reprimand and a fine and was then put on guard duty at the sewage works. But worse than that, word got round the villages that he was bested by a lass and everyone's laughing at him. Serves him right, I say. I've never been so angry in my life. It was awful, being manhandled like that.'

Rose giggled. 'Guarding the sewage works? Oh my. Whyever do they need a guard there? I'd've thought the smell would put off anyone going near.'

Daisy shrugged. 'I don't know, but they're guarding all sorts of places like that these days.'

Elsie took a sip of her tea. 'I think it's to make sure the enemy can't destroy our infrastructure – you know, water, sewage, electricity, gas. If any of those were cut off, life could become pretty uncomfortable rather quickly.'

'Mmm,' said Daisy. 'And if the waste isn't properly treated it could contaminate the water supply. The last thing we need is a cholera outbreak on top of everything else.'

'So guarding the sewage works, as smelly and unpleasant as it is, is really rather important,' observed Rose.

'It is,' said Elsie.

Daisy smiled. 'And it couldn't have happened to a better man for the job.'

Rose sighed. 'I wish they'd send Jimmy off to guard the

sewage works for a while. I'm sure the miserable beggar is up to no good.'

'What do you mean?' asked Elsie. 'I thought he was just grumpy because he fancies you.'

'So did I,' laughed Daisy. 'He can't keep his eyes off you as far as I can tell. That's a sure sign of a man with a crush.'

'Don't talk so daft,' Rose scoffed. 'He's always glaring at me, or looking at me with that rotten smirk on his face. He doesn't like me at all. And these days he's always sneaking off and staying out all night.'

'A lot of men do that. Their Home Guard duties can take up all their spare time,' Elsie pointed out.

'I know. But there's times when he's gone for a couple of days or even a week,' she said. 'He takes off on that motorbike of his without a by-your-leave for his mother and his only excuse is Home Guard special duties. Yet Mr Morgan and Ivor are Home Guard as well, but they always get back in good time for work. They never seem to know where Jimmy is, though. It's very strange.'

'I'm sure it's all above board,' said Elsie. 'But it's best not to ask.'

'Mmm.' Daisy nodded. 'Aunt Kate says Uncle Ted is all over the place. She hardly sees him at weekends, and last half term he was away for the whole week on what he said were Home Guard duties. It's definitely strange.'

Elsie took a long drink from her cup, not looking at either of them.

The bell over the door tinkled as someone came in. Rose, who was facing the entrance, looked up. 'They'll be lucky,' she said. 'This place is packed.' It was indeed, with every table occupied and no one showing signs of being ready to leave. 'Shame though, because there's three of them and they look rather tasty.' She winked at her friends.

Daisy turned to see what she meant and groaned.

'What? Do you know them?'

'Just one of them,' she said. 'The one in the middle is Mattie.'

Elsie twisted to get a better view, looking delighted. 'Your unrequited love?' she asked.

'Shhh! Not so loud,' Daisy hissed, not daring to look round. 'What if he heard you?'

'Oho,' said Rose. 'We'll soon find out. He's heading this way.'

'Daisy? It is you!' Mattie's voice reached them just before he and his friends did. Rose hid a smile as her friend took a deep breath and turned to face him.

'Mattie, what are you doing here?'

He grinned at her. 'You mean, the gossip hasn't filtered through the family yet?'

'What gossip? What have I missed?'

'I've got a new job. I'll be training to be a GP here in Wells.'

'Really? I thought you were set on hospital work.'

He shrugged as one of his companions spoke up. 'He was until he realised he couldn't make up his mind about a specialism. Aren't you going to introduce us to your friends, Musgrove?'

Mattie nodded towards Daisy. 'Nurse Daisy Selway, who I've known all my life, meet Drs Simon Carter and Richard Needham. They're both junior doctors at Exeter and have been helping me move.'

'Hello,' she said, shaking their hands. 'And this is Elsie Bloomfield and Rose Flaherty.'

'I don't suppose we can squeeze in with you at this table, ladies?' asked Simon with a charming smile. 'Considering we're practically related through Matthew and Daisy here.'

Rose responded in kind to his smile. He was pleasant-looking, with hazel eyes and well-cut brown hair. 'Of course,' she said, budging up on the window seat she was occupying. 'Any friend of Daisy's is a friend of ours, eh girls?'

'Aha!' he said, sliding in next to her while the others purloined chairs from other tables and crowded round the table with the girls between them. 'Is that a Brummie accent I hear?'

Rose narrowed her eyes. 'It might be. Depends on whether you're going to insult it or not. Be warned, I won't appreciate anyone denigrating how I talk.'

He held up his hands. 'Wouldn't dream of it, I swear. I did my training there.'

'Yet now you're in Exeter. You can't have thought much of it.'

He laughed. 'I loved it actually. But my family live near Exeter, so I wanted to be closer to home when the war started. I wouldn't mind going back one day. What brings you here?'

'I'm a land girl. I work on a farm a ways from here at Catcott.' She explained it was a few miles south on the road towards Bridgewater.

A waitress arrived and took their orders, including some more hot water for the girls' teapot. Rose relaxed, enjoying the chance to chat to someone who wasn't a surly farmer.

Richard was sitting between the two other girls. 'Are you a land girl or a nurse, Elsie?' he asked.

She shook her head. 'Neither. I'm with the ATS.'

'Should we salute you?' he asked with a teasing glint in his eye.

She laughed. 'Hardly. I'm just a clerk who does a bit of driving when needed.'

Rose thought she was doing herself down, because she knew that Elsie had been sent off on a lot of courses lately, so they must think she was capable of much more.

'Which surgery are you with, Mattie?' asked Daisy. 'I can't believe no one told me.'

Mattie mentioned the doctor he'd be working under and she nodded, recognising the name. 'I was coming up for an interview the day after the train crash,' he explained. 'I meant to tell you myself but never got round to it. I expect our folks thought you already knew.'

She nodded, looking down at her hands. 'Probably,' she said.

Rose leaned forward. Daisy had given her friends the bare bones of what had happened, but they could see it had been a difficult experience for her. 'It was quite a night for you both,' she said, her tone gentle as she searched Mattie's face.

'It was,' he agreed, his gaze on Daisy's bent head. 'Our Daisy was a real trouper, though. Crawling through the wreckage to minister to people trapped inside.'

'You were right behind me,' Daisy pointed out, looking up.

He was as handsome as Daisy had described and Rose decided he seemed nice. She could understand how her friend had carried a torch for him for so long.

He didn't notice Rose's regard because his attention was on Daisy. 'I contacted a pal at Taunton Hospital after,' he said. 'I'm told that Muriel and little Albie are doing well. By some miracle, neither of them had any serious injuries. Muriel's leg had a clean break that is expected to heal well.'

Daisy's face lit with relief as she smiled at him. 'Oh, thank goodness. I was worried about possible crush injuries, and the baby seemed unconscious when we found him. I've been fretting about them.' She blinked as her eyes filled with tears. 'Goodness! Look at me, getting emotional over people I hardly know.'

'It's understandable,' said Mattie, his tone gentle. 'It was an awful night. It's hard to banish the images of what we saw, isn't it?' She nodded, looking down at her clasped hands again. 'But you have no need to fret over the mother and babe now. They're fine. Ah, here comes our tea.'

Rose watched with concern as Daisy took a deep breath and pasted a smile on her face. She hoped that the news that Mattie had brought her would help her friend get over the trauma of that night. She'd been so brave, it would be so cruel if she continued to suffer over the memory of it.

They spent a jolly hour with the doctors until Simon and Richard declared it was time they left. It seemed they had all driven their own motorcars, laden with Mattie's worldly goods.

'Why didn't you call your Uncle George?' Daisy asked Mattie. His relative ran a haulage business. 'He'd have sent a lorry down to do it all in one trip and save you all your petrol rations.'

Mattie shrugged. 'I was going to, but these two have just got their vehicles and were intent on wasting their rations, so I let them.' He laughed.

'You came in three cars?' asked Rose. 'Goodness.'

'It's not as bad as it sounds,' said Richard. 'I'm going on to spend a few days on a course in Oxfordshire, and Simon's heading back to Exeter for his shift tomorrow, so we couldn't come in the same car.'

'Elsie's been to a few courses in Oxfordshire lately, haven't you?' said Rosie.

'Oh really?' he said. 'Whereabouts?'

She nodded. 'Not a hospital,' she said. 'Just an admin course or two at a place called Coleshill.'

He regarded her thoughtfully. 'Really? That's where I'm going. Small world.'

Elsie stared at him, a strange expression on her face for a moment before she wiped it clear. 'I suppose so. There's all sorts going on around there. I hope your course is interesting.'

He smiled and inclined his head to the side. 'Thanks. Maybe I'll see you there sometime.'

She shrugged and looked away. 'I doubt it. I think I'll be too busy where I am to go on any more courses. And none of mine are medically related.'

Daisy checked her watch. 'Well, it's been lovely, gents. But we need to get going if we're to catch our bus back.' She went to pick up the girls' bill, but Mattie snatched it up before she could.

'My treat, ladies, as a thank you for putting up with us,' he said. 'And you don't need to get the bus. I can drive you back as far as Glastonbury and Street. I'm going to spend the evening with my folks, so it's not out of my way.'

Rose smiled. 'That's so kind. I can get the bus from Street the rest of the way.'

Simon turned to her. 'Hang on. As I'm going beyond there to get back to Exeter, I'd be happy to deliver you all the way back to Catcott if you like?'

'Really?' she asked, delighted. 'That would be lovely, thank you.'

* * *

He'd been a charming companion on the drive, asking about her and her family.

'Six brothers? Good grief!' he'd exclaimed, making her laugh.

It wasn't until Simon pulled up in the farmyard that Rose began to have misgivings. He didn't need to worry about any of the Flaherty brothers as he got out of the car and came round to open the passenger door and help her out. It was Jimmy Morgan, standing at the open front door in his Home Guard uniform, glaring at them that persuaded Simon to say a pleasant goodbye, shake her hand and make a swift exit.

She stood and watched him leave, wishing he'd stayed and chatted a bit, but she didn't blame him for not wanting to put up with Jimmy's glowering.

'Who was that?' he asked.

'A friend,' she said. He wasn't really, just an acquaintance. More a friend of a friend's friend. Someone she wasn't likely to see again. But Jimmy didn't know that. 'He's a doctor.'

'Huh,' he muttered. 'A bit posh for the likes of you, ain't he?'

Rose sighed and turned to face him. 'Do you realise how rude you are, or do you just open that great big gob of yours and stuff your foot in it for fun?'

'I'm just saying—' But Rose held up a hand to stop him.

'Well, don't. If you haven't got anything nice to say, then just do me a favour and shut up, Jimmy. Just because I'm a working-class girl from Birmingham doesn't mean I'm not worthy of some respect. Simon didn't look down on me like you do. He was very nice. Something you've failed to be the whole time I've been here.'

He took a step towards her so that they were standing toe to toe. He was a good head taller than her, so she was forced to look up into his glowering face.

'I don't look down on you,' he said.

'Yes, you do. You hate me.'

'No, I don't.'

She scoffed. 'Well, you've got a funny way of showing it, because you're always scowling at me. Can't you ever be nice to me?'

'Like you are to me, you mean?'

She blinked. 'I'd be nice enough to you. But I give back what I receive. When all you do is glare and complain, why should I do anything different? Are you going to change your ways? Because if you do, I might, too. Do you actually know how to be nice?'

She didn't like the fact that she was sometimes as nasty to him as he was to her. She wasn't horrible to people as a rule, but he pushed her buttons every time. She wouldn't let her brothers do her down, so why should she let Jimmy?

'I know well enough,' he said, his voice almost a growl. 'How about this?'

Before she had time to step away, his hands were on her shoulders, drawing her towards him, and his lips were on hers. If she expected his kiss to be rough, she was wrong, and the shock of his gentle caress held her still for a few moments before she couldn't help herself and she began to kiss him back, her arms creeping round his waist as she moved closer to him.

A door slamming inside the farmhouse brought them both back to their senses and they sprang apart. Rose's hand went to her mouth, her eyes wide as she stared at him. His eyes glittered in the moonlight as he searched her face.

'I'll not apologise for that,' he said, his voice soft and low.

She didn't know what to say. She only knew that she didn't want it to be a mistake.

Inside, the clock in the hallway chimed the hour and Jimmy looked away. 'I've got to go,' he said, striding off across the farm-yard to the barn. A moment later, she heard the rumble of his motorbike engine and he rode off without a backward glance.

Rose stood by the farmhouse door, her hand still touching her lips. Her tongue crept out to moisten them and she tasted the essence that she recognised as Jimmy Morgan.

'Oh my,' she muttered softly before she sighed and turned to go into the house.

* * *

Elsie sat in the back of Mattie's car so that Daisy could sit in the passenger seat. She could see why her friend liked the young doctor so much; he was very pleasant, and nice looking as well. She admired the way Daisy treated him with affection without turning into a silly girl around him like so many do when faced with the object of their crush. She supposed that poor Daisy had had a lot of years of practice, otherwise all her family and friends in Street would have known how she felt about Mattie, and that would have been humiliating.

She sighed, relaxing back into the leather upholstery as Mattie confidently negotiated the roads out of Wells towards Glastonbury and Street. She hoped that now that he was going to be living closer to home he might recognise what a super girl Daisy was.

She wondered how Rose was getting on with Simon. He seemed quite taken with their red-haired friend. Maybe a little flirtation with the doctor would take her mind off what Jimmy Morgan was up to. It had been awkward for Elsie when Rose started complaining about him and speculating why he wasn't carrying out regular Home Guard duties. She ought to mention it to the CO – maybe he would be able to have a word with Jimmy and tell him to be more careful in future. Elsie didn't want Rose getting into trouble, which she well might if she mentioned her suspicions to anyone else.

That train of thought led her to think about her suspicions of Mattie's other friend, Richard. If he was going on a course at Coleshill, he must surely be an Auxilier or a Stay Behind, but there was no way of knowing for sure. She couldn't expose her own secret role, any more than he could tell anyone what he was up to. No, it was better that it wasn't discussed. The less each of them knew, the better.

But it was good to know that there were other Auxiliers and Stay Behinds out there, ready to take up the fight.

* * *

After they'd dropped Elsie off, Daisy turned in her seat and watched Mattie as he drove the final couple of miles back to Street.

'I can't believe you've come home.'

He glanced at her briefly, before turning his attention back to the road. 'I'll not be moving back with Ma and Pa,' he said. 'I'm renting a house near the surgery but if I like the job, I'll probably buy one.'

It made sense. A professional man could afford a mortgage. His pa, Lucas, was a foreman in the Clicking Room at Clarks these days and he'd been encouraged by management to buy a home when he had moved up the pecking order at the factory. 'We've come a long way from the days when our families were all renting workers' cottages from Clarks, haven't we?'

'We have indeed,' he agreed. 'You know Clarks gave me a grant when I went to university, don't you?'

'I heard,' she said. 'But I'm sure you'd've succeeded whether you got it or not.'

'I like to think so.' He smiled.

'But I wouldn't be in a rush to buy right now,' she said. 'I mean, what if we're invaded? Or, God forbid, we lose the war? It doesn't seem a good time to invest in property, does it? What if you bought a house and it got bombed?'

He shrugged. 'I don't know. Maybe you're right. Who knows what the future holds, eh?'

She could've kicked herself. What on earth was she doing, talking like that? If he bought a house near here, it would mean he intended to stay. By persuading him to keep on renting, she was giving him free rein to up and move away again.

'Well whatever happens,' he said, 'there's plenty of work for the likes of you and me, eh, Daisy? Folk always need doctors and nurses.'

'I know. I suppose we're lucky here. At least we're not dealing with air raid casualties like they are in London and Bristol.'

'Mmm.' He glanced at her. 'How were you after the train wreck?'

She shrugged, not looking at him. 'It was difficult at first. I had a few nightmares about missing people who might have been saved. But it's getting easier.' She looked at him and then away again. 'Getting the good news about Muriel and Albie helps.'

'I had nightmares as well,' he said softly. 'I didn't expect it, given my training, but I suppose nothing prepares you for something like that, does it?'

She shook her head. 'No. But I talked to my friends about it and they helped me to see that we did everything we could, and that's all we can do, isn't it?'

'Exactly.' He glanced up through the windscreen. 'Looks like Jerry's early tonight. The searchlights are at work already.'

She could see the beams of light reaching up into the dark sky. It was barely five o'clock, but the nights were drawing in earlier each evening as the winter solstice approached. She shivered, more from nervous anticipation than cold. 'Ma says this war's different from the last one. Back then, the folks round here were kept safe, well away from the fighting. But this time we have planes flying over every night, bombs dropping on homes and churches. Even without a full invasion yet, we're still living in fear that any day could be our last.'

'I know,' he said, looking grim. 'But that shouldn't stop us living our best life. We can't let Jerry win by just giving up and giving in to the fear. And folk will look to people like you and me to set the example. To keep calm and carry on.' He brought the car to a halt outside the farmhouse. 'Here we are, safe and sound.' He turned to her and for a moment, she dared to hope that he didn't want to drive off and leave her just yet.

'D'you want to come in? Ma and Pa will be glad to see you. We were all in a bit of a state last time, weren't we? It took me a few hours to calm down after. It's just as well everyone insisted I took the day off.'

He sighed. 'That was a rotten night, wasn't it? It's a miracle it wasn't much worse.'

'I think it gave Ma a fright, seeing me covered in blood and dirt like that. But she's learning not to fuss too much, thank goodness. I had to keep reminding her that I'm not a child any more.' She rolled her eyes. 'She was married and had two children by the age I am now.'

'You're almost in your dotage,' he teased, making her laugh. 'No sweetheart calling round?'

She gave him a side eye. 'When have I got time for a sweetheart?'

He shrugged. 'If the right lad came along, I'm sure you'd find the time. Do you regret moving home after the freedom of living in hospital accommodation?'

'Not really,' she said. 'It's fine most of the time and home's a lot more comfortable than a draughty nurses' hostel.' She tilted her head to one side. 'Aren't you tempted to move home and enjoy your ma's cooking? It's only a few miles from Wells and you'll have extra petrol coupons for your work, won't you?'

He laughed. 'I don't think so. Besides, when I went to university Ma took over my old bedroom as her art studio. I have to sleep on a camp bed when I stay. But Ma's doing well for herself, producing her postcards of local views again. Lots of people buy them from her to send to their menfolk while they're away.'

She nodded. Mattie's ma was a talented painter who'd begun selling her paintings to earn some pin money when her children were little. Some of her pictures had been used in greetings cards. She had also illustrated several children's books. Daisy's own pa had been sent some of Louisa Musgrove's original watercolour scenes from around Street when he was a prisoner of war during the last conflict. He still had them, properly framed now. 'Pa always says it was Aunt Louisa's pictures that kept him going, reminding him to hold on against the odds so that he could get home to Somerset and his family one day.'

The low wail of the air raid siren cut through the air, rising in tone as it got louder.

'I'd better go,' said Mattie. 'Will you be all right?'

She nodded, feeling that familiar ache of dread in her gut at the sound of the mournful siren. 'I'll join the family in the shelter.' She knew that some of their neighbours didn't bother, believing that an attack on farmland was unlikely. But Pa insisted the family used the shelter when the sirens went. He'd kitted it out with lamps and blankets, books and boardgames as soon as war was declared. 'Do you want to take cover with us?'

He shook his head. 'I'll get to Ma and Pa's. If I don't turn up when they're expecting me, they'll fret.'

'All right. Thanks for the lift.' She hesitated, wishing she had the nerve to tell him how she felt.

'You're welcome, Daisy. Anytime.' He smiled. 'It'll be good to see you more often now I'm back in the county.'

She looked into his dark eyes and her heart swelled. 'That would be lovely,' she said. 'Maybe we could go to one of the Crispin dances together?'

She held her breath, wondering if she'd pushed her luck too

far. It had sounded as though she was asking him on a date. Would he even notice? And if he did, how would he react?

He nodded. 'Maybe. As the junior doctor at the surgery, I seem to be on-call every weekend at the moment, but as soon as I get a Saturday off, I'll try and get down for it. I know Ruby and Henry enjoy them. We could have quite a good party there, couldn't we?'

She stifled a sigh. He didn't want to go just with her. She had her answer. 'That'll be nice,' she said, looking away.

He leaned over and kissed her cheek. 'Say hello to everyone for me.'

She got out of the car, and waved as he drove away, resisting the urge to touch her cheek. She wished she was brave enough to have turned her head so that their lips had met instead, but she couldn't bear the thought that he might have been embarrassed if she'd tried to turn his friendly peck into something more. And he *would* have been embarrassed, because he had never seen her as anything other than part of his extended family, even though she had no blood tie to him. His reaction to her suggestion of a night out for just the two of them showed her that.

The siren continued to wail as she sighed and made her way to the shelter and her family.

19

Jimmy cursed himself all the way to the rendezvous. He shouldn't have kissed Rose, no matter how sorely she'd provoked him. What was she playing at, coming home in some uppity doctor's car? Didn't she know that posh fellows like that would only be after her for one thing?

He'd been shocked by the strength of his feelings when he'd seen her with another man. Never in his life had he ever thought of himself as a jealous man. But tonight he'd nearly lost his mind, seeing Rose smile and take that chap's hand when she'd got out of his car. It was just as well that when he'd seen Jimmy watching, the doctor had the sense to say goodbye to her and make a quick exit. Jimmy's hand had been itching to reach for the pistol he always kept concealed under his shirt these days.

As he neared his destination, he did his best to calm himself. He stowed his motorcycle out of sight and waited. A few minutes later a soft whistle heralded the arrival of another Auxilier on foot and not long after that four others arrived on bicycles. They all moved off the lane and Jimmy showed them where to hide their bikes by his vehicle.

Above them, they could hear the drone of planes in the clouds, but they were high enough that they weren't an immediate threat.

Jimmy peered through the gloom at the men as they huddled together in the shelter of a hedgerow. There was Sergeant Hayes, their unit leader. He'd fought in the trenches in the Great War and lived to tell the tale. These days he was a grocer, but he was also a keen marksman and outdoorsman. Beside him was Arnold Armitage, another farmer, on whose land their arms cache was located, and his son, Stephen, who at fifteen was too young to enlist but still a useful lad to have around with an old head on his young shoulders. Another young lad was Terry Stafford, alongside his pa Bill. They both worked in the local quarry, so knew plenty about explosives. They were also believed to be poachers, but no one had ever caught them at it. Jimmy was inclined to keep a close eye on them, not quite trusting them.

'Right, lads,' said the sergeant, keeping his voice low. 'Our orders are to infiltrate the airfield, mark as many vehicles and planes as we can to confirm we could have destroyed them if they'd belonged to the enemy. Everyone has their target areas. We are to get in, mark 'em and get out without being detected.' He paused, handing each of them a stick of chalk. 'If you've got any questions, ask 'em now, because I don't want to hear a squeak out of any of you once we leave this position.'

'Do we know how many guards there are?' asked Jimmy.

He nodded. 'Half the men based here are on standby, the rest have caught the bus into town for a night out, so they're not at full strength. There will be a couple of regular patrols around the base, so watch out for them and time your movements accordingly. Don't take any stupid risks. These fellows don't know we're coming, so if they find us, they'll assume we're the enemy and act accordingly. I don't want to have to tell any of your kinfolk that you got shot, so make sure you do what you need to do and get back here without any drama.'

They blacked up their faces, pulled on dark woollen caps and moved out, splitting apart and moving silently towards the perimeter of the airfield from different directions. Jimmy pulled a wire cutter from his knapsack and made quick work of a portion of the fence low to the ground so that he could roll under it and push it back into place so that it wouldn't be obvious someone had entered there. Once he was on the other side he pulled a hank of sheep's wool from his pocket and hung it on the fence at the right height so that anyone looking at it would think an animal had been rubbing itself against the fence. It would be his marker to lead him back to the section of loose fence and save him the trouble of having to create another gap through which to escape. Too many breaches in the perimeter fence would soon be spotted.

He stayed low, getting his bearings. They'd been shown a plan of the airfield and he knew where he was supposed to go, but it was completely dark, with clouds covering the moon and blackout blinds obscuring the light from inside the hangars and other buildings.

A door opened and a guard stepped out of one of the buildings, his silhouette bright against the light behind him. From inside, Jimmy could hear the clatter of cutlery, so it was safe to assume that that was the mess building. Once he had that position fixed in his head, he knew which direction he needed to go in. He watched, not moving as the guard moved away, before finally standing and heading to his target area while keeping an eye out in case the man came back or someone else left the mess. The other Auxiliers disappeared into the darkness.

Within moments, he was standing with his back to one of the hangars. He listened carefully at the side door but there was no sign of any activity inside. As silently as he could, he opened the door, grimacing as it creaked on rusty hinges. It sounded loud in the silence. Once it was open just wide enough for him to slip inside, he paused and listened again before entering. He didn't close it behind him, for fear of that damned noise, reasoning that it would be better to leave it and hope none of the guards patrolling the airfield would notice it.

Almost afraid to breathe, he moved silently into the hangar, feeling his way. Away from the door, he took out his torch and chalk and swiftly worked through the hangar, marking a white cross on the underbellies of each of the planes inside. He was soon back at the door. He had to stifle the urge to rush out, instead waiting and listening to make sure the way was clear.

He was just about to leave the sanctuary of the dark building when he heard footsteps and he shrank back out of sight behind some crates. While there, he chalked them as voices grew louder and then receded as men passed by. They were so busy discussing the merits of their favourite cowboy films that they failed to notice the open door. Jimmy stifled a nervous chuckle as they moved on, oblivious.

He slipped out of the doorway and left it open rather than draw attention with the rusty hinges. He moved swiftly along the edge of the hangar. The sight of a torch beam cutting through the gloom at the corner of the building sent him down onto the ground, where he rolled into the darker space against the wall. He held his breath, hoping the guard couldn't hear his heart beating, which he swore was drumming clean out of his chest. A voice called out in the dark.

'Oi, did you nick my lighter?'

The torch bearer stopped and turned round. 'Nah, I gave it back to you. Did you ask Lofty? He was lighting up a couple of minutes ago.'

'The bugger's probably nicked me smokes as well,' the first voice grumbled. 'Just wait 'til I catch up with him.'

Jimmy tried not to laugh along with the guard as the other man ran back in the direction he'd come, but he had to breathe, or he'd pass out and be sure to be discovered. He quietly exhaled and then slowly drew in fresh air, not daring to move as the remaining man chuckled and pulled a pack of cigarettes from his pocket and struck a match. Jimmy winced and closed his eyes tight, praying he wouldn't notice him sprawled out against the hangar wall. It occurred to him that closing his eyes was a stupid move as he wouldn't know if he'd been seen or not, so he quickly opened them again. To his relief, the guard was now walking away, completely oblivious to Jimmy's presence.

He waited a few minutes before moving on, aware that, funny as it seemed right now, if those guards had been German there would have been nothing amusing about the situation. He crouched and ran across a section of the grass runway back towards the fence. Out of the corner of his eye he saw movement, so he changed direction, then dropped to the ground again amongst the longer grass, praying he hadn't been spotted. He risked a quick glance, breathing a sigh of relief to see that it was young Armitage and not a guard. The lad moved fast and was soon out of sight. Jimmy checked around again and started off as soon as he saw the coast was clear.

A dark shape loomed out of the gloom and Jimmy realised he'd gone too far left as he reached what appeared to be the side of another building. Rather than retrace his steps, he rested by the structure he'd almost run in to. It wasn't until he ran his hands over it that he realised it wasn't a building, but he'd stumbled across a large stack of fuel barrels. With a grin, he quickly chalked as many as he could reach before making a dash for the fence. Once he reached it, he crouched and moved swiftly along it, his hand brushing the wires until he felt the wad of wool he'd wedged into it.

He'd just dropped and rolled under the fence when he heard a shout on the other side of the airfield. It sounded like someone had been spotted. He got to his feet, cursing as his jacket caught on a piece of jagged wire, ripping his sleeve, and ran.

* * *

He was back at the rendezvous within minutes. The sergeant was there, as were the two Armitage men.

'Right, lads,' he told them. 'Get yourselves back to the OB. We'll debrief there.'

'Did the others get caught, Sarge?' Jimmy asked as the Armitages rode off on their bicycles.

'Not sure yet,' he said, grim-faced. 'No shots fired, so we'll have to wait and see. Now, get going. Make sure you don't start that motorcycle of yours until you're well away from the rendezvous.'

He nodded and headed off, waiting until he was far enough away before he kick-started his motorbike. He soon overtook the two on bicycles. On arrival at the woods, he stowed his vehicle in the undergrowth and made his way to the OB. He pulled on the rope for the trap door, which swung open silently and he climbed down the iron ladder. He was contemplating putting the kettle on when he realised that someone was already there.

He froze. The others were behind him and likely wouldn't get there for another ten minutes or so. Apart from the local CO and his clerk, no one else should know about the location of this OB, let alone how to get into it. He pulled his pistol out of his belt as his heart rate increased. Was this another test? Or had some poacher mate of the Staffords found it and decided to make use of it? God forbid it was a German spy. Should he shoot first and ask questions later?

As all these thoughts flashed through his mind, he crept forward until he stood just outside the metal door into the main chamber and listened. He could hear the hiss of an oil lamp and... he tipped his head to one side, not sure if his mind was playing tricks on him. Was that someone whistling under his breath?

'Bugger this,' he muttered, pushing open the door with his shoulder, his gun at the ready. 'Hands up!' he yelled as he rushed in.

Captain Jackson carefully put down his mug of tea and raised his hands.

Jimmy swore, and raised his weapon so that it was pointing at the arched ceiling of the bunker. 'I thought you was an enemy spy,' he said.

The captain smiled. 'How do you know I'm not?' he asked.

He narrowed his eyes at the older man and levelled his pistol at him again. 'I don't, do I? How did you even know where this place was?'

He nodded. 'Good point. Always keep your guard up. You never know who might betray you. But in this case, I'm not the enemy.' He tilted his head towards the radio. 'If you contact unit HQ they'll vouch for me.'

Jimmy shook his head. 'I'll not be using that when you could jump me the moment I turn my back.'

'Quite right, too,' he said, his tone mild. 'If I was an enemy, I'd definitely be looking for the opportunity to overpower you.' The captain regarded him calmly, although Jimmy didn't believe for a moment that he wasn't alert. No man could really be that calm with a loaded pistol aimed at him.

'How did you know where this place was?' he asked again. He

couldn't help wondering if it was that ATS lass who'd told him. The CO might think she was on the level, but Jimmy wasn't happy about her knowing so much about the unit.

Captain Jackson shrugged. 'I've been observing this OB and a number of others over recent weeks.'

Jimmy shook his head. 'We'd've seen you,' he said.

He smiled again. 'And yet, here I am. I've far more experience than any of you when it comes to remaining undetected. It kept me alive during the Great War. That's something I'll be teaching all of you so that, God willing, you'll survive this one.'

Jimmy was still wary, not sure whether the man's confidence was an act, when the radio burst into life.

'Sparrow calling Robin,' came a woman's voice – he recognised the clear tones of Elsie Bloomfield. 'Come in Robin. Over.'

'Aren't you going to answer her?' asked the Captain. 'Or would you like me to?'

Jimmy shook his head, keeping his gun levelled at the captain. 'Step back,' he said. 'On the bunk over there.'

He did as he was told, giving Jimmy some space. With his free hand he reached for the microphone and switched it on. 'Robin calling Sparrow,' he said. 'We've got an intruder. Requesting orders. Over.'

'Understood Robin. Be advised that Bulldog is due to visit you. Is that your intruder? Over.'

It was. Jimmy hadn't taken his eyes off the captain, so he saw his lips quirk at the name.

'My French comrades called me *Bouledogue*,' he said, sounding like a real Frenchman. Jimmy knew he taught French at the grammar school in Wells. 'They seemed to think I had the stubborn nature and tenacity of the beast. It seemed appropriate to continue using it as my codename.' He nodded towards the radio again. 'She'll be expecting a response, lad.'

He blinked and nodded, realising that he was holding a gun on an officer. He raised the microphone and confirmed. 'Bulldog is here,' he said. 'Any idea how he knew where we were?' There was silence for a moment before he realised what she was waiting for. 'Over,' he said.

'I can't tell you that, Robin, but be assured he has Apollo's full confidence. He should not be regarded as an intruder. Over.'

Apollo was Captain Crick's call sign. Jimmy sighed and lowered his pistol. 'Understood Sparrow. Over.'

He turned his back on the captain as she requested a report on the evening's mission. He responded, using the codes that had been agreed, so that she was aware that the men were still making their way back to the OB. She signed off, requesting a full report once they arrived.

'Well done, lad,' said the captain as Jimmy turned to face him. 'You handled that well.'

He still wasn't happy about the situation. 'I don't like that you know about this place. The less people know the better.'

'You're right. And I can assure you that no one will find out the location from me. Nor am I going to tell you how I found you.' He picked up his mug and took a drink, grimacing. 'Ugh! This has gone cold.' He checked his watch. 'The others should be back at any moment. Let's get the kettle on and make a fresh pot, shall we?' He rubbed his hands together. 'It's getting mighty cold out there, we'll probably have a frost.'

Jimmy filled the kettle from the keg of water and lit the camping stove. By the time it boiled, the others had arrived. The sergeant wasn't surprised to see Jackson sitting there enjoying a brew, which made him feel even worse. Wasn't it just his luck that he'd challenged an officer? He took his tea when it was poured and sat on one of the bunks and listened as the others gave their reports.

'Thought we'd copped it,' said Bill Stafford. 'Someone started shouting. But it turned out that some squaddie had nicked his pal's lighter and smokes and he wasn't best pleased,' he chuckled. 'Bloomin' idiots were having a right set-to while they should've been on guard duty. They had no idea we was but feet away from 'em.'

'It were hilarious,' said his lad. 'I had to bite my fist to stop from laughing out loud. 'Course, we had to wait while they argued. I didn't think they'd ever bugger off.' He took a loud slurp of his tea. 'Ah, that hits the spot. It was flippin' cold, lying there, waiting for a chance to run for it.'

'Well done for waiting it out,' said Jackson. 'It's important to exercise patience. If you'd run, you'd have been spotted. If those guards had been doing their jobs properly, you'd have been rounded up and interrogated – if you weren't shot first.'

'What about you, Morgan?' asked the sergeant.

'I managed to mark all the planes in the hangar, sir. Plus some crates in there. Oh, and on the way back I found some barrels of fuel and marked all of them, n'all.' He was pretty pleased with this.

'Did you check the contents of the crates?' asked Jackson.

Jimmy frowned. 'No, sir. I was just told to get in there, chalk everything and get out. That's what I did.'

The captain nodded, looking thoughtful. 'Fair enough. But I'd strongly recommend always checking the contents of crates. When you're working underground, you need to obtain new supplies any way you can. Those crates could have contained weapons, ammunitions or rations. All of which would be useful to us. In future, even on training missions, if you get the chance to requisition things like that, do so.'

'But we're on the same side,' said Mr Armitage. 'We can't be nicking supplies from our lads.'

'Listen to the captain,' said Sarge.

'Thank you,' said Jackson, inclining his head. 'Actually, while we are indeed on the same side in this instance, it's still important for you to learn how to supplement your supplies in any way you can. While we have our orders from the very top, the secret nature of the auxiliary units means that we will only receive the bare minimum of supplies through official channels in the same way that most Home Guard units do. For example, most of your hand guns were donated by America; they're New York Police Department issue weapons, not standard British forces issue. Anyway, after the invasion, you'll be on your own, with no chance of new supplies through official channels. We are therefore subject to an additional order, which is to obtain anything else we might need from *all* sources – and I quote – *by fair means or foul*. That includes from our own side if the opportunity arises. That order comes from the very top.'

They were silent for a moment, thinking on that. 'So,' said Jimmy. 'You're saying that if Stafford and son managed to *requisition* some fuse wire and extra sticks of gelignite from the quarry, the top brass would approve?'

Jackson smiled. 'Exactly. And if you're on another mission like tonight's and discover that your RAF comrades are leaving crates of weapons or whatever around, feel free to requisition some of them also.'

'Just make sure you're not caught,' said Sergeant Hayes, his voice gruff even as his eyes brimmed with mirth. 'Because as the captain here will agree, as far as most folks are concerned, we don't exist, so bailing you out of gaol won't be easy.'

20

By December, the Blitz had torn the heart out of cities around the country and the war seemed to be coming ever closer to Somerset with enemy planes flying overhead most days and nights.

Bristol had been raided at the end of the previous month, leaving the city centre devastated and two hundred civilians dead. Only the bare facts had been reported – rumour had it that the government was now embargoing the reporting of civilian casualties so as not to cause panic. But Daisy's friends at the Bristol Royal Infirmary told her about the terrible injuries they had treated amongst the hundreds of casualties. Patients had been moved out to hospitals in neighbouring towns and cities like Bath, because there were simply too many of them to cope with.

'I do wonder whether I should go back to work on the wards,' she sighed as she told Elsie and Rose about the latest letter she'd received from a pal who was bemoaning the shortage of both medically trained staff and supplies to treat the wounded.

'But you're needed here as well,' said Rose. 'And I don't suppose your folks will want you going back to Bristol while it's being bombed.'

'I know,' she grimaced. 'We've already had that conversation at home and Pa made it very plain I was to stay put unless I got specific orders to go. It's bad enough that Peggy Jackson is doing her nurse's training in Bristol. Aunt Kate is beside herself, wanting to either bring her home or transfer her to somewhere else. Uncle Ted says she's to stop fussing because at the rate the Germans are going, they'll be bombing all the cities, so no matter where she is there's a risk. Of course, with all those casualties, she'll be needed sooner rather than later.'

Elsie looked shocked. 'But if she's only in her first year of training, they won't be expecting her to do much more than sponge baths and wiping fevered brows, surely?'

Daisy shrugged. 'In normal circumstances, yes. But our Peggy has been in the St John's Ambulance for years. I used to go as well, so did Mattie. So she's got useful skills. There are some women who volunteered for nursing duties who've had no experience at all. They've been working in places like London after only a week of training. From what I heard, it's all hands on deck, doing what they can.'

'A bit like when you helped out at that train wreck?' said Rose.

She shivered. 'Yes. Although I hope she doesn't end up having to crawl through the dark to treat casualties. Let's hope the hospitals don't get bombed. I heard that they have their own Home Guard unit at Peggy's hospital and a team of fire watchers on the roof all night.' She sighed again. The memory of the night of the train wreck still made her feel anxious and nauseous.

'It doesn't sound like the Germans care whether they hit a military base, a hospital or a residential street,' said Elsie. 'They just fly over, high above our beams and guns, and drop thousands of bombs as they go. It's awful.'

'I know,' said Rose. 'Did you hear? The ones coming from the Bristol raids have been dropping their spare bombs all over the place. It said in the local paper that they'd dropped a whole load of them in a line from Bristol all the way south to Chard one night.'

'Our lads have managed to shoot a few of them down, though,' said Daisy. 'Some German aircrew have been captured, but most of them didn't survive.'

Rose nodded. 'I heard one plane crash landed in a field the other side of Bridgewater and when they tried to get out, the farmer was there with his pitchfork. He kept them in the plane until the Home Guard arrived to take them away. Can you imagine? They probably had guns, but he just poked at 'em with his pitchfork and they cowered in the plane.'

Daisy laughed. 'You can't mess with an old farmer,' she said. 'Although if they'd just crash landed their plane, I doubt they were thinking straight.'

'They were probably glad to be captured alive,' said Elsie. 'It must have been terrifying, being shot down. I'm glad they were caught though.'

'Well, the war's over for them,' said Daisy. 'My pa was a prisoner of war back in the Great War and they treated him and his pals like slaves – making them work and keeping them on starvation rations.' It occurred to her that his current poor health might be connected to his ill treatment back then, combined with the worry of the current conflict. 'Those German airmen should be grateful we don't treat our prisoners like that.'

'Of course not,' said Elsie. 'Anyway, when are you going home, Rose? I expect your parents are looking forward to seeing you over Christmas, aren't they?'

Daisy watched as Rose started talking about her short break over the holiday, when she would be able to spend Christmas Day and Boxing Day in Birmingham before having to get back to the farm. She'd begun to notice that Elsie tended to change the

subject when anything the least bit sensitive about the war was
mentioned. She suspected that she knew far more than she was
letting on, just as Daisy was convinced that Uncle Ted did, too.
She noticed that a lot of local men saluted him when they saw
him, even though he didn't seem to do local Home Guard duties
like many men did. He also went to a lot of meetings when he
wasn't teaching at the school, according to his young sons. Aunt
Kate had grumbled about it at first, but since the Blitz had started,
she had thrown herself into working with the Women's Royal
Voluntary Service and had gone strangely quiet on the subject,
which was not like her at all. It made Daisy think that maybe her
aunt knew more than she should about what Uncle Ted was up to.

She would have liked to question Elsie, but she knew that it
wouldn't be fair on her friend, who was no doubt under strict
orders about what she could and couldn't talk about. Everywhere
she went these days she saw posters – on buses, noticeboards, in
shop windows and on advertising billboards – reminding people
that it was dangerous to talk without thinking. *Walls Have Ears,*
they said. *Careless Talk Costs Lives.* Who knew who might be
listening? Enemy spies could be anywhere, and the most
innocuous piece of information might help them.

But Daisy was beginning to realise that it was no good
thinking that just because they were in the wilds of Somerset that
what they said didn't matter and that they were safe. There were
airfields and garrisons all within a few miles, as well as mines
producing coal around Radstock and Midsomer Norton. Docks
around Bristol kept supplies going in and out of the country.
Factories across the county were producing planes, munitions
and God only knew what else. So Somerset was as important to
the war effort as any other part of the British Isles.

These thoughts made Daisy stop listening to Rose's happy

chatter about her impending trip home. *I want to do my bit,* she realised. She looked at Elsie, who was smiling and nodding as she listened to Rose. Daisy realised she couldn't say as much to her friend, no matter how sure she was becoming that the ATS clerk and driver seemed to be far too well-trained for such a lowly job. Elsie would be bound by all sorts of rules and regulations and wouldn't be able to discuss anything with her. If she tried to get her to talk, she might well end up getting them both into trouble. No, she would have to try something else.

I'll bet Uncle Ted will know how I can play my part.

With that thought, she turned her attention back to her friends with a smile and her mind made up. She would talk to him the first chance she got. He might well act as though he didn't know anything about it, but she was pretty sure that if she told him how she felt, he would find a way to help her.

'So, I'll be back on the 27 December,' said Rose, unaware that Daisy had been so engrossed in her own thoughts that she'd missed most of what she said. 'It'll be strange, just being me and Mammy and Daddy. Liam's going to be on duty, then he's going to his wife's parents' after work on Christmas Day. I think he's seen far too much of our parents since the rest of us left home, so I don't blame him. I hope I'll get to see him on Boxing Day, though.'

'What are you going to do for Christmas, Elsie?' asked Daisy. 'Have you heard from your sister?'

Elsie shook her head. 'No, I haven't heard from her.' She smiled, although it seemed to Daisy that it was a little forced. 'But I'm on duty over the holiday. Most of the others in the unit have family they can get home to, so it made more sense for me to volunteer to hold the fort while those that can be spared can have a proper break with their loved ones. I'd hate for someone to miss out on a family Christmas when I'm perfectly happy to take the duty.'

'Surely you won't be on your own for Christmas?' said Rose, looking horrified. 'If you'd said, you could've come with me. Mammy and Daddy wouldn't mind, I'm sure.'

'My folks would welcome you as well,' said Daisy.

Elsie shook her head. 'Thank you both, it's very kind of you. But I really don't mind, you know. I've never been much of a fan of this time of year. Not since our parents died. We never had any money after that to make it special, so Gertie and I used to pretty much ignore it. We both always worked over the holiday, so this year is no different for me. It's not as though I'll be completely alone. There'll be some others there to keep the unit functioning. I expect it will be quite jolly.'

Rose and Daisy were silent as they studied her. Elsie remained calm and serene, while both girls struggled to understand how someone could be happy to miss out on time to spend with their nearest and dearest.

'Right,' said Daisy. 'Then we must have our own little Christmas celebration when Rose gets back. Just the three of us.'

'Good idea!' cried Rose, beaming as she clapped her hands together. 'The cider girls' post-Christmas party. It'll be something nice to look forward to.'

* * *

As her train chugged slowly into Birmingham on Christmas Eve just before sunset, Rose looked around her with horror. Buildings she'd grown up around were reduced to rubble, parts of the city were wasteland. She'd known that the bombings had been bad, but knowing and seeing it with her own eyes was another thing.

By the time she met her parents at the station, she was

fighting tears – grief for her home city warring with fear for Mammy and Daddy and Liam and his wife who were living through the raids; dread that her other brothers might never make it home and guilt that she was feeling sorry for herself while she was living in the relative safety of Somerset.

She ran to them, flinging herself into their arms and sobbing.

'Ah, there's our cider girl,' said Mammy, kissing her and holding her close. 'Don't cry, pet.'

'I've missed you so much,' Rose said, trying to mop up her tears.

'And we've missed you as well, princess,' said Daddy, patting her back. 'But you're here now and we're going to have a jolly time. So wipe your face and let's get out of here before the blackout starts.'

Buses were still running – a miracle in Rose's eyes, considering that several roads were closed to traffic.

'Some of the walls that are left standing after the last raid need to be demolished,' her father explained. 'They're that precarious, a bus rumbling by could bring them down. So they have to go round the long way, but this'll get us home, don't you worry.'

Rose was quiet as their bus made its slow progress through the ruined streets. The other passengers were all cheerful, talking about their Christmas plans and the prospect of a couple of days off work. No one spoke about the possibility that their festivities could be spent in air raid shelters if Hitler decided to attack during the holiday. No one talked about those who wouldn't be seeing another Christmas. No one seemed to want to spoil the mood by mentioning all the men and boys who were spending their Christmas in foreign parts, not knowing if this one was their last.

21

Only a skeleton staff remained at Edgely Hall over Christmas and Boxing Day, but those who were there made the best of it, sharing a hearty Christmas lunch, including a flaming Christmas pudding. They even had home-made crackers that someone's relative had sent as a gift.

The CO was a keen winemaker in his spare time and his present to the staff who were left on duty over the holiday was a case of his best vintages. They included wines made from blackberries, plums, elderberries, even rhubarb, and the small team who enjoyed a tipple with their lunch agreed that they were all surprisingly good.

'Are you ready for a top-up, Bloomfield?' asked Jameson, a lieutenant who'd only been at the unit for a week.

She put a hand over the top of her glass. 'I'd better not,' she said. 'I've a feeling that stuff is stronger than it looks.'

He laughed. 'It's delicious, though, isn't it? Go on, one more won't hurt, will it?'

She shook her head, smiling as she didn't want to seem rude.

'I'm really not much of a drinker,' she said. 'You have it. I'm sure you'll appreciate it far more than I can.'

'Fair enough,' he said, pouring himself a large one. 'Cheers and Merry Christmas.'

There was a record player in the drawing room and someone put on some music. Elsie was persuaded to dance with each of the half a dozen men there in turn, laughing as they apologised for missing a step as the CO's home-brew took its toll. After she'd been trodden on a couple of times, she insisted that someone go and get the cook and housekeeper to come and join in, if only to save her own poor toes. The older women, both widows with no family, were happy to take a turn around the room in the arms of the motley crew of soldiers. It was a jolly afternoon, with everyone determined to make the best of a Christmas away from home.

Eventually, the cook announced she was going to make some turkey and piccalilli sandwiches for their tea and the housekeeper went with her. Elsie relaxed on one of the Chesterfield sofas, wondering if she could manage a sandwich after such a good lunch.

'So,' said Jameson, coming to sit next to her. 'Who did you upset to get stuck with Christmas on duty?'

She smiled. 'No one. I volunteered.'

'Really? Why?'

She shrugged. 'I've nowhere to go, to be honest. If I wasn't here, I'd have to find a hotel to stay in and I can't imagine it would be more comfortable than here.'

'Mmm. It's not very comfortable in our quarters. You've landed on your feet getting a room in the house.'

Most of the men were housed in a Nissen hut in the grounds while the senior officers were in the house. Elsie, as the only ATS personnel on site, was given a room in the attic that had previously been accommodation for one of the servants. It wasn't very grand, but it was neat and quite warm and she had lovely views across the surrounding countryside. She felt awkward about that, because she'd heard the men complaining about how cold and damp their quarters were.

'Sorry about that,' she said with a smile. 'If there had been more women personnel, I'm sure we'd have been put in a Nissen hut as well. Being the only girl has its advantages sometimes.'

He took another sip of his drink. Elsie was pretty sure he'd got through most of one bottle of rhubarb wine on his own, but he still seemed quite lucid; he hadn't trodden on her toes once while they were dancing, so maybe he was one of those chaps who could hold his booze. Not like her brother-in-law. A shadow crossed her face as she thought about him. He'd not been a happy drunk; it made him sour and unpleasant and best avoided.

She blinked, forcing away her memories. 'So, from your question, can I take it that you upset someone and somehow managed to get picked for holiday duty?'

He laughed. 'No, not really. It was more a case of the last one in gets stuck with it, having missed the chance to put his case forward for having some festive leave.'

'Ah, I see. Would you have gone home if you'd managed to get some time off?'

He looked thoughtful for a moment. 'Probably not, to be honest. Christmas at home has never been a cheerful prospect since my father died when I was about ten. Now my mother's remarried after years of playing the poor widow and is making the most of her new life.'

'It must be nice for her to have someone again after all this time.'

He wrinkled his nose. 'I've no objection to her finding someone to replace her husband, but I do object to my stepfather thinking he can take over the role of my father even though I'm of age.' He took another drink. 'Especially when he's a pompous pen-pushing killjoy who wouldn't know fun if it smacked him in the face.'

Elsie laughed at his mildly delivered but harsh words. 'Ah, I see. That's why you're so cheerful about being here.'

He grinned. 'That and the company.' He raised his glass to her. 'Are you sure you don't want another glass before I finish the damned bottle?'

She looked around. The other men were smoking and chatting amongst themselves about motorcars, football and whether Cook would bring in more mince pies with their sandwiches. Most of them had switched to drinking beer, although she noticed that one of the older chaps was sipping from a hip flask.

'Goodness, no, really,' she said. 'Someone's got to stay sober. If the invasion came tonight, everyone here would be too squiffy to resist.'

He shook his head, relaxing with his arms stretched out along the back of the settee. Elsie couldn't be sure, but she thought he might have touched her hair. It felt quite nice, so she didn't move or complain. 'Hitler won't come tonight,' he went on. 'He's probably in some Bavarian castle, drinking schnapps and messing around with his mistress.'

'I certainly hope so,' she said drily, making him chuckle. 'Although I can't imagine anyone finding that odious man attractive.'

'Some women are attracted to power,' he said. 'That's why officers do so well with the ladies.'

She wrinkled her nose. 'I'm afraid power does nothing for me.'

He regarded her thoughtfully. 'Good to know,' he said.

They chatted on for a while, joining in with the other conversations, until Cook and the housekeeper returned with trays of sandwiches and pots of tea.

Jameson persuaded her to dance again as evening drew in. He was handsome and charming and Elsie felt the stirring of excitement when he smiled at her. When she said goodnight to the assembled company, he accompanied her to the bottom of the stairs and kissed her cheek, startling her. He pointed upwards. Someone had hung a small sprig of mistletoe. 'Sorry,' he said. 'I couldn't resist.'

She smiled. 'That's all right. Merry Christmas, Charles.'

'Merry Christmas, sweet Elsie,' he said. Then he kissed her again, this time on the lips, before taking his leave. She floated up the stairs, her heart feeling lighter than it had for a long time.

It wasn't until later, when she was alone in her room, that she allowed herself to think about Gertie and the baby. Even though she and her sister had parted on less than friendly terms, Elsie couldn't help but miss her. The baby, Frances, would be nearly a year old now. She wondered how she was getting on. She might even be walking. It hurt to think that, having lived with Gertie throughout her pregnancy and after helping her with the baby in those early weeks following her birth, her niece wouldn't even remember her. And if she didn't survive the war, would Gertie ever tell her daughter about her Aunt Elsie?

And what of Charles Jameson? Her stomach fluttered with butterflies. She'd enjoyed his attention and his kisses had been sweet. While her head was cautious about getting involved with anyone, her heart was singing with joy that someone had found her attractive enough to want to spend time with her and to kiss her under the mistletoe.

* * *

Christmas on the Selway farm in Walcot was a happy affair, with a plump home-grown roast goose for their festive lunch.

That evening they gathered at Aunt Kate and Uncle Ted's house in Street. They had a jolly time of it with songs and games like charades, and mulled cider.

Daisy noticed Uncle Ted slip away to his study. She supposed that Christmas Day wasn't the time to talk to him about what had been on her mind, but then again, the sooner she spoke to him the better. She left the others chatting and drinking tea and knocked on his door.

'Come in.'

Inside, she found Uncle Ted behind his desk, smoking his pipe. She smiled, knowing that Aunt Kate wouldn't allow him to light up anywhere else in the house. 'Caught you,' she said.

He chuckled, holding up his hands. 'A man's got to have the odd indulgence,' he said. He indicated the chair on the opposite side of his desk and she sat down. 'What can I do for you, lass?'

'I've been thinking,' she said, suddenly feeling foolish. 'About the Home Guard.'

'What about it?' he asked.

'I wondered if I could join?'

He raised his eyebrows. 'Why would you want to do that? You're doing an important job already.'

'So are you, but you're still doing plenty with them,' she pointed out.

He shrugged. 'I'm not doing much,' he said mildly. 'Just providing a bit of training, that's all. There's a limit to how much an old man like me can offer.'

She was pretty sure he was deliberately underestimating his importance. She remembered the Jackson children showing her their pa's medals from the Great War, and her own pa's hints, when she'd mentioned the ones Uncle Ted had been awarded by the French and Belgian and Dutch governments, that still waters ran deep but that no one would ever know exactly what Ted had been up to in the war. All he would say was that Ted hadn't fought in the trenches but had been in a much more precarious situation with only his own wits to rely on. Nor did she think that Elsie's boss would have sent her to collect him or taken the trouble to come to Uncle Ted's house for meetings if what he was doing was trivial.

'I don't know,' she said with a smile. 'You equipped me to deal with the likes of Ronnie. It seems to me I'd be more useful to the Home Guard than he is. I managed to disarm him, after all. I don't see why I can't join up.'

He chuckled. 'Ronnie's not typical of our men, you know. And even he's learned his lesson.'

'That's not the point, Uncle,' she said, leaning forward and resting her elbows on the desk. 'I don't want to sit around and wait for some lad to defend me if we're invaded. I want to do my bit. Won't you help me?'

He shook his head. 'I'm sorry, Daisy, love. The Home Guard is for men only.'

She huffed. 'That's not what I've heard. They say some farmers' wives and daughters have joined up because they're handy with a gun. I can use a shot gun as well as any man.'

He inclined his head to one side. 'I heard that as well, but from what I understand it's only where there simply aren't enough men available. We don't have that problem round here. And anyway' – he held up a hand to silence her when she would have argued – 'do you really want to spend time with the likes of Ronnie after a hard day's work?'

She huffed, resting her chin on her hands. 'I suppose not. I wasn't impressed with him or the men who came to see what he was up to. But surely there must be something I can do? I'd not rate our chances if we've got to rely on those idiots to save us, would you?'

'They're getting better, lass. Your little incident highlighted some gaps in their training that we've been addressing. And most of the men in our Home Guard unit are far more conscientious about their duties than young Ronnie.'

'I still put him on his backside, though,' she muttered. 'And I could any other man who thought they could take advantage.'

'That you could, lass.' He grinned. 'I taught you well.'

She rolled her eyes. 'Then why can't I—?'

His hand came up again, silencing her. 'I'm sorry, Daisy. It's not up to me. Home Guard is intended to be a male defence force. Besides, wouldn't it hurt your pa's pride if you did that? It's hard enough for him that your brothers are on parade and he's not.'

She sighed. 'I suppose. We're all worried about him, but he won't go to the doctor. I've half a mind to get Mattie round and make him examine Pa. I know he's not right, but if he won't see anyone about it, he could end up in a right pickle without treatment.'

Ted nodded. 'I've noticed he's lost weight. But men can be stubborn. I'll have a word with him, if you like? But maybe Mattie might be the right man for the job. He'll know what to ask him to get to the bottom of it all.'

'Yes. I'll ask him. But that doesn't mean I'll let you distract me from what I came in here to ask about.'

He shrugged, giving her a sly smile. 'It was worth a try. But I can't help on that score, I'm afraid. I really think you're doing enough, working as a nurse for the community. If there's an invasion, your first aid skills will be even more valuable.'

She sighed and sat back, not knowing what else she could say. 'I just want to do my bit,' she said, aware that it sounded like she was whining. She knew that she could go back to a city hospital, or enlist in the Nursing Corps. But with Pa being so stubborn about his health, she didn't want to leave the farm. She needed to be there to keep an eye on him and offer Ma some support.

Uncle Ted regarded her as he tapped the tobacco out of his pipe into the ashtray on his desk. 'Tell me,' he said. 'Are you still riding round on that bicycle of yours?'

She nodded. 'I do most of my visits around the village on it, and then ride out sometimes on my days off. I can get to Catcott to see my friend Rose in about half an hour these days.'

He looked impressed. 'That's a good turn of speed. It's what, six miles or so out to Catcott from here?'

'I think so. Not as fast as your motorcycle, of course. But I don't scare the cattle as I pedal past them.' She grinned. 'When I'm working, it helps to be able to cycle quickly to get from one appointment to the next. I can see a lot more patients that way.'

He nodded and stood up. 'Well, I'm sorry I can't be of any more help to you, Daisy, love. But if I hear of anything you can do, I'll let you know.' With his trademark charming smile, he ushered her out of his office and followed her into the parlour where the rest of the family were chattering without even noticing that the two of them had been gone.

22

The journey back to Somerset from Birmingham was long and arduous. When Rose finally stepped down from the train at Bridgewater Station, she was in no mood to find Jimmy waiting for her next to the farm truck, even though getting a lift was infinitely better than waiting around in the cold for the next bus back to Catcott and the long walk from the village to the farmhouse.

'What are you doing here?' she asked, not caring that she sounded ungrateful.

'Ma thought you'd appreciate a lift,' he said. 'But if you don't want one, I'll leave you to it.' He opened the door and climbed into the truck.

She closed her eyes and sighed. He might leave her if she didn't get a move on. Sure enough, the engine rumbled and she had to scramble to open the passenger door and throw her bags in before climbing in and sitting beside him.

'Thank you,' she said, not feeling inclined to put much warmth into it.

'What's that?' he asked, cupping his ear. 'I couldn't hear you.'

She scowled at him as he let off the handbrake and the vehicle lumbered forward. 'I said thank you,' she said, raising her voice.

He glanced at her with a grin. 'There, see. That wasn't hard, was it?' When she didn't respond, he concentrated on manoeuvring the truck away from the station. 'So,' he said after a few minutes. 'Did you have a good Christmas?'

It was too much for Rose. She looked out of the side window, hoping he didn't notice the sob that escaped her before she put a hand over her mouth. But she couldn't stop her shoulders from shaking.

He cursed, making her sob even more. She'd been determined not to cry, had been so strong through all the hours since Mammy and Daddy had waved her off this morning. But she was just so tired and heart-sore that she couldn't hold it in any longer.

'I'm sorry,' she said, her throat tight with emotion, making her voice squeaky. 'I'll be all right in a minute. Just ignore me.' She kept her head turned away, feeling weak and embarrassed. No doubt Jimmy would mock her and make her feel even worse than she already did.

To her shock, he turned a corner and brought the truck to a halt in a side road. He engaged the handbrake, turned off the engine and pulled her into his arms. He didn't say anything, but held her tight against his chest, his chin resting on the top of her head.

The warmth of his strong arms around her was the last thing she expected but, she realised, it was exactly what she needed at that moment. She breathed in the scent of his tweed jacket and gave in to the flood of emotion that had been coiled tight within her for the past couple of days.

She didn't know how long she cried for, but eventually she became aware of his hands stroking her back and hair and the steady beat of his heart against her cheek. She took a deep breath, feeling it shiver in her chest as she moved back a little, already missing his warmth. She scrambled in her pocket and retrieved her handkerchief and wiped her face before blowing her nose. She couldn't look at Jimmy. She knew that she wasn't a pretty crier so she must look a sight. Her face would be red and blotchy and her eyes puffy.

'What happened?' he asked, his tone gentle for a change.

She risked a quick glance at him but looked away straight away. She didn't think she could hold herself in check if he was genuinely being nice to her. 'One of my brothers is missing in action and another has been wounded,' she said, blinking back more tears. 'And Birmingham... oh lord, it's a mess. Whole streets reduced to rubble... So many people killed... The bombers hit the water supply as well and the firemen had to use water from the canals to fight the fires.' She sniffed and wiped her eyes again. 'I tried to persuade Mammy and Daddy to come to Somerset, but they won't. Daddy says he's got to stay and do his bit – he's an ARP – and Mammy refuses to go anywhere without him.'

'Sounds rough,' he said. She realised he still had his arm around her shoulder and he was stroking her hair. With a nod and a sigh, she relaxed against his side. It was the first time she'd felt safe since she'd arrived in the wreckage of her home city. Even coming home on the train, she kept thinking about the train wreck that Daisy and her doctor friend had been involved with, and she expected the one she was on to crash or be attacked at any moment. She hadn't been able to get it out of her mind and her fear had made the journey to Somerset seem so much longer than before.

'It was such a shock,' she admitted. 'They knew about Michael being missing for a few days, but decided not to tell me in a letter. I'm so cross about that. I wondered why I hadn't heard from him and I'd avoided mentioning it to Mammy in case it worried her. But she knew, and I didn't.'

'Missing doesn't mean dead,' he said. 'You know that, don't you?'

She nodded. 'I know, but it means they don't know where he is. He could be hurt, or captured, or... or lying dead in a ditch somewhere. The last anyone knows, he was somewhere in the Mediterranean – might be Italy or Greece or even North Africa. The army won't say. All they told Daddy was that we had to keep the faith and wait for news.' She sighed, feeling exhausted by it all.

'What about your other brother – are his wounds bad?'

'We don't know much. It's Patrick, who's in the navy. He was in a road accident while on shore leave, apparently. He's written to Mammy and Daddy, says he's in hospital and will be shipped home soon to recuperate. Said he's broken his leg. I suppose that's better than us being told his ship's gone down, isn't it?'

'Yeah.' He didn't need to tell her that the chances of surviving a sinking ship were pretty awful, especially in the northern seas at this time of year.

'We don't even know where he is. Somewhere abroad,' she said, ''cause he said they're waiting for a hospital ship before he can come home.'

'But your other brothers are all right?' he asked.

She nodded. 'As far as we know. There have been letters from them over the last week or so.' She didn't want to say that Mammy was still fretting something awful and barely sleeping, waiting for news of each of them.

'Well, that's good, isn't it?'

'Is it?' she asked, feeling irritable. 'All it tells us is that they were alive when they wrote their last letter. Who knows what's happened to them since then?'

She expected him to get cross with her and braced herself for a scathing response, but he merely nodded. 'You're right,' he said, his tone still gentle. 'But at least you've heard something, eh? You can't go thinking the worst. That's how Hitler will win. That's why he's bombing women and children and reducing the cities to rubble. He's trying to wear us down. We can't give in and let him beat us.'

She felt bad now in the face of his patience. She blew her nose again and nodded. 'I know. We've got to stay strong.' She looked up at him, realising with a little surprise that she was comfortable, snuggled into his side like this. 'Sorry to be such a wet blanket,' she said.

He shrugged. 'It's all right. I know you were excited about going to see your folks. It must have been a rough couple of days. You ready to go home now?'

For a moment, she thought he meant to put her on a train back to Birmingham, but then she realised he meant the farm. It made her feel a little better, knowing that the farm was a safe haven for her. With a measure of reluctance she hadn't expected, she sat up straighter, finally breaking the contact with his warm body. 'Yes, please. Let's get going.'

On the drive back to Catcott, he told her what she'd missed over the past couple of days, which wasn't much, other than that Ivor had drawn the short straw and had to do her milking duties and he'd managed to land face first in the freezing mud when one of the cows took against his cold, rough hands and kicked him. 'So don't expect him to cover for you again any time soon,' he told her.

She smiled, appreciating that he was being nice and trying to make her laugh, but she was exhausted by all that crying and the stress of the past couple of days. She closed her eyes, intending to rest them for a few minutes. But the next thing she knew was that

Jimmy was lifting her out of the truck and into his arms. She started protesting.

'Shhh,' he said, holding her tighter. 'You're worn out. You've been dead to the world most of the way home. Let's get you inside.'

Too tired to argue, she relaxed against him and let him carry her into the farmhouse and up to her room. She barely noticed that he kissed her cheek as he laid her on her bed before he covered her with the eiderdown and left her to sleep.

23

After a lull over Christmas, air raids began again with a vengeance in late December. 1941 came in with bitterly cold weather and more bombings. Jam and cheese were added to the list of rationed foods in early January.

In an effort to keep life as normal as possible, Daisy persuaded Elsie to go out to Catcott to join Rose and the Morgan family and their neighbours for the annual Wassail ceremony on the early evening of Twelfth Night. The Selways had had their ceremony in their farm's small orchard earlier in the day before Daisy went to work. The Catcott farmers preferred to have theirs later in the day.

'Are we really going to stand in an orchard in the freezing cold for this?' asked Elsie, shivering as she pulled her scarf around her neck and ears. 'I don't understand what this is all about.'

'I know, it sounds daft to me,' grumbled Rose, stamping her booted feet in the hope that she could get some feeling back in her freezing toes. 'But they say it's important. They've been wassailing around all the orchards around here all afternoon.' It was now getting late and the sun was going down, leaving them in the dusky gloom.

'It is important,' confirmed Daisy. 'This is a pagan ceremony, going back to the dawn of time. We have to feed the trees and wake them up, to chase away any bad spirits and make sure there's a good apple harvest this year. If you're going to be proper cider girls, you need to take part in the Wassail.'

'Well, I wish they'd get on with it,' said Rose. 'And they shouldn't be waving them torches about. What if there's planes up there?' She pointed skyward. 'We could be machine-gunned, or bombed if they spot us.'

Rose clearly wasn't the only person thinking this, because the flaming torches they'd followed towards the trees were quickly extinguished. Some people brought out battery torches, but they used them sparingly and turned them off completely once everyone was gathered in the Morgans' orchard, so they could only see by moonlight.

Mr Morgan took the lead in the ceremony, pouring a cup of cider onto the roots of one of his trees in the middle of the orchard that had been decorated with ribbons and flags. This was to nourish the tree. He also spiked a piece of toast onto one of the branches, to encourage wildlife to come to feed on the tree and keep it healthy and also help pollinate the blossoms when they appeared in the spring. He intoned traditional words, and then the gathered crowd joined in singing the traditional Wassail song, exhorting the trees to wake up and provide a good harvest.

Although Rose and Elsie had no idea of the words, everyone else sang with gusto, ending the song with a cacophony of noise as people banged drums, clapped sticks together. Some of the women, with colourful artificial flowers and real evergreen leaves decorating their hats, had brought saucepans and metal ladles to bang.

Daisy laughed as the other girls covered their ears. 'Make a noise!' she told them as she clapped and whooped. 'We've got to chase the bad spirits away.'

Eventually the noise died down and the cheerful crowd remained among the trees, drinking from flagons of warm cider. Even Rose accepted a small drink in the hope that it would chase the cold away. She suspected that the locals had had enough warm cider through the afternoon and evening that they didn't notice the freezing temperatures now.

'I must tell Charles about this,' said Elsie with a smile.

'Who's Charles?' asked Daisy.

She blushed. 'Oh, just one of the chaps at work. We've... er... we danced together at Christmas and then he kissed me under the mistletoe.'

'You dark horse,' said Rose. 'So are you courting now?'

'No! Well, not really. We're just friends. We can't be anything else, not with the fraternisation rules, can we?'

Daisy frowned. 'Why? Is he a senior officer?'

Elsie shook her head, looking embarrassed. 'He's senior to me. He's a lieutenant, so a junior officer. But even at our basic training, ATS girls were warned not to fraternise with any of the men. They said it wasn't good for morale and could ruin a girl's reputation.'

'Yet he danced with you at Christmas,' said Rose.

Elsie shrugged, her cheeks still warm. 'I danced with all the men there. So did the cook and the housekeeper.'

'But I assume only this Charles kissed you under the mistletoe,' said Daisy.

Elsie put her hands to her cheeks. 'I know. And he's asked if we could go out together, even though we shouldn't.'

Rose grinned. 'He must really like you. Do you like him?'

Elsie nodded. 'I rather think I do. He's very nice. But I'm not sure about getting involved in some secret liaison.'

'It does seem a bit sordid,' said Daisy. 'Do you really want to be sneaking around to see him?'

Elsie sighed. 'Not really. But he is very nice.'

'Well, just be careful, love,' said Rose. 'I wouldn't want to get involved with a chap if I couldn't be seen walking out on his arm.'

Elsie took a deep breath. 'You're right, and he says he understands. But he's so handsome and I suppose I'm rather flattered that he's paying me so much attention. Is it wrong of me to be tempted?'

'Handsome is as handsome does,' said Rose. 'You deserve someone who's proud to be seen with you.'

'You should get him to come to one of the dances in Street so we can make sure he's good enough for you,' said Daisy.

'Maybe I will,' she said with a smile.

Once the Morgans' orchard had been wassailed, the crowd moved onto the next orchard in the village, until the ceremony had been completed in all of them.

The party didn't last much longer as most of the men were in their Home Guard uniforms and they were expected on duty. The older women didn't hang around after that, each heading back to their respective homes with their children.

Elsie and Daisy walked back to the Morgan farmhouse with Rose, where they would visit for a bit before catching the late bus back to Street and Glastonbury.

'Now we're all proper cider girls,' said Daisy. 'We've done our bit to ensure a good apple harvest.'

'I can't say it makes me feel any different,' said Rose. 'Apart from having frostbitten toes.'

'It was an interesting experience,' said Elsie. 'It's a shame they don't do it in the warmer months, though.' She shivered, rubbing her arms through her coat as they entered the farmyard.

'Ah, but the whole point is to wake up the trees from their winter slumber and chase away bad spirits who might have been hiding there from the cold,' pointed out Daisy. 'Before the war, the farmers would fire their shotguns as well, to make sure they made enough noise. Of course, they've been ordered not to now, in case anyone mistakes the shots for an invasion.'

As they walked into the farmyard, the rumble of a motorcycle engine disturbed the night air. Jimmy rode out of the barn and across the yard to disappear up the road.

Rose narrowed her eyes as she watched him go. 'Look, he's off up to no good again.'

'What d'you mean?' asked Elsie, looking confused. 'It looks like he's off on Home Guard duty. He's wearing his uniform.'

Rose sighed. 'That's what he says he's doing. But the local unit meets in the church hall, which is in the other direction. And none of the local lads seem to know what he's up to. He doesn't go to the parades there any more. He says he's on *special duties*, whatever that means.' She blew out a breath. 'I've heard him come back in the early hours sometimes and other times he doesn't come home at all. One night when he got back it was nearly dawn and the sleeve of his jacket was ripped, like he'd caught it on something or been in a fight. I'm really worried that he's doing something he shouldn't. What if he's poaching or is involved with black market shenanigans? Or what if he's been sucked into something and he's become an enemy spy? It'd break his mammy's heart.'

Daisy watched Elsie's reaction to Rose's words. She'd noticed that the ATS girl tended to avoid Jimmy's gaze when he was around and often smoothed things over or changed the subject when he was mentioned. Sure enough, after looking a bit nonplussed, Elsie shrugged. 'Surely his parents would have something to say about it if Jimmy was up to no good, wouldn't they? They seem like upstanding citizens. There's bound to be a logical explanation. Are you sure he isn't with the next Home Guard over? I heard they've had to move men around between units so that they have the right numbers in each area.'

Daisy could see the sense in what she was saying, but she had a feeling that Elsie knew a lot more than she was letting on to both of them.

'If that's the case, why does he tell me to mind my own business when I ask him about it?'

Elsie chuckled. 'He probably wants to create the illusion of mystery to keep you interested.' She winked. 'You are interested in him, aren't you?'

Even in the moonlight, Daisy could see that Rose's cheeks were blooming as she shook her head.

'I am not,' she said, sounding outraged.

'Really?' asked Daisy as she looped her arm through Rose's. 'Because I agree with Elsie. You seem interested in each other, but you're both fighting it.'

Rose huffed out a breath, creating a cloud of condensation in the cold air. 'I don't know what makes you think he's interested,' she said. 'Because I can't see it from where I'm standing.'

'Ah, so you're interested and you're not sure if he is?' said Elsie, grinning.

Rose rolled her eyes. 'I *might* have been interested,' she confessed. 'And he *might* have *seemed* interested a time or two. But then he goes all surly and snappy again and I just want to box his ears.'

'Ooh, do tell,' said Daisy. 'When has he seemed like he *might* be interested in you, Rose?'

She grimaced. 'He *might* have kissed me,' she murmured. 'But it clearly doesn't mean anything.'

'You dark horse,' said Daisy with a smile. 'When was this?'

Rose looked like she wished she'd never said anything.

'Come on, Rose,' said Elsie. 'Spill the beans. We need details.'

'It really was nothing,' she said. 'That day we went into Wells, he was here when your Mattie's friend dropped me off. We had a row and he grabbed me and kissed me.'

'Oh my,' said Elsie. 'Why didn't you tell us?'

She shrugged.

Daisy frowned. 'He didn't take advantage against your will, did he?'

'What? No! At least, I thought he might be rough when he grabbed me, and I would've fought back if he had. But... the kiss was actually rather sweet and gentle. Then he said he wouldn't apologise and took off on his motorbike. By the next day, he'd reverted to his usual grumpy self, so I decided to forget about it. Then...'

'Then?' said Daisy.

'What else has happened?' said Elsie.

Rose sighed again. 'He picked me up from Bridgewater Station when I came back from Birmingham. I was upset over the news about my brothers and all the mess the air raids have made of the city and when he asked me if I'd had a good Christmas, I couldn't help but burst into tears.' Her eyes filled and she blinked rapidly, clearly trying not to cry again. 'He stopped the truck and held me in his arms while I wept all over him. He was so kind.' She shook her head. 'Anyway, I was so worn out, I fell asleep on the way home and he carried me to my bed.'

At the sight of their startled expressions, she held up a hand. 'Don't worry, he didn't do anything, apart from pull off my boots and coat and tuck the eiderdown over me. But... I'm not sure, I might have been dreaming, but I think he kissed my cheek before he left the room.' She covered her eyes. 'Can you see why I'm so confused? Most of the time he's teasing me, which makes me want to punch him, but sometimes he's... I don't know. It's as though he's a completely different lad. And on top of all that there's all these nights when he's going off on his own and won't tell anyone what he's doing and... I don't know how to explain it, but I can't trust him.' She lowered her hand and looked worried. 'Elsie, do you think I should report him? I mean, the government keeps saying we should report any suspicious behaviour.'

Elsie shook her head. 'I really don't think he's a spy, Rose. What on earth could a simple farming lad know that would be useful to the enemy?'

'I don't know, that's the trouble. Am I being extra suspicious because he's playing around with me and keeping me confused? For all I know, he could be having a secret romance with someone and that's why he's acting so strange. But if that's the case, why did he blinking well kiss me?'

They'd been standing in the farmyard all this time, so caught up in their conversation that they hadn't even noticed the cold any more. The kitchen door opened and Mrs Morgan called out.

'Is that you, Rose? It's getting on, love. Did your friends get the bus yet?'

'Oh heck,' said Daisy, checking her wristwatch. 'It's due any minute. We'll have to run to make sure we catch it.'

With a quick goodbye and promise to meet again soon, Daisy and Elsie took off running across the farmyard towards the village to catch the bus.

Rose watched them go before going into the farmhouse and up to her room.

* * *

On the bus, the two girls caught their breath, laughing at how close they had come to missing it.

'So,' said Daisy as they settled in their seats. 'What do you think about Rose and Jimmy? I can't say I'm surprised. She gets far too cross about him.'

Elsie grinned. 'I know. But he's not exactly a charmer is he?'

Daisy regarded her thoughtfully. 'What makes you say that? I can't say as I've spent enough time talking to him to know one way or another.'

Elsie shrugged, looking away. 'Neither have I,' she said. 'I just got that impression from what Rose has told us about him. It sounds like he takes himself far too seriously.'

'Doesn't your job involve supplying Home Guard units?' she asked quietly, although there weren't any other passengers within earshot. 'Maybe you could check to see what Jimmy's up to, so that you can put Rose's mind at rest.'

Elsie looked startled. 'Oh, no. I can't do that. I mean... no. It's not done. I could get into a lot of trouble.'

'Even if all he's doing is sneaking around with another lass? That's hardly a crime, though that does make him a horrible person for kissing Rose when he's spoken for. At least then we'd know. But what if he *is* up to no good, like Rose is thinking?' she persisted. 'Surely it would be our duty to report him?'

Elsie sighed, lowering her voice. 'Look, I shouldn't be telling you this. So you must promise me you'll not breathe a word of it to anyone – even Rose.'

Daisy nodded but didn't say anything.

'All right, I'm going to have to trust you not to get us both into trouble, but, well, I know that what Jimmy's doing is legitimate. He doesn't take his orders from the local Home Guard unit because he really is on special duties.'

She nodded, feeling a bit smug. 'I thought as much. A bit like whatever Uncle Ted is up to.'

'What?' Elsie stared at her, horrified. 'No. Absolutely not. You mustn't go saying such things.' She glanced around, keeping her voice low and urgent. 'Please Daisy, stop talking about this and don't ask me anything or you'll be in a whole mess of trouble. I should be reporting this conversation as it is. Please don't put me in a position where I end up landing us both in hot water.'

Daisy took pity on her friend. 'Don't worry. I can keep secrets. And I won't do anything to put my own godfather at risk now, will I?'

Elsie still looked uncomfortable. 'I don't suppose so. I'm sorry, but... I really can't tell you anything. I shouldn't have said what I just did.'

'It's all right, Elsie, really. My lips are sealed and I promise I won't ask any more.' After all, her friend had pretty much confirmed what she had been suspecting. Her Uncle Ted was definitely in deeper than he let on judging by her reaction to just the mention of his name, and she was beginning to get an idea of what he was up to. Maybe it was time to have another conversation with him about how she could help? 'So,' she said, nudging Elsie's shoulder. 'Tell me more about this Lieutenant Charles. Is he handsome? Has he got any good-looking pals who might take pity on a nurse and a land girl? We could have some jolly times together as a group of friends so that you don't get into trouble.'

24

Elsie fretted about what she'd said to Daisy regarding Jimmy and Captain Jackson. She really shouldn't have said a word. By rights, she should report the conversation and her part in it to her CO. But she was afraid that she'd be for the high jump if she did.

However, after a sleepless night, she decided the best she could do would be to tell the CO that Rose was suspicious of Jimmy's activities and had mentioned it to both her and Daisy. She would ask him if there was anything she could do to put her friends off the scent.

'Are either of your friends aware of the auxiliary units in the area?' he asked her when she broached the subject.

'No, sir. They haven't got a clue. I think that's why the suspicion of Jimmy's activities arose. Rose sees him leaving the farm and going in the opposite direction to his father and brother who are regular Home Guard. She's come to the conclusion that he's up to no good.'

'And your other friend – the district nurse?'

'Daisy believes he's up to something, although she's inclined to think he's not likely to be a spy. But she suggested it was our duty to report anything suspicious, even if it did turn out to be innocent.' She tried not to look uncomfortable as she said this.

'Mmm.' The CO regarded her with his level gaze. 'And what did you say to that?'

She shrugged. 'I asked what a simple farm hand could possibly be up to that the authorities might need to know about? There's no evidence that he's involved in black market activity or poaching. The conclusion we came to was that he was conducting an illicit affair, although as a single lad, it seems unlikely. Their main concern was that he was going off in his uniform and claiming to be Home Guard when he's clearly not attached to the local unit.'

'I see.'

'The thing is, sir,' she went on, not sure whether she should mention this, but feeling now she really ought to say something. 'Daisy is Captain Jackson's goddaughter, and I think she suspects he is more involved in special duties than he's letting on.'

He raised his eyebrows. 'Why does she think that?'

She sighed, wondering whether she was making things worse. She'd resolved not to mention it, but she knew that the CO trusted her to report everything that might represent a danger to the integrity and secrecy of the Auxiliers. But Daisy's perception was sharp and she seemed to be adding a lot of things together and reaching her own conclusions. 'She mentioned that her uncle won't ever talk about what he did in the Great War, but she remembers his children showing her his medals once. Did you know he was awarded the *Crois de Guerre*, as well as awards from the Dutch and Belgian governments? She says no one in the family will talk about what he did, but Captain Jackson's wife mentioned to me in front of Daisy that he disappeared for most of the war years and no one knew whether he was alive or dead. Daisy's father said he didn't serve with a regiment, but rather he was behind the scenes, working on his own most of the time.' She paused. 'She concludes that he was some sort of spy.'

'Does she indeed?' he asked, showing no surprise.

'Yes, sir. And I think she believes he's doing something similar now.'

The CO looked thoughtful. 'And she's mentioned that to you and the land girl?'

She shook her head. 'No, sir. Just me,' she said. 'But I think that, because she's seen me with her uncle when I've been on duty, she suspects my job is rather more than a clerk and driver. She's also mentioned that I seem to have been on an awful lot of courses.' Her shoulders slumped. 'I expect you'll want to transfer me away.'

He tilted his head to one side. 'Why?'

She frowned. 'Because a civilian is suspicious of me. It could compromise the local network.'

'You haven't confirmed her suspicions, have you?'

'Of course not, sir. I signed the Official Secrets Act.'

'Quite. Well, I think I need to have a word with Captain Jackson, but I don't think we need to send you into exile just yet, Bloomfield.'

'Thank you, sir,' she said, part relieved and part alarmed that he used the words *just yet.*

* * *

After Elsie had returned to her office and was busy on her typewriter, the CO put through a call to Ted Jackson.

'I've just had a very interesting conversation about your goddaughter, the district nurse,' he told him.

'Daisy? What about her?'

'It seems she and their land girl chum have been asking my

clerk whether they should be reporting Jimmy Morgan for being up to no good.'

'Really? What's he been up to?'

'Nothing other than following orders, so far as I'm aware, and to keep his own counsel about why he's going off for Home Guard duty in a different direction to his father and brother. It's got their tongues wagging. They're trying to work out whether he's a criminal, a spy or involved in an illicit affair.'

Ted laughed. 'I see. And our Daisy is part of this discussion, is she? Do you want me to ask her not to discuss it? She'll want to know why, so my interference might actually make the situation worse.'

'No, don't worry, that's what I thought as well. Bloomfield can deal with them. But I thought I should mention that your goddaughter also told my clerk that you were probably a spy in the Great War.'

'Really? I'm not sure how she came to that conclusion.'

'Apparently your children showed her your medals and she noticed that some of them were... rather unusual for a regular soldier, shall we say?'

Ted was silent for a moment. 'Ah. I remember they were showing them off at one time. I put them under lock and key after that.'

'And some of the older generation have suggested that you were behind enemy lines for a lot of the time back then.'

'Did they now? It's not something I've ever confirmed or denied. Like many men, I simply chose not to discuss it.' He sighed. 'I suppose you'll want me to head young Daisy off and persuade her not to talk about this again?'

'You might want to ask family members to keep their opinions to themselves,' he replied. 'But I don't think you should be too harsh with the girl. In fact, I'm wondering whether, given her sharp perception, as well as her job as a district nurse, she might well be a useful addition to our network. Do you think she's up for it? We need more civilians to act as messengers.'

'I don't want her put in danger,' he said. 'And my wife and her parents would be more dangerous to me than any Panzer division if they found out.'

'Understood. It's always a difficult balance between family loyalty and duty. But think about it. Even if the worst happened and we were occupied, she would be one of the few people able to move around without attracting suspicion. She wouldn't even need to know anything about other members of the network – her role would simply be to pick up coded messages from one location and pass them on to the next. No need to know anything or anyone. Get her to sign the Official Secrets Act. Speak to her. Once she knows what's what, she may not want to get involved but she'll know to hold her tongue, in which case the problem is solved. So long as we can count on her discretion.'

Ted sighed. 'I don't think she'll turn down the chance. She's already told me she's keen to do something and suggested joining the Home Guard. I told her our local units are only recruiting men. She wasn't very impressed by that, given she'd had cause to disarm one of them a while back.'

'Ah, so she's the one? Sounds like our sort of lass, don't you think?'

'All right, I'll ask her. But I'll also do my best to dissuade her. The family would have my guts for garters if I didn't.'

'Well, they don't need to know, do they? God willing, they'll never know.'

'We can only hope so.'

* * *

Uncle Ted turned up at the Selway family home one day when Daisy was there alone.

'Hello, lass. Have you got a minute?'

She nodded, standing back to let him in. 'Everyone's out,' she said. 'I was just making a drink before I go back to work.'

He nodded and hung his hat on the hook by the door. 'A brew would be nice. I won't keep you long.'

They didn't speak until they were sitting at the kitchen table with their drinks. 'So, what can I do for you, Uncle?' she asked, unwilling to wait for him to broach the subject.

He sipped his drink before he replied. She waited patiently. He never could be hurried if he didn't want to. 'Have you ever heard of the Official Secrets Act, Daisy?' he asked.

She nodded. 'It's about keeping the government's secrets safe from the enemy,' she said.

'That's a good summary of it,' he agreed. 'And to safeguard the country's secrets, some people are required to sign it.'

She frowned. 'How do you mean?'

'When someone signs the Act, they're pledging to keep quiet about whatever it is they know or anything they're doing on behalf of the government. The consequences of breaking that pledge and revealing official business to unauthorised personnel are severe. It amounts to treason,' he said, his gaze grave.

She stared back at him, her own gaze clear. There was no way she was going to say anything about what Elsie had said to her. She wasn't about to get her friend into trouble. 'Sounds serious, Uncle.'

'Oh, it is, lass. Which is why I've been reluctant to let you get involved.'

She raised her eyebrows, but tamped down hard on her growing excitement. Instinct told her it wouldn't do to let him know what she was thinking. She must have given it away though, because she saw the hint of amusement in his regard.

'You've *been* reluctant?' she observed with a small smile. 'Does that mean you've changed your mind?'

He scratched at his cheek. 'Not willingly,' he conceded. 'If I could, I'd keep you and all the family well away from anything to do with the war, lass. But with the threat of invasion growing, we need to be prepared, and you've made it quite clear that you'd like to do something to help.' He reached into his jacket and pulled a sheaf of papers out of his inside pocket and placed them on the table in front of her. 'This is the Official Secrets Act. I want you to take your time and read it through carefully. If you believe you can adhere to its conditions, then you have the opportunity to sign it or not, it's up to you. If you do, then I can tell you something about how you can help the war effort. But if you choose not to, then we'll forget we ever had this conversation and that will be the end of it. Whatever you do, you must never discuss this with another living soul. Not family nor friends. Lives could depend upon it.'

She could see that he was in deadly earnest, which cooled her excitement a little. But not by much. This is what she wanted. To do something – anything – to help the war effort. 'Do you have a pen, Uncle?' she asked, ready to sign straight away.

He shook his head. 'Not yet, lass. Take your time to read what it says and think about it. Then if you still want to do this, sign it and bring it to my house tomorrow after four o'clock. Be discreet when you pass it to me, signed or unsigned. There's no need for anyone else to see it, d'you understand?'

She nodded. She could imagine what Ma, Pa and Aunt Kate would have to say about it.

He stood up, checking his watch. 'Right, I need to be off. I'm teaching in less than an hour. I'll see you tomorrow.'

She got up and saw him to the front door.

'Remember, you don't have to do this,' he reminded her. 'I know the family would rather you didn't.'

'I know. But if none of us did, we'd be in a right pickle, wouldn't we?'

'Maybe,' he conceded. 'We'll have to see.'

When he'd gone, she gathered up the papers and ran upstairs to her room, where she hid them under her pillow. She would take her time and read them tonight after work. She was almost certain she would sign them, but she appreciated that Uncle Ted wanted her to be aware of the gravity of what she was agreeing to. She had no idea what he would be asking her to do, but if it would help win the war against Hitler and his evil allies, then she would do it, whatever the cost.

25

January passed into February and the cold and rain didn't let up and nor did the battles in the skies night after night as the RAF and the ground-based anti-aircraft gun emplacements fought to stop the Luftwaffe raining terror down on the country. There was no news of Rose's brother Michael. Patrick was transferred to a hospital on the British mainland and was recovering from his injuries, although he was too far away from Rose to go and see him for herself.

'Did you hear?' said Mrs Morgan as Rose came into the farmhouse kitchen after morning milking. 'Buckingham Palace has been bombed, and on Friday the thirteenth as well. I heard it on the radio.'

'Oh my lord,' said Rose, pulling off her gloves and putting them on the range to dry off and warm up. 'Even the King and Queen aren't safe. They haven't killed them, have they?'

'No, lass. They're safe. But they say they're refusing to leave London, even though the government is asking them to. The Queen refused to go without the King and he won't budge. They took themselves off to the East End to see what the Nazis have done to the folk down there. Apparently the Queen said now the palace had been bombed she felt she could look these good people in the eye. Bless her heart. Such a brave woman.'

Rose helped herself to a bowl of porridge as Mrs Morgan poured her a cup of tea. She wasn't sure whether the royal family were brave or just plain stubborn. Most folks didn't have much choice but to stay where they were because they couldn't afford to leave.

Mrs Morgan pottered around the kitchen while Rose finished her breakfast. When she'd finished, she quickly washed her bowl and cup.

'I'd better get back. Do you know where Mr Morgan is? I'm not sure what he wants me to do today.'

'Ah, he's gone over to Shapwick with Jimmy and a couple of the hands while Ivor does some deliveries for me. There's a chap over there with some cattle stranded after the rains. The moors over that way have flooded and the beasts took themselves off to an island and now they can't get back. If they can't be moved, the men'll have to get some feed across to 'em. It's beef cattle, so at least they won't need milking.'

'Oh. Right. So what should I do today?' At this time of year there wasn't much growing in the fields but there was always something to do on the farm such as building maintenance, clearing the rhynes, and ploughing fields ready for planting when the ground wasn't frozen, as well as looking after the livestock.

'Can you give me a hand in the dairy? I've butter to churn and cheeses to check. I know it's boring work, but you'll be out of the cold wind, lass. With the two of us we'll manage to finish early, so you could have the afternoon off if you like?'

It wasn't her usual day off, but Rose was happy to have some unexpected free time. 'All right,' she said.

It was nice to be working with another woman for a change,

and Rose enjoyed the older woman's chatter and two pairs of hands made sure they finished quickly.

They were done by eleven, so she spent an hour in the office. She'd been working her way through the crammed drawers in the desk, throwing out old papers that were too old to be of any use. The only one left was the bottom drawer on the left. When she tried to open it, she realised it was locked.

Frowning, she thought for a bit. She had seen a key in a tin on the shelf above the desk with some paper clips and hadn't known what it was for, so she'd left it there. She wondered now if it would fit this lock?

Sure enough, it fitted and the lock opened smoothly. Rose opened the drawer, expecting it to be crammed full of the same rubbish she'd cleared out of the others, but there was barely anything in it.

'What on earth is this?' she muttered, picking up the green coloured booklets resting in there. '*The Countryman's Diary 1937,*' she read. '*Sponsored by Highworth Fertilizers.*' That was odd. She hadn't seen any paperwork mentioning that company. The Morgans get their fertilizer from a local company. She'd seen the invoices. The other booklet was buff coloured and was a diary from 1938 with the same sponsor. Maybe a salesman had been visiting in the hope of gaining a new customer and left the calendars. But why put them in a locked drawer?

She had just flicked open the first one when the door opened. She glanced up. Jimmy stood there. 'Oh, it's you. Did you get the cattle off the island?'

He nodded, his gaze on the booklets in her hands. 'Where'd you get those?' he asked.

'They were in the bottom drawer here. Your ma asked me to chuck out anything we didn't need. I don't suppose a couple of old calendars are of any use now, are they?' She flicked another page over and glanced down, but she didn't have a chance to register the contents before Jimmy was standing right in front of her, his hand snatching them from hers.

'You're right,' he said. 'Don't know why we kept 'em. I'll chuck 'em on the fire.' He turned away and was heading out of the door before she could draw breath. 'You've done a good job in here. The place is looking a lot tidier. Don't work too hard.'

'All right, thanks,' she said, amused and pleased by his words. 'Were you coming in here for a reason?'

'Nothing important,' he said, not looking round as he strode away down the hall towards the kitchen.

Rose sat down, frowning. Something was off. Jimmy rarely came near the office when she was there, and he'd never complimented her on a job well done before. It was strange that he was so keen to take those booklets off to burn when there was an even bigger pile for burning on top of the desk. Maybe she should've said something.

She was still thinking about it when she heard the back door slam. No doubt Jimmy was going back to work. She sighed and stood up, going into the kitchen to get a cup of camp coffee. The old paraffin heater in the office kept the chill out, but she still wasn't warm, so she fancied a hot drink. She put the kettle on the range and decided to put some more wood on the fire. It wasn't until she was staring into the flames that she realised there were none of the usual tell-tale signs that any paper had been burnt there in the few minutes between Jimmy leaving the office and her getting to the kitchen.

What had he done with the booklets? And why was she sure that the one word she'd read of the text inside the one she'd opened was *gelignite*? She might be a city girl but even she knew that that wasn't a fertilizer. She shook her head. She must have imagined it. She had to stop thinking so badly of Jimmy and thinking she was finding sinister things when it was clear it was just some old calendar that was no good to man nor beast. It was strange though. Maybe she should ask him what he'd done with them when she saw him later. She turned back to the range to lift the kettle and make her drink.

* * *

Jimmy walked quickly towards the elm woods, cursing. He'd thought the booklets would be safe in the locked drawer. But then Ma had mentioned she'd asked Rose to clear out the desk and he'd known she'd not be stopped by a lock. He ran an agitated hand through his hair. He should've just ignored them and let her shove them on the pile of other rubbish, but she'd been in the process of opening one of them. If she'd seen what was in there it would've been disastrous. He paused as he reached the woods, more cautious now so that he could avoid the traps and trip wires the unit had set up to deter folk from walking through there.

Leaning against a tree, he pulled out his cigarettes and lit up. He took his time smoking and thinking. When he was done, he stubbed out the butt and buried it. No point in letting people see he'd been there. As he stood he pulled the booklets out of his inside pocket. It had been a good idea of the powers that be, making their instruction manuals look like old calendars. They said the reason was that if the enemy came searching, they would dismiss an old calendar as nothing of interest. But it seemed they hadn't taken into account inquisitive girls like Rose, who just had to open it and have a look.

He grimaced, wondering whether he had to report what had happened. They were supposed to keep them safe, and he was sure they were in that locked drawer. But in hindsight, he realised he should've kept the key with him instead of in the paperclip tin.

He hoped he'd acted quickly enough that she hadn't seen anything she shouldn't. She didn't need to know that she'd had the auxiliary unit's bomb-making instruction manuals in her hand.

He'd have to think on it. He didn't want to get himself or Rose in trouble. He needed to find another hiding place for the booklets as well. Maybe somewhere away from the farmhouse. There was already a copy at the arms cache. In the meantime, he had better get on.

* * *

After Rose had had a quick meat paste sandwich for her dinner, it was just gone one o'clock. She'd missed the bus going through to Bridgewater and it wouldn't be coming back towards Street and Glastonbury for another hour, so she decided it wasn't worth hanging around for it as by the time she got anywhere it would almost be time to turn round and come back again to do the evening milking. She'd have a quick walk and then return and read a magazine in comfort.

She wished she had a little motorcycle so that she could explore the area without having to walk everywhere, but thought it might be too much trouble. Getting a petrol ration would be difficult if she couldn't justify the journeys she would take. She wondered how Jimmy got away with it. He was always riding off on his motorcycle. Her regular worry that he was doing something he ought not to niggled at her again but she tamped it down, unwilling to spoil her unexpected break with thoughts of him.

She set out on her walk, her gas mask box over her shoulder. She put her purse in there as well, in case she decided to go to the village shop on the way home. Her back and shoulders were aching from churning butter and rotating wheels of cheese that were maturing on shelves in the cold room behind the dairy. Until she'd come to Somerset, she'd been used to getting those products from the local grocery shop. It had never occurred to her how much work went into making them.

She set off, heading up the lane towards the main road. As the lower moors were flooded and she would be heading back down to the fields where the Morgans' cows were currently grazing on the edge of the moor later, she decided to climb up to the ridge where the main road ran. From there she would have a good view of the countryside, right across to Glastonbury Tor, over six miles away.

At the top, she stuck to the edge of the elm woodland where she had a measure of shelter from the bitter wind. She knew that Mr Morgan had warned her about animal traps up here, so she kept a careful eye on where she trod. High overhead, she saw planes going east. She felt the familiar dread in the pit of her stomach as she stopped and watched them. It took a little while for her to establish that they were Spitfires, and therefore friendly. She leaned against a tree trunk, watching them through the branches. When spring came she wouldn't be able to see them for leaves, but today she had a good view of the planes against the clear blue of the winter sky. She hoped that all of them got home safe from wherever they were going.

It made her think about her brother Declan who was in the RAF. She had no clue where he was. All she knew was that he was working on the engineering side of maintaining planes. Whether that was on an airfield in Britain or abroad, she had no idea.

With her thoughts on her brother, Rose nearly missed the movement further in the woodland. She caught it out the corner of her eye. Frowning, she turned her head to see a man emerge from the undergrowth about twenty yards from where she was. She wondered if he was an old tramp who'd fallen asleep, but then she saw that he was cleanshaven and quite young. She recognised him as the son of the neighbouring farmer. She froze, not wanting to be discovered watching. This must be the poacher Mr Morgan had warned her about. Another man emerged behind the first, rising up out of the ground. She couldn't work out where he'd come from until she saw them pull something and what she realised was a trap door camouflaged by ground-hugging plants slid silently across to cover the hole they'd emerged from. As soon as it was shut, it became hidden in the undergrowth. If she hadn't seen them with her own eyes, Rose wouldn't have known there was anything there, it was that well concealed.

She didn't move, holding her breath for fear that she would give herself away as the two of them stood there, chatting and sharing a cigarette. She was reluctant to let them know she was there because she recognised them. It was Jimmy and the lad from the Armitage farm next door. There was something decidedly odd about this situation. What were they doing, hiding underground like that? And why would they be poaching from their own fathers?

She wished she had the courage to show herself and challenge them, but she wasn't that foolish. Whatever they were doing, they were trying to keep it a secret. While she might have managed to fight off one, she didn't fancy her chances against two. So she stayed as still as she could, hoping they'd either go back inside their lair or leave sometime soon. She began to feel quite light-headed. As the two men laughed over some joke between them, she slowly let out the breath she'd been holding, hoping they didn't turn and notice the steamy condensation forming around her head as her warm breath met the cold air.

Then she slowly inhaled. It wouldn't do her any good to faint and fall in a heap where they could see her.

After what seemed like ages, but was probably not that long, they finished the cigarette and finally walked away down the hill, leaving Rose watching after them, wondering whether she had the courage to check out their hideaway.

She didn't move until they were long gone, scared that they'd turn around and see her. She was freezing by now, having stood so still, and her toes felt numb as she walked slowly towards the spot where she'd seen them emerge. She spotted one trip wire and carefully stepped over it.

She looked around, listening for any sign that they might be coming back. But it was silent in the woodland. Even the planes overhead had disappeared. She might have missed the concealed lever under a fallen log that opened the trapdoor if the stupid idiots hadn't thrown down the cigarette butt at their feet when they'd been standing right next to it. With her hand on the lever, she hesitated. What if there was someone else inside? She listened, wondering whether there was another man hiding down there, listening to her movements? What should she do?

She had a choice. She could pull on the lever and go down and see what they'd been up to. If they were poachers or spies then she would need to take something from their hideout to prove her case. If they were black marketeers, then the same logic applied. She looked around again. She would need to make careful note of where this place was as well, so that she could lead someone back here. Her other option was to simply note the location and run like billy-o, and let the authorities deal with it.

The latter was the safest choice, no doubt. But now that Rose knew it was there, she just *had* to see what was inside.

After another careful look around, she took a deep breath and pulled the lever. The trapdoor opened silently to reveal a shaft with a metal ladder. She reached into her coat pocket and pulled out her torch. She kept it there because she hated going out to the privy in the dark without it. She shone the beam down the shaft, still listening for signs of occupancy. It remained still and silent all around her, as though the world was holding its breath.

Rose climbed down the ladder. At the bottom, she saw another lever, which she pulled. The trapdoor above her closed, leaving her alone in the silence. She felt a shiver go down her spine and hoped like heck that she wouldn't be trapped down there.

She shone the torch around her before following a short passage to a metal door. Again, she paused and listened. Silence. With trembling hands, she opened the door and gasped.

The chamber was filled with rough shelves, upon which were large cans marked with skulls and crossbones to indicate that their contents were poisonous; others were marked *kerosene* and *paraffin;* there were also crates marked in chalk: *fuses, grenades, bullets, gelignite.* At the end of the room was a rack of guns. She sank down onto a bench and stared around.

'Oh God. They really are spies,' she whispered. Only an enemy would be stockpiling all these weapons. The realisation felt like the sharp pain of a dagger plunging into her heart.

The pain set her in motion. She reached into the first two crates, pulling out a grenade and some fuses and stuffing them into her pockets. Then she whirled away, rushing back down the passage, pulling on the lever and clambering out of the bunker as quickly as she could. She barely remembered to close it behind her before she was running – not back to the farm, but in the opposite direction towards the road.

She had to report this. She had to stop Jimmy Morgan and his accomplice from committing treason.

26

Elsie was just taking a document out of her typewriter when Jameson came into her office. She smiled. He often popped in to see her and his gentle flirtation always brought colour to her cheeks.

But today he looked more concerned than flirty.

'Sorry to bother you,' he said. 'But there's a land girl called Rose at the door asking to speak to you. She says it's important.'

She frowned. 'Goodness!' What on earth could Rose want?

'Shall I bring her in?'

She glanced at the CO's door and wondered whether she'd get into trouble, letting a civilian into the office. But Rose's appearance here was so unusual, she really ought to find out what she wanted. 'I'll come out,' she said. 'I'm due a tea break.'

When Elsie got to the entrance lobby where her friend waited, Rose let out a sigh of relief.

'Oh, thank goodness you're here,' she said. 'I didn't know who else to turn to. You'll know what to do.'

'What's wrong?' Elsie asked. 'You look like you've run all the way here.'

Rose nodded. 'I managed to catch the bus as it came through, but yes, I did run a long way before it turned up and I rushed here from the bus stop. You need to get someone out there as soon as possible.'

'Out where? Rose, you're not making any sense. What's happened? Has a plane come down on the farm or something? Why didn't anyone telephone?'

Rose shook her head. 'No, it's not that. It... it's worse than that and I couldn't use the telephone at the farm – I don't know if they're in on it or not. Oh, lord... I won't be able to go back there, will I?' Tears welled and overflowed. 'You've got to help me, Elsie. It's terrible.'

She put an arm around the distressed girl's shoulders. 'Hush now, don't cry. You need to tell me what's going on, Rose.'

Rose took a shaky breath and nodded. She scrubbed the tears from her face and glanced at Jameson, who was watching them with interest, and away again. 'Can we talk in private?' she asked. 'I don't know who we can trust.' She turned her back on the soldier and pulled open her pocket, indicating that Elsie should look inside.

Elsie gasped and her eyes widened when she saw the grenade in her friend's coat pocket. She looked over her shoulder at Charles. 'Thank you, Lieutenant,' she said.

'See you later?' he asked.

'I'm not sure,' she said. 'Maybe tomorrow?' She didn't wait for him to reply before turning away. 'Rose, where did you get that?' she asked softly, steering her friend out of the lobby and towards her office.

'In an underground bunker in the woods,' she whispered. 'I saw two men coming out of it and went in to see what they were up to. There's guns and ammunition and fuel and all sorts of things. I'm sure they're planning something terrible.'

'You went inside?' Elsie was horrified. Rose could have compromised the whole operation.

Rose nodded again. 'I wanted to bring you proof. There are spies operating in the woods above the farm and I know who they are.' When they reached Elsie's office and closed the door behind them, she reached into her pockets and brought out the grenade and fuses she'd stolen. She put them carefully on Elsie's desk and stepped back. She looked at her friend. 'I came straight here. I didn't dare go back to the farm. You'll know who this should be reported to, won't you?'

She ushered her friend into a seat by her desk and sat opposite her, holding her hands. 'Tell me what happened, Rose. I need to know what you saw and heard.'

Within minutes, Elsie knew she couldn't shield her friend. 'Can you wait here a minute? I need to have a quick word with my CO. He's going to want to speak with you.'

Rose nodded and slumped back in her chair. 'All right. I thought I'd have to. I was just worried that no one would believe me. But these are proof, aren't they?' she asked, pointing to the items on Elsie's desk.

'Yes,' she agreed, picking up the grenade and fuses as she stood up. 'I won't be a minute.'

She was reluctant to leave her friend, but had no choice. She was only glad that she'd come here and not to the nearest police station. At least they could take steps to ensure the network of Auxiliers in the area wasn't compromised. She knocked on the CO's door and entered as soon as he granted permission.

'I'm sorry, sir, but we've got a bit of a situation,' she said, carefully placing Rose's booty on his desk. 'My friend Rose has found an arms cache out at Catcott. She's come here to report the presence of spies in the area.'

'Has she now?' he said, regarding the items with interest. 'She went inside?' She nodded. 'But she wasn't spotted?'

'I don't think so, sir. She came straight here.'

'Mmm. Who did she see?'

'Jimmy Morgan and another man who she thinks she recognised from a neighbouring farm.'

'Where is she?'

'In my office, sir.'

He nodded. 'Give me a few minutes to make a phone call, then I'll need to speak to her. Maybe take her into the break room and make her a cup of tea, then bring her in here. I wouldn't mind a fresh cup as well.'

'Yes, sir.'

'Oh, and Bloomfield,' he said as she reached for the door handle.

'Yes, sir?'

'Don't discuss it with her. We'll need to get her to sign the Official Secrets Act before we take this any further. Get the forms ready.'

'Of course.'

* * *

Rose looked up when Elsie came back into the room.

'My CO wants to talk to you, Rose,' she told her. 'Come with me and we'll make some tea before you go in and meet him.'

Rose bit her lip. 'I'm in trouble, aren't I?' she asked as she followed her friend to the break room where she set out making a pot of tea.

Elsie shook her head. 'Of course not. Why would you think that?'

She shrugged. 'I don't know. I just feel like this is really serious and if they arrest Jimmy, the Morgans aren't going to want me back at the farm, are they? If he's a traitor, he could hang, couldn't he?' She felt sick to her stomach. 'For all the aggravation there's been between me and Jimmy, I never truly believed he was a real bad'un until I saw the evidence for myself.' She scrubbed at her eyes. They felt gritty. She hoped she wasn't going to burst into tears. 'His poor mammy and daddy. It'll break their hearts.' She wouldn't admit that her own heart was breaking right now.

Elsie patted her arm. 'I can't discuss it with you, but don't fret. Wait until you've spoken to the CO. Now, come on, I've just got to type up a quick form for him and then we'll take in the tea. Don't worry, I'm sure it will be all right.'

Rose wasn't convinced and she continued to fret as Elsie completed her task and whipped the document out and put it into a folder. She knew it had been her duty to report what she'd seen, but if she were honest, she'd hoped that Elsie would tell her there was a perfectly reasonable explanation for what she'd seen and that it wasn't as bad as she thought it was. She really didn't want to think that Jimmy would do something as terrible as treason; not the lad who'd held her while she cried over her brothers, or the same one who had kissed her so softly – twice! It just didn't make sense. She knew he could be a miserable beggar sometimes, but that didn't mean he would betray his country, did it? But then what about those booklets she'd found and the fact that she thought she'd seen the word gelignite in one and Jimmy had whisked them away before she could check?

Elsie knocked on the captain's door and waited for permission to enter. When it was granted, she opened the door and ushered Rose in.

Rose gulped as she went in to face Elsie's boss. Her friend followed her and put the tray and folder on his desk. He rose from his chair and held out his hand.

'You must be Rose,' he said. 'Thank you for coming in today. I'm interested to hear about your adventure.'

She shook his hand, feeling the strength behind his grip. He was a tall man, about forty or so. Despite his charming smile, Rose felt that she was being judged by his shrewd eyes. 'Nice to meet you, sir. I'm sorry to arrive without an appointment.'

'We're always available to see anyone who might have vital information for the war effort,' he said, indicating that she should take a seat opposite him. 'And you're just in time for afternoon tea.'

Elsie was already pouring and handed Rose a cup of tea before she served the CO. 'Would you like me to stay, sir?'

He shook his head. 'That won't be necessary. The captain will be arriving soon. Can you send him in as soon as he arrives, please?'

Rose felt a little panicky when Elsie nodded and left the room. She had hoped that her friend could stay with her but of course she would have to follow orders. She wondered who the captain he mentioned was. The more officers who needed to hear her story, the more serious the situation seemed. She was beginning to feel real fear that her eavesdropping and search of the underground bunker might well lead to a death sentence for Jimmy and while part of her was angry with him and felt he should face the consequences of his actions, another part of her was horrified that she might be condemning him when he'd showed himself to bc kind and caring when she'd needed it most. She picked up her cup with both hands, hoping that she wouldn't reveal how badly she was shaking.

When the door closed behind Elsie, the CO turned his attention to her. He held up the grenade and fuses. 'Before we begin, can you confirm to me that these are the only items you removed from the bunker?'

She nodded. 'I wanted to show you proof,' she said. 'In case I couldn't find it again, or they realised that I'd seen them and they moved it all out.'

'Very wise, my dear.' He smiled, putting them to one side. 'Now, before we can discuss this, I need to ask you to sign this document.' He took some papers out of the folder Elsie had given him and offered them to her.

She put down her cup and reached for them. 'What is it?' she asked.

'It's the Official Secrets Act. By signing it, you're pledging to keep everything we discuss today to yourself. You must not discuss it with anyone else – not Bloomfield, your family, your employers or your friends.'

'But I already told Elsie,' she said. 'I'm sorry. I didn't know who else to turn to.'

He gave her a reassuring smile. 'You did the right thing, Rose – it is all right if I call you Rose? Or would you prefer Miss Flaherty?'

She felt a bit discombobulated by his charming manner. She knew this was serious because why else would they ask her to sign the Official Secrets Act? Yet he seemed so calm, not as scary as she'd expected.

'Rose is fine,' she said.

'Good. Now, in signing this document, Rose, you will be making a solemn promise to keep the government's secrets. Can we rely upon you to live up to that promise?'

She nodded. 'I promise,' she said.

He handed her a pen. 'Take your time and read it first, my dear.'

She skimmed the papers, frowning a little at the official language, but she got the gist of it. She was required to keep the secrets she might be privy to and if she didn't she would be liable for prosecution and the penalties would be severe. 'But if I haven't done anything wrong,' she said under her breath as she read it, 'I shouldn't have to go to prison.'

'Quite right,' he said, making her jump when she realised he'd heard her. 'No one is planning on sending you to prison for what you've discovered today, Rose. We just need to ensure that you realise the importance of secrecy before we discuss what happened.'

Once she had finished reading it, she signed it where he indicated. It struck her as odd that he already had her name and the address of the farm typed at the top of the form. That must have been what Elsie had been typing.

The CO gathered up the papers and returned them to the file. Her throat suddenly dry, Rose picked up her cup again and drank some tea. She had just put it down on the saucer when there was another knock at the door. Rose jumped at the sound. She breathed a sigh of relief that she'd put her drink down, otherwise she might have thrown it all over herself.

'Come,' called the CO.

The door opened and the man she recognised as Daisy's godfather entered. He was in mufti, wearing a tweed jacket with leather patches on the elbows.

'You wanted to see me?' he said to the other man. 'I got the impression it was urgent, so I came straight from school.'

The CO nodded. 'I believe you've met Miss Flaherty – Rose – before?'

He came further into the room, studying her with interest. 'Ah, yes. The land girl who broke her ankle. You're good friends with my goddaughter now, I believe.'

'That's right, sir,' she said, trying but failing to give him a shy smile.

Seeing her discomfort, Ted Jackson glanced at the CO with raised eyebrows.

'Sit down, Captain. Rose was just about to tell me how she discovered a bunker in the woods above Catcott.' He pointed to the grenade and fuses. 'She brought us these as proof and has identified some men she saw leaving the bunker.'

'Ah,' he said, sitting next to her and studying her with interest. 'I'd be interested to hear that as well.'

Rose took a deep breath and began to tell them about what she'd seen. They asked the occasional question, but otherwise let her recount the story in her own words.

* * *

Elsie stayed at her desk, wishing she knew what was going on in the CO's office. She wished she'd been allowed to stay in there to offer Rose some moral support, but she understood that it was probably best that Rose didn't become aware just how involved in the auxiliary unit network Elsie really was. Just because her friend had found out about Jimmy and his unit's weapons cache, it didn't mean she should be allowed to know *everything*. Even Elsie's knowledge of the units operating in the area was limited to what she needed to know in order to do her job. She only knew that Jimmy was involved because she'd recognised him when she'd visited his OB and trained him and his comrades to use their radio. She didn't know the names of any of the other men in his unit, just their code names for communications purposes. In the event of an invasion, the less she knew about the identities of Auxiliers and the locations of OBs and arms stores, the better.

It therefore followed that the less Rose knew, the better. Otherwise, if either of them were captured and interrogated, they could jeopardise the lives of each other and everyone in the network.

She hoped that the CO and the captain were reassuring Rose, though. She was obviously very upset at the thought of Jimmy being a traitor and if he had truly been one, Elsie dreaded to think about the consequences. No wonder poor Rose was worried about going back to the farm.

It was a good half an hour before the CO came out of the room. Elsie wanted to ask him what was happening in there, but she didn't dare.

'Bloomfield, I need you to call the Morgan farm and the Armitage farm and get Jimmy Morgan and Stephen Armitage over here.'

'What shall I tell them, sir?' she asked, reaching for the telephone directory.

'Just say I have an urgent mission for them.'

27

Rose's head was spinning as she sat in the back of the staff car while Elsie drove her into Street. They decided she should be prepared to duck down behind the driver's seat if Jimmy was spotted coming the other way on his motorcycle.

'Are you all right, Rose?' asked Elsie, watching her in the rear-view mirror.

'Yeah,' she sighed. 'I feel a bit daft, though. I know we're not supposed to discuss it, but how the heck could I have got it so wrong?'

Elsie chuckled. 'Don't beat yourself up about it. You weren't to know. You did the right thing, although going into the bunker might have been a dangerous move if there'd been someone else there.'

'I know,' she groaned, covering her face. 'My brothers are always saying I'm too nosy for my own good. Once I saw them come out, I had to take a peek inside. I wasn't expecting what I saw, though.' She put her hands down. 'But now I've signed those papers and I've got to shut up and keep my nose out of it.' She shook her head and caught Elsie's eye in the mirror. 'I won't ask how much you know about it. You did try to warn me, didn't you?'

Elsie shrugged, keeping her focus on the road ahead. 'I couldn't possibly comment,' she said.

'Of course you can't,' grumbled Rose. 'But next time you suggest I don't know what I'm talking about, I promise I'll listen, all right?'

They got as far as Walton Church without seeing Jimmy and Elsie dropped her off at the bus stop there. She stood waiting for the bus, sure that at any moment Jimmy would appear on his motorbike and demand to know where she had been, but she didn't see him before the bus arrived.

She sat by the window, her mind awhirl. The officers who'd spoken to her hadn't told her much, but they had confirmed that Jimmy wasn't a spy but was in fact part of a special group of men who were preparing to go underground to work behind the lines if the Germans invaded. They'd told her that not even Mr and Mrs Morgan knew about this and reminded her that the document she'd signed meant she couldn't tell anyone – not even Jimmy, nor his parents when the invasion happened and he disappeared to keep the fight going. It would put them at risk.

The little they had told her made perfect sense. Despite complaining about him and saying she thought he was up to no good, Rose had been sure deep down that he wasn't really that sort of chap. Despite his arrogance and grumpiness, she thought he was an honest man. She'd been so upset, seeing him and that bunker this afternoon, sure that it proved she'd been wrong about him. She could hardly believe how relieved she'd been to learn that he was in fact a loyal soldier, ready to lay down his life if need be.

It had been such an incredible revelation that it had set her head spinning. So much so that, when they asked if she had any more questions, she'd blurted out that she wanted to do her bit as well.

As soon as she'd said it, she expected them to tell her to forget about it and go back to being a land girl and leave it up to the men. But, to her shock, they hadn't done that.

'Good lass,' Captain Jackson had said. 'Your actions today show that you're bright and resourceful. You won't be expected to fight in the same way as our Auxiliers, but there are other things, vital things, that you can do to support them. Now, we need to get you back to the farm before Jimmy arrives here. Give the Morgans a call from the telephone in Elsie's office. You can tell them you were visiting Daisy and forgot the time. Remember, don't discuss any of this with him, with Elsie or anyone else. We'll be in touch.'

So here she was, heading back to Catcott with the knowledge that Jimmy was likely a hero even though no one else knew about it, and she had been recruited to do her part in the defence of Britain in the awful event of an invasion.

Mammy and Daddy would be furious, and then they'd worry themselves sick, she thought. *It's just as well I can't tell them. But if what I do can help keep them safe, then I'll do whatever is necessary.*

28

Jimmy was furious. No one knew where that damned land girl had gone so he'd had to do the milking, and now he'd been summoned to the area headquarters. He had no idea why they'd called him in because Ma had taken the message. So he'd had a quick wash and put on his uniform before leaving the farm. He hoped he didn't still smell of cows. He'd have a few choice words to say to Rose when she got back – she'd called and spoken to Ma just before he left to say she'd forgotten the time.

He thought about Rose as he wheeled his motorcycle out of the barn. He wouldn't admit to himself that he'd been worried about her. After her accident a few months back, he'd felt guilty that he'd left her alone for so long before going to check on her. It hadn't made him any kinder to her, but she'd held her own against him and as time had gone by he'd begun to respect her and enjoy their encounters. When she'd come home with that doctor fellow, he'd been shocked by how jealous he'd felt. He shouldn't have kissed her then, but he hadn't known what else to do. He'd just been so riled up at the thought of another man kissing her. Then earlier today he'd acted like an idiot, snatching the 'calendars' out of her hand and rushing off with them. He'd realised later that he should've asked if there were any other papers that needed burning. That would've put her off the scent. He was pretty sure she hadn't had a chance to see the contents of the booklets, but if she had, his grabbing like that would've made things worse.

And now she'd *'forgotten the time'* when she should have been back to do the milking. Was she running from him? Was she with that other fellow? Or had she met someone else? He'd thought they were getting on all right since she'd come back from Birmingham. He hadn't complained when she'd cried all over him. He thought he'd been quite kind to her, although he'd felt pretty inadequate in the face of her distress.

Well, if she was going to be unreliable, it would be better if they sent her back to Birmingham. He refused to acknowledge the ache in his chest at the thought of her leaving for good. It would be for the best. He couldn't get involved with any lass at the moment. When the Nazis invaded, he had a job to do that meant he'd have to walk away from everyone he knew and loved in order to keep them safe. Rose was a distraction he couldn't afford to have.

He parked his motorcycle and went into the offices at Edgely Hall. It was gone six in the evening, so he expected the place to be deserted. But a soldier was waiting at the door to lead him through to the CO's office. Stephen Armitage was already there.

'Ah, Morgan, here you are,' the CO greeted him. Captain Jackson stood by the window. He was in mufti. 'Come in and close the door.'

Jimmy did as he was told and took a seat next to Armitage when the CO pointed to it.

'I expect you're wondering why I called you both in this evening?'

'Yes, sir. Are the rest of the unit coming? Have we got another mission?'

The CO shook his head. 'Not a mission as such tonight. You'll rendezvous with the rest of your unit later. No, we've called you in today because your arms cache has been compromised.'

Jimmy frowned. 'But... are you sure? Only we was there earlier, sir, and nothing was amiss, was it?' he asked the other lad.

'No. It was dead quiet,' he said.

'So we understand,' said Captain Jackson. 'Unfortunately, you were careless leaving it and someone saw you both.'

He felt a chill run down his spine. 'What? We didn't see anyone.'

'Clearly not,' said the CO. 'But someone was observing you. And whoever dropped their cigarette butt on the ground right next to the access lever was beyond careless. It led the observer straight to your entrance.'

Jimmy grimaced. He hadn't dropped it, but he'd shared the smoke. 'Sorry, sir. We should've made sure we didn't leave anything like that around. We'll make sure it doesn't happen again.'

Stephen nodded but didn't say anything.

'Good. Make sure it doesn't. If it had been a German spy watching, you could have been in serious danger. As it is, you'll need to move the arms store to another location. I've informed your sergeant. It will have to be a priority.'

Jimmy wanted to groan. Digging out the bunkers for the OB and the arms store had been back-breaking work over several nights, even with the help of a team of army sappers. None of the unit would be happy about having to do it again, but he understood the reason for it. 'Yes, sir,' he said.

He glanced at the captain. He'd somehow found their operations base and Jimmy still hadn't worked out how he'd done that.

Had he also found out where the arms cache was? But the older man looked like he'd come straight to HQ from the school where he worked, so it wasn't likely to have been him who had seen them in the woods this afternoon, was it? It might have been the CO. He knew where the OB was, but as far as Jimmy knew he hadn't seen the location of this arms cache. If it had been him, Jimmy didn't understand why he'd wait until now to call them in about it.

'Who was it who saw us, sir?' Armitage asked.

The CO gave him a cool look. 'Who it was is irrelevant. The fact that you were seen is the important issue here. You're also damned lucky that they reported directly to me and not to the local authorities. Your carelessness could have compromised the whole network.'

For a moment, Jimmy wondered whether Rose had followed him. But Ma had said she'd gone to see the Selway girl at Walton, and anyway, Pa had warned her off going into the woods, so it couldn't have been her.

'Yes, sir, sorry, sir,' he said.

Jimmy was angry with him for even asking the question. The CO was right. This was bad and could have proved fatal if an enemy had spotted them. Whoever it was wasn't important. That they were careless enough to be seen leaving their arms cache was what really mattered.

'You'll both need to be more vigilant from now on,' said the captain.

Jimmy nodded. He was glad he wasn't the only one getting it in the neck, but if he had, he would have thought twice about ratting on a comrade. They had been telling them all along that the unit members needed to protect each other at all costs. It wouldn't look good if Jimmy had started blaming the other lad, even though he'd been the one to toss his cigarette butt on the ground. It was such a stupid thing to do, Jimmy was mentally kicking himself for not noticing and making sure he'd picked it up or buried it. All the work they'd done to camouflage the bunkers would count for nothing if they left butts and boot-marks on the ground outside them.

The CO checked his watch. 'Right, you need to get along to your OB where your sergeant is looking at possible new locations for the arms cache. Dismissed.'

They stood and saluted and Armitage gave him a rueful look before he preceded him out of the room. As the lad left, the captain gave Jimmy a narrow-eyed stare. 'I hope that you've learned an important lesson from this, Morgan. You're showing signs of becoming a valuable Auxilier and I've had good reports of you on your missions. But silly mistakes like this could cost lives in the event of an invasion, so make sure it doesn't happen again.'

'Yes, sir. I've definitely learned my lesson.'

'Good. Off you go then. You've work to do.'

* * *

Back at the farm, Rose made her apologies to the Morgans, promising not to do it again. She hoped they never thought to check her story with Daisy because the men she'd spoken with had told her not to mention today to her friend, so she would be unaware that Rose had used her as an excuse.

She ate her supper in silence, not feeling hungry at all, but aware that it was wrong to waste food in these days of rationing. Mrs Morgan was already fretting about Jimmy missing his evening meal.

'He got called out by the Home Guard for something and had to rush off on that motorcycle of his. I don't know why they sent him off to another unit when we've got one right here in the village. Whoever's running his mob seem to be a bit big for their boots, telephoning and demanding his presence at the drop of a hat. The local guards are much better organised. At least they allow a man time to eat his daily bread before keeping them out all hours.'

Now that she knew a little about the important work that Jimmy was really doing, she found it hard to know what to say to Mrs Morgan. But she had promised to keep the secret, so she gave the older woman an apologetic smile. 'I'm sorry, it's my fault for missing the milking. Jimmy could've had his supper if he hadn't had to cover for me. I'll apologise to him as well. If there's anything I can do to make up for it, I will, I promise, and I won't do it again.'

Mrs Morgan sighed. 'What's done is done. We all make mistakes, lass. I'm just glad you were able to telephone to let us know you were all right. I was fretting that you'd had another accident.'

'I'm so sorry,' she said, blinking away tears.

'Ah, don't upset yourself, now. So long as you don't make a habit of it, the odd mistake isn't going to kill us, is it?'

She rubbed her eyes. 'I suppose not.' She sighed. 'I've got a bit of a headache. Would you mind if I went to bed?'

'Of course not, lass. You're looking a bit peaky. You're not sickening for something are you?'

'No, I just feel bad about letting you down. I'm sure I'll be all right after a good night's sleep.'

'Right, well you get off to bed then, lass, and we'll see you in the morning.'

In the privacy of her room, she lay in bed, trying to make sense of everything that had happened today. She was so relieved that Jimmy wasn't a traitor. She wouldn't have been able to stay here if he was. She'd come to love Somerset since she'd moved to Catcott. Even though the work at the farm was back-breaking, dirty and exhausting at times, it wasn't nearly so bad as it had been at the last farm. She had new friends in Elsie and Daisy. They might not see each other much because they were all busy, but as Elsie had proved today and Daisy had already shown, she knew she could rely upon them. If she had to move, she would miss them. She'd quite enjoyed being one of the cider girls and she would hate to be the one to break the bond that they'd been building together.

She wished she could talk to them about what Elsie's boss and Daisy's godfather had told her, but she didn't dare. She realised that her actions today could have caused a lot of trouble not only for Jimmy but also all of the unknown men who were doing the same thing as him – preparing to defend this land and halt the enemy's progress. If she'd gone to the wrong authorities about what she'd seen, it might have been awful for Jimmy because he wouldn't have been able to talk about what he was doing. Being in possession of so much ammunition and weaponry would look really bad for him and the Armitage lad. Her worry about him facing charges of treason and the consequences might well have come true, given that the men who were controlling the Auxiliers, as they had called them, might not have been able to get them released without possibly compromising their whole operation.

She turned over in bed and punched her pillow, frustrated and a little scared. She wished this rotten war was over. Her daddy had said the Great War was supposed to have been the war to end all wars, yet here they were again. There was still no news about her brother Michael, missing the lord only knew where. She worried about him and all her brothers every day. Was Michael lying dead in a field somewhere? If so, would they ever know his fate? Had he been captured? If that were the case, surely they'd have been told by now. Or was he hiding, waiting for his chance to get home? She'd heard rumours that some people in occupied Europe were helping our lads – harbouring them and helping them to escape. But it was a dangerous business because the Nazis showed no mercy to anyone who helped the Allies. After today's shenanigans, Rose now realised that Jimmy would face the same dangers if the enemy ever managed to set foot on English soil.

'Dammit! Now I'm worrying about him as well,' she grumbled into her pillow.

She wished she could talk to him about it, but it had been expressly forbidden. They weren't going to tell him that it was her who had brought so much trouble to his door today. She hoped he'd never find out. It would be awful.

Eventually her mind quietened and she was able to fall into a troubled dream in which Jimmy spotted her watching him and he threw a grenade at her. She woke up before it exploded, shaking and sweating. He'd looked so damned angry!

* * *

She was sitting at the kitchen table eating her morning porridge when Jimmy came home. He looked grubby and worn out and Rose felt even more awful than she did already.

'Morning, Jimmy,' she said. 'I'm really sorry about last night.'

He gave her a sharp look. 'Last night?'

'Missing the milking,' she said, realising that he was suspicious of her. Maybe she should try to look more contrite and less sympathetic. 'I just lost track of time and missed the bus. By the time I got back, your mammy said you'd had to go out on Guard duty. You missed your supper. Sorry.' She looked down at her bowl. 'Come and sit down. I'll make you some tea. Do you want some porridge?'

He slumped down onto a chair. 'Anything. I'm flipping starving.' He scrubbed at his face. 'I'll have that then I'd better wash and change. Are Pa and Ivor out in the fields already?'

'They are,' she said as she put a bowl of steaming porridge in front of him then busied herself brewing a fresh pot of tea. 'But your daddy said you're to get a couple of hours' sleep before you go out on the farm. He says you'll be a danger to yourself and others if you try and work without having any rest.'

Mrs Morgan bustled into the kitchen with some fresh eggs. 'Ah, there you are son. Is Rose making you some tea? Good. We've got some extra eggs so I'll make you a nice pile of scrambled eggs for you to have after your porridge. There's a couple of sausages left from last night as well that I saved for you. I'll heat them up.'

'Thanks, Ma,' he said as he practically inhaled the porridge. 'I'll be fine once I've eaten.'

'You'll be even better after you've had some sleep, lad.'

'I told him Mr Morgan said he should go to bed,' said Rose.

'Quite right, too,' said Jimmy's mother.

Jimmy looked like he was going to argue, but then he gave a huge yawn. With a groan he rested his head in his hands. 'All right. I give in. A couple of hours. That's all I need. Then I'll be back at work.'

Rose left them to it, heading out to work. She was glad he was home. And even gladder that he didn't seem to realise that it was her who had betrayed him.

29

March 1941 arrived with more frosts and chill winds, but there were odd days of milder weather and on the farms, fields were ploughed ready for planting. The shortage of labour resulted in the government conscripting unmarried women aged twenty and twenty-one into jobs in industry and farming as well as the forces, where they took on clerical, driving and technical jobs to release more men for combat.

Elsie finished typing the coded message, carefully folded it and placed it into the tobacco tin under the tobacco and cigarette papers inside as she'd been instructed. She handed it to Captain Jackson who slipped it into his pocket.

'Thank you,' he said.

'You're welcome, sir,' she replied. 'Is there anything else I can help you with?'

'No, that's all for now. But keep your eyes and ears open for me, will you? I'm building on the network of messengers in the area and there are a few places where we're on the lookout for suitable recruits.'

She nodded. 'Of course, sir. Can you tell me what constitutes a suitable candidate?'

'Local knowledge is helpful, that goes without saying. But these folk need to be able to move around without attracting attention. If we are invaded, it will be vital to be able to deliver messages to the Stay Behinds through our dead letterbox system. It won't work if whoever is carrying the communications is picked up the moment they go outside.'

She thought for a moment. 'So maybe someone who regularly does deliveries, such as a butcher or baker? Or a doctor or nurse who does home visits?' She immediately thought of Daisy, but dismissed the thought. After all, she doubted the captain would want to recruit his own goddaughter into such a potentially dangerous operation. 'What about vicars?'

'Yes, that's the sort of thing. And maybe even teachers going from home to school, eh?' He smiled, patting his jacket pocket.

She chuckled. 'Quite. Although I imagine people notice you out and about even when you're in mufti.'

He shrugged, still smiling. 'A crusty old teacher is no threat.'

Elsie frowned. 'But a lot of people hereabouts have seen you in your uniform, sir. Isn't there a risk that someone might inadvertently betray you to the enemy?'

He sighed. 'You make a good point. But, should the invasion happen, I won't be hanging about, waiting to be betrayed. I have plans in place, as I'm sure do you.'

She glanced at him, wondering if he was expecting her to tell him. But the CO had stressed that she shouldn't share her plans with anyone – not even someone attached to the unit. The whole network's survival relied upon secrecy. The less each member of the Stay Behinds knew about the others, the better. Hence the need for the dead letterboxes to pass intelligence. If the messengers didn't see the senders or recipients of the coded communications they carried, they couldn't betray them to the enemy.

As for herself, she didn't think even Captain Jackson knew of the existence of a radio sub-station located under the chicken coop in the grounds at Edgely Hall.

Before she could reply, he held up a hand to stop her. 'Not that I want or need to know.'

She gave him a grateful smile. But then a thought occurred to her. 'But won't the Germans be likely to round up all able-bodied men, sir?'

'Probably, if they have the manpower to deal with them. The news coming from the Channel Islands since Germany invaded them last June is that most men of fighting age have been rounded up and either taken to German prison camps on the mainland or forced into slave labour. Whether they would have the capacity to do the same throughout the whole of Britain, I don't know, but we must assume that men will be more restricted than women.'

She sighed. 'I dread to think what it must be like over there. It's awfully close to home, isn't it?'

'Yes, but I imagine it was too risky to try to stop the invasion of the Channel Islands when we're fighting on so many fronts in Europe. Let's hope we can turn the tide sooner rather than later. No one wants the islanders to suffer under Nazi rule, but sometimes it's just not strategically possible to fight.'

'Do they have any Stay Behinds on the islands, sir?'

'I couldn't possibly say,' he said with an enigmatic smile. 'But I certainly hope so. We don't want Hitler to have everything his way, do we?'

After he had gone, Elsie sat for a moment in the quiet office, thinking about their conversation and what they hadn't said. She knew that her role, should the invasion come, would become very dangerous. If possible, she would retreat to the secret bunker under the chicken coop, where she could monitor radio transmissions and pass on coded messages.

But, if for any reason she couldn't get to her bunker, she had an alternative plan. She would have to abandon her uniform – she'd been instructed to burn it if necessary – and she would aim to blend into the civilian population. She had false papers, components to build a radio, together with a pistol and ammunition secreted in her luggage. If caught by the Germans, she would be shot as a spy.

She would be told where to go at the last moment and only her CO would know where she was. She assumed that Captain Jackson would also go underground. To remain in his post as a teacher would be suicide – too many people knew he was working with the military, albeit only ostensibly with the Home Guard. That alone would attract the attention of an occupying force and he would be rounded up. No, he was far too useful to the Auxiliers, so of course he should go to ground with them. She wondered what his family would think about that. Would they be surprised? They'd certainly worry about him. Whereas Elsie didn't think anyone apart from her cider girl friends, and maybe Charles, would notice that she was gone.

She checked the time. The CO had been out at a number of meetings for most of the day, but he'd be back soon. She should put the kettle on. He'd want a cup of tea as soon as he returned. She stood up, smoothing down her skirt as she did so. She was a little frightened at the thought of abandoning her uniform. Since she enlisted, it had given her a sense of belonging she hadn't had since her parents had died and her sister had married. The army had become her family.

That's the whole point, she reminded herself. *Since Gertie left me high and dry, the army has been my anchor, my reason for living. So, if*

I have to abandon my uniform in order to do my duty, I'll do it and not complain. I'll be protecting my family and my country. I'd rather do that than simply give up.

She wondered what the invasion would mean for her and Charles. They talked most days, enjoying walks in the grounds and sharing meals in the mess hall. It was all very light-hearted at the moment but she thought it might become more serious if only they didn't get into trouble for fraternisation. She was growing very fond of him and was hopeful that their low-key relationship could one day develop into something deeper and long-lasting. Yet she'd not once been tempted to tell him about her plans. If she thought about it, she decided that she had kept silent so as not to put him in danger, that she was following orders. He was trustworthy, they were on the same side, so she should be able to tell him. But she knew she wouldn't. She couldn't. Instead she would simply disappear and carry out her mission. She hated to think how worried he would be then. She'd feel the same if he vanished. But there was nothing she could do about it.

She hoped and prayed that the expected invasion never came.

* * *

The next day, Daisy made sure that no one was around before she checked the hidden space behind the loose brick in a garden wall. Inside was a tobacco tin. She frowned and wondered whether she should open it. After all, for all she knew, some young lad had discovered the hiding place and was using it to hide his smokes from his ma. But then she remembered her instructions: *Collect whatever is in the dead letterbox and move it to the next one. Do not read it. Do not try to remember what you collected. The less you know, the better.*

With the memory of her uncle's voice in her mind, she quickly retrieved the tin and put the brick back into place. She put it in her bicycle basket underneath her medical bag and rode off.

* * *

After Rose's near-disastrous discovery of the arms cache in the woods above the farm, she waited impatiently to hear what she was going to be required to do. When she'd heard nothing for a couple of weeks, she began to suspect they had simply told her they would get in touch in order to put her off. She was disappointed that they had fobbed her off so easily.

She was coming back into the farmyard from the moor with a full milk churn balanced precariously in a wheelbarrow when the postman arrived.

'You're doing a grand job, lass.' He grinned as she stopped and lowered the barrow to the ground, huffing out a breath that created a cloud of condensed air around her face. It had been an effort to keep the churn upright as she'd trudged up the hill with it, even though she'd tried to wedge it in place with sacking, her gas mask box, the bucket and the three-legged milking stool. She flexed her cold fingers inside her gloves. Her hands were painfully stiff.

She suspected he was laughing at her, but he was a nice man who reminded her of her granddad, so she chose to take it in good cheer. 'Thank you very much.' She smiled.

He grinned and opened his postbag. 'Got a few letters for the farm today.' He took out a batch and sorted through them. 'There's a couple for you, as well. Got a sweetheart in Birmingham, have you? You get a lot of post from there.'

She shook her head, taking the letters from him. 'Not much

chance of that with six older brothers,' she sighed. 'It's probably from my mammy.'

'Ah,' he said, needing no further explanation. Big brothers around the world were put on this earth to make sure no lads got anywhere near their sisters. 'Well, maybe the letter you've got from someone in Glastonbury is the one you've been waiting for. You sweet on a local lad, eh?'

She looked at him, confused as she took the letters from him. She didn't know of any lad from there who might be writing to her. 'No local lad either. It's probably from my friend Elsie. She's in Glastonbury. She's likely wanting to know when I've got my next day off.' But even as she said it, she realised two things: first, that it wasn't Elsie's handwriting on the envelope and second, there was an envelope with identical handwriting addressed to Jimmy.

'Right,' said the postie, unaware of the fact that Rose's heart had missed a beat as she realised this could be her orders from Elsie's boss. 'I'd best be off.' He looked up at the grey sky. 'It don't look like it's going to get any warmer today. I'm surprised them cows' udders don't freeze up solid in this weather.'

Rose laughed at the idea. 'I know. I'm looking forward to getting inside for a warm up.' She stuffed the envelopes in her pocket.

He took his leave as she bent and grasped the handles of the wheelbarrow again and steered it over the cobbled yard towards the dairy. Once it was in there, she left the churn and scrubbed down the bucket and milking stool. She'd been told in no uncertain terms that a grubby stool could result in contaminated milk, so it was an important job that she had to do as soon as she finished milking. That done, she went into the farmhouse, kicking off her boots and walking into the kitchen in her thick socks. She was glad she'd thought to wear two pairs this morning.

The frosted ground had been hard and freezing cold, so she'd soon lost all feeling in her toes. Now, as she walked over to the range, warmth began to curl around her and she felt the sting of pins and needles in her fingers and toes as sensation returned.

She moved the full kettle to the hotplate and leaned against the range, placing her gloves on the top so that they would be warm when she had to go out again. She took the letters from her pocket and sorted through them, leaving those addressed to the Morgans on the dresser before turning her attention to the two letters she'd received.

She bit her lip as she looked at them, trying to decide which one to read first. Mammy might have some news of Michael. It had been nearly three months since he'd been reported missing. The longer it went on, the harder it was for the family to believe that he had survived and would be able to come home to them. And what of Patrick? She knew that he'd been shipped back to Britain after his accident, but he had been sent to a hospital in Scotland – so far away from all the family that no one had been able to visit him. She was dreading the news that he had made a full recovery and was being sent back to war. Then she felt guilty for wishing her brother's injury had been bad enough to have him deemed unfit for service. And then, what about her other brothers? Every time a letter arrived from home, Rose had the same dilemma – whether to rip it open and learn what it said, or to put it off a little longer in case it was news she dreaded?

Today, she had an alternative. She had no idea what the letter postmarked Glastonbury might contain, but she knew it was important. She was still a little shocked that she'd volunteered, but the experience of discovering the arms cache and believing that it posed a threat to the community had made her realise that even a girl like her could do something to help keep everyone safe.

The kettle began to boil, so she put both letters in her pocket and set about making a drink. She knew she would be expected to get back to work soon, so she couldn't hang around. One of the farm hands had enlisted, so she had been given his job of caring for the pigs. Those beasts were as stubborn and difficult to handle as the cows, and trickier when she was dealing with them inside the pig shed because she didn't have much room to run if she needed to escape them. But at least it was warmer in there as she cleaned out the pens, filled the food and water troughs and kept a watchful eye on the weight of the young pigs. They were much faster than the cows and one or two were always trying to escape by slipping through her legs and out of the gates of their pens. She was sure that sooner or later, she'd end up on her backside in the sty, which would amuse everyone.

With a cup of tea in hand, she sat at the kitchen table with her letters. A few more minutes wouldn't hurt or change the news from home. She opened the local one first. It was from Captain Jackson, she was sure. The handwriting was exactly as she'd expect a teacher's to be. But it wasn't signed and there wasn't a return address. It merely said that she should present herself at an address in Taunton at a certain day and time. That it was on her usual day off didn't surprise her. The captain could have found out about that from a casual chat with Daisy or Elsie. It would be a shame to miss meeting up with the other girls, though. Perhaps she could suggest they met in the evening instead of the afternoon as they usually did?

Before she could ponder on it, she heard the back door open and the familiar thud of boots on the floor that told her Jimmy had arrived. Rose quickly shoved the letter and envelope into her pocket and pulled out the other one. She had it open and was scanning it as he walked into the kitchen.

She glanced up briefly and nodded at him. 'Tea's in the pot,' she said before turning back to Mammy's letter.

'Thought you'd be out with the pigs by now,' he said as he poured himself a cup.

She didn't answer, her attention caught by a line on the page. 'Oh!'

'What's wrong?' he asked, moving towards her. 'Bad news?'

'What?' Rose looked up as he stood next to her seat. 'No. It's quite good, actually.' She glanced back at the letter. 'My brother Declan thinks he might be posted to an airfield somewhere in the South.' She smiled. 'Mammy doesn't know which one but has told him to let me know and to be sure to come and see me when he can.'

'There's a lot of airfields across the South of England right now. Is he a pilot?'

She shook her head. 'No, he's ground crew, thank goodness. I don't think any of us would sleep at night if he were flying.' She held the letter to her chest. 'It would be so lovely to see him. But I doubt if he'll end up round here. Like you say, there's a lot of airfields right across the country.'

Jimmy sat down next to her. 'I thought all your brothers were annoying? You complain about them often enough.'

Rose huffed. 'Well, of course they're all annoying. It seems to be compulsory for all males to irritate girls, especially their sisters. But when the others aren't around, me and Dec get on all right.' She laughed. 'Mind you, I've missed them all and I think I'd be glad to see any of them right now.' Her smile became bitter-sweet. 'Especially Michael.'

'Is he the one who's missing? Still no news?'

She shook her head. 'Not a word,' she sighed, folding the letter and putting it in her pocket. She hoped Jimmy didn't notice the crinkle of another sheet of paper as she did so. 'Mammy says it's making Daddy ill, the worry of it.'

'That's rough,' he muttered before drinking down his tea. 'Still, at least he's not confirmed dead, is he?'

She closed her eyes briefly. 'I'm sure you're saying that to reassure me,' she said slowly, 'but, honestly, Jimmy, it's not helping. What if he's lying dead in a ditch or a bomb crater somewhere and we never know where he is? This not knowing is so horrible...' She took a deep breath and shook her head. 'Anyway, I need to get to the pigs.'

She quickly rinsed her cup and left it on the drainer.

'I'm sorry,' he said. 'It must be awful. I hope you get some good news soon.'

She nodded, not looking at him. 'Thank you, Jimmy. I appreciate it. Oh, by the way, there's the post on the dresser,' she told him as she grabbed her gloves and headed out.

* * *

Jimmy waited until he heard the back door slam and saw Rose hurrying across the farmyard to the pigsty before he tore open the letter addressed to him. He grinned as he read it.

He was just absorbing the contents when the back door opened again. He stuffed the letter into his pocket before his ma came into the kitchen.

'I hope that pot's got another cupful in it, lad. I'm that cold.'

'Sit down, Ma. I'll get it.'

'Thank you, son. We're a bit short on eggs this week. The hens don't like laying in this weather, and who can blame them?' She placed her egg basket on the draining board before sinking into her rocking chair by the range. 'Ah, that's better,' she said, rubbing her chapped hands together. 'I'll be glad when the spring comes. I'm that sick of winter. What's Pa got you doing today?' He handed her a cup of tea. 'Thanks, lad.'

'I fitted a new part to the tractor.' He rolled his eyes. 'You'd think Ivor could do it. He drives the blooming thing all the time. But he's useless at anything mechanical.'

He'd had to make sure Pa knew how to remove certain parts of the tractor as well as the farm truck to disable them in the event of an invasion. He'd shown Ivor as well, but he didn't have a clue, which is probably why he hadn't been recruited as an Auxilier.

His ma shook her head. 'I don't know where that lad got his brains from. He's the only Morgan man who can't maintain his own tractor.' She took a sip of her tea and sighed, content. 'Did the post arrive?'

'Yeah. On the dresser. Actually, I got a letter,' he said, taking it out of his pocket. 'I'm being sent on a course for a week.'

Mrs Morgan frowned. 'What kind of course?'

He shrugged. 'Not sure, Ma. The Home Guard are organising it. I'm to get myself up to a place in Oxfordshire next week.'

'They're not sending your pa and Ivor as well are they? We need all hands these days. If we lose one more farm hand to the army, we'll be hard put to keep the farm running. Pa's even talking about finding another Land Army girl, although she'd have to share with Rose and I'm not sure how well that will work. The poor girl's in the smallest bedroom as it is. There's no room for another bed. Pa's suggested bunk beds, but I don't like the idea of a girl having to climb up and down after a long day's work.'

'Huh,' he huffed. 'Me and Ivor have had to put up with it since she arrived, so why can't they? I hear in some farms, the land girls are billeted in bunks in the barn.'

'Oh no, I wouldn't let them do that. They'd catch their death in that draughty old barn. The least we can do is make sure they've got a decent roof over their heads at night.'

He drained his cup. 'Well, let's hope no more of the hands enlist, eh, Ma?'

She nodded. 'And that this rotten war ends sooner rather than later.'

He didn't respond to that. No one wanted war, but now that he was an Auxilier, he was learning all sorts of things about himself that he'd never have known if the world was at peace. 'Anyway, I'd best get on. Pa said I should keep an eye on Rose while she's getting used to the pigs.'

'You didn't say whether the others are expected to go on this course with you, son,' she reminded him.

'Oh. No, they won't be. It's just me.'

He didn't hang around for any more questions. All he'd been able to tell his family was that the Home Guard had selected him for special duties that he couldn't talk about. Pa had been curious, but hadn't asked any more. Jimmy thought he might have an inkling of what was going on because a few other farming folk had been pulled out of the local platoon for the same reason. Ivor wasn't interested, spending all his spare time with his sweetheart in Street. Ma was more suspicious, asking lots of questions he couldn't answer. Jimmy had learned to make a quick exit whenever the subject arose.

So, instead of being interrogated by his ma, Jimmy headed towards the pigsty to check on Rose. The fact that he felt a lift in his spirits at the thought of seeing her again after such a short time irritated him. He had better things to do than to get involved with some city girl who would be rushing home to Birmingham one of these days. There was a war to win and a country to defend before he could let himself think about finding a woman for himself.

With that thought in mind, he changed direction and headed out to the fields. Rose could cope on her own for now. He'd check on her later.

30

By Easter 1941, the days were getting longer and the trees had awoken from their winter slumber. Cities across the British Isles were still being attacked from the air. In London, people slept in bunk beds set up far below the surface in the London Underground rather than risk their lives in flimsy Anderson shelters. Rationing was making shopping difficult, with long queues and short supplies.

Even rural Somerset hadn't escaped the conflict. Army and RAF camps sprung up, housing men being trained to fight, either on land or in the air. At the Crispin Hall dances, Daisy, Elsie and Rose met soldiers and airmen from all over the country and commonwealth who had been sent to their usually sleepy part of the world.

On Good Friday, there was an attack on Bristol resulting in hundreds of deaths and injuries. Fire engines and first aid teams from all over Somerset were sent to the city to help with the recovery operation. Yeovil was attacked as well, killing soldiers and civilians alike. Bombs landed on towns and villages across the county, at Chedzoy and at Shepton Mallet.

Despite Prime Minister Churchill's rousing speeches and the government's assurance that everyone should keep calm and carry on, all three of the girls were feeling the strain. Rose fretted about her parents in Birmingham as well as all of her brothers, but especially Michael who was still posted as missing. She hadn't heard about Declan's new posting either, so assumed he wasn't anywhere near cider country after all. Elsie still worried about her sister and niece and Daisy worried about all the lads she knew who had gone to fight, as well as her friends who were nursing in Bristol.

To try and keep their spirits up, they met regularly to attend the dances in Street and to see the latest films at the picture house there.

One Saturday afternoon the three of them emerged from the cinema on Leigh Road after watching the matinee showing of the Crazy Gang's latest film, *Gasbags*. They were all giggling as they made their way down the road towards the high street.

'Oh I do like a bit of Flanagan and Allen, they're so funny. No wonder they call them the Crazy Gang. They're so daft!' laughed Daisy.

'I know,' said Rose. 'Fancy tethering a great big barrage balloon to a mobile fish and chip shop.' She shook her head as she giggled. 'It was hilarious, the way it flew away.'

Elsie smiled at her friends' amusement. 'I have no idea how they filmed that. But I can't imagine it would've flown all the way to Germany without being shot down in real life, can you?'

'Of course it wouldn't, it's just a chance to have a poke at the enemy,' said Daisy. 'But it was good fun, wasn't it? And it all ended well with them getting back to England with one of the Nazis' secret weapons.'

Rose sighed. 'I wish our Michael would turn up like that.'

'Still no news?' asked Elsie, linking arms with her.

'No,' she said. 'But we keep telling ourselves that no news is good news. He could still be out there somewhere, just waiting for his chance to get home.'

'Quite right,' said Daisy, linking with Rose's other arm. 'Don't give up hope.'

Rose nodded, so grateful that these two girls were so keen to encourage her. 'I'm not giving up on him, I keep praying we'll hear soon.' But the longer it went on with no news, the harder it was to hold onto hope. She squared her shoulders. 'Now, are we going to have a cuppa in the tea shop? If we're staying around for the dance this evening, I want to take the weight off my feet for a bit.'

They were soon sitting at a table with a pot of tea and three buns in front of them. As always, it was busy and also as usual, Daisy greeted many of the people in the tea shop.

'Do you know *everyone* in Street?' asked Elsie with a smile. 'You seem to know a lot of people.'

'Not really,' laughed Daisy. 'I went to school here, and now I work here. But Street's bigger than you think and growing all the time. Why, in my lifetime, I've witnessed lots of houses being built as well as expansions at the factories. I couldn't possibly know everyone. You know there's thousands of people who work at the Clarks shoe factory, don't you? That said, I do know a good few people.' Her eyes sparkled. 'Why? Do you want me to introduce you to someone?'

Elsie's cheeks went pink. 'No thank you. I've actually got a date with Charles next week.'

'Ooh.' Rose's eyes sparkled as she leaned forward. 'Do tell!'

She shook her head. 'Well, you know we've been quite friendly for a while now, but we've tried to keep it quiet at work. Anyway, he's going to take me to the theatre in Bath.'

'Posh,' said Rose, looking impressed. 'You wouldn't get a farm hand taking you to the theatre.'

'Very nice,' said Daisy. 'Good idea to go into Bath. Less chance of being seen by your bosses.'

'I know,' she agreed. It still worried her, but she was a little tired of pretending she wasn't getting involved with him.

'Is he handsome?' asked Daisy.

'He is.' She smiled, her cheeks going pink.

'When are we going to see for ourselves? Are you going to bring him to a dance?' Daisy pointed out.

Elsie shrugged. 'I don't know,' she said.

Daisy watched her, wondering whether Elsie's new beau had anything to do with Uncle Ted's work, but she wasn't about to get either of them in trouble by asking her. She was curious to know who else was involved in the clandestine work that she was doing now.

She was doing her little bit for the war effort by delivering and collecting messages as she went out and about on her rounds. She never saw anyone else while she was doing this. All communications were done through what they called 'dead letterboxes' – hidden, secret places where she would collect coded messages and deliver them to the next one. It amazed her, the ingenuity of some of these places. They were secreted behind loose bricks in walls, inside gateposts, pipes or tree trunks, hidden in gutters or even holes in the ground. She had her own set of places which she had to check and move along anything she found there to specific drops.

It all seemed a bit cloak and dagger, considering the country wasn't actually occupied. But she'd been told that it was important that everyone involved in the secret messaging network was well-practised so that when the invasion came they could move information around without being detected. Uncle Ted had also mentioned that observers were already in place, recording movements around their areas, reporting anything unusual that the authorities might need to investigate. Who knew how many enemy spies might already be active in the country?

'You must ask him. We'd love to meet him,' Rose said, unaware of Daisy's wandering thoughts.

'Yes,' said Daisy, bringing her mind back to the matter in hand. 'We've got to make sure he's good enough for you.'

Elsie rested her elbows on the table and her chin on her hands. 'I don't know. He really is nice, and handsome, too. We get along well. I'm just a bit scared of falling in love, only to have him sent off and killed in this damned war. Charles is so nice that I think I could fall for him easily and I'm not sure I could bear it if anything happened to him.'

The others were silent for a moment, lost in their own thoughts.

'We all worry about that,' said Daisy. 'But wouldn't it be better to just seize the day? To take our happiness where we can and hope for the best?'

Elsie closed her eyes, as though she was in pain.

'Oh my. What did I say to bring that look to your face?' asked Daisy.

Elsie sighed and looked around. Busy as the tea shop was, there was no one paying attention to the three girls. Her heart contracted at the sight of a young mother cuddling her baby. 'Can I tell you a secret?' she asked.

They both nodded. Daisy beckoned them both closer with her finger. 'A little tip, cider girls. A lot of folk round here work in the factory where it's so noisy that you can't hear what your neighbour is saying. So they've all developed the ability to lip read. If you don't want anyone else to know your business, we need to keep our heads together while we talk so they can't see what we're saying. Aunt Kate taught me that. She and her friends Jeannie and Louisa worked together in the machine room with three hundred other women. She said you have to get crafty to keep your secrets.'

Rose and Elsie moved in closer until their foreheads were almost touching over the small table and Elsie put her hand up to the side of her face to make sure that no one else could see what she said. 'I don't know why I'm worried about anyone knowing this. None of you know the people involved, but... I'm afraid it doesn't reflect well on my sister. She's the only family I have. And her little girl, of course. But that's the secret. You see, my brother-in-law saw the writing on the wall when Herr Hitler rose to power in Germany. He was sure that war was coming. So he joined the navy back in early 1938. My sister was furious, wanting him to at least wait and see. But his father had been a mariner and he wanted to follow in his footsteps rather than be conscripted into the army.' She paused. 'Sorry, I'm rambling, but the thing is, after he went to sea, she met someone else. She decided to seize the day and had an affair. And her daughter is the result.'

'Oh my,' said Rose.

'Does her husband know?' asked Daisy. 'If he's been away at sea, he's bound to realise the child isn't his, isn't he?'

Elsie shook her head. 'No, he doesn't. But only because my sister lied to him. She was sure she'd get away with it, only I wouldn't play along.'

'What did she do?' asked Rose.

She sighed. 'She wrote to him and told him that *I'd* been the one to have an affair and that *I* had the baby. She said that they should take on the child because they'd been trying for one without success for a while before he went away. She made it sound like she wanted to save me from disgrace.' She huffed out a breath. 'It still makes me furious when I think about it. She thought it was the perfect solution and wrote and told him all this before she bothered to tell me. I got an angry letter from him, telling me I should be ashamed of myself, expecting them to take on the expense of my bastard child and that I would have to give up more of my salary if I wanted to continue living with them.'

Rose gasped and Daisy blinked.

'Your own sister did that to you?' said Rose. 'That's horrid.'

'It really is,' said Daisy, squeezing Elsie's hand.

'That's why I joined up,' she said. 'I couldn't bear it. I could hardly write back to my brother-in-law to tell him the truth, could I? So I left. Gertie took the baby and evacuated when war was declared, but now she's back in London and even though I'm still angry about what she's done, she's my only family and I'm worried sick about them.'

'Understandable,' said Rose. 'I can't believe someone could be so cruel as to lie like that about their only kin.'

Daisy frowned. 'I agree, it's a nasty thing to do and you did the right thing by walking away from the situation. You certainly shouldn't be expected to pay your hard-earned money to keep your sister's secret. But what has that got to do with your date next week?'

Elsie pulled a face. 'I'm not sure, really. Maybe I just felt the need to tell you the awful truth about my sister. I haven't told another soul and it's been getting me down. But I think the connection between the two things might be a matter of trust. If I couldn't trust my closest family, am I really brave enough to put my trust in someone I hardly know, who might be here today and gone tomorrow?'

'Good point,' said Rose, looking a little lost.

'Are you feeling the same way?' Daisy asked her.

'I think I might be. Sometimes I think I really want a sweetheart. But then I see the news and I think about all my brothers and what they're going through, and I wonder if it might be too dangerous to trust my heart to anyone while there's a war on.'

'Not even a lad who's in a reserved occupation like Jimmy?' asked Daisy, nudging her shoulder. 'He'll not be going anywhere.'

Rose and Elsie exchanged a brief look before Rose shook her head. 'Even a lad like Jimmy,' she said. 'After all, I'll be wanting to go home to Birmingham when the war's over. He'll be staying here in Somerset, no matter what.' A shadow crossed her expression for a moment before she banished it. 'So there's no point in me getting involved with him. Besides, he's still a miserable beggar most of the time. I'd rather have a man who can at least smile now and again.'

'Which leaves you, Daisy,' said Elsie. 'Are you making any progress with your Dr Mattie?'

She sat back and rolled her eyes. 'He's not mine,' she said. No matter how much she wished for it to be otherwise. 'He's busy in his surgery in Wells most of the time, and I'm busy here in Street. I see him at family gatherings, but not that often.'

'But you're not related, are you?' asked Rose, looking confused.

'No, just family friends. But I doubt he'll ever think of me in the romantic sense. It's driving me mad.'

All three girls sat back and sighed. 'Why does everything have to be so confusing?' asked Rose. 'I always thought I'd grow up, meet a chap, get married and live happily ever after. But truth be told, I'm too exhausted most of the time to want to make the effort to pretty myself up for a date. I'd rather relax and enjoy time with you two.'

'I'm sure you would manage it if you met the right lad,' said Daisy. 'Haven't any of the lads you dance with at the Crispin Hall taken your fancy?'

Rose wrinkled her nose. 'Not really. Mind you, the last couple of times someone asked me, Jimmy was there, glowering at them. He's put a few off, I can tell you.' She rolled her eyes. 'He's as bad as my brothers. It's not like I'm some silly girl who gets taken in by a handsome face and some sweet words. I've seen my brothers turning on the charm with unsuspecting girls too often to fall for that. But I'm still annoyed by Jimmy interfering, especially now I'm finally free to make my own decisions without the Flaherty brothers breathing down my neck. At this rate, I'm going to end up a spinster, watching everyone else get married and have babies.'

'You're not over the hill yet, Rose, love. Maybe you should dance with Jimmy,' laughed Daisy.

Rose shook her head. 'He's already told me he doesn't dance, not that I would with him, anyway. I don't know why he bothers going to the dances at all. He just stands against the wall, watching and making me feel uncomfortable.'

'Right,' said Daisy. 'It seems to me we need to forget about anyone else and concentrate on what *we* want. I for one intend to say yes to any decent-looking lad who asks me to dance this evening. I'm not going to care about what Mattie thinks or whether my partner is worthy of me. They aren't, of course,' she said, her chin in the air, making the friends giggle. 'But I'm in the mood to dance, so that's what I'll do.'

'Why not?' asked Rose. 'I'm in. I don't know how much dancing I can manage before I'm too tired to do any more. But I'll do my best. I'll accept any lad who is clean and polite. I won't dance with any of those drinkers.'

'Of course not,' agreed Daisy. 'No drinkers, just dancers for us cider girls.'

Elsie looked undecided. 'I'm not sure,' she said. 'Now I've said I'd go out with Charles next week, I don't know whether I should be dancing with other fellows.'

'There's no harm in a dance, is there? Why shouldn't you have some fun? It's not like you're going to rush off and have a torrid affair with one of them, is it?'

'It seems to me,' said Daisy, 'that none of us is expecting to find our forever love tonight, so what's the harm in a bit of a dance with a chap or two?'

'I'm only likely to accept offers of a dance in order to annoy Jimmy,' said Rose. 'As awkward as it is when he's glaring like that, it's good to know I'm annoying him as much as he annoys me.'

'That's decided then,' said Daisy. 'A few dances with chaps if we feel like it, and the cider girls will enjoy ourselves together the rest of the evening.'

31

There were more people than usual at the dance, including a lot of young men in uniform. They seemed to travel in packs and took up most of the tables around the dance floor, although the three girls were lucky to get a small table near the stage where the band were warming up.

As soon as they were settled with some drinks, someone waved at Daisy from across the hall.

'There's Ruby.'

'Mattie's sister?'

'That's right, and the chap with her is Henry, her other brother,' she told Elsie and Rose as the two of them made their way over to their table. When they arrived, the girls invited them to join them and soon they were all chattering and laughing. Ruby and Daisy got up to dance together and Henry shyly asked Elsie if she'd like to take a turn around the floor with him.

'Go on,' said Rose with a smile. 'I'll guard our table and enjoy watching for a bit. Then perhaps Henry will have a little dance with me?'

His ears went red as he nodded. 'Of course,' he said. 'If Elsie doesn't mind.'

She waved them off, thinking that Henry Musgrove seemed like a sweet lad. She knew from Daisy that he was a Quaker in his early twenties. He had been able to gain exemption from fighting because he worked for his Uncle Tom, who ran a company that made prosthetic limbs and other aids for folks with injuries or disabilities. Now, with the world at war again, the demand for their products was greater than ever, and so Henry had been allowed exemption to stay at home to carry out this vital service.

Rose sighed and rested her elbows on the table and her chin in her hands. She couldn't help but tap her feet to the lively music, but she was content to watch for the time being. It had been a busy week on the farm and she had also been busy with her secret work. The meeting in Bridgwater had been with an officer she'd never seen before. He had explained that the task they had in mind for her was to be an observer and messenger.

For the time being, she was simply to note any traffic she saw in the lanes across the moor at specific times as well as planes moving across the sky above Catcott – their types and numbers if possible as well as direction of travel, although on cloudy days and at nighttime it was difficult to see them. She had been taught how to identify different planes by their shapes and also by the sounds of their engines. She noted them down and every twenty-four hours she would put her reports into a secret 'dead letterbox' in a gatepost on the edge of the moor. By the time she placed her next report in there, the previous one had gone. It wasn't very exciting work, but it was something. They had assured her that there would be more to do as she became more proficient, but this was good practice for now. And if the invasion came, she would be required to record all enemy movements in the area – troops, tanks, lorries, staff cars. Anything that passed by the farm would need to be listed and sent in the usual way. As she understood it, she was one of many who were secretly involved in the clandestine network and the information she gathered would be passed from letterbox to letterbox by messengers until it reached the appropriate people who could make use of the intelligence to plan their attacks against the occupying enemy.

She was trying to get used to surviving on little sleep, knowing that her brothers fighting abroad were all having to manage in far worse conditions than she was. At least she had a warm bed, if only for a few hours, and hot food for her belly. It was difficult, though. Right now she felt exhausted. She hoped she could stay awake long enough to enjoy the evening with her friends.

The music changed and Elsie and Henry came back to the table. As promised, he offered her his hand and although she would rather just rest for a little longer, Rose didn't want to be rude. With a smile, she joined him for a dance while Elsie had a rest. As they took their first turn around the hall, Rose spotted Jimmy with a couple of other lads from the farm. As usual, he was glaring at her. She considered sticking her tongue out at him, but didn't want to appear rude in front of her dance partner. Instead she ignored Jimmy and smiled up at Henry, making his ears go red again.

'You're a good dancer, Henry,' she said.

'Thank you,' he said. 'My sister uses me for practice.'

'Well, I must thank her. I think you're the first chap I've danced with who hasn't stepped on my toes.'

He groaned. 'Don't say that. Now I'm bound to do it.'

She laughed. 'No you won't. You're too good a dancer for that.'

He grinned. 'I do tread on Ruby's toes sometimes, especially when I've had enough of being made to dance with her.'

'I'm sure. But no doubt she makes you pay for it, just as I would my own brothers.'

They carried on dancing with no mishaps. Rose ignored Jimmy and chatted happily with Henry, who had a sweet manner and a dry sense of humour. Daisy and Ruby joined them, and the four of them chatted as they danced, laughing together until the end of the song and the band leader announced they were taking a short break.

'I need a sit down,' announced Daisy.

'Me too, I'm that worn out. I've been up since five this morning,' said Rose, thanking Henry again for not stepping on her toes. In fact, she was feeling quite light-headed now. Maybe she should have had more than an apple at lunchtime, but she'd been too worn out to eat and she'd missed supper because she'd got an early bus to come into Street and meet the other cider girls. That bun in the tea shop was the most substantial thing she'd eaten all day.

Henry laughed, then something caught his eye behind her.

'Mattie's here,' he said, causing Daisy to spin around to see. Sure enough, her handsome doctor was standing just inside the entrance to the hall, amongst a crowd of airmen who'd just come in. 'He said he might try to get here tonight.' He lifted a hand to attract his older brother's attention.

Rose glanced sideways at Daisy, noting her flushed cheeks and radiant smile as Mattie made his way through the crowd to them as they reached their table. She couldn't understand how the man didn't notice how keen on him Daisy was. He was obviously fond of her, as evidenced by the hug he gave her in greeting. He looked as pleased to see her as she was to see him. *What's holding him back?* she wondered.

'Well, well, Doctor. What brings you to the dance tonight?' Daisy asked.

'The chance to dance with you, Nurse,' he said. 'No one's stood on my foot since the last time we danced.'

'Oh, you,' she grumbled, smacking his shoulder. 'I mis-stepped once, when I was all of ten years old. I'll have you know I'm a decent dancer these days.'

He grinned, looking very much like his younger brother. 'Really? I noticed Henry was dancing with your friend rather than you or Ruby. I think you're all talk and the minute I fall for your smooth words, you'll trample all over me.'

Rose giggled at his teasing. 'She really is a good dancer,' she told him. 'You should try it. You can't hold one stumble against her after all these years.'

He gave an exaggerated sigh. 'All right, I'll give her one more chance.' He winked at Rose as Daisy huffed.

'Well, you'll have to wait,' she said. 'I'm ready for a sit down and a fresh drink first.'

As Rose sat down, she stifled a yawn. She was glad of the chance to rest. She noticed that Jimmy was still there, still scowling at her. She rolled her eyes before she made a great show of smiling broadly at him and waving. One of his pals noticed and elbowed Jimmy. It looked like he was getting some ribbing. With a satisfied smirk, Rose turned her back on him and gave her attention to her friends.

'Oh my,' said Elsie. 'There's a lot of flyboys in here tonight.'

'I know,' said Ruby, looking hopeful. 'Some of them are eyeing us. D'you think they'll ask us to dance?'

Mattie frowned. 'Don't go letting a uniform turn your head, sis.'

She sighed. 'Chance would be a fine thing. Do you and Henry *have* to be here tonight?'

Rose laughed. 'Brothers do tend to make it difficult to find a sweetheart, don't they? Be grateful you've only got two to contend with. All six of mine used to follow me around, jumping out when some poor lad showed me any interest.'

Ruby's eyes widened as she looked at something behind Rose. The others all seemed to freeze as Rose became aware that someone had come to stand just behind her chair and was leaning towards her. Out of the corner of her eye she saw the blue of an RAF uniform before she felt his warm breath against her cheek and he spoke softly into her ear so that the others didn't hear.

Rose's eyes widened. She stood quickly and spun round as he stepped back, grinning down at her. As she saw his face for the first time, three things happened. First she felt dizzy after jumping up so quick, then the wail of the air raid siren cut through the air, and moments later Rose's eyes rolled back in her head and she fell into a dead faint.

Daisy jumped up, knocking over a chair. *What the heck?*

The stranger, who had been closest to Rose as she'd fallen, had caught her in his arms. His cocky grin had disappeared.

'Put her down!' she ordered.

'Where?' he snarled. 'I'll not let her lie on the damned floor.'

'Clear the table,' said Mattie. 'Put her there.'

'She needs a doctor,' he said, still not relinquishing his hold on her.

'I'm a doctor,' said Mattie.

'And I'm a nurse,' said Daisy, 'so do as he says and put her down here.' She pointed at the table.

The others jumped to move their glasses and gas mask boxes so that Rose could be laid out on the table. Daisy pulled off her cardigan and rolled it up to act as a cushion for her friend's head.

Someone blew a whistle and shouted that everyone had to evacuate to the nearest shelter, but the small crowd around the stricken Rose ignored them. An ARP warden came over to chivvy them. Henry had a quick word and he moved on, urging the onlookers to get a move on.

The stranger hovered over Rose's prone body until Daisy literally pushed him out of the way. 'Let me see her.'

'What's wrong with her?' he asked moving closer again, trying to get around her.

'She's fainted, obviously,' she said. 'Now move back.' She elbowed him in the gut. He grunted but barely budged.

'But our Rose never faints,' he said, sounding confused. 'Is she ill?'

Daisy glanced at him, frowning. 'You know her?'

Before he could answer, a rough hand grabbed his shoulder and pulled him away. 'What did you do to her?' Jimmy Morgan demanded, looking furious.

'Nothing! I'm—'

Daisy winced as Jimmy's fist connected with the man's jaw, sending him flying. Someone in the crowd heading out of the doors cheered. Others in RAF uniforms would have turned back and joined the fray, but the ARP warden shouted and ordered them towards the exit.

'For God's sake, Jimmy!' Daisy yelled. 'You're not helping. Stop being an idiot. Pick him up. He knows Rose.'

Shaking her head, Daisy turned back to her unconscious friend. Mattie was on the other side of her. 'Can you check that that flyboy hasn't got a broken jaw while I deal with Rose?' she asked. 'And make sure Jimmy doesn't throw any more punches or he'll end up in a cell for the night.'

'Right.' Mattie nodded and left her to loosen the collar of Rose's blouse and check her pulse.

'Come on, Rosie, love. Wake up.' She turned to Ruby and Elsie. 'Can you lift her legs up? Let's get some blood to her head.'

The girls jumped to help while Mattie and Henry picked up the groaning stranger and helped him into a chair. Jimmy stood by, looking furious.

'What did he do to her?' he asked Daisy.

'I don't know, Jimmy,' she said as Rose's eyes fluttered open. 'But punching him doesn't help.'

Rose blinked and looked around. She frowned as she saw Jimmy. 'Who did you punch?'

'The beast that did this to you,' he said, waving a hand towards her as she lay prone on the table.

Daisy put a hand on Rose's shoulder as she tried to get up. 'No stay there for a bit. You fainted. That RAF lad said something to you and you fainted dead away.' She nodded her head towards the stranger.

'Help me up,' said Rose. 'Let me see him.'

'In a minute. Are you feeling dizzy? Does anything hurt?'

'Daisy,' she said, her voice shaking but her gaze determined. 'Let me up.'

With a sigh she nodded. 'All right. But take it slowly.' The other girls lowered Rose's legs and Daisy helped her to sit up so that she could see the young man who had so shocked her friend that she'd fainted. She watched carefully as Rose looked at him, noting the catch in her breath.

'He says he knows you,' Elsie told her.

'Of course I do. I'm her damned brother,' the stranger snarled, glaring at Jimmy.

'He is,' said Rose. 'This is Declan.'

'Your brother?' asked Jimmy. 'Then why did you faint? What did he do to you?'

Rose blinked, still a little out of sorts after being unconscious. Without answering his questions, she turned her head and looked at him. 'Did you hit him?'

Jimmy flexed his right hand and nodded. 'I thought he'd hurt you.'

'Of course I didn't,' Declan grumbled, rubbing at his jaw. 'I just wanted to surprise her. How was I to know she's gone soft since she's become a cider girl? Most times when we sneak up on her, she comes out fighting.' He scowled at Jimmy. 'She punches harder than you do.'

The small group around the two casualties stood watching. The hall had emptied of everyone else and the siren had fallen silent. No one seemed to know what to say. Daisy, with her arm around Rose's shoulders to keep her steady, noticed her friend was shaking. She glanced at her, worried that she might be succumbing to shock, but one look at Rose's face reassured her. Her friend's eyes were brimming with mirth and her lips were squeezed tight even as her shoulders shook.

When their eyes met, Rose couldn't hold it in any longer. She began to laugh from deep in her belly. 'He's right,' she gasped. 'I'd have broken his nose like Daisy did to that Home Guard lad.' She giggled, looking at Jimmy. 'But he caught me by surprise good and proper. That must be why I fainted.' She grimaced. 'I've never done that before. So I missed you hitting my brother. I'd have liked to have seen you put him on his backside, Jimmy. I'm sorry I missed that.'

'Oi!' Declan cried. 'You're supposed to be on my side. Flahertys together, remember?'

That sent Rose into further gales of laughter. 'Don't talk daft, you big lump. It serves you right for not telling me you were coming.'

'I thought you'd be pleased to see me,' he complained.

Rose rolled her eyes, still chuckling. She shuffled her bottom to the edge of the table and let Daisy help her to stand. 'Of course I am, I was just surprised is all. But I'll bet you sneaked up, expecting me to be with a lad, so it serves you right. Now shut up complaining and come and give me a cuddle.'

Declan narrowed his eyes. 'I don't know. Am I likely to get

hammered again? Since when did you have so many protective friends?' He pointed at Daisy. 'Even that one got handy with her elbows.'

Daisy glared at him. 'Didn't do much good though, did it? I was trying to look after my patient and you were getting in the way.'

'All right, hold your horses. I was looking out for my little sister. How was I to know you're a nurse? You sound like a proper cider girl to me.'

Rose laughed again. The others watched, all but Jimmy and Daisy highly entertained by this turn of events. 'Oh, take no notice of him, Daisy. Just be glad it was only one of the Flaherty brothers causing mayhem. I'm used to having to sort out all six of them at once. Now, get yourself on your feet, Declan, and say a proper hello to your favourite sister.'

She held out her arms as he shook his head and reluctantly got to his feet. 'You're my *only* sister, thank God,' he muttered as he engulfed her in a hug and lifted her off her feet.

Outside they heard the all-clear siren sound and a few minutes later the crowds were streaming back into the dance hall, complaining that it had been a false alarm.

Someone handed Rose a glass of elderflower cordial and Daisy insisted she drank it down. She did as she was told and felt a lot better for it. She agreed with Daisy that her blood sugars must be low on account of her not having eaten properly today.

As the band struck up again, Declan kissed her cheek. 'We'll talk in a minute, sis. Now go and dance with your friends and tell them I'm your favourite brother. I'll be wanting to dance with them before the night's out.'

She narrowed her eyes as she studied him. 'And what will you be doing now while I dance?'

He grinned. 'I'm going to get acquainted with the cider boy who punched me.'

'Don't you dare fight him,' she demanded. 'He's got a lot of friends around here.' She could imagine the chaos that would ensue, with a mob of farm hands fighting the flyboys.

He raised his eyebrows. 'I didn't throw a punch, he did. But don't worry, I just want to talk to him.'

* * *

Jimmy watched Rose drag her friends onto the dancefloor, insisting that she was fine.

'He just surprised me, that's all,' she laughed.

'Don't you want to talk to him?' asked Elsie.

'Not yet. Let him stew for a bit. I want to dance. Come on, that siren might have been a false alarm, but the next one might not be.'

Her brother seemed to have got his humour back, despite the bruise blooming on his jawline. He laughed and shooed the girls away. Jimmy sat beside him, feeling foolish.

'I'm sorry I hit you,' he said. 'I was just trying to protect Rose.'

Declan regarded him coolly. 'And why do you feel the need to protect my sister?'

'She works on our farm,' he said, unwilling to say anything else about his feelings for the land girl. 'My ma and pa said I should watch out for her.'

'Is that right?' he asked. 'Do you wade in with your fists when someone bothers your other farm hands?'

Jimmy let out a bark of laughter at the thought of it. 'Not likely,' he said. 'I'm usually trying to stop them from getting into fights. And I suppose you're going to tell me I don't need to look out for Rose. But from where I was watching, you was sneaking up on her and then she fainted. I wasn't going to hang around and let you get away with it.' He lifted his chin. 'Don't go telling me you wouldn't do the same if you were in my place.'

Declan took a sip from the glass of dandelion and burdock someone had given him, pulling a face at the taste. 'Christ, I could do with a Guinness right now.'

'This place is temperance,' Jimmy told him. 'You'd have to try the pubs. But they mostly stock cider and ale. Not sure if they have much stout.'

Declan shrugged. 'I'd better not. I'm already going to have to explain to my flight sergeant why I've got a bruised face. At least I can tell him honestly that I hadn't let the demon drink get the better of me. The last man that ended up in a drunken fight got put on a charge.'

Jimmy winced. 'Damn, I'm sorry. It was a misunderstanding.'

He looked at him, his gaze measuring him. 'I know. You was protecting Rose.' His mouth lifted to one side. 'My brothers are going to be mighty glad someone's looking out for her. The question they'll be asking, though, is whether you did it because you want her for yourself?'

He frowned. 'I told you, my ma and pa—'

Declan held up a hand to stop him. 'I know all that. But I also know you were too riled up thinking I'd hurt Rose to be just doing your duty by your mammy and daddy. You'd never have got the better of me otherwise.'

If Jimmy had had any doubts about whether this really was her brother, his use of those words convinced him. No one round these parts but Rose called their parents *mammy and daddy*. And now that he had calmed down, he recognised his Birmingham accent and could see that Declan had the same bright eyes as his sister, although his hair was a dark auburn rather than Rose's bright red curls.

This time it was Jimmy who shrugged. 'She's a good land girl, better than the last one we had. I didn't want to see anyone messing with her.'

Declan smirked, although his eyes were cool. 'Good. Me and the rest of the family are grateful for your concern. It's good to know someone's looking out for her, even if she can handle herself most of the time. Just make sure you don't take any liberties with her yourself, then we can stay friends.'

Jimmy bristled. 'I said I'm sorry I hit you, not that I wanted to be your friend.'

Declan laughed and slapped him on the shoulder. 'Ah, don't get all riled up again, cider boy. If you always take everything so serious, our Rose will be making your life a misery.'

He didn't dare react to that comment. Rose Flaherty was indeed making his life a misery for reasons he didn't want to think about. But when he'd seen her faint like that, he'd realised he'd rather be miserable with her around than to be without her. Yet, considering the mission he was being prepared for, the fact that Rose couldn't stand him most of the time, *and* the fact that there were five other men like this Declan ready to jump to their sister's defence, he would be a damned fool to get any more involved with her.

* * *

Rose seemed to have found a second wind now that the shock of Declan's appearance had waned. She kept glancing over at him, deep in conversation with Jimmy, wondering what on earth they were talking about.

'You don't have to stay with us,' said Elsie, who she was dancing with. 'I'm sure you're dying to talk to your brother.'

She shook her head. 'I'll have a chat with him in a minute. But he's talking to Jimmy right now. I hope that oaf is apologising for hitting him like that,' she said. 'Although I'm cross with myself for fainting when I could have witnessed someone other than our older brothers managing to knock Declan onto his backside.'

Daisy, who was dancing with Ruby next to them, shook her head. 'He just piled in.'

'It was rather magnificent,' said Ruby. 'I don't condone violence, but I think it was rather heroic of Jimmy to rush to your defence. He must really like you, Rose.'

Rose felt her cheeks warm, even as she shook her head. 'He really doesn't,' she insisted. 'I don't know what came over him.'

'You could always ask him,' said Elsie.

She did want to ask him about it. Jimmy must have been really riled up to have hit Declan, who was as tall as him and no lightweight. If he hadn't caught her brother by surprise, it might have developed into quite a fight, with them being well-matched. Was it because she'd fainted? It had never happened to her before and although she'd been feeling a bit light-headed, she was sure she'd been fine until she'd had the shock of seeing Dec when she'd least expected him. But why Jimmy had rushed in and bashed him, she had no idea. She ought to be angry with Jimmy, but when she'd realised what he'd done, she'd been delighted. Not that she could confess that. Declan would be furious.

'It seems that my brother has got plenty to say to him,' she said, making herself look away. 'I'll catch up with him when he's finished gossiping with Jimmy.'

Someone tapped her on the shoulder. Rose paused and looked round. The soldier standing there looked familiar, but she couldn't place him. He smiled.

'Sorry to interrupt ladies, but I wondered if I could have a dance with Elsie?'

Elsie blushed. 'Charles,' she said. 'I didn't know you were coming tonight.'

Rose remembered now where she'd seen him – at Elsie's office. So this was the soldier who had asked her friend out. She hoped he didn't say anything about meeting Rose before. She needn't have worried though, because he only had eyes for Elsie.

'Are you all right with that, Elsie?' she asked softly.

She nodded, her cheeks pink. With a smile, Rose stepped back and the lieutenant swept Elsie into his arms and away from her friends.

'Oh, I say,' said Ruby as the three of them watched the couple dancing. 'What a night! First Jimmy comes to Rose's rescue and then a handsome soldier sweeps Elsie off her feet. Whatever next?'

'She looks rather glad he's here, doesn't she?' said Rose.

'She does,' sighed Ruby. 'I wish someone would sweep me off my feet. The only lad I seem to dance with is Henry when I can bully him into it.'

The others laughed. 'Don't be in such a rush,' Daisy told her. 'I'm sure there's plenty of lads who'd like to dance with you.'

'It's obvious most are keeping their distance because both of my brothers are here tonight,' she complained.

Rose giggled. 'I know how that feels,' she said. 'How about I get Declan to dance with you?'

Ruby looked thoughtful. 'He's quite handsome, your brother.'

'Really?' She turned to look at him where he sat at the table with Mattie and Henry now. Jimmy was nowhere to be seen. She wondered briefly whether he'd gone home and if so how she was likely to get back to the farm this evening. But then she dismissed the worry and took Daisy and Ruby's hands and pulled them with her back to the table. 'Let's see if you think so after a dance, eh?'

They looked up as the girls arrived. 'Declan,' said Rose. 'I've been telling Ruby here that you're a terrible dancer, but she's still willing to give you a try. Just don't go getting handsy, because both of her big brothers are here.' She turned to Henry. 'Did you hear the announcement? It's the "ladies' excuse me", so it's our turn to ask the lads to dance. Will you do me the honour, Henry?' As he stood up and came around the table, she winked at Daisy and whispered in her ear. 'That leaves you and Mattie. Knock his socks off!'

* * *

Before Daisy could catch her breath, Rose had organised partners for all of them, leaving her with Mattie. Thinking he wouldn't really want to dance, especially as the current song ended and the band began to play a slower one, encouraging couples to hold each other close, Daisy went to sit down. But he surprised her by standing and holding out his hand to her.

'Shall we?' he asked with a smile.

With a nod, she took his hand and let him lead her onto the dance floor. She was prepared for him to hold her at arm's length, but he pulled her close and wrapped his arms around her. Daisy melted, breathing in his essence as she rested her cheek against his chest.

'This is nice,' he said. She felt his words rumble through his body.

'Mmm,' she said, not daring to try and make conversation for fear that she would spoil this perfect moment. She closed her eyes, savouring his warmth and wishing that this dance would go on for ever.

'Do you think that Ruby is all right with that Declan chap?' he asked eventually.

'I expect so,' she sighed, wishing he would concentrate on

her and not his little sister, who wasn't so little any more and perfectly capable of deciding whether a chap was good enough for her or not. 'Rose is fond of him, and she's not impressed by many lads, I can tell you, even her brothers. But it was Rose who suggested Ruby dance with him, so I think he must be all right.'

He chuckled. 'I've noticed she gives Jimmy short shrift.'

'Mmm. They seem to be locked in a cycle of mutual loathing and magnetic attraction,' she said. 'Although they both deny it.'

'I did wonder why he was so keen to punch Declan,' he mused. 'I think maybe still waters run deep. I hope Henry doesn't get in his way. He seems quite smitten by your friend Rose.'

Daisy raised her head and looked at him. He was watching the other couples dancing. 'If you'd rather just people watch, we can go back to the table,' she said.

He frowned. 'But I like dancing with you.'

She raised her eyebrows. 'Do you? You seem to be focussed on everyone else. Maybe I should leave you to it and ask someone else to dance. I see Jimmy's back at our table now. Shall we swap? Then you can stand guard over your siblings' hearts without any distractions.'

He looked confused and Daisy wished she'd just shut up and enjoyed the moment. But his lack of attention on her had stung and now she was too far gone to make the best of it.

'If you'd rather dance with Jimmy, then of course,' he said, looking a little hurt.

She didn't want to, she could hardly tell him what she was really thinking and feeling, could she? She felt a wave of disappointment. In his arms, she'd let herself hope that he was at last beginning to see her as a woman worth romancing. She stepped back, breaking contact with him.

'Actually, I'm feeling rather tired. I think I'll call it a night.

Could you let the others know I'm leaving? Tell them I'll see them next week.'

Before he could respond, she spun around, collected her cardigan, bag and gas mask and headed out.

* * *

Mattie was at the table with Jimmy when the others came back.

'Where's Daisy?' asked Ruby.

'Gone home. She was tired and asked me to say goodnight to you all,' Mattie said.

'Why didn't you go with her?'

Mattie sat back and regarded her, confused. 'Why would I? She knows her way home and it's not far.'

Ruby rolled her eyes. 'That's beside the point. It would have been nice. You could've had a romantic walk in the moonlight.'

Mattie laughed. 'Don't be daft, lass. A romantic walk? This is Daisy we're talking about.'

His laughter died as he noticed everyone except Declan, a newcomer, was looking at him with exasperation.

'Oho,' said Declan. 'I take it the doc is clever, but not very bright.'

'Spot on, brother,' said Rose, giving Mattie a disappointed look.

Mattie shook his head. 'I'm lost. What are you talking about?'

'Honestly Mattie,' said Ruby. 'When are you going to see what's right under your nose? If you don't do something soon, someone else is going to snap her up. Haven't you noticed how many chaps ask Daisy to dance?'

He huffed, not liking the idea of her dancing with other lads. Which was ridiculous. He had no say in who Daisy danced with. 'Well, she's a pretty lass. Why wouldn't they?'

His sister growled. 'Oooh, you idiot. You're the only lad she wanted to dance with, and you've obviously upset her or she wouldn't have left early without speaking to any of us.'

Mattie felt as though someone had sucked the air out of his lungs. 'Daisy? No. She was tired.' She couldn't possibly have *those sorts of feelings* for him, could she?

* * *

'...so I decided to come along to see if you were here. I hope you don't mind me cutting in when you were dancing with your friend.'

Elsie regarded Charles, pleased to see him, but a little concerned that he might have arrived when she was dancing with Ruby's brother and jumped to the wrong conclusion. 'It's nice to see you. I haven't seen you at any of the other dances here.'

He shrugged. 'I didn't think they'd be much fun, being temperance. But that was before someone mentioned that you come here regularly.'

She wasn't sure how she felt about people in the unit offices gossiping about her, but she supposed there was no harm done. Charles was a good dancer and handsome, too. It was rather thrilling, being in his arms again. 'It's nice to see you,' she said. 'I'll introduce to you my friends. They're a jolly lot, although you missed all the drama this evening.'

'The air raid?'

She shook her head. 'No, we barely noticed it. Someone approached Rose and she fainted at the sight of him.'

'Good grief! What spooked her? Was it a spurned lover?'

She chuckled. 'Hardly. He's one of her brothers. He's just been posted to the county and decided to surprise her. Then her farmer's son rushed in and knocked him flat, thinking he'd hurt Rose.'

Charles grinned. 'Sounds like I missed quite a show.'

'It certainly was.'

'I take it all ended well? Your friend seems fine now.'

'Yes, she is.' She looked around to see Rose back at their table, talking to her brother, whose arm was slung casually around his sister's shoulder. 'No harm done.'

'Good. Well, I'm glad I'm here now. You fit perfectly in my arms.' He pulled her a little closer.

Elsie blushed, not sure what to say to that. It was nice, dancing with a chap rather than another girl, and she was rather thrilled that he was holding her so close against his body.

'I haven't seen much of you at work this week,' she said. 'What have you been up to?'

'Nothing exciting,' he said. 'I've been working with some of the local Home Guard units on their defence plans. The chaps in Wells have set the standard and we're trying to get more towns as well prepared as they are to hold the stop line across the county. The trouble is, some units are seriously lacking in arms and munitions. They keep asking for more supplies, but there's a limit to what we can get hold of.'

The problem of equipping Home Guard units wasn't something that Elsie had much to do with, she had been more involved with supplying the auxiliary units. The problem was that, with those units being secret, it was difficult to arrange things through the usual channels. However, she didn't know how much, if anything, Charles knew about these secret groups. The CO had stressed that she should not discuss anything with anyone – not even work colleagues. She was surprised therefore that Charles was so blasé about this.

'It's all rather tedious, to be honest,' he went on.

'But valuable work, nevertheless,' she pointed out. 'In fact, I don't think you should be telling me this here. Do you realise that anyone could overhear you?'

He laughed. 'No one's going to hear us with all the racket the band is making.'

He might be saying all this close to her ear, but that didn't mean she was comfortable with it. 'I'm told a lot of the workers at the shoe factory can lip read,' she told him. 'They like to gossip while they're working despite the noise of the machines. Your conversation could be reported all around the factory by tomorrow.'

The music changed and the band picked up the tempo. She took a step away from him, a little relieved. She really didn't want to be having this conversation. She didn't want him to think she was a nag. She only hoped he took notice of what she said and was more careful in future. 'Can I introduce you to my friends?' she asked in an effort to change the subject.

He inclined his head. 'If you must,' he said. 'I was rather hoping to have you all to myself.'

She laughed, flattered. 'But I did come with them. It would be rather rude of me to ignore them now, wouldn't it?'

'You're right. Sorry. I can be a selfish beggar sometimes.'

As she led him to the table, she hoped that he would be nice to the others. Her brother-in-law had been possessive of Gertie, not wanting her to stay in touch with any of her friends after they'd married, so he'd been rude and surly in company. If he could have cut Elsie out of their lives as well, he would have. She felt a shiver run down her back at the thought of his reaction if he ever learned that Gertie had been unfaithful to him. He would never forgive her.

But that was something to worry about another day. The Musgrove siblings and Rose and her brother looked up as she approached. She introduced Charles to all of them and he greeted them with smooth charm, showing no sign that he'd been reluctant to meet them. She breathed another sigh of relief, glad that he hadn't made her feel uncomfortable around the people she was coming to regard as good friends.

'Where's Daisy?' she asked.

The others all glanced at Mattie, who scowled back at them.

'Gone home,' said Rose.

Elsie frowned. It wasn't like her to leave without saying anything. 'Is she all right?'

'Probably,' said Ruby. 'Although no thanks to Mattie. My brother is clueless when it comes to love.'

'Goodness.' She sat down. 'What happened?'

Mattie rolled his eyes. 'Nothing happened, as I keep telling everyone. We danced, we chatted, then she said she was tired and she went home.'

32

The Great Fire Raid hit London on the night of 10 and 11 May 1941. Over two thousand fires raged while wave after wave of incendiary bombs were dropped over the city. German bombers following behind the first planes could see the fires burning from miles away, making their targets even easier to hit. Over a third of roads in London were impassable and the Palace of Westminster was hit, burning the Commons chamber, causing Prime Minister Churchill to weep at the sight of the destruction of the heart of the country's democracy. It did nothing to weaken the people's resolve though. Outraged by the destruction of buildings and lives, the population continued to stand behind the armed forces, to support the war effort in any way they could and to mock Herr Hitler in songs and cartoons.

In Somerset, the training of the Auxiliers and Stay Behinds carried on apace as the apple trees blossomed in the orchards.

It was a fortnight before Daisy saw Mattie again. She'd kept herself busy, determined to give up on her feelings for him. She'd thought she was doing quite well until he arrived at the farm one evening and asked her to take a walk with him and her foolish hope blossomed again. As she pulled on her shoes, she was aware of her parents and brothers chatting to Mattie behind her. Ma beamed at her when she straightened up.

'Off you go then, you two. Enjoy your walk.'

Daisy's stomach was tied up in knots. She wondered whether she was being foolish, agreeing to this. After all, he wasn't likely to suddenly declare his undying love, was he?

'Come on then,' she said, walking out of the door without looking at him.

They walked across the fields for a while in silence. It wasn't their usual comfortable silence, but Daisy wasn't inclined to break it. Eventually, Mattie cleared his throat.

'So, how's work?' he asked.

She shrugged. 'Busy. There's measles going round at the Board School. Most of the children are fine with it, but a couple have had to go into hospital. They're both evacuees, so don't have their mothers around, the poor little mites. I organised a few books and a teddy bear for each of them. I hope that helps. A few lads have come back from fighting with medical discharges. One's an amputee. He's struggling with the false limb he was issued, so I asked Uncle Tom to see if he can help him.' She realised she was rambling, so she shut up.

'Good... actually, not good for the patients, of course. But, well, I'm glad you're busy. They must all be grateful for everything you do.'

She shrugged. 'I'm just doing my job, same as anyone else.'

They paused as they came to the edge of the Selway land. 'I don't think many would think about a teddy bear for a child or getting an amputee a better prosthetic.'

'I'm sure they would.' She looked around, noting that it wouldn't be long before the rest of her family would be busy with haymaking. The potato and willow crops were all doing well, as were the mangolds that would be used to feed the livestock in the winter months. 'Are you getting on all right in Wells?' she asked.

He nodded. 'I'm enjoying it. I was worried that I'd regret leaving the hospital, but I think being a GP suits me better.'

'That's good. I'm pleased for you.'

He put a hand on her arm. 'Daisy, look at me.'

She really didn't want to, but did as he bid. 'What?' she asked, pasting on a smile.

He frowned. 'Have I done something to upset you?'

She shook her head, her smile becoming even more fixed. 'No. Of course you haven't.'

'Only my sister said I must have at the dance the other week, and I've been thinking about it ever since—'

She stepped back so that his hand dropped. She didn't want to have this conversation. 'I don't know what nonsense Ruby's got in her head, but she's wrong. Shall we head back?' She began walking without waiting for him to answer.

He caught up with her and matched his pace to hers as they walked back towards the farmhouse. 'I thought she was wrong,' he said, sounding relieved. 'She had this daft idea that you fancied me and I should've walked you home that night.'

Daisy took a deep breath, trying to stay calm. 'I'll bet you were horrified. I mean, the last thing you want is someone like me who you've known all your life making doe eyes at you, eh?' She kept her gaze on the uneven ground, not wanting to humiliate herself further by falling at his feet.

'It's not that,' he said. 'It's just that I'm sure you wouldn't want people thinking that. I mean, you're a lovely girl...'

'But I'm not your type?' she said. 'Don't worry, I know that. Don't go letting Ruby make you feel uncomfortable.'

'Now you're putting words in my mouth,' he protested.

She shook her head. 'I'm just saving you the trouble of saying it.' She slowed her pace as they came into the farmyard. 'Look, Mattie. If you liked me like that you'd've said something before now.'

'Like what?' he asked, coming to stand in front of her.

She looked up at him, wishing she could throw herself into his arms but knowing it would only embarrass him and make things worse. 'Romantically, Mattie,' she said, feeling unutterably sad. 'But I know you don't, so let's forget all about this, all right? Let's just carry on as we are – good friends – and ignore what anyone else says.'

'If that's what you want,' he said, studying her guarded expression.

She nodded.

'All right,' he said. 'Friends, as always.' He leaned down and kissed her cheek. 'So, friend, do you fancy coming to the pictures with me on Friday?'

Daisy's heart sank. 'Actually, I've got a date then.'

'Oh? I didn't know you were courting.'

'Hardly courting,' she said. 'But the teacher of those evacuees I was telling you about invited me out and I said yes. He seems like a nice chap and I think he's a bit lonely being away from the bright lights of London.'

Mattie frowned. 'A city boy?'

'A man, Mattie, not a boy. We're not children any more.'

His frown deepened. 'Well make sure you don't end up in the back row with him. You've got a reputation to maintain.'

She laughed at that. 'Thank you for your concern. But I'll be fine, thank you. I'd better go in. I'll see you again soon. Give my love to your family.'

She left him and closed the door behind her. Mattie stared after her, feeling oddly unsettled. He wasn't sure what had just happened. Had Daisy really said that she wasn't his type? He gave a little shake of his head and turned towards his car. He didn't know what he'd thought to achieve by coming here this evening, but he hadn't expected her to say that – nor to tell him that she had a date.

He got into his vehicle. As he drove away, he wondered what had gone wrong between them and why he felt so sure that he had made a huge mistake where she was concerned and that things were never going to be the same again.

* * *

As Mattie drove away, Daisy leaned her back against the door, shaking. Had he asked her out on a date? Or was he just being his usual, clueless, friendly self? If he had meant it as a date, it was ironic that he'd chosen the very day when she'd accepted a date with another man.

She sighed. Well, it was too late now. She'd accepted the teacher's invitation and she wasn't about to stand him up. He seemed nice and she had been determined to forget Mattie. She'd done the right thing. Just because he was worried he'd upset her, it didn't mean that Mattie was any closer to seeing her as a potential wife, did it? She was done with waiting. Who knew what the future held? With an invasion imminent, she needed to grasp her opportunity for happiness while she could.

But she couldn't help worrying that turning Mattie down was the biggest mistake she'd ever made, but it was done now, so she had to live with it.

* * *

Elsie looked up and smiled as Charles came into her office on a sunny afternoon in July. 'Hello,' she said. 'Have you come to see the CO?'

He shook his head, his eyes on the new epaulettes on her jacket. The two pips on each matched those on his own uniform. 'I came to see my favourite girl. What's with the pips?' he asked.

Her smile widened. The ATS had finally been given full army status, after years of being regarded as a voluntary supplement to the forces. 'I've been promoted. I'm a subaltern now.'

'But you've got lieutenants' pips,' he said, looking confused.

'I know. It's the equivalent rank. Isn't that fun? We're equals now.' She needn't worry now about Charles getting in trouble for fraternising with a lower rank.

He gave her an odd look, one side of his mouth lifting in a half-smile. 'So are you moving to a new job?'

She shook her head, a bit puzzled by his reaction. 'No, I'm needed here.'

'But you're a junior officer now. Anyone from the ranks can type a few reports and do a bit of driving for the captain. If they're not moving you, why on earth did they promote you?'

Her hurt must have shown on her face because he sighed. 'Look, I'm sorry, darling,' he said, leaning on her desk, 'but don't you see? It seems a bit rum that you've been given the same rank as me when you're not commanding any men and you won't be sent into battle. You can imagine what people are going to think.'

Elsie held her tongue. She wanted to tell him that she was far more than a clerk and a driver, but she knew she mustn't.

'They're going to think you're offering more than secretarial services to the CO, that's what,' he went on. He ignored her gasp and delivered the final blow. 'It's certainly got me wondering.'

Elsie was hurt beyond measure that he would think that of her. She was not promiscuous, he knew that. She caught his gaze. Charles's usual pleasant regard was cool. 'Is that really what you think?' she asked, her voice scratchy as she tried to maintain her composure. She couldn't tell him that she was far more than a clerk and driver, that she was highly trained and prepared for a vital mission when the invasion came. The unfairness of his calmly delivered words stung.

He shrugged, looking away. 'Come on, old girl. It's not easy to work your way up the ranks, and you've got to admit you're hardly leadership material running around for the CO, are you? Yet here you are with two pips on each shoulder, just like that. What are we supposed to think?'

Neither of them had heard the door to the CO's office open. When Captain Crick cleared his throat, Charles jumped to attention and saluted. Elsie sat, frozen at her desk.

'Ah, Jameson, I was just going to send Bloomfield to look for you. Come on in. I've got a job for you.' He stood back, waiting for Charles to walk into his office before turning towards Elsie.

She blinked rapidly, determined not to cry in front of the CO.

'Are all the reports up to date?' he asked her.

'Yes, sir. There's just some post for you to sign.' She held out the folder containing the letters.

'Good.' He reached into his breast pocket and pulled out his fountain pen. 'I'll do those now.' He opened the file, scanning each letter before signing it. 'Right. Can you get those in the post immediately, except this one?' He held out one addressed to Captain Jackson, to which he'd added a post script note. 'Can you deliver this by hand?'

'Of course, sir. Do I need to wait for his reply?'

He shook his head. 'No need. Get this delivered and the rest in the post then you can finish for the day. Maybe go and visit one of your friends, eh?'

She had kept her head down, not sure how much he'd heard

of her conversation with Charles, but now she looked at him. His regard was as professional as ever. She nodded.

'Good show. Off you go then.' He lowered his voice. 'And don't worry about the rubbish our friend in there was spouting. Well done for keeping your cool. I'll deal with him now.'

Elsie gulped. So he had heard them. *Oh lord!* She was only glad that she'd let Charles do most of the talking. She had no idea what the CO meant about dealing with Charles, but she wasn't about to ask. Instead, she nodded and began folding the letters and sliding them into their envelopes.

The office door closed and she sagged a little. She was shocked. How could she go from being thrilled to see him and share her news to feeling dirty and tainted by his cutting words? Did he really think that the only way she could get a promotion was to sleep with the CO? The captain was a married man, for goodness' sake! 'Well, if that's what he really thinks of me,' she muttered under her breath, 'then he's not the man I thought he was.' She'd thought he'd be pleased for her. She huffed out a breath as she folded the letter to Captain Jackson. As she slid it into its envelope, she couldn't help but notice the post script the CO had added: *I've made a decision about who to send in response to Stirling's request. He'll be on his way tonight.*

She had seen a memo from a Lt David Stirling, requesting suitable personnel to join a new special air service brigade which would be training as paratroopers at a camp in Egypt. She wondered who the CO had in mind. He hadn't asked her to type any orders.

She sealed the letters, put the ones to be posted to one side. She would drop those with the postal clerk on her way out. The letter to Captain Jackson, she put in her handbag. All other paperwork was locked away in her filing cabinet before she put on her jacket, picked up her gas mask box with her handbag and left the office.

* * *

It wasn't until she heard someone at breakfast the next morning saying that Jameson had been given an urgent posting and wouldn't be coming back to Edgely that she put two and two together. Elsie was alone. Again.

She wasn't sure how she felt about Charles's sudden departure. Probably part hurt, and part relief. Their last encounter had been unpleasant and had killed any hope she'd had that he might be the man for her. She had learned a painful lesson. It would be better to avoid romantic entanglements for the time being. Maybe when the world was at peace, she could open her heart again. But for now she had a job to do and she would do her bit to the best of her ability. She was only thankful that she had her cider girl friends. They were true and steadfast and all she needed for now.

* * *

Rose got back from morning milking and went into the farmhouse for breakfast. It was much easier in the warmer months when she didn't need gloves and layers of socks in order to keep out the cold. She noticed that the sun was bringing out her freckles, but there wasn't much she could do about it.

'Morning, lass,' said Mrs Morgan as she poured tea. 'Come and take a load off. Ivor and my James have already had their breakfast, but Jimmy's just taking a phone call in the office. I've boiled some eggs for you both.'

'Thanks, Mrs M.' She smiled as she took her cup and sat at

the long kitchen table. 'Is he being called in for more Home Guard duty?'

'I hope not. It was ringing as he came in the door, so he went to answer it. I expect we'll find out soon enough.'

'Right. I'll eat this then I've the pigs to clean out. Do you want any help in the dairy after that? If not, I'll get down the fields and see what Mr M needs doing if Jimmy doesn't know.'

She was dipping some bread into her soft-boiled egg when Jimmy came into the room. She looked up, smiling. 'You'd better eat your eggs quick,' she told him, 'or I'll have yours as well. These are so fresh and lovely.'

He stood in the doorway, looking at her, a strange expression on his face.

'Come and sit down, son,' said his mother, putting his plate on the table next to Rose.

'Sorry, Ma. I, er...'

'What is it? You've gone mighty pale, boy. Are you sickening for something?'

He shook his head then scrubbed at his face. Rose frowned. His mammy was right. He didn't look right. Seeing her watching him, he looked up at the ceiling and took a deep breath. 'Rose,' he said, coming to sit next to her. 'Declan was on the phone.'

She stilled. 'What's he doing telephoning in the middle of the morning? Is he all right?'

He nodded. 'He is. But... he's had some news.'

'He's not being posted away is he? I was just getting used to having him around.'

Jimmy swallowed, his lips thinning. He glanced at his mammy as though silently asking for help. 'No, he's not being posted. His CO called him in to tell him... I'm sorry, love. It's your brother Michael.'

Rose felt as though the air had been sucked out of her lungs as she stood up. 'What about him? Have they found him? Is he coming home?'

He shook his head, taking her hands. 'No. He's gone, Rose. It's official.'

She tried to pull her hands away but he held her fast. 'No,' she said, shaking her head. 'No! He can't be... No!'

'Oh my love,' said Mrs Morgan, coming to put an arm around her shoulders. Rose collapsed into Jimmy's chest, sobbing. He released her hands and put his arms around her, holding her close. As she cried, mother and son tried to soothe her but she couldn't be consoled.

* * *

Jimmy held her tight, hating himself for having to deliver the news. But Declan had been just as distraught on the phone and he couldn't make the poor lad come and have to tell his sister. He'd offered and her brother had gratefully accepted.

As he rocked her, Ma stroked her hair. He gave his mother a helpless look.

'What can we do?' she asked him softly as Rose continued to weep.

'Declan's getting a lift over here. He's been given a forty-eight-hour pass on compassionate grounds. He wants to take Rose with him to Birmingham so they can be with their parents. I said I'd give them a lift to the station.'

She nodded. 'I'll go and pack a bag for her. You stay here, son. She needs you.'

Jimmy continued to hold her, stroking her and whispering to her. 'Let it out, love. I'm more sorry than I can say. Declan's coming. He's taking you home to your ma and pa.'

Rose's grief was so deep that he didn't know whether she

heard any of it. She certainly didn't notice when he kissed her hair. Jimmy knew he shouldn't do it, but he couldn't help himself. If he could've taken away her pain, he'd have done it gladly.

Ma came downstairs with Rose's bag just as Declan arrived. Jimmy was reluctant to let go of Rose, but one look at her brother's tortured expression persuaded him that the siblings needed to take comfort from each other and he relinquished his hold on her into Declan's care.

'I'll bring Pa's car round,' he said, leaving the room as Declan tearfully explained to Rose what he'd told Jimmy on the phone. It seemed that Michael had been injured and hidden by the French resistance and was almost recovered when someone had betrayed them. He and his saviours had been ambushed. Most of them, including their brother had been killed immediately, but one had escaped long enough to get a radio message out before the whole network in that village had been shut down. It was thanks to that message that they knew his fate. Otherwise they might never have known.

Jimmy drove the silent pair to Bridgewater, wishing there was something he could do to ease their pain. He wished he could tell Rose about the mission that he was being trained to undertake, to reassure her that he would do his damnedest to make sure that the enemy never triumphed, but that wouldn't bring her brother back, would it? As he watched them disappear into the station, he realised that, when the invasion came, he and his unit would be facing the same dangers that Rose's brother had encountered. It brought home to him that just one careless word could betray and condemn them. No matter how much he wanted to reassure Rose, he couldn't tell her anything. Not only would it put him in danger, but it would put her and his family at risk. All he could do was to be kind to her while he could, and then be the best

Auxilier he could be to keep her safe, even if she didn't know where he was.

* * *

Jimmy was waiting for them when they arrived back at Bridgewater Station two days later. She didn't know how he knew, but his presence was reassuring. She remained silent as Declan thanked him and accepted his offer of a lift to his base.

It had been an awful couple of days. They had done their best to comfort each other – she and Declan were the only ones who were able to get home to their parents, along with Liam who had also been given a day's leave on hearing the news. Together they had composed letters to her other brothers, breaking the news in case they hadn't been informed. It was the hardest thing she'd ever done, and she prayed that she wouldn't have to do it again in this lifetime.

There had been air raids over Birmingham as well, so they'd followed Mammy down into the public shelters while Daddy did his ARP duty. It was awful. Crowded, noisy, smelly. Yet no amount of pleading on Rose's part, backed up by her brothers, could persuade their parents to move out of Birmingham to the relative safety of Somerset.

'Now, now, princess, don't fuss so,' said Daddy. 'We've got work to do here and what would we be doing with ourselves out in the country? No, we'll stay here and keep busy and you must go back to your farm and stay safe there so we don't have to worry about you.'

'And if the good lord decides it's our time,' said Mammy with tears in her eyes, 'you can be sure we'll be resting in the comfort of our sweet Michael's arms. So you mustn't fret, my darling girl.'

Now back in Somerset, she stared out at the countryside. The orchards, the willow beds, the cattle and sheep in the fields. Nothing could take away her grief, but she felt a measure of peace as they pulled into the farmyard.

Jimmy gave her a gentle smile as he turned off the engine. 'Welcome back, Rose.'

'Thanks for the lift,' she said. 'I hope I didn't put everyone out, rushing away like that.'

'Don't be daft, lass,' he said. 'I'm only sorry you got the news you didn't want to hear.'

She nodded, not wanting to talk about it. She turned and got out of the vehicle. He waved her away when she reached for her bags, picking them up for her. As they approached the farmhouse door, Rose glanced at him. 'I also want to thank you for being so kind to me the other day.'

He shrugged. 'No thanks necessary. I just wish I had had better news to give you.'

'I know. I just wanted you to know how much I appreciated you being there for me.' They entered the building.

'By the way, Ma rang Mrs Selway and asked her to tell Daisy your news. I think she was going to let your other friend know. They've both sent notes.'

'Thank you. I haven't had a chance to think about contacting them.' She was grateful she wouldn't have to tell them. Just the thought of saying the words hurt.

'Pa says don't worry about work today. Rest up after your journey. We'll cover the milking later and I've already seen to the pigs.'

She shook her head. 'No, I'm fine. I'll be doing the milking as usual. I've already taken up enough of your time.'

'Are you sure?'

'Yes. I need to keep busy. Maybe I'll do an hour in the office first. Check what's come in since I left.'

'All right. Ma's in the dairy. I'll drop your bags upstairs and get back out to the fields.'

She watched him go before going into the office. She sat at the desk and sighed. There were only a few envelopes so it wouldn't take long to deal with that. She also needed to report in and explain why she hadn't been observing for the past couple of days. She found some paper and an envelope and wrote a coded message. She would deliver it to the nearest dead letterbox on her way out to milking.

She wondered whether she should just give up, she felt so broken down. But then she thought about all the people across Europe who were risking their lives to resist the enemy; about Jimmy, secretly training to protect his community and keep the German advance at bay; her friends, the cider girls, each serving the country in their own way, and she knew she wouldn't stop. When the invasion came, she would do her bit and try and make life as difficult as possible for the occupying force. If she could join a unit like Jimmy's – learn to fight and blow up things and do to the Germans as they did to her brother and his saviours, then she jolly well would.

She was tempted to talk to Jimmy about it, but knew she couldn't. She had to keep his secret, keep him safe. Maybe one day they might be able to share their secrets. But in the meantime, she had work to do. She picked up the first envelope on the pile of post and slit it open.

33

At the beginning of June 1941, British forces withdrew from Crete after a fierce battle for the island. German air power overwhelmed the Allies and, exactly a year after Dunkirk, a new evacuation – of 18,000 British soldiers – took place under fire. Three destroyers were lost along with over 2,000 men.

The cider girls met on their half day and climbed to the top of Glastonbury Tor. Daisy walked them around the tower, pointing out landmarks. They could see for miles.

'I can't believe I haven't been up here before now,' said Elsie. 'Edgely's just down there at the bottom on the hill.'

'It's a long time since I've been here,' said Daisy. 'The climb seems harder. I must be getting old,' she laughed.

'You can see it all the way from Catcott,' said Rose, trying to work out which woodlands in the distance were the ones above the farm.

They sat down with their backs against the tower, enjoying the sunshine.

'Thank you for your notes,' said Rose. 'Both Dec and me

appreciated them. But, if you don't mind, I don't want to talk about it today.'

'Of course, love,' said Daisy. 'But when you do want to talk, we're both here to listen.' Elsie nodded.

'Thank you.' Rose blinked rapidly against the tears that still threatened on a regular basis. 'So, what have you two been up to?'

'Charles has been posted overseas,' said Elsie.

'Oh, I'm sorry. You were getting along so well, weren't you?'

She sighed. 'Actually, I think things were going to end anyway. I got a promotion to subaltern, which is the equivalent of his rank of lieutenant, and he was rather cruel about it.'

'What do you mean?' asked Daisy.

'He said people would think I'd been sleeping with the CO to get my pips because a clerk/driver wasn't worthy of the rank.'

'Good grief! What a horrible thing to say.'

'I hope you put him straight,' said Rose.

'I didn't get a chance. As soon as he said it, he was called away and he left for his new posting without saying goodbye.'

'How rude,' said Daisy. 'Sounds like good riddance to him.'

'Mmm. It did rather put me off him. I don't wish him ill, but I'm glad he's gone. It's taught me a valuable lesson. I won't be getting involved with anyone else at Edgely, that's for sure.'

'A few weeks ago, I'd have said don't give up on finding love,' said Rose, 'but now I think you're sensible. I won't be looking for a sweetheart until I know we're at peace. I've enough to worry about with my brothers. I haven't the energy to fret about another man as well.'

'What? Not even Jimmy? He's not going anywhere, is he?' said Daisy.

Rose exchanged a brief glance with Elsie before answering. 'Even Jimmy,' she said. 'I'm grateful for his friendship, but nothing more, thank you very much.'

Daisy sighed. 'You're both right, of course.'

'Does that mean nothing's happened with Mattie?'

She shook her head and explained about his visit to the farm. 'So I went to the pictures with Geoff the teacher instead.'

'And how was it?'

She shrugged. 'He's nice enough. But like you two, I think I'm giving up on men for the duration.'

They were all silent for a few minutes, each lost in their own thoughts. Each wondering whether they were fooling their friends or themselves. And each keeping their secrets – which played a part, alongside their recent disappointments and losses, in persuading them that while the future was so uncertain, love wasn't on the cards for them.

'All right,' said Rose. 'So that's decided. No looking for love. Just the cider girls against the world until this rotten war is over.'

'Agreed,' said Elsie.

'Cider girls against the world,' said Daisy. 'I rather like the sound of that.'

* * *

MORE FROM MAY ELLIS

The next instalment in the heart-stirring Cider Girls Series is available to order now here:

https://mybook.to/CiderGirls2BackAd

ACKNOWLEDGEMENTS

There are so many stories around about the heroic deeds of the countless men and women in wartime, but I recently discovered one that has hardly been mentioned. Few people knew that there was a whole secret army of people in Britain who were prepared to make the ultimate sacrifice during World War Two. In the event of a German invasion, they would become the British Resistance. They were required to sign the Official Secrets Act and couldn't tell anyone what they were doing. They would simply disappear from their homes, hide out in secret bunkers, emerging only to carry out acts of sabotage aimed at halting the enemy advance and to cut off their supply routes. They were trained in explosives, weaponry, unarmed combat and survival techniques. They could move around the countryside undetected, but due to the nature of their mission they weren't expected to live more than a few weeks.

These Auxiliers and Stay Behinds were ordinary people – farmers, quarrymen, doctors and others in reserved occupations, as well as older men, veterans of the Great War and younger lads who had useful skills but were too young to enlist. Women were also involved in the secret army as radio operators, observers and messengers. All would risk their lives. None could tell their nearest and dearest.

One might think that the rural county of Somerset didn't need a secret army. But Churchill, who ordered the creation of this secret army, recognised that the fifty-mile coastline of

Somerset was vulnerable if the Germans decided to come up the Severn Estuary to invade. From there, they could march north to Bristol and east to London, bypassing the defences along the south and east coasts. As a result, Somerset was the setting for many units of this secret army, creating a wide network of defenders and saboteurs. Their training was so good that a significant number of men were later enlisted into the new SAS and served with distinction across Europe, Africa and the Middle East.

Thankfully, Britain was not invaded and eventually the secret army was stood down with a simple letter of thanks. None of those involved could tell anyone what they had been trained and prepared to do. They received no medals. Yet they were heroes, ready to lay down their lives. That's why I wanted to tell their stories.

This series is about some of the secret army operating in Somerset. It is thanks to researchers at the British Resistance Organisation Museum at Parham Airfield in Suffolk, writers such as Tim Wray, who wrote *The Somerset Underground* and others now sharing information about this hidden history now coming to light. This story is based on information I have gleaned from these sources. I am grateful for the assistance I have received from the museum staff and volunteers, as well as the information available online at www.staybehinds.com.

I'd also like to thank Mrs Mary Heck of Street for her entertaining chats about life in the area during World War Two, including the revelation that her older brother, a farmer, was part of what she knew as 'the Secret Home Guard'.

I also dedicate this story to the memory of Mrs Elizabeth Anne Selway, June 1941 – July 2025.

ABOUT THE AUTHOR

May Ellis is the author of more than five contemporary romance and YA fiction novels. She lives in Somerset, within sight of Glastonbury Tor. Inspired by her move to the area and her love of social history, she is now writing saga fiction – based on the real-life stories of the Clarks factory girls.

Download your exclusive bonus content from My Ellis here:

Follow May on social media here:

facebook.com/alison.knight.942

bookbub.com/authors/alison-knight

ALSO BY MAY ELLIS

The Clarks Factory Girls

The Clarks Factory Girls at War

Courage for the Clarks Factory Girls

Dark Times for the Clarks Factory Girls

New Hope for the Clarks Factory Girls

The Cider Girls

Wartime with the Cider Girls

Standalone Novels

Lily's Choice

Sixpence Stories

Introducing Sixpence Stories!

Discover page-turning historical novels from your favourite authors, meet new friends and be transported back in time.

Join our book club Facebook group

https://bit.ly/SixpenceGroup

Sign up to our newsletter

https://bit.ly/SixpenceNews

Boldwood

Boldwood Books is an award-winning fiction publishing company seeking out the best stories from around the world.

Find out more at www.boldwoodbooks.com

Join our reader community for brilliant books, competitions and offers!

Follow us
@BoldwoodBooks
@TheBoldBookClub

Sign up to our weekly deals newsletter

https://bit.ly/BoldwoodBNewsletter

Printed in Dunstable, United Kingdom